NEW
Stories
FROM THE
Midwest

NEW
Stories
FROM THE
Midwest

2012

INTRODUCTION BY

GUEST EDITOR
JOHN McNALLY

EDITED BY

JASON LEE BROWN AND
SHANIE LATHAM

an imprint of
INDIANA UNIVERSITY PRESS
Bloomington & Indianapolis

This book is a publication of
Quarry Books
an imprint of

Indiana University Press
Office of Scholarly Publishing
Herman B Wells Library 350
1320 E. 10th Street
Bloomington, Indiana 47405 USA

iupress.indiana.edu

Telephone orders   800-842-6796
Fax orders   812-855-7931

© 2013 by Indiana University Press

⊖ The paper used in this publication
meets the minimum requirements of the
American National Standard for Information
Sciences—Permanence of Paper for Printed
Library Materials, ANSI Z39.48–1992.

Manufactured in the United States of America

Library of Congress
Cataloging-in-Publication Data

New Stories from the Midwest 2012 / edited by
Jason Lee Brown and Shanie Latham ; with an
introduction by guest editor John McNally.
     pages cm
     ISBN 978-0-253-00818-3 (pb : alk. paper)
— ISBN 978-0-253-00825-1 (eb) 1. Short
stories, American—Middle West. 2. American
fiction—21st century. 3. Middle West—
Social life and customs—Fiction. I. Brown,
Jason Lee, 1973- II. Latham, Shanie.
     PS563.N373 2013
     813'.0108977—dc23
                                            2012047305

1 2 3 4 5   18 17 16 15 14 13

For Jay

CONTENTS

ACKNOWLEDGMENTS

"Mr. Scary" by Charles Baxter. Reprinted from *Gryphon: New and Selected Stories.* Copyright © 2010 by Random House, Inc., with permission of Random House, Inc. "Mr. Scary" first appeared in *Ploughshares,* vol. 36, no. 2 & 3 (Fall 2010).

"To Psychic Underworld:" by Dan Chaon. Reprinted from *Stay Awake.* Copyright © 2011 by Random House, Inc., with permission of Random House, Inc. "To Psychic Underworld:" first appeared in *Tin House* vol. 12, no. 46 (Winter 2010).

"Townie" by Roderic Crooks. First published in *Gulf Coast* vol. 22, no. 2 (Summer/Fall 2010). Copyright © 2010 by Roderic Crooks. Reprinted by permission of the author.

"The Amnesiac in the Maze" by Michael Czyzniejewski. First published in *Ninth Letter* vol. 7, no. 2 (Fall/Winter 2010–11). Copyright © 2010 by Michael Czyzniejewski. Reprinted by permission of the author.

"The Deep" by Anthony Doerr. First published in *Zoetrope: All-Story* vol. 14, no. 3 (Fall 2010). Also published in *The Sunday Times Magazine* as winner of The Sunday Times EFG Private Bank Short Story Award. Copyright © 2010 by Anthony Doerr. Reprinted by permission of the author.

"Circling in the Air" by David Driscoll. First published in *Mississippi Review*

EDITORS' NOTE

New Stories from the Midwest, 2012 showcases twenty stories set in the Midwest by midwestern and non-midwestern authors. The goals of *New Stories from the Midwest* are to celebrate an American region that is often ignored in discussions about distinctive regional literature and to demonstrate how the quality of fiction from and about the Midwest (Illinois, Indiana, Iowa, Kansas, Michigan, Minnesota, Missouri, Nebraska, North Dakota, Ohio, South Dakota, and Wisconsin) rivals that of any other region.

To collect the stories, we solicited via flyers, letters, and e-mails for contributions from more than three hundred magazines, literary journals, and small presses. We received more than three hundred nominations from more than one hundred publications and editors. We narrowed the selection to fifty finalists, which were passed on to the guest editor, John McNally, who chose twenty stories for inclusion. The thirty stories not selected are listed at the end of the book.

Jason Lee Brown and Shanie Latham
Series Editors

NEW
Stories
FROM THE
Midwest

Introduction

John McNally

WHAT DOES IT MEAN to be a midwestern writer?

I first became aware of the idea of the "regional writer" in eighth grade when my father drove me to Greenfield, Indiana, for the city's James Whitcomb Riley Festival. On weekends, my father and I sold concert T-shirts at small festivals and fairs throughout Illinois and Indiana, so I became intimately familiar with the peculiar histories of each small town across I-80, up and down I-57, and beyond. But who was James Whitcomb Riley? I wanted to know. Turns out, he was a famous Hoosier poet born in Greenfield in the nineteenth century. With the hope that Mrs. Davis, my eighth grade reading-and-writing teacher, would notice and be impressed, I bought a James Whitcomb Riley Festival T-shirt and wore it to school. But Mrs. Davis *didn't* notice. And when I pointed it out to her, she had no idea who he was. How was it possible that she had never heard of this writer who had his own T-shirt? Was it possible to be *too* regional?

Well, no, I don't think so. In an essay about the importance of place, Richard Russo writes about the fear (by some writers) of being labeled a regional writer: "The real fear of being labeled regional—in the sense of, say, Hamlin Garland or Sarah Orne Jewett—is its unstated implication. These writers weren't more regional than Mark Twain and Faulkner; they, I believe, were less talented, less visionary, less true." In other words: Fear not, O regional writer! Just make sure you're good. *Damn* good.

If all politics is local, as Tip O'Neill once famously declared, then so is all fiction. The best fiction, it seems to me, is always strongly rooted in place. I can't read Theodore Dreiser's *Sister Carrie,* Willa Cather's *O Pioneers!,* or Louise Erdrich's *Love Medicine* and separate the characters and their stories from the places those books are set. What would a Dickens novel be like without London? What would a Faulkner novel be like without Mississippi? In the very best writing, place is already part of the story or a novel's DNA, not something simply plopped in.

I try to impress upon my fiction-writing students every semester the importance of place. And when someone turns in a short story with the sentence, "It was a typical small town," I write in the margin, "No, no, no! There's no such thing as typical." And then, during workshop, I'll talk about how a "typical small town" in southern Utah, for instance, is not the same as a "typical small town" in Iowa, and how, in fact, one small town in Iowa isn't even the same as another small town in Iowa. A reader doesn't read a story or novel to discover the *typical.* They read to discover the *individual.* By semester's end, the students' stories I remember most vividly are almost always the ones with a strong, idiosyncratic sense of place. Often I feel as though I've been to the places they've written about or have visited the stores and restaurants they've described, even if I've never been anywhere near the actual city itself. Why is this? "Writers have to recognize and accept an essential artistic paradox," Richard Russo writes, "that the more specific and individual things become, the more universal they feel."

I'll admit that I was slow in coming to this realization. When I first began writing fiction, the settings of my stories were often amorphous, sometimes nonexistent, or they were rural, probably since I had spent several years living in southern Illinois, where, as an undergraduate, I had decided to become a writer. It took years for me to be able to write about where I had grown up on the southwest side of Chicago. My first attempts turned out maudlin, and the things I focused on were always gratuitously gritty: the crumbling sidewalks, the bent and twisted guardrails, the broken glass. That sort of thing. But then I started using real place names—Ford City Shopping Center, Guidish Park Mobile Homes, the corner of 79th and Narragansett—and I began seeing my stories with a clarity that my earlier stories, set in nebulous rural towns, never achieved. What I eventually discovered was that characters were a product of a place, often a very specific place, and that all place had to do was *be.* Faulkner's books couldn't be set in Anchorage, Alaska, any more than *One Hundred Years of Solitude* could be set in Poughkeepsie, New York. Place provides a context for the many characters in a novel or short story, and it begins to provide a basis for why they behave the way they do. The more specific the place, the more intensely those characters become defined. After all, every place has its own urban legends, its own mythologies. The people who live there have their own peculiar ways, whether it's the food they eat (in my case, that would be beef sandwiches at Duke's on 85th and Harlem) or the way they insult each other.

A reader's relationship with place is a complicated one, however, and writers may want to tread with caution before writing *too* specifically about what they know. Thomas Wolfe's thinly-veiled autobiographical novel *Look Homeward, Angel* caused a bit of a commotion in his hometown of Asheville, North Carolina—enough so that Wolfe eventually wrote a novel about a novelist whose first novel caused a commotion in, you guessed it, his hometown. The latter was, of course, the posthumously published and appropriately-titled *You Can't Go Home Again.* One of my favorite reactions to a novel of mine is from a reader on Goodreads, who wrote, "The main reason I like this book so much is the author is from my hometown and most of it is set there. This guy really captured the feeling of that shitty little place and reminded me why I love and hate Burbank." What better compliment could a writer ask for? Not surprisingly, there is a flip-side to that coin, as when the owner of a bar that I had (gently) poked fun of in another novel came up to me at a high school reunion, introduced himself, and then suggested that I didn't live in the real world. Fair enough. I'm a fiction writer. It should go without saying that I don't live in the real world! The look in his eyes, however, said, "I'll meet you by the bike rack later, McNally. You'd better be there!"

I honestly don't know what it means to be a Midwestern writer, and yet I'm deeply committed to, and proud of, being one. I always make it a point to note in my biography that I'm a native of Chicago's southwest side. The problem is that I'm lying. The truth is that I grew up in a suburb that bordered Chicago's southwest side, the city of Burbank. There's a difference, as anyone who lives east of Cicero Avenue, on the *Chicago* side, will tell you. In fact, they would be offended that I appropriated Chicago, the city proper. But let's face it: Chicago comes with a host of connotations that Burbank, Illinois, simply doesn't. And I suppose what I'm really trying to do is hitch my wagon to a tradition that includes Nelson Algren, Studs Terkel, and Stuart Dybek, to be a part of *that* continuum rather than admit that I'm just slightly on the other side of that margin. (Of course, Hemingway was born in a suburb, so I suppose I could reassess my literary lineage.)

To a certain extent, regionalism spawns territorialism, and territorialism is all about *not* being the other person. And yet "what we're not" is always shifting. What constitutes one's territory keeps dividing and subdividing, *ad infinitum,* like an amoeba, until the very patch we're standing on becomes our turf. Within the Midwest, there are state rivalries. When I was growing up, Indiana never got any respect from Illinois. Likewise, when I told friends and family that I was heading to Iowa for graduate school, the general response was, "Iowa? What the hell's in Iowa?" Within states, there are divisions. As a student—and, later, a college professor—in southern Illinois, I became acutely aware that Chicago was seen as a city full of people who thought too highly of themselves, and there was great resentment (understandably) that so much state money was funneled north instead of south, which needed more than it received. In Chicago, there are north side and south side rivalries, as any Cubs or White Sox fan can tell you. But it's deeper than that. South Siders view North Siders as elitists, and I still meet North Siders who, upon learning where I'm from, will ominously refer to the South Side as "another world altogether," which, I suppose, is true. Not that we are united on the South Side. We have our own rivals. Are we citizens of Burbank, superior to those who live in nearby Argo or Oak Lawn? Back when I was in high school, we sure thought so! (I write all of this now in pure wonderment. And yet, if I'm perfectly honest, I can still feel the hackles of rivalry rising.) But even Burbank itself is conflicted—those who go to one grade school as opposed to another, or those who live on one side of 79th Street or State Road as opposed to the other side.

I could keep going, of course. The point is that regionalism is at once an artificial construct and a completely real facet of the contemporary world. I've been living in North Carolina for almost a decade now, yet my Midwestern dialect stamps me as an outsider as soon as I open my mouth. Local bumper stickers read, "We Don't Care How You Do Things Up North." Which brings me back to my original point: Territorialism is all about *not* being the other person. Being a Midwestern writer living in the South is both illuminating and frustrating—illuminating because I see the built-in support system that comes with being a Southern writer (a network of conferences and book clubs populated by readers with a deep and abiding loyalty for their own); frustrating because I'll sometimes show up to give a reading from my new novel *set in Chicago,* only to find an empty bookstore. I hear that voice whispering: *We don't care how you do things up north.*

My deep-seated territorialism is thrilled that there is now a series (long overdue, in my opinion) titled *New Stories from the Midwest,* and I'm extraordinarily proud of Jason Lee Brown and the late Jay Prefontaine for getting it up and running. This year's series editors, Jason Lee Brown and Shanie Latham, did a superb job of picking the initial batch of stories, which they forwarded to me so that I could choose the very fine stories you'll discover here. When I sold my first anthology fifteen years ago, my editor told me that he thought all anthologies, regardless of the subject, were just an excuse to celebrate the short story. I don't entirely agree with him, but I've always respected this theory because it's so old-fashioned in its optimism. In that spirit, I hope you enjoy this celebration of some excellent stories, no matter where you're from.

One

Mr. Scary

Charles Baxter

for Richard Bausch

THERE WAS SOME SORT OF commotion at the end of the check-out line. Words had been exchanged, and now two men, one tall and wide-shouldered, the other squat and beefy, were squaring off against each other and raising their voices. Their shoes squeaked on the linoleum. The short one, who had hair from his back sprouting up underneath his shirt collar, was saying a four-letter word. The other man, the tall one, shook his head angrily and raised his fist. An elderly security guard was rushing toward them. He didn't seem up to the task, Estelle thought. He was just a minimum-wage retiree they had hired for show.

"Good God," Estelle said to her grandson. "There's going to be a fistfight."

The boy didn't glance up from his phone gadget. He held it in his palm and was rapidly clicking the letters. "They're just zombies," the boy said quietly and dismissively after a glance.

"Well, how do you know that?" the grandmother asked, trying for conversation. "I've never met a zombie." The men seemed to have calmed down a bit. They were just rumbling at each other now.

"Zombies *like* discount stores," the boy, whose name was Frederick, said patiently, as if he had to explain everything. He still wasn't looking at the two men. "They eat plastic when they can't get brains." The boy glanced up, showing his grandmother his bright blue eyes. "Just look around if you don't believe me," he said. "This junk? It's all *theirs.*" The fight between the two men seemed to bore him, before the fact. Almost everything bored him.

Another security guard had arrived, a red-faced fellow with a crew cut. He would put a stop to things. Together with the older security guard, he herded the two men toward the service area. So: that had happened. Now it was over. Estelle handed the baseball bat she was buying for Frederick to the check-out clerk, who scanned it and who then held out her palm for money.

"You don't see *that* every day," Estelle said to the clerk, who was frowning.

"Ain't none of my business," the clerk said with shrug.

Estelle handed the bat to her grandson, who took hold of it in his left hand while keeping up his writing with his right.

"You're giving this to me because *why?*" the boy asked, glancing up.

Estelle sighed. She no longer waited for thanks for anything from him. Gratitude was simply beyond his abilities.

"For your baseball games," she said, over her shoulder.

"What baseball games? I don't play baseball."

"*Thank* you," the checkout clerk said behind her, belatedly, as if prompting Frederick. He followed his grandmother, his eyes downward again, oblivious to her, to the partly cloudy sky outside the automatic doors, to the untied shoelaces on his left foot, to his own waddling walk, to the folds of fat under his T-shirt, to the gift of the unthanked aluminum baseball bat. The poor child. He had been so beautiful once, years ago, with a smile to light up the world, and now . . . well, just look at him.

They drove across Minneapolis and stopped for a red light in front of the Basilica. At the corner traffic island stood a bearded panhandler with a cardboard sign that read, "HOMELeSS VetERaN. ANYThING WILL HeLP. GoD BLeSS." The man's face was wreathed in sunburned desolation, and she was reaching into her purse for a dollar when her grandson spoke up from the back seat.

"Grandma, don't give him anything."

"What? Why?" Estelle asked.

"He's a pod," the boy said.

"What?"

"*You* know. A *pod.* A replicant."

Estelle looked in the rearview mirror and saw the boy scowling malevolently at the homeless man.

"No, I don't know. Why do you say such things?"

"See, for starters, he's in the stare-at-you army," the boy said, with his eerie talent for metaphor. "They stare at you. That's the pod game plan. I can always tell. I have *radar*. That guy is garbage." Frederick laughed to himself. "He's the lieutenant colonel of garbage."

"No human is garbage," his grandmother said defiantly, rolling down her window, "and I don't want to hear you talking like that."

"Okay, fine," the boy said, "but I'm just saying? How come you *like* these creeps?"

But she had already reached through the car window and placed a dollar bill in the man's palm, and when he said, "Thank you, and God bless you," Estelle felt a small feeling of satisfaction and pride. He might be a bum, but he knew how to be thankful.

"I suppose you think he's a zombie too," Estelle said, as she rolled the window back up.

"*No*," the boy replied. "He's a . . . *replicant*. Like I told you. He looks like a human being, but he isn't. Just like this car we're in now *seems* like a real car." Frederick smiled at his grandmother, a private smile, but the smile seemed to be poisoned somehow by the baby fat on his twelve-year-old face and by the boy's customary malice, a thin screen for his unhappiness. Often his face was unreadable: it was as if he had trained his facial expressions to be ungrammatical. The poor child: he even had a double chin, making him look like a preteen Rotarian. Curled into himself, having returned to his phone gadget, Frederick irradiated waves of unsociability and ill will. His being hummed with animosity toward the world for having staged the enactment of his various miseries. His revulsion at life had a kind of purity, Estelle thought.

Really, all she wanted to do was to take him into her arms and hold him. But he was too old for that now. What had worked once, all that love she had given him, no longer did.

"Mass times force equals velocity," the boy said, just before his grandmother dropped him off at Community Day Camp. "It's true. Did you know that?"

"No, I didn't. But actually, Freddie, that doesn't sound quite right."

"Well, it's true. *Absolutely*. I've been studying physics. And mass times force equals velocity. That's why a baseball travels faster if you hit it hard. You're forcing the ball to, like, accelerate." He waited for his words to sink in. "To escape inertia. You want to hear something else? This is even more amazing. *Gravity equals weight times voltage.* That's Yardley's Theorem."

"Yes. Well, OK. We're here," Estelle said, pulling to a stop in front of the Community Day Camp building, a grim yellow concrete-block affair with a flagpole hoisting a limp flag just inside the turning circle. During the winter, the building served as a community center. During the summer, they offered activities for kids from ages eight to twelve, with trips to spots of local interest. Last week the boys and girls had visited an institution for assisted-living, giving each old person a gift of their own devising. Frederick had given his own old person an African violet. The day camp counselors also staged sports activities on the playground in back. Frederick hated all of it and performed his sullen silence with great majesty whenever Estelle picked him up.

"Do I have to go in there?" the boy asked, once she had stopped.

"Well, I *did* drive you over here. Kiddo, give it the old college try."

"I've done that all summer."

"So do it again."

"They all hate me," Frederick said. "They throw their lunch food at me."

"Throw it back."

"Yeah, *that'll* work. They throw sandwiches. Which *explode.*"

"Well, can't you—"

"—I got a cupcake in my hair yesterday."

"—Make an effort—"

"—All right, all *right*," he said.

"—to go in there—"

"—I said *all right*."

There was a brief air-pocket of dead silence.

"See you in a few hours," Estelle muttered, as her grandson heaved himself out of the car. He was still writing something on his phone. He also had words penned on his arm.

"Don't bother coming back. Just call the coroner," the boy shouted, closing the car door and causing the baseball bat to roll again on the floor.

Her husband Randall, down on his knees in the garden, waved to Estelle absentmindedly with his trowel as she pulled up on the driveway. "Not enough fertilizer for the pansies," he said to her once she was out of the car and behind him, leaning on him. Using his customary tone of comic despair, he said, "And

I've been overwatering the snaps, damn it. Look at them." He stood up, shaking his head before turning and giving Estelle a quick kiss on the lips. When he did, the brim of his sun hat poked against her forehead. "Drop him off OK?" Randall asked.

"So I bought him a baseball bat," Estelle said, putting her hand on her husband's shoulder. "It was a hopeful gesture." She straightened her husband and dusted him off. "But he stayed grumpy. Oh, and this is interesting: there was a fight in the checkout line at the K-Mart."

Randall nodded, gazing at her carefully. "Sure. Of course there was," he said. As always, she was taken aback by his capacity for understanding her, for knowing her least little mood. "Stel," he said, "I've made some lemonade, and . . . Freddie's disposition isn't your fault, you know."

"I know," she said. "I know." She whistled to the dog, who regarded her with indifference from his shade under the crabapple tree. "I just wish sometimes that Freddie were, oh, I don't know, more . . . *normal,* and I hate myself for wanting that. Who wants normal?"

"You do," he said. "Well, let's have a softball game on the vacant lot when he gets home. Us and a few normal neighbors. With his new baseball bat."

"A softball game?"

"Yes. With Freddie. Or maybe we should just *let him be.*" He gave her hand another squeeze and preceded her into the house, holding the door open behind him. How considerate! Randall had always been considerate: he was one of those easygoing persons—affable, graceful, thoughtful—on whom the sturdy world depended, and although her little secret was that she was fatigued with him and felt almost no passion for him, she still needed to have his calm presence around. He was like a preservative, and she would fight to keep him if she had to. He played poker once a week with his chums; he drank one beer per evening; he was semi-retired from his veterinarian practice; he never raised his voice. He was even a graceful and attentive lover. What a paragon of virtue Randall was! Nothing to excess, this husband. But he had never been wild, and Estelle couldn't help herself: she was bored by people like him. Secretly, men who started fistfights attracted her. They had sap. But it was boredom that had the staying power.

"Here," Randall said, handing her a lemonade in a Dixie Cup.

"Thank you," she said, leaning forward into him again. His skin had a kind of slippery silkiness, an odd texture for the exterior of a middle-aged man. Her first husband, the dreaded Matthew, whose nickname had been "Squirrel"—winsome womanizer, alcoholic, self-centered bum, gate-crasher, liar, charmer, deadbeat, and cheat—had felt like hair and sandpaper. Sex with him had always been burningly raw and fecund. Children came from it, three of them. Where was Squirrel Van Dusen now? Pittsburgh? Or was it Tucson he had recently called from, yes, somewhere in the Southwest, that sunny haven for bums, asking for a tide-over loan for his newest harebrained scheme? It was hard to keep track of him: Randall had taken the most recent call and kept her from whatever Squirrel had asked for. She still had a soft spot for the guy. The flame could not quite be extinguished. Human wreckage *had* always attracted her. "The Bad Samaritan," Randall had called her once, in that not-quite-teasing way of his.

"It's a stage he's going through," Randall said, sitting down at the dinette. "Frederick's going through a stage. All boys go through a stage. They have to practice at being bad before they become men."

"*You* were never bad."

"Well, okay. I guess I never was," Randall said thoughtfully, nodding his head once and turning away from her. "Not like that."

"You always got up at five o'clock. To pray. With the birds. Like Saint Francis. You were a boy scout," she said, knowing she was being petty. "You still are."

"That's unkind. And I never *prayed,* not like that. I prayed to someday meet someone like you. Actually, Estelle," he said, fixing her with a look, "what *are* we talking about? This isn't about me, is it? Or Frederick?'

"No, I don't suppose so."

"Well, my dear, what is it about?"

She looked at him. Behind her, she could hear the leaves of the ash tree stirring in the dry summer wind. She could even hear the electric clock in the stove, which gave off a dull but thoughtful hum, as if it were planning something.

"It's about the usual," she said. Of course he knew what it was about. He always knew.

They'd run off together as teenagers forty-five years ago, Estelle and Squirrel, and when their kids were still toddlers, they'd crisscrossed the country in the Haunted Buick. What fun it was, being young, rootless, those hours of driving when music would start up for no apparent reason underneath the car's dashboard and then stop a few minutes later. There was a short in the radio, but Squirrel liked to say that the Buick was haunted. An announcer would begin speaking in mid-sentence from that same place under the dashboard, and Squirrel would say, "Where did *he* come from?" You couldn't switch the radio off: the dial didn't work. The Buick was beyond all that.

In those days, Estelle and Squirrel never stopped anywhere for longer than a few months. They would cross the border into yet another state they hadn't yet ravaged looking for opportunities, surefire moneymaking projects to *put them on the map*, as Squirrel liked to say. That was the expression he used after dark in bed with Estelle in one motel or another, whispering to her about what and where they would be, some day. They'd be settled, and happy, and rich. They'd be *on the map*. The children, the two boys and Isabel, the youngest, whom they called Izzy, slept in the other bedroom, a clutch of little snorers and bed-wetters.

All the trouble had been manageable at first. In Maine, there had been midnight phone calls from a girlfriend Squirrel had acquired somewhere, and a day later they were treated to her sudden arrival on the doorstep of their rented duplex. She'd been coarsely attractive, this girlfriend, furiously chewing bubble gum, and her waitress name-tag was still pinned to her blouse over (Estelle could not help noticing) her plump right breast. *Cheryl.* She was pregnant, this waitress, this Cheryl, said. She wanted satisfaction. *Satisfaction!* What a word. Or else. Or else what? She would be back, she said, with a court order. Estelle and Squirrel packed the car that night and were gone the next morning, the kids still asleep in the back seat by the time the sun came up. Estelle didn't speak to Squirrel, except about necessities, for a month after that.

In Montana, Squirrel's partner-in-business threatened them all—another midnight call!—with a court suit and, if that didn't work out, personal revenge Western style with a semiautomatic. By the time they had relocated in northern Minnesota, as temporary managers of the Trout Inn on Nine-Mile Lake, Estelle thought they were finally free of adventures. They'd come to the calm expository part of the movie, the part after the big opening attention-getting mayhem. Squirrel's mischief-making had been all used up, she thought, just flushed right out of him, and she was relieved.

And then one night Estelle had awakened to find that Squirrel had entered her while she'd been sleeping and was thrusting into her with a wild look on his face, with his hands around her neck as if he planned to strangle her, and she screamed at him and shook him off. She loaded the still-sleeping kids into the Buick, against Squirrel's pleading, and took off for Minneapolis. She remembered to take what money there was, and the credit cards, Squirrel pleading with her but not stopping her, and the children crying.

That was Part One of her life. Now she was in Part Two. There would never be a Part Three. Of that she was sure.

⟡

Mid-afternoon, Estelle pulled her car into the turning circle for Community Day Camp. Of course, Freddie was already there out in front, staring up into the sky as if he were waiting for helicopter rescue. He lumbered toward the car, opened the front passenger-side door, and poured himself in. He aimed the air-conditioning vents toward his face.

"How was it today?" Estelle asked, too brightly.

Freddie sat silently as if the question was much too complicated to be answered. Finally, he said, "We're going to put on a play."

"Yes, I think you told me that," Estelle said. "What is it? What's the play?"

"We're all writing it. Or *they* are. The kids and the counselors." He gave her his best sour look. "It's called *Wonderful World.*"

"And who do you play?" Estelle asked.

"Me? I play Mr. Scary."

"Mr. Scary? Who's that? And what do you do?"

"I stand up at the beginning of the play, and I recite my fear monologue and scare everybody."

"Well, that's nice," Estelle said, trying to put the best face on things. "Do you have it? The monologue? Could you read it to me?"

"Yeah," Freddie said. "I got it right here with me." He heaved himself upward, trying to get his hand into his trouser pocket. After much poking, he pulled out a grimy sheet of paper. Her grandson unfolded the paper and began to read. His delivery sounded like a voice-over in a horror movie. "*Fear,*" Freddie intoned. "What *is* fear? You and I live with it, interact with, fear. We know fear, but we *shun* it. But what if one were to *embrace* fear? Not to *live* with it, but to *be* it, to *become* fear. In our everyday lives we *divorce* ourselves from *fear.* We tell ourselves it is *distant,* it is *unreal,* it is *abstract.* But this is *not* so. Fear is *tangible,* more tangible than you or I. What if a man *became* fear? Where would fear *live?* He would dwell among us, *hidden* but not unseen. *Who* would fear be? For *what* would fear strive? What would be the *face of fear?* Ha ha ha ha."

"Very good, Freddie. But, well, that's a strange monologue to give to a twelve-year-old," Estelle said, after recovering herself. "The words are awfully big. What does it have to do with a wonderful world?"

"It's like what you have to get out of the way? *Before* the world is wonderful? And yeah, well, that's what they gave me," Freddie said, slumping down in the car. "The counselors wrote it. That's what Mr. Scary says. I've got to memorize it. Also we also made T-shirts today. I mean, we wrote words on T-shirts. So they became ours."

"What did you write?"

Freddie held his shirt up. With laundry marker, he had written *GOT HERPES*? on his. "Well," Estelle said, "that's not very nice."

"It's supposed to be a public health warning," Freddie said. "A wake-up call."

"And the other kids, did they throw food at you?" Estelle asked.

"Not today," Freddie said. "Today was a good day. They liked how I did the Mr. Scary monologue."

"Freddie," Estelle asked, "do you really have to laugh at the end of that? It's a little corny."

"The ha ha ha ha part? I added that," her grandson told her. "That's my contribution." He took out his phone gadget and began tapping letters.

"Are you texting someone?"

"No," Freddie said. "I'm writing a story."

"Oh, good," Estelle said. "What's it about?"

"The underworld," he told her.

Sometimes, on certain days when Estelle had found herself sitting on the front stoop of the house, her coffee cup cooling between her palms, and the morning breeze riffling her hair, Freddie still eating his breakfast cereal inside, she would imagine that the way her grandson had turned out, with his sorrow and obesity and malice, had its own logic. But then at other times, particularly when the breeze stopped, time halted as well. And when that happened, Estelle was no longer sitting on the front stoop with her coffee but was back *there*, in time, in Part One, taking her daughter Isabel to a guidance counselor, and then to that killingly expensive, pill-dispensing psychiatrist in the circular building with curved interior walls that made Estelle think of a gigantic brain, and they, all of them, the brilliant professionals and Estelle herself, were trying to *talk* Izzy out of the sullen and then manic rages—shoplifting, a stolen car, drug-taking, car wrecks, god knows what kinds of sex, and with whom—that had overtaken her daughter and turned her into this oblivious bingeing adolescent force-of-nature who'd actually driven once into a parked fire truck. Well, at those moments nothing had its own logic, or it had the wrong kind of logic, because you couldn't *talk* anybody out of anything, could you? No. How many young women had managed to do what her daughter had accomplished? Had smashed a stolen car into a fire truck? An achievement. Her teenage accomplices had fled, but Isabel had stayed there, dazed behind the wheel but boldly confident that such an excellent accident gave her special monster status. Who else, among Estelle's acquaintances, had also hit, though not very hard, a pedestrian in a parking lot? Her daughter Isabel had, and had been unrepentant. *He shouldn't have been there,* she had said of her victim, a retired dentist. In her taste for mayhem, Isabel had truly been Squirrel's child. So there *was* a logic to her actions, of a sort.

Estelle thought that her own life had veered between long patches of drudgery, weeks and months filing claims in an insurance office during the day and then racing home to cook dinner for her children and to put them to bed, typical single-mom scheduling, and then, the next job, working in the front office at the veterinarian hospital where she'd met Randall, accompanied by a choral background of barking. Yes, all that domesticity. And classes taken at the community college including art history, her new passion. Then other stretches of time superimposed themselves on the dull ones, the moments of high drama, first the ones staged by Squirrel and then the ones staged by her daughter. Her two sons, Carl and Robert, seemed frightened by their little sister and had landed jobs after school at grocery and hardware stores; poor souls, solid citizens before their time, they almost didn't count, those boys.

But Isabel! Even on medications, she drank anything, she took anything, she went anywhere at night; she seemed to have no home place except the deep nothingness that she sought out. In Squirrel, those traits had been charming, for a while—they looked good on a boy—but with Isabel they were as charmless as her scowling face. There was really something demonic about her, almost bestial. Estelle imagined her as she saw her back then: twisted up with imagined injuries, avoiding eye-contact, the blond hair matted and unwashed, her jeans caked with dirt, her fierce young woman's sexuality attracting the worst of the boys who gleefully hovered around her waiting for her next bold move.

One night, one of many late nights, Isabel had come home at three in the morning. Estelle had awakened out of a shallow and dream-infected sleep and went into Isabel's room, where Isabel had thrown herself on the bed in the dark. She was muttering, and after Estelle had switched on the lamp, she noticed that the pillow where her daughter rested her head had turned gray at the indentation. Her daughter never showered anymore, and she smelled like a feral child.

"Where have you been?" Estelle asked her, trying not to yell.

"I've been inside and outside," Isabel said. "I've covered the world." She giggled. "Like that paint? That covers the world? I've done that."

"Jesus. What am I going to do with you?" Estelle said to herself, to the walls. "At least get undressed. At least get some sleep. And you're grounded," she said, automatically.

"Undressed?" Isabel asked. Every facial expression she gave her mother indicated that any and all requests were, at that moment, preposterous. "You want me undressed, Mom? Like those nine-to-five people who are undressed? Who go to sleep?"

"Yes," Isabel said. "Like those people."

Isabel glanced up at her mother. Picking herself up, she stood next to the bed, then lowered her jeans. "See?" she said. "I can do this." She swayed and laughed at herself. "Wanna see something?" She laughed again. "I'm a magician. I can do this amazing trick. Just watch. You've *never seen this before in your life*. I can make my panties stick to the ceiling."

"What?" Estelle said.

After stomping her blue jeans to the floor, Isabel lowered her underwear and clumsily stepped free. She bent down and picked up her underpants—pink, Estelle noticed, her heart breaking—and then threw them up at the ceiling. They fluttered back down to the floor.

Isabel gazed upward and said wonderingly, "I thought it would work. I had such a good time."

Estelle was staring, too. Her mind moved slowly. "What are you talking about?"

"Oh, poor Mom," Isabel said. "You're so sheltered. Can't you guess?"

"No."

"Well," Isabel said, putting her hand on her mother's shoulder to keep herself from swaying, "I was with a boy tonight. And we . . . you know. And Mommy, did you know, that after you do it, I mean when you do it with a boy, it drains out of you? Later? Onto what you're wearing? And it makes your clothes . . . sticky. And that's why I thought my underwear would be there up on the ceiling!" she concluded, triumphantly. "Except it isn't."

Of course Isabel would become pregnant. There was no such thing as safe sex with Isabel. Of course she would have a baby and give it to her mother to raise after naming the baby Frederick (who came out of his mother brown, so his father must have been African-American, or something), and of course she would disappear quickly afterwards, leaving no known address.

Poor crazy Isabel. Poor Freddie, her son. It wasn't about individuals anymore; it was about the generations, and what they handed down. The courtrooms, the hospitals, the doctor's offices, the classrooms, the jails where they had put Izzy overnight: sometimes, sitting on the back stoop with her coffee cup, Estelle felt all those places descending over her, as if another person had lived that part of her life and had *not* yet survived it but now was inhabiting her own body. Clouds would cross the sky, cumulus clouds puffy with their own complacency.

In the car, with Freddie explaining about his hero, Argo, and his descent into the underworld, Estelle turned toward Lake Calhoun. When she parked near the beach, Freddie sat up and said, "What're we doing here?"

"I thought it would be nice to go outside," Estelle said. "Just a stroll. It's summer, Freddie. We've got a little time before dinner."

"Of course it's summer. I mean, what are we *doing* here?"

"Well, look at the swimmers." Outside the car, she walked ahead of him in the mid-afternoon glare on a sidewalk that ran parallel to the beach. At some distance from them, young men and women were playing volleyball. Out on the lake she could see swimmers splashing each other, and, beyond them, hazed in the hot Impressionist light, the sailboats. The air smelled of suntan oil and lake vegetation. People were bicycling past on the bike paths, and everywhere men and women, children and dogs were enjoying themselves. Pop music floated on the air from some radio.

"I hate it here," Freddie said, from behind her. Estelle could hear the shuffling of his shoes on the sidewalk. "I need to practice my Mr. Scary monologue."

"We should have brought your swimming trunks."

"I can't swim."

"You could learn."

"Not if I don't want to, I can't," he said. "I'd rather sleep with the fishes."

"The fish. Not fishes. *Fish*. You shouldn't be so negative," Estelle told him.

"You mean I'm supposed to be *happy*?" He inflected the word with scorn. "Happiness sucks."

"Well, you could try," his grandmother said, feeling a wing-feather of hopelessness. Just to her right, a boy about Freddie's age, maybe a bit older, bronzed with the sun, a kid who obviously lived outdoors, was tossing a football to a friend. The wing-feather beat against Estelle as she watched him. Happiness only came to those who never asked for it.

"I'd rather be Mr. Scary," Freddie said. One of the boys close to them threw their football unsteadily, and it landed near the sidewalk. Freddie stared at it before kicking it out of the way. One of the boys said, "Throw it here!" while Freddie continued on.

Estelle raised her head, closed her eyes, and breathed in. "You could have thrown that ball." she asked. "Couldn't you?"

"No," Freddie said. "It's just a trick. They're trying to mess with us."

"Incidentally, I think," Estelle said, "that Randall is organizing a softball game for after dinner. We'll use your new bat!"

"Oh, that's great. That's just great."

"Don't you want to try it?"

He treated her to his silence.

Well, at least there was the Bakken Museum. After they had returned to the car, Estelle drove Freddie to his favorite place on the southwest side of the lake, the museum where they had a working Theremin installed. Freddie had been here half a dozen times, and each time he would push impatiently past the exhibits near the front door to the Theremin in the middle of the museum's stairwell. He'd turn on the old instrument and raise his hands in the air between the two antennae.

Here, he was in his element. His hands raised like a conductor, with his fingers out, Freddie would tap and poke the air in front of him, and from the old Theremin came pitched noises that sounded like music but really *weren't* music, Estelle thought, any more than screaming was like singing. According to the information on the explanatory wall plaque, other Theremins had been used for the Beach Boys' "Good Vibrations" and the movie scores for *Spellbound* and *The Day the Earth Stood Still*. Freddie, when he played this thing, had a beatific smile on his face, as if he were summoning his monsters from the deep. Once he had played "Jingle Bells" for her on it, and Estelle thought she would jump out of her skin with revulsion. He had learned through trial-and-error where to poke the air for certain pitches. Apparently he had a musical ear. He was getting good at it. Soon he would be playing "My Funny Valentine" on this thing and scaring away everybody.

But you couldn't take a kid down to the MacPhail School of Music for Theremin lessons, and you couldn't bring out your grandson in front of the guests to have him play his Theremin, causing the other grandmothers to applaud, because Freddie wasn't really *presentable,* and neither was this music, which sounded like the groans of the dying, oscillating at sixty cycles per second.

Still, she watched him, poking and prodding the air and producing the hellish glissandos, with something like admiration. Her own sons were not like that. There was no other boy like him.

"There's no one else like him," Estelle said to Randall, who was bending over the grill, the left side for the hot dogs, the right side for hamburgers. He had put on his chef's apron and was worrying the hamburger buns on the edge of the grill with a spatula. Freddie sat writing his story, sitting on a picnic bench, on the other side of the back deck. He was concentrating with fierce inward energy.

Late summer evening, and Estelle sat watching Randall cooking the hamburgers and Freddie working on his story. Somewhere in back, the cicadas, harbingers of autumn, were chirring away. Their neighbor, Jerry Harponyi, who played cello in the city orchestra, was watering his garden, and when he saw Estelle across his back fence, he raised his hand, still holding the garden hose, to wave. The water gubbled, airborne, in a snake-like line, before falling.

"No, there isn't," Randall said. "But let's not talk about this now. By the way, I've drafted about seven of the neighbors to play softball in the park in an hour. And Freddie said he'd join us."

"Freddie said that?"

"Yes. I used all my persuasive skills."

"What did you say?" Estelle asked.

"I said it'd be nice if he played."

"He didn't object?"

"I just said that it'd be a nice gesture." Well, Estelle thought, that was Randall, all right: the King of Nice Gestures. "After all, you bought him that baseball bat. And he loves you, you know."

"Who?"

"Freddie, your grandson."

"No, he—"

"—Of course he does, Stel. Please. You're the only thing in this world holding him on." He looked at her with a smile, his face disfigured momentarily by smoke from the grill. "I can't do it the way you can. You're his lifeline. Don't you know that? Can't you see it?"

Harponyi waved again. "Looking forward to the game!" he shouted, and the water from his hose flung itself out again in patterns in the air.

"Me?"

"Yes. My dear, you. You're a rock, an anchor. You're all he's got. I love you too, you know, but I'm not desperate. Anyway, you know what position you should play?"

"No," she said. "First base?" She always liked it when Randall told her he loved her.

"No," Randall said. "Outfield. You need a rest. You can just stand out there and wait for balls to fall into your glove. Like a nun. Like a little sister of mercy."

"I'd enjoy that, I think," Estelle said.

Standing in the outfield, with the sun setting below the park's trees to the west, Estelle felt the early evening breezes blowing across her forehead, the same breezes that blew Randall's hair backward on the pitcher's mound, so that he looked surprised, or like one of the Three Stooges, she couldn't remember which one. With grown children of his own, and his own sorrows—his wife had pitched herself through a window eight stories up two months after learning that she had inoperable cancer—Randall had every right to be moody, or grumpy at times. Or just sour. But, no: he was relentless in his cheerfulness. And tiresome, if you didn't share it. Somehow the tragedies he had lived through hadn't altered him. They had no relevance to him. There he was. In the fading light, he still gleamed a little.

Randall had just struck out Harponyi, the cellist. The first baseman, a fifteen-year-old from across the street, whistled and cheered. His name was Tommy, already chunky with muscle, a real athlete who in a year or two would be playing high school football, and for a moment Estelle wondered whether it wasn't a bit unfair to have boys like that playing on their side. But it all balanced out: their second baseman was an office temp who lived down the block and who was, at this very moment, talking on her cell phone, and their shortstop was old Mr. Flannery, a retired social studies teacher who lived on the corner and who looked a bit like Morgan Freeman. He was old but wiry. Freddie, when he came to bat, wouldn't have a chance if the ball went toward Mr. Flannery.

These are my people, Estelle thought, and bless them all, here in Part Two. Strange how one's heart could lift sometimes for no particular reason. On the other side of the park, the sounds of the soccer players, their outcries, rose into the air and made their way toward her. A fly buzzed around her head, and she smelled the strangely green smell of the outfield grass. She pounded her fist into the baseball glove, a spare that Randall had found somewhere in the basement.

Freddie was up. He was practice-swinging the bat that Estelle had bought for him that morning. His swings were slow, and even without a ball anywhere near them, they seemed inaccurate, approximate.

Stepping up to the plate, Freddie took one hand off the bat to shade his eyes against the sun. When he saw his grandmother, he waved. Estelle waved back.

Randall's first pitch hit the ground a few feet in front of Freddie and rolled to the catcher, Tommy's brother, who threw it back to Randall. "Good eye," Estelle shouted, and people laughed.

The next pitch went into the strike zone, and Freddie swung at it and missed, by a considerable margin. His physical movements were like those of an underground creature rarely exposed to the light. The umpire, an insurance adjuster who lived with Harponyi, called the first strike.

Freddie took another practice swing.

When Randall threw the next pitch, Estelle could see that it would go into the strike zone and that Freddie would swing at it and connect with it, and when he did, the ball soared up, a high fly, slowly ascending, and as it rose into the air, Freddie headed toward first base, not really looking at where he was going but watching the ball instead and then glancing at his grandmother underneath it. For a brief moment they exchanged glances, Estelle and Freddie, and he seemed to grin; and then the ball began its descent, as Freddie, watching it again, headed toward Tommy, the first baseman, a boy as solid as he, Freddie, was soft. Tommy had taken up a stance and had braced himself with his elbow out, and Estelle saw that when Freddie got there, he would slam into Tommy like an egg thrown into a wall. Estelle tried to shout to Freddie to look where he was going, but her shout caught in her throat out of fear or terror, just before the ball dropped in its leisurely way, with perfect justice, into her outstretched glove.

Two

To Psychic Underworld:

Dan Chaon

CRITTER WAS STANDING OUTSIDE the public library with his one-year-old daughter in his arms when he saw a dollar bill on the sidewalk.

It came fluttering by, right next to his tennis shoe, carried by the wind along with a leaf.

He hesitated for a moment. Should he pick it up? He adjusted Hazel's weight. She was straddled against his hip and watched with silent interest as he bent down and snagged it.

He'd had the feeling that it wouldn't be just a normal dollar and he was right. There was writing on it. Someone had written along the margins of the bill in black ink, in a clear deliberate handwriting that he guessed might be a young woman's. *"I love you I miss you I love you I send this out to you I love you please come back to me I will wait for you always I—"*

This written all around the edges of the bill, and he was standing there studying it when his sister, Joni, came down the steps of the library toward them. He had come to pick her up. That was one of the conditions of his current circumstance. He used Joni's car during the day so long as he was there at the library to pick her up from work.

"Hello, soldiers," Joni said brightly. "How goes the war?"

"Mm," Critter said, and Hazel stared at Joni sternly.

"And what have we here?" Joni said, indicating the dollar bill he was still clutching between his fingers. "A little offering for your dearest sister, perhaps?"

She took the love-dollar from him and looked it over. He watched as she read the writing on it, one eyebrow arching. "Ye Gods!" she said.

"I just found it," Critter said. "Just right here on the sidewalk."

Their eyes met. She was still his older sister, though she was also a tiny librarian woman with short hair and a pointy face, and he was an unemployed sasquatch of a man a foot and a half taller than she.

She handed the dollar back to him. "Yikes," she said. "Geez, Critter, you're quite the magnet for freaky notes lately, aren't you?"

He was, yes. *A magnet,* he thought, as they drove back to Joni's house. That was one way to look at it.

He'd found the first note a few weeks after his wife's funeral, on the sidewalk not far from his apartment. It was written in spiky block letters on an index card:

TO PSYCHIC
UNDERWORLD:
STOP ASTRAL
TRAVELING TO
MOLEST/DECEIVE
OTHERS (ANIMALS TOO.)
ANIMALS ARE NOT
MADE OF HATE.
CEASE AND DESIST.

"Jesus," Critter thought. This was when he was still in Chicago, still in the old apartment that he and his wife, Beth, had been living in when she died, still thinking that he would probably be able to pull himself together. He was pushing Hazel in her stroller, they were on their way to the park, and he looked around to see if there were any noticeably insane people nearby.

But there was nobody. It was Sunday morning, and the street was quiet except for a jogger a few blocks up. A pigeon rustled at the curb, pecking at the bone from a discarded chicken wing.

Back in the days when his life had been normal, Critter might have been kind of pleased to find such a note. Beth had loved this kind of thing. So had Joni, for that matter. Beth was a middle school science teacher and Joni was a librarian and they both had collections of weird stuff they had found. Bizarre, misspelled letters written by lovelorn eighth graders. Obscene Polaroids left between the pages of library books. They used to call one another on the phone to share their latest discovery, and Critter had always remained a little off to the side, never feeling quite as sharp or ironic as they were. Critter was an electrician, primarily home repair, and so he didn't usually come across anything except bad wiring and faulty lighting fixtures.

Several days after he found the first note, he was sitting in the pediatrician's office with Hazel—he was feeling kind of proud of himself for remembering to keep the appointment—when another note fell out of an old copy of *Sports Illustrated* that he was perusing. This was a piece of light-blue unlined paper, and written on it, in the careful cursive handwriting of a ten- or eleven-year-old, was a little list:

1. Go for a walk with someone
2. Go out somewhere with someone
3. Talk to someone
4. Watch TV
5. Go on the computer
6. Play PlayStation 2
7. Go to the cemetery and talk to my mom
8. Listen to music
9. Go in my room

For a moment, Critter thought he might completely lose it. It was, he thought, possibly the most heartbreaking thing he had ever read, and he heard himself make a soft, involuntary sound.

Across from him, a young woman with a sleeping infant looked up sternly. Here was Critter, thick beard and shaggy long hair, making snuffling sounds, and the little mother didn't like the look of him at all. It would not be appropriate for him to start weeping in the pediatrician's office, obviously, he realized, and he lowered his eyes and tightened his jaw, and he felt a repressed tear run out of his nose and into his mustache.

Shit, he thought. He needed to get a grip on himself, this was ridiculous.

Nearby, Hazel was sitting in the play area, among some wooden blocks. She gave him a thoughtful expression. Then she lifted two cubes in her hands and touched them together carefully, as if they might give off sparks.

"Boom," she said.

He had been having a fairly hard time of it. Which was natural, he supposed. His wife had been killed in a car accident and he was living alone with his baby daughter and he hadn't been to work since the funeral; customers would call with their electrical needs and he would just let the answering machine pick up, he hadn't even checked the messages in almost a month—there was in fact a sticky note still posted above the telephone in Beth's handwriting:

> Mrs. Palmarosa
> 343-7622
> Her doorbell gives a shock!

Which was the last thing on earth that Beth had written to him before she died.

"Listen," Joni said. "I want you guys to come and stay with me for a while. Just for a visit. Get out of that apartment for a while. Get out of Chicago. And—you know what?—you might find that you actually like Toledo. You can be an electrician anywhere."

"Mm," Critter said. He was sitting on the couch with the portable phone, staring at the muted TV. "I'll think about it," he said.

"You don't have to do this all by yourself, you know, Critter," Joni said. "There are no prizes for being stoic. You realize that, right?"

"I know," he said.

And so now here he was. It was September, and he and Hazel had been living in Joni's apartment for more than two months, and he guessed that he was basically kind of losing his mind.

Not completely, obviously. He continued to do a decent job as a father, he thought. He kept an eye on Hazel as she toddled around, he kept her diapers clean and made little plates of food with cut-up fruit and cheese and crackers, he took her to the park in the stroller, and they never watched any television that had sex or swearing in it.

He was not yet ready to start looking for a job, but he was helping a little bit with various chores. He rinsed off the dishes and put them in the dishwasher.

He took some letters to the post office, and put gas in Joni's car, and went grocery shopping with a list that Joni had made up—though there was a moment where he became kind of frozen in the aisle of condiments and crackers; it was another note, a shopping list stuck to the cage of the shopping cart:

Roach Spray
Batteries
Water Mellon

Which, really, what was so surprising or disturbing about that? But nevertheless he didn't know how long he had been standing there looking at the scritchy, pathetic handwriting when a middle-aged lady had spoken to him firmly.

"Sir, I need to get access to that ketchup, if you could please move forward."

And Critter awakened from his trance with a little shudder.

It was foolish, he knew, to feel so unnerved by such stuff. He had never been a superstitious person, and in any case it wasn't as if there were anything particularly uncanny at work. He was living in a city—Chicago, Toledo—of course there were all kinds of flotsam drifting around.

But he hadn't noticed it before, that was the thing. Beth used to tease him, in fact, about how inattentive he was, she always pointing out the weirdness of the world that he was missing—hot air balloons in the sky over the park; the woman in the bear suit sitting on the El train a few seats in front of them, her bear's head in her lap; the pool of blood in the foyer of their apartment, right there underneath the discarded catalogs and junk mail. "Oh my God!" Beth said. "I can't believe you didn't notice that!"

But now, suddenly, he did. Now, suddenly, it seemed that there were notes everywhere, emerging out of the blur of the world. Something had happened to him now that Beth was gone, he thought—something had opened up, some part of his brain that had been deaf before was now exposed, it was as if he were some kind of long-dormant radio station that had begun to receive signals—tuned in, abruptly, to all the crazy note writers of the world.

"Please," someone had written on a napkin and left it on the table in McDonald's, where he had taken Hazel for a little peaceful snack, a casual Toledo afternoon, but now here was this other voice poking its head through the surface of his consciousness like a worm peeking up out of the ground. "Please," in ballpoint pen on the napkin. And then "Please" on the napkin underneath it, and "Please" again on a third. Someone either very polite or very desperate.

Probably, it wasn't such a big deal. When he had first come to live with Joni, he had shown her some of the notes he had found, expecting, he supposed, that she would find it as eerie as he had—the accumulation of these strange little documents, popping up wherever he went, all of them sad or desperate or slightly creepy. She was the type of sister who had liked to tell him ghost stories when they were younger, back when she was a teenager and he was eight or nine. He'd figured that she, too, would see some kind of omen in the array of notes. But she didn't.

"These are awesome," Joni said. "I love the 'psychic underworld' one."

She had a scrapbook full of stuff that she had come across at the library, and she showed it to him as if she had discovered that they shared the same hobby. As if they were stamps or coins or some such thing.

"Oh, you have to see this one," Joni said, and opened the scrapbook to show him a note written on a powder blue memo page with pictures of kitties on it:

Hi, I
had cyber
sex!! With
a guy named
eric! I love sex!!

"I found this next to one of the computer terminals on the second floor," Joni said. "Can you believe it? The handwriting looks like she's about—what?—twelve?"

To Joni, he guessed, it was something a bit like gossip. Mildly titillating. Something like a glimpse into a window across the street, or an overheard conversation at a restaurant. How weird people were! Her eyes got a kind of conspiratorial glint.

"I love that it's written in pink ink!" Joni said. "It's probably one of those strawberry-scented markers!"

"Yeah," Critter said. "Ha ha."

They were sitting at the kitchen table together, and Joni had opened a forty-ounce bottle of beer, which she poured into two highball glasses. He had a bed in the guest room, and they had set up a crib for Hazel against one wall.

He lifted the glass to his lips. How to explain that he was afraid? How to explain that it felt as if these notes were like the stories she used to tell him about ghostly hands that reached up to grasp your wrist when you weren't expecting it, hands that tightened and wouldn't let free?

"What?" Joni said. "What are you thinking?"

When Beth was killed, she was reading. It was around four on a Thursday afternoon, school was done, and she was on her way to pick up Hazel at day care, hurrying down the sidewalk toward the bus stop. Walking and reading, which he always warned her about, her feet moving automatically beneath her as she flipped through a stack of quizzes that her students had taken in preparation for their sixth-grade proficiency test.

What is a hypothesis?
What is the relationship between a food chain and a food web?
What holds the solar system together?

And then she'd taken a step out into the street without looking. That is what the police said. Stepped out into the street without looking both ways. The practice tests fanned out, flew up, fluttering, and were carried away, wafting into the gutters or caught in fences or flattened against the side of a building.

He started to imagine this, and then he made a choice not to imagine it any longer.

He had always prided himself on being a steady sort of person. Not prone to anxiety. Stable. Even a little intimidating because of his size.

People always assumed that he was called "Critter" because of how he looked. The mane of red-brown hair and heavy beard and eyebrows, which he'd had since his late teens, the bear-paw hands, broad chest, imposing gut. Very few people knew that his real name was Christopher, and that he had become "Critter" because as a child he'd had such a speech impediment that he had a hard time pronouncing his own name. "Chri'er," he called himself. "Cridder," he said, and even now he had a hard time pronouncing "Christopher." Even now at age twenty-nine he stumbled over the syllables, there was still a slight lisp and sputter as he spoke his own name: "Chrithdopher Tremley," even when he pronounced it slowly. He dreaded the various official encounters—banks and government offices, doctors, policemen, the man at the funeral home—which were always the worst times to try to force the hated name out of his mouth. It was a terrible, exposed sort of feeling.

He was a very private person. Beth used to tease him, she thought it was funny, all the things that he felt uncomfortable about, all the stuff he thought of as *personal*. He disliked being barefoot, he hated to talk on cell phones when people could overhear him, he didn't like to sit in the window of the El train where people from the street could see him as he glided past. *My poor shy man,* Beth murmured, and he blushed when she kissed him in public.

He would never, ever, have written a note for people to find lying around the library or the sidewalk. It would have seemed grotesque to him. Maybe that was what bothered him so much about these things that he kept coming across. He had the image of his own personal thoughts softly detaching and carried off by the wind like dandelion seeds, floating through the city. That was one of the things that grief felt like, he thought. *Astral traveling,* he thought.

And now, as if the notes themselves were not enough—

Lately, he had begun to imagine that he saw notes that weren't even there. They weren't hallucinations. Not exactly. Just little misfires, he guessed.

Like, for example, one day he and Hazel were walking to the grocery store to get a few things that Joni had listed for him, he was pushing Hazel's stroller down the shady block and she was quiet, fingering her teething ring, and then he hesitated. Stiffened. He could see a piece of paper that had been stapled to the side of a tree.

YOU SUCK! it said in big capital letters.

And then when he got closer he realized that he was just imagining things. It actually said: YARD SALE!

And then there was another time when he thought he saw something written in the mud outside of the library where Joni worked. He glanced down to the bare corner of the lawn where the grass had been worn off and it looked for a moment as if someone had printed something there. IM . . . WATCHIN . . . YVV. That's what it looked like at first. And then when he looked closer he saw that it wasn't words, after all. Not English words at least. Some kind of Chinese characters? But no, it wasn't that either. It was just the tracks of birds, pigeons, probably. Their three-toed feet marking a line across the wet ground.

He was surprised by the disappointment that settled over him. Nothing, he thought, and his throat tightened. Nothing, nothing.

If the world was trying to send him a message, what was it?

It was a little after midnight, and he sat there in his room in the dark, the guest room in Joni's apartment, staring out the window while against the opposite wall Hazel slept in her crib, her face leaned gently against the wooden bars.

There was nothing to look at outside the window, but he kept looking. The sky was starless and purple-gray, and the silhouettes of tree boughs reached up into it. Through a gap in the trees and buildings, he could see a sliver of a busier street, the red taillights of cars sliding past and then disappearing.

If you have a message for me, he thought, what is it?

There was the wall across the street with the lines running between the bricks in Ts and Ls and Hs and Is, there were the strings of high wires that ran from the buildings and connected to poles and then to other buildings and then to poles again, there were the gestures of tree branches and the smattering of leaves running together down the middle of the street in a formation. You might be able to read such things, maybe. Someone might: not him.

He wondered. He was not the man he had been anymore. He thought: *you are still you, but changing fast.*

It seemed so obvious, once he thought it, but still the idea sent a little shudder through him. He would never be the same person. He would never be able to go back.

He could imagine himself, the way that he had once been just five or six months ago. What would he have thought, driving by down there on the street, glancing up to see a big bearded man sitting at the third-floor window of an apartment building. A grown man, almost thirty years old, peering out at the street, mumbling to himself.

He would not have recognized himself, bent over a dollar bill that he'd spread out on the sill of the window, carefully writing with a pen.

What a weirdo, he would have thought, as the man held his note out in the air, letting the wind take it from his fingers.

Back then, he probably wouldn't have even noticed. He wouldn't have been looking up toward the windows, and he certainly wouldn't have seen the dollar bill lift up in a gust of autumn wind, carried off with a few leaves and scraps.

Off to join the others in their conversations—all the little messages that the world was bearing away.

Three

Townie

Roderic Crooks

AT THE DEADWOOD INN, THE WOMAN on the bar stool to my right whistles when I tell her I'm from New York City, then starts in on a long, rambling spiel about the five seasons of Iowa that leaves me unclear as to what constitutes the extra season. A football game is playing on a set above rows of multi-colored bottles lit from underneath, but this woman cannot keep her eyes off of me. She says, "So you visiting then?" She points her drunk, glassy eyes at me while the guy at the seat on my left mumbles about the ineptitude of whatever franchise is on the television. I can't tell which side is ours or if they are winning.

I tell her that I live here now, that I've taken a job in town and wait for her to turn her attention back to the game, or to the man on my left, or anywhere but at me. She keeps her chin turned up and her gaze locked, so I add, "At the university museum." I hope this helpful detail will satisfy her curiosity and send her back to whatever she was doing before she told me I didn't look local.

Instead, she whistles again. I figure all this whistling must mean she feels sorry for me, being so far from home. I have never been this far into the American Heartland and begin to fear that all women in the bars of the Midwest will be this friendly. The way this lady keeps staring at me with her mouth open makes me feel like a unicorn, magic and impossible. I don't know what it is about me that has this effect on the woman, if it's that I'm a shade of brown she's not used to seeing or if it's my clothes, or something more basic, something so obvious to everyone else as to be invisible to me.

My new coworkers sit at a table a few feet from the bar and as hard as I try to ignore them, I keep straining to listen in on their conversation. The kid who works at the security desk, Ben, is talking about a trip to London with his girlfriend during Thanksgiving break, over two months away. This kind of planning strikes me as excessive, presumptuous even. Who knows what could happen in two months? In sixty days, we might wake up to find that England no longer exists, or has declared war on us again, or is simply missing. The most terrible things are happening even as we sit in this bar, drinking our cheap liquor. Less than thirty days ago, as an example, I had a home and someone in it who loved me, but now I have neither. Take your eyes off what you love for one second and it can disappear.

Martin, the guy on tech crew who showed me a secret hammock mounted in the rafters above the loading dock, has tickets to Paris. Hearing all these romantic vacation plans infuriates me. I bite down so hard the pressure makes my ears ring. Nancy comes up behind me and puts her hand on my back. Even with all the smoke in the bar, I smell her, the heavy rose scent of some drugstore perfume.

Nancy is the only one at work I like. I taped the postcard of the Hawkeye State she gave me on my first day to the wall of my office. My job is to sift through boxes of old, useless things that have become lost in the museum's collections. No one can tell if they are broken-off parts of art or garbage. I dust them, photograph them, then put them back in their boxes. I spend entire days in my little office reading magazines and napping.

Nancy smiles at me, and the woman next to me, now on my left because I have turned my stool around, at last stops staring. Nancy says, "You doing all right here, kiddo?" I think she must be pushing fifty, but I haven't asked. The makeup on her face forms a flat death mask of Maybelline color that she painstakingly retouches throughout the day, penciling on eyebrows in startled-looking arches. It gives her face a pleasant, naïve quality, like she is constantly in the process of being amazed, but there is something sad in her eyes. She has an ass like a bread truck, so that when we walk around in the museum, I have to slide behind her to let people on the other side of the hall get past us. Nancy has to pretend not to notice I have dipped out of her peripheral vision and then popped back in to accommodate foot traffic. She says, "Are you thinking about Paul?"

I say, "I wasn't, until you said it." I watch the ridge of muscles in-between her *trompe l'oeil* eyebrows bulge out. She would be scowling, if she could.

She says, "Sorry. You looked so unhappy over here. Why don't you join us?" She sweeps an open palm out in the direction of the table like a stewardess showcasing an escape hatch. The people on the side of the table that can see us look up and smile without knowing what they are smiling at. I let Nancy stand there for a long time, until her little grin dies out gradually and she lowers her hand down to her side.

Finally I say, "I'm all right, Nancy. It's a little hard for me to be here. I'm home-sick, is all." To me, Iowa is simply a brown square smack dab in the middle of the map I looked up the week before I came.

The man on my right, who used to be on my left, says over his shoulder, so quietly that only I hear, "Love it or leave it." I look over to him, not sure if I heard what I think, and see that he is wearing a shirt with the logo of the Kum & Go gas station on it. He squinches up the side of his face I can see, makes two quick clicking sounds with his tongue, then tips his glass at me.

When Nancy moves to go back to the table to rejoin our work friends, I say I'm too drunk to sit with those assholes. She looks around to make sure no one overheard, then slinks back to the group. I turn my stool back front-ways and watch the guy next to me in the mirror behind the bar. He looks back and, for a while, we study one another's faces in the second-hand light of bar neon. He's younger than I thought, late twenties maybe, which is already old in a college town. The pale hair sticking out of the sides of his hat would be blond in daylight. When I shake the last of the ice out of my empty drink a second later, he grabs an empty pilsner from the row of glasses the bartender has assembled near a caddy full of maraschino cherries and slides the glass over to me. He fills it from his pitcher without saying anything about the terms of this invitation.

A girl with a tiny dog in her purse walks behind us at that moment, down the aisle between the bar and the table with my coworkers. The guy spins around on his stool and reaches out to pet it. The stupid little thing jumps right at him and he catches it in the cradle of his arms. It licks his face. The girl, who looks too young to be in a bar and too dumb to care for a pet, snatches the dog back and slurs an apology. He holds up his hand to stop her and says, "That's all right. Animals love me. Everybody loves me."

When the girl leaves, I tell him that when I was a kid, we got a dog from the pound. They warned us he was a biter and showed signs of having been abused, but I picked him anyway. His legs were so short and his body so long, we figured he was part Weiner, but you could have named any breed and it wouldn't have been entirely off. They say people look like their dogs.

Listen, I tell him. This dog had no understanding of the word "obedient." He refused the leash. He bit every man that ever knocked on the front door of our apartment: the landlord stopping by to pick up the rent check; a cop coming to give us a ticket for the expired tags on the car; my father dropping in to wash his clothes when he got out of the halfway-house. I called this dog Buddy.

Six years after we got him, Buddy bolted into traffic on Lenox Road and a livery cab clipped him and kept on going. I carried him home in my arms and he wheezed and coughed up blood the whole way. I made him a bed on the sofa in the living room and called my mom at the bar she liked to drink in, next door to the one where she worked. She promised she'd be home right away to take him to the vet. By the time she came, well after last call, the dog was dead. I held his face in my lap even after his ribcage stopped moving. There was a stain on the sofa from his blood, and for a long time, whenever I saw it, I felt like I was noticing it for the first time. I thought of Buddy when my eyes happened to run over that spot, how he whined when I put him in the kennel, how he walked me to school in the morning. That's what it's like when you miss someone that much: it takes months before you know he is never coming back.

When I reach the end, he holds up his splayed out fingers and wags his hand at the wrist as if he were hailing a taxi. He says, "That's a sad fucking story, man." The bartender comes over and refills our pitcher. The guy fills my empty first, then his. He picks up his beer and sucks down the whole thing in seconds. Then he curls his lips over his teeth to clear off the foam. He says, "But it sounds to me like that dog was an asshole. You should really let it go."

Later, he tells me his name is Jimmy, by the way. When he stands up to go take a piss, I am shocked to see how small he is, maybe five-seven. Most of these Nordic college girls out here are taller.

We drink together until bar close. One by one, my coworkers take off without making eye contact, except for Nancy, who says to call if I get in any trouble. Jimmy takes me to an after hours at the house of some dude he used to work with at the gas station and when we go in, he warns, "Nothing good ever happens in this town after two in the morning." He asks me for a twenty, which I cough up unquestioningly. Ten minutes later, he brings me to the bathroom and we do a few lines together. Even the cocaine in Iowa tastes worse than at home. When the party breaks up, we walk on the rusted-out train tracks and trellis bridges I have never before noticed, all through downtown, over the river, and out to the edge of the city.

I live behind a strip mall in an Eisenhower-era complex, a horseshoe-shaped two-story surrounded by a vast parking lot scarred with craters and potholes. The only road in curves sharply and dead-ends in a rundown park. There's a sign sticking out of a bramble of thorn bushes carved with the words "Mormon Winter Park."

The dingy one-bedroom I rented over the phone looks out over the blacktop and a patchy lawn abutting the park. Inside the two rectangular rooms in the unfurnished apartment, the floors are peel-and-stick, the walls made of fallout shelter cinderblocks covered in lead-tinted paint. I own half-sets of almost everything—dishes but no silverware, chairs without a table, cases for pillows I don't have anymore.

Jimmy does not seem to mind the living conditions here. He kicks off his shoes at the door and heads right through to the bedroom. We strip and climb onto the air mattress I bought at a camping store. It sags so low from our combined weight that I can feel the floor beneath us. The mattress is a twin, but when I wrap myself around Jimmy's smaller frame, we can both fit. I look out the window into the park and see a stream of smoke coming from the woods. Jimmy's eyes are still open, and I ask if he sees it too. He closes his eyes, yawns, and says, "Forget about it. It's just the Mormons." His breath slows immediately and he starts to snore.

We stay in bed all day the next day, until it's time to go drink again. When he gets up to leave, I ask for his number, so I can call him later. He says he doesn't have one. "Relax," he says, "I know where to find you." Off the top of my head, he might the only person in the world of whom this is true.

Paul nagged me for months to apply to jobs out of state, to quit my job as a technician at the Brooklyn Museum and find something far away so we could clean up and start fresh, as if all you had to do was snap your fingers and everything about you would be changed and made orderly. The only place that took me was the museum at the university. On the Friday afternoon they called, I told them I needed a week to talk it over with my boyfriend, but mostly I was stalling to see if I could find a reason not to go. Iowa, Ohio, Idaho. In my mind these places were one, an endless tundra dotted with shitkickers and slaughterhouses.

Two days later, I woke up on the floor next to our bed a little high still, but feeling good, rested even. I knew I would be hungover later, but there were still enough chemicals in my blood to keep me from hurting. The skin around my eye felt tight and I realized then that I couldn't open my eye. In the mirror on the closet, the skin there looked puffed up and about to turn all kinds of ugly colors. I figured it was Paul that hit me, because we'd fought before. I couldn't remember exactly how it happened, if I said something to set him off or even if I had it coming. I found him on the couch, and no matter how loudly I yelled or how hard I shook him, he wouldn't wake up.

His mother met me down at the emergency room at New York Methodist. She bullied the doctor into letting her see Paul and asked all kinds of questions about the long-term effects, treatment options, and payment plans, as if she were comparison shopping for a dishwasher. It never occurred to me to be so demanding. After a few hours of this, she finally acknowledged my presence by saying, "I think it would be best if you left now." I wanted to tell her that speed-balling was Paul's thing and not mine, but what was the point? It was easier for her to hate me than to admit what her son was.

Days later, when he came home, he stood in the living room and held his hands at his sides while I hugged him. He pressed the tip of his finger on the edge of my eye socket, right where the bruise started, and said this would never happen again. It took me a second to understand that he meant he was leaving me, not that we weren't going to hit each other anymore. I agreed it was probably a good idea for us to quit, that eight years of drinking, drugs, fighting, making up, and doing it all over again was enough. That night he went to an NA meeting in the basement of a church and slept over at his mother's house. Within a week, I had made the arrangements. The day I left, I kept waiting for him to show up and announce that he had reconsidered, but at the end there wasn't even a kiss or a handshake or anything. When I deplaned at the runty airport in Cedar Rapids, I expected him to be waiting in the terminal with flowers.

I am the only one not wearing a costume at the Halloween party thrown by the girl from the office across the hall from mine. These kids I work with. They're all nice, but they have to be at least a decade younger than me, maybe more.

Their display of good will and faith in the future makes me feel old and ruined, even though I'm only thirty-four. They all look so hearty and sincere.

Except for the costumes, this party is the same party I have been going to almost every night since I came to town. It moves from house to house, but I keep seeing the same people engaged in the same conversations. You can tell time by what's on the stereo: hip-hop means last call. A pretty white girl from Human Resources tells me I have to get the dancing started, I guess because I'm the only one at the party who is not exactly white. She says it like that, You *have* to dance, and so I dance with her in the living room, shaking unenthusiastically under the bright lights with the same dozen people I see almost every day looking on. I don't even like dancing.

I walk out onto the porch to have a cigarette. Wind cuts through the pillars of the covered terrace, so fast and strong you can hear it whipping down through the trees. The temperature has dropped thirty degrees since the afternoon. I pull my shoulder blades up toward my ears, flatten myself against the house, and smoke with the cigarette pinched between two shaky fingers. A girl with dreadlocks that look like they stink comes out a second later with a bulldog pipe and offers me a hit. I can tell from her straight teeth, her messy clothes, and the brand-name sandals that she comes from money. We pass the weed back and forth a couple times and bullshit about how it might snow soon and how much longer the beer at this get-together will last. I keep forgetting her name. I have a bottle of Old Style in my hand and a can of beer in each of my jacket pockets.

Jimmy walks up from off the street, wearing only a T-shirt and some jeans. He rubs his hands over his thin biceps and I feel colder looking at him. He trips climbing onto the porch and walks into the bubble of light formed by the single bulb over the door. The lids of his eyes droop down and his mouth is slightly open. It's only been a few weeks since we met, but I feel like I've been waiting forever for him to come find me.

He waits on the top step, then before he even greets me he says, "Do you think I could hit that real quick?" I start to tell him it isn't mine to share, but before I can get a word in, he walks closer and says, "C'mon. Be nice." He puts his arm around my neck and tips forward like he might fall over. I look at this girl Cindy or Mindy or Candy and squint my eyes and suck through my teeth, the way you do when you see a wound that looks like it hurt. I stuff my hands in my pockets, next to the beers, and fold my jacket over Jimmy like a bird closing its wings.

She packs the bowl again and while she tamps a little pinch into it, she says, "This a friend of yours?" She thinks she knows already, so I don't say anything.

Jimmy says, "Yeah. I'm his new boyfriend." He staggers forward, crunching the toe of my shoe with his. His left hand slips inside the opening of my jacket and he puts his other hand on my stomach, under my shirt. The hippie girl gives me the weed. I hold the bowl for him and light it so he can smoke, his face inches from mine. He blows the smoke out into my eyes and whispers in my ear, "I told you everyone loves me." I hold him there, feeling the heat from my body seep out through my skin to warm him and think how good it is that someone has found me.

He steps away and I offer the bowl back to the hippie. When I reach over toward her, Jimmy claps one of the beer cans in my pocket between his palms. I hold my hands up as if I were being frisked while he fishes it out. He tries to tell that joke about not having to tell a lady with two black eyes anything because you already told her twice, but he is so completely ripshit that he keeps screwing up the punch line.

The girl can see the joke is not going to end well. She tells me she's going inside to find her girlfriend and get away from all this misogynist crap. Jimmy looks her up and down and says, "Why don't you do that, you fucking dyke? What kind of fucking hippie are you supposed to be, anyway?" He grins as he says it, but his head is stuck out far over his neck and drifting side to side. I worry he's going to keel over.

The girl screams that she will kick his ass and puffs her chest out. She's swinging her arms around and yelling. He eggs her on, steps closer to her with that silly, stoned expression. I plant myself between them and put both my hands on his chest. I say, "I think it would be best if you left."

He leans in close to me and murmurs in my ear, "I wish you would hit me, you fucking faggot. I wish you would." Then he slaps my hands away and stomps off the porch. He walks all the way to the end of the block. When he gets under the streetlamp at the corner, he flips us off over his back without turning around. The hydraulic gasp of carbonation escaping from the can hisses from his direction.

That night, after all the other guests have gone, I sit on the couch in the living room and tell the girl whose house it is how lonely I am. I accidentally knock over a leftover beer on her coffee table and spill on the rug she has bought especially for the party. She says, "You have to go." When I reach the corner, I flip off her house with both hands and yell out into her street, "You fucking bitch."

I pass through downtown on my way back home. The bars have recently let out, spilling drunken undergrads from every doorway onto Dubuque Street. None of them are dressed up as anything anymore. They have all lost most of their costumes and are parading around in mismatched props, fairy wings and tiaras mixed up with toy guns and smudged grease paint. They must be immune to this wind, having grown up in it. The constant display of health here is stunning. I have never encountered a people so well fed and polite, so happy. Except for Jimmy, who is staggering toward me with that same ghoulish smirk plastered on his face. He says, "What took you so long?" and falls into me. I know I should be mad at him, but in this moment, I feel something like relief.

We cross the river by the museum. The bridge has a sign that, as a warning, shows the date when last a person died from jumping or falling. Jimmy runs ahead of me, leans out over the railing, and shouts, "I'm going to make them change this fucking sign." He plants his feet up on the bottom edge of the rail and holds his arms out in front of him, his fingertips reaching out over the water.

I say, "Are you planning on jumping or falling?" I grab his belt and pull him back from the edge. He takes me on a shortcut near the big dorms. From the top of the hill, in the acres and acres of parking behind the hospital, I can see smoke coming from the park behind my apartment building again. It looks like a curtain of silver fog rolling across the open fields, swallowing up the scenery as it spreads.

I get tired of him borrowing my clothes all the time, so we swing by the place Jimmy sometimes stays and pick up his stuff. We go in the middle of the afternoon, when the guy who lives there won't be around to hassle Jimmy about the rent he owes. All Jimmy's things fit in one carload: a couple garbage bags full of clothes in the backseat, some books on the floor, a busted ten-speed hanging out of the trunk. Jimmy says when he gets off paper, he'll look for some other state to live in. I don't contradict him, even though he never does anything to finish his parole or pay off his fines. Every time we see a cop, he gets skittish.

A few days later, Jimmy and I lie together in bed, the remnants of a twelve-pack on the floor next to the air mattress. Jimmy picks up the phone and hands it over—Nancy calling to say she just got home from break. She laughs when I tell her who has answered. She says, "Well I hope you're being careful. He sounds like trouble to me. You don't know where he's been."

I let her laugh at us for a while, and then I make an excuse to hang up. When I got off the phone, Jimmy, who has been listening to the whole conversation, says, "I hope you had a good laugh, you dick. I guess your fat friend thinks she's better than me because she's got some stupid job that no one gives a shit about." He picks a plate up off the floor and stabs his cigarette into it.

I try to calm him, to pull him back down into bed, but he swats my hand and says, "Keep your fucking hands off me." He slams the rest of his beer, gets up, and goes into the front room. He comes back a few minutes later, grabs the rest of the beers and stands in the doorway. He says, "You think you're too good for me. You act like you're so together, with your job and all that stupid bullshit. But you're a fucking mess up here." He taps his finger on his temple a few times. He bangs the front door shut on his way out, and I suppose it's going to take a lot of apologizing to talk him down.

That night, I cave in to Nancy's complaining and we all go out to dinner together, the three of us, Nancy, Jimmy, and me. Nancy is big on introductions. She wears a dress and even more makeup than usual to the restaurant, which is full of boys and girls who look as if they are playing dress-up. Jimmy forgoes the food altogether and pounds three whiskeys before Nancy's appetizer gets to the table. He gets antsy, maybe because we have been holed up for so long, and he's smoking like a factory. Nancy complains and coughs unconvincingly, so Jimmy grabs his drink and plops down over at the bar to finish his cigarette.

Nancy folds her hands in her lap and stares down at the floor. After a few minutes, she says, "He's a real charmer."

"He's nervous," I say, even though I don't know this to be true.

She drops her hands into her lap and says, "What the heck are you doing? This guy's a loser. I mean, look at what you're throwing away." She holds up one hand to count, and successively loops the index finger of the other hand around each digit as she counts off my good points: "You're smart. You're good-looking. You've got a decent job. What's so bad about your life you want to let this guy ruin it?" She leans her head far back as if to examine something on the ceiling. "You could have any guy you wanted."

I want to explain to her that I do have the one I want, but instead, I say, "He's not so bad, once you get to know him." Across the restaurant, I see Jimmy order himself another drink. When I look back at Nancy, she is shaking her head.

She says, "Every time someone is nice to you, you act like they're crazy." She waves an imaginary pen in the air to summon the check.

We drop Nancy off after dinner. She kisses us each on the cheek and turns off the porch light as soon as she gets in. Jimmy and I head over to another bar. I meet a girl at the cigarette machine and, for a while, we chat about music or politics or drugs, or maybe all of these things at once. By the time I excuse myself to find him, a half hour has passed. I catch up to him at the pool table, as a guy a head taller than Jimmy jabs a finger into his chest and tells him he better shut his fucking mouth. Before I can get over to separate them, Jimmy nods at the guy, takes a step back, then swings at him. The guy dodges out of the way easily, then pops Jimmy right on the bridge of his nose. The crowd pulls them apart. I drag Jimmy out the front and around the corner to the alley by the wrist. Even though I'm irritated with him for fighting, I admire his willingness to take a punch.

Next to a dumpster out back, he shakes himself free and shoves me. I fall back against the wall and hold my palms out toward him. I say, "Easy, easy." He has his fists up again.

He clenches the front of my hoodie and pulls my face close to his. He says. "You love it, don't you, you sick fuck. You love to see me get hit, don't you? Since you're too much of a pussy to do it yourself."

I say, "Jimmy, I'm not going to hit you. I won't do it." But even as I say it, I ball my fists up at my side. He's begging for it.

A group of big and fratty boys approaches from the other end of the alley. Three or four of them have on baseball caps with the brims turned to the back. They look like mannequins, all of them perfectly proportioned and dressed in variations of the same outfit. It's hard even to tell how many of them there are exactly. Jimmy and I stand closely together, his hand still on my sweatshirt. He unclenches his fingers and spreads his palm out over my chest. We wait there together as the group, abruptly quieted, passes us. One of the boys in the pack says, "Fucking faggots." We watch them make their way down the alley, the sound of their laughter bouncing off the concrete and brick.

Jimmy backs up and looks down the alley the way the boys went. He turns his face toward me and I wait for him to say something. His jaw moves, like he is trying to work something out. He spits in my face.

I wipe my cheek with my palm and when I look back up he is already halfway down the alley. When I get home, I lumber through the apartment with the lights turned out, kicking the clothes and papers on the floor out of my path. I consider tossing all his things out, but it seems so ambitious at this hour. I fall asleep on top of the covers with my clothes on.

He comes back late and climbs into bed with me. I wake up when the door opens but don't move. I hold my body stiffly, but he crawls onto the bed on all fours and pushes his forehead into my shoulder until I roll over. He presses his back into my chest and pulls my arm around him. I hold him like that while he cries.

The next morning, I wake up before he does and make the coffee. He comes out, still in dirty clothes from the night before, the bridge of his nose plump and deformed. I ask, "What happened to you last night?"

He sits down on one of the chairs in the kitchen part of the front room. The chairs are spaced out around an imaginary table that I have never gotten around to actually buying. He says, "All I remember is being on the bridge. I wanted to jump off it and make them change that fucking sign, but I came back home, to say sorry first. I guess I passed out." He exhales loudly, puffing out his cheeks, then says, "Sorry."

I sit down at one of the other chairs, and say, "Jimmy, listen. You keep trying to get me to fight you, but I'm not going to. If you get like that again, I'm going to have to get rid of you."

He nods. He pulls his knees into his chest and rests his heels on the edge of the chair. He stretches his T-shirt out over his knees and ducks his head into the little tent he has made. I pour some coffee and wonder if he'll wait for the bruise on his face to heal before he starts in again.

Twenty minutes into Martin's Christmas party, at his tastefully appointed and seasonally festive home on Brown Street, Jimmy tells Martin's wife that she should lose weight if she wants to wear those leggings. I grab our coats from the bedroom before the shocked silence ends. I shoo Jimmy out the door without apologizing to Martin or his wife. Jimmy drapes his coat over his shoulders like a cape and charges off, to a bar, I am sure. I ask him why he got so nasty, so quickly this time and he says, "Who the fuck cares? You hate those people as much as I do." Before I can get in another word, Nancy calls out from the porch and I jog back to see what she wants.

She meets me in the yard in front of Martin's house. There are three steps down to the sidewalk. She stands above me and says, "You know, you really can't bring him to places like this. People are getting mad." This is the second week of December, but already the air stings my skin like rubbing alcohol. Nancy is out here in a holiday sweater, her arms folded, foot tapping the sidewalk.

I say, "I didn't really want to come anyway. I didn't want to be rude and skip altogether." I look down the street in the direction Jimmy has gone.

She says, "So you're going to keep this loser and let him drag you down?" She sounds tired.

I shrug and say, "No, it's not like that." I button up my coat and put my hands in my pockets. I wait for her to give up and go back inside, but she keeps standing there in that homemade sweater. The light comes from behind her so I can't see her face. I say, "I don't know. I guess he's what I'm used to."

She comes down onto the sidewalk and makes me look her in the eyes. She says, "That's bull. You're not the only one who ever had it bad. I guess you were too busy thinking that we are all a bunch of hicks. Some of us had lives before you got here, you know." The smile she tries to muster for me comes out as a twitch in the corners of her mouth. She says, "Not everyone here is as provincial as you like to think." When she walks back up to the house, she hugs herself tightly, and it occurs to me that the sadness I have always perceived in her is not for herself.

I catch Jimmy at the closest bar to Martin's house. He is already arguing with some girl inside, his voice audible over the jukebox. I stand close to him and wait for him to finish. After listening to him rant, I butt in, "Jimmy, can I talk to you a second? Outside?"

He says, "Give me a minute," and holds his index finger up to my face without looking at me. He rips into the girl, even though they have obviously just met. He looks tiny and sickly. I watch him reel off his points and browbeat this girl with his faulty reasons until I can't take it anymore. He looks so weak all of a sudden, so frail.

I say, "Jimmy, listen. I'm going home and I want you to leave tonight." He looks at me for a minute, as if he is not sure what I said. I let it sink in, and then I head for the door.

He runs after me. He says, "Fine. Fine. You've made your point." When I don't stop, he trots ahead and blocks me with his whole little body. He whines, "You can't throw me out like this. Give me some notice or tell me what's wrong or something." He holds my elbow and digs his fingers in. I can't tell if his eyes are wet from being so drunk or if he's going to cry. He says, "You can't fucking do this."

I say, "Or what?" I pull his fingers off my arm. I look at him, all pumped up and ready to fight, but I don't feel angry. I tell him, quietly, there will be no fighting and no making up and if he wants to get melodramatic about it, he knows where he can find a bridge to jump off. I leave him there on the street, his complexion red from the cold and drink.

I think he's going to follow me, but he says, "Goodbye," in a breathy voice. I don't turn around to see the look on his face. I hear the words again, drifting over from somewhere behind me, oscillating from ear to ear.

He doesn't come home at all that night. The next day, I go to work, but all day I expect a call. I tell Nancy what happened and she says, "It's about time. Now you can get on with your life." I feel better, until I realize going back to my life means shutting myself in my office and dusting bits of rubble with a sable brush. I keep hearing that pitiful, desperate "Goodbye." I can hear it at my desk, coming in from the window.

I walk by the bridge on my lunch break. They have not yet changed the sign to commemorate his jump, but I am sure the adjustment is in progress. The brown surface of the water shows the direction of the wind in shifting flat spots and depressions. The shallow parts nearest the riverbanks are already frozen. I see Jimmy here at the highest part of the bridge, as he must have stood on the railing, put his arms in Olympic position, then jack-knifed up, out, and over. The currents here are wicked, a whole cosmos of black holes waiting to drag a body under. I swear I can make out his discolored face down there, smiling up from the river grass. That afternoon, I watch the news expectantly, waiting to hear his name and see the sheriff pull the bloated corpse out of the ice and weeds.

After the late news, every time I drift off to sleep, I hear his voice again and feel him in the room with me. I am so exhausted after what seems to be hours, that I ask him out loud to leave me alone, to stop haunting me. I dream I see his face, outside the window, twenty feet off the ground. He grins at me and begs to come back in. Some time around midnight, I toss the covers off, dress, and go out to a bar close by that Jimmy showed me. I need something to take the edge off.

He is sitting at this bar, dressed in cowboy boots and a flannel shirt. He leans heavily to the left, as if he might slip off his seat at any second. It takes a full minute after I sit down next to him for him to see me. There is a scabby patch on his cheek, the kind of scrape you get from having your face on the pavement. He leers at me for a while, then says, "You look terrible. Have you been crying?" I flag the bartender down and get to business.

After we have finished our last round, and the bartender has put up the chairs and turned on the lights, we walk back down the strip, the lights of all the stores turned out for the night. I am too drunk to drive, so I prop Jimmy up on the side and try to steer him in a more or less straight line. When we get close to my apartment, in the park, I can see smoke again. Two distinct plumes rise up from under the canopy of black trees, spreading out and disappearing as the columns rise to meet the nighttime clouds. Jimmy tells me when the Mormons came through here on foot just after statehood, before the transcontinental railroad, a group got stuck out there in the woods, just a few hundred yards from the Iowa River. The fifth season in Iowa is winter, a winter so premature and unrelenting it must be counted twice. When that first killing frost set in, they knew they were too loaded down to make it over the mountains in time. They dumped everything they could possibly live without, but with the snow already falling, it wasn't enough. Half of the men over sixteen decided to stay behind, while the rest of the caravan, lighter and more agile now, made a break for the Great Salt Lake. Most of the stragglers died out there in the snow, all those boys huddled up together, checking every morning to see who had gone in the night and who had lived. The city fire department knows now not to take the reports of fire in the park seriously. The country dirt is lousy with them, marooned Latter-day Saints, deathless and inconsolable in their yearning for the ones who left them.

The Amnesiac in the Maze

Michael Czyzniejewski

HE DOESN'T KNOW HOW LONG he's been in the corn, but that's not because of the amnesia: he's just lost. His disorder affects the longer-term things like not knowing his name, where he was born, what his mother looks like, if he ever knew her in the first place. Now, without a watch, calendar, or phone to tell him of the world, he's wandering along. He remembers visiting this farm, drinking a cup of warm cider, buying a bag of decorative gourds, chatting with the farmer's wife. He petted their dog, a black lab that was part Pekingese. He was about to leave, just drive off with his gourds and return to his nameless existence. But the maze was free, looked fun, something to do instead of watching TV, instead of hoping to remember. He entered the maze twenty minutes before closing and hasn't emerged since. It's been weeks, maybe two, maybe four: He's lost track to that degree. But since he doesn't know who he is, doesn't have any particular place to go, why not stay? And maybe that's how the amnesia comes into play: no motivation to emerge.

Eventually, the amnesiac does get out. While there is only one exit to the maze, there are many ways for him to free himself, to be freed. The maze is only made of corn, after all. And as stated, the amnesiac's amnesia is not related to his being lost, nor does it affect his common sense.

The amnesiac, during his time in the maze, is by no means alone. Other people, other visitors to the farm, come and go through the maze every day. The amnesiac assumes that the busier days, always two in a row, are the weekends, and starts to count time in that way. Before long, he knows when it will be Saturday and that gives him solace, to know at least that much. Like most people out in the world, he starts to look forward to the weekends. He enjoys others and, most of all, hopes that one of them will help him find his way. So far, they haven't, but he looks forward to running into them, anyway. He decides he is sociable, wonders if he was always sociable. If that's the first piece of the puzzle.

At night, the amnesiac sleeps in the dirt, nestled against a row of stalks like he would lie against the wall in his bed. Corn is firm enough to support his weight, yet surprisingly pliable, like an outstretched arm from a lover, or maybe his mother. Occasionally, he wakes with something crawling on his face, inside his clothes. Even in the moonlight, he does not check to see what it is. He'd rather let it be, let it cross him like a road and allow it to move on. He'd rather become part of the ecosystem that is the corn maze than disturb it any more than he already has.

The amnesiac tries, several hours a day, to recoup his past. Without any distractions, without outside stimuli, he figures he will be able to concentrate. Everywhere he looks, it is either corn, dirt, or sky. As he ambles along, he expects flashes of his memory to come back to him, for his subconscious to kick in, offer up some clues. There is no scientific evidence to back this, nor are there documented cases of this theory proving correct. But the amnesiac doesn't know that. He's trapped in a corn maze and speculation, along with hope, is all he really has.

The farmer's teenage son is named Theo, the amnesiac discovers. The amnesiac confronts him upon their third meeting, recognizing him from the two previous encounters. Theo walks the maze once a week, the amnesiac notes, to troubleshoot. He makes sure no paths are blocked by fallen stalks. He looks for lost items, which he will put in a box near the counter back in the market. He checks on the progress of the corn, measuring height, palming an ear to determine its weight. He looks for lost visitors.

I'm a lost visitor, the amnesiac says.

I've heard about you, Theo says. *Nice to meet you.*

Theo tips his cap, and with two turns of the maze, is gone.

⁂

Of course the amnesiac has thought of the obvious solution: He, at any time, can just bull through the stalks, through the rows, until he reaches an edge. The first few days in the maze, that path seemed destructive. Not only would he be cutting short the growth time of so many ears of corn, but he'd ruin the maze. How much fun would it be, for those guests who have the ability to find their way, to stumble across a straight line that led out? But as the days turn into weeks, when that angle seems less and less important, the amnesiac finds that the maze won't *let* him make this choice. The amnesiac tries pushing through one wall, leading to another passageway, which he is to cross to the next wall of corn. But once through one wall, the amnesiac can't resist the lure of the path, to turn right or left, try again, believing he is one choice away from freedom. This goes on for an entire day, the amnesiac forcing down one wall of the maze, only to stop and tread down the next dirt decision. At the end of the day, no closer to freedom than at the start, the amnesiac cannot deny the maze's power over him.

⁂

The maze is the size of three football fields, stacked sideline to sideline, virtually a square. It is an atrociously large area for its purpose. The corn is over ten feet high and still growing, mid-August when the amnesiac first walked in. Brown now begins to tinge the stalks and husks. The entrance to the maze was at the southeast corner, the amnesiac recalls, just past the farm's goat pen, while the exit lies right next to it, in the same corner, just a thin row of corn in between. What this means is the amnesiac has to somehow circle back to that same corner, that the maze ultimately leads toward the entrance. The path is complicated, however, with forks at every turn, two, three, four options where there could just have easily been two. Each dead end proves just as complicated, intricate retracing necessary just to undo one bad turn, one poor choice. The amnesiac wonders how the farmer made such an elaborate design, how he was able to execute such a busy scheme while sitting on a tractor, let alone get out himself. The amnesiac pictures a helicopter circling above, transmitting directions to an earpiece. Maybe someone in a very tall tower doing the same. Or maybe the farmer is a genius. The amnesiac, though lost, frustrated, and losing hope, is impressed. The maze is an accomplishment and his predicament is living proof of that.

⁂

To the amnesiac's dismay, the corn isn't growing into sweet corn. Instead, it's becoming the barely edible feed corn, or maybe decorative Indian corn, which doesn't taste any better. He feels certain he is malnourished, though he'd been a bit heavier than he'd wanted to be, anyway. The nights are starting to grow cool, and as the corn loses its green, the weather may become unbearable. This is when the amnesiac starts to weave an outer layer, something to put over his T-shirt and khaki shorts. Even the most amateur tailor can weave a decent poncho from corn leaves, stiff yet giving. He is even able to make a better pair of shoes, the flip flops he wore into the maze long since disintegrated. He is soon covered in corn leaves, a walking, talking part of the maze.

⁂

Several of the other farm guests offer to help the amnesiac, lead him out of the maze. Often, the amnesiac will follow these people, sometimes even make conversation.

How long have you been in here? they want to know; he cannot answer.

Has anyone asked about me? he wants to know. *I'm missing, two times over.*

Some guests are more than willing to help, but it's hard for him to keep up, to stay focused. Often he will linger behind, lose them around a turn. Or get drawn in another direction, certain it is the right way. The amnesiac vows to be more proactive, to simply ask for help, to concentrate. Otherwise, he'll have to get used to the path his life has taken.

⁂

The amnesiac, in another attempt to reclaim his past, tries envisioning himself in different roles, hoping that if he chooses the right situation, his memory will kick in. He starts high, imagining himself a doctor, shouting out, *I'm a doctor!* but it doesn't stick. He tries astronaut, lawyer, engineer, actor, architect, submarine captain, tennis player, filmmaker, and billionaire, but nothing seems familiar. He works his way through different occupations, and for the entirety of a day, nothing seems to be the person he is or was. Just before giving up, the amnesiac shouts out, *I'm a farmer!* and he sees himself in a field, harvesting crops, smelling foul, corn all around him. For a second, he believes this vision to be true, then the next second, realizes why it seems so familiar.

⋆⋇⋆

One day, at least a month into his predicament, the amnesiac sees a familiar face in the maze. It is a woman, a woman who looks as disheveled and tired and frustrated as he, a woman he saw days or weeks earlier. The amnesiac runs toward her, grabs her by the arms.

Why did you come back to the maze? he says.

Come back? she says. *I've never left.*

The woman, the amnesiac discovers, is lost as well. The amnesiac asks if the woman, like he, has amnesia, and the woman says she does not, is taken aback by the question.

Have you hit your head? she asks.

Maybe, the amnesiac says. *But not in here—I came in like this.*

The amnesiac and the woman walk along together, discuss their routines, trade secrets of survival, propose strategies for getting out. Then the amnesiac stops to adjust his cornhusk shoes, to rewrap the outer structure. When he looks up, the woman is gone. He can hear her talking and he calls out to her. She calls back. Somehow, in that second, she took a turn, then another, and another, and they became separated. They yell out, trying to find each other again, but the more they look, the farther apart they get, the harder it is to hear each other's voices. Soon the amnesiac is exhausted and sits to nap. When he wakes, he calls out again, but doesn't hear anything. He and the woman never see each other again.

The amnesiac likes to think she got out, that right after they lost touch, she found the exit. More so, he's happy he has someone to lament, someone to miss. Since the amnesia, he's longed for this. Even sadness for someone is better than nothing for anyone.

⋆⋇⋆

The loneliest nights for the amnesiac are the nights it rains. The amnesiac understands the necessity of the rain, sees how it fits into the grand scheme. But in the rain, there is nowhere to go, nowhere to hide. The amnesiac weaves elaborate hats and umbrellas and other coverings, but the rain is still the rain, and the amnesiac, in the rain, gets wet. A rain of any real depth will make the paths through the maze unwalkable, meaning the amnesiac has to sit and wait for the rain to stop, for the mud to return to dirt, for evaporation and saturation to occur on a grand scale.

Rainy days are the longest days, the days the amnesiac most wishes he had someone to talk to. The days it rains are the days nobody else comes into the maze.

⁂

The amnesiac, one day, comes across a family in the maze, and the smallest child, a girl with red hair and freckles, says, *There he is!* pointing at the amnesiac.

The amnesiac is suddenly filled with joy, thinking he's found someone who knows him, who knows his real name, who can fill him in on the rest of his life. This man might be his brother, these children his niece and two nephews. They could even be his own children, his loving brother caring for them in his absence. He could go home, piece everything together. Best of all, know who he is.

Who am I? the amnesiac asks. *Where am I from?*

Suddenly, the family appears frightened.

You're from the corn, the older boy says.

The amnesiac's heart sinks.

You're the scarecrow, says the father. *It's what the farmer calls you. What it says on the sign outside, on the billboard on 6, and in the ad in the paper.*

The amnesiac realizes many things at this moment. He is silent. The red-haired girl takes a picture with her phone. The amnesiac thinks, suddenly, of asking her to use it, to call someone, but there is no one to call. He poses for several more pictures, tells the family the corn is safe, that the crows dare not enter his domain. And it's true—in all the days he's been trapped, he's not seen a single crow. For some reason, this makes the amnesiac proud.

⁂

The amnesiac has an apartment. Or had. It's a state-issued place in the town closest to the farm, about six miles away. It's just one room and a bath, a box he existed in when they released him from the state-run hospital. He began to collect things there, some old furniture, a few books, silverware and towels and a toothbrush and changes of clothes. He lived there just over a month before coming to the farm, to get his cup of cider and bag of decorative gourds. He had a car, a blue Focus, parked out in the farm's gravel lot, though the farmer has probably moved it by now, or had it towed. The amnesiac thinks of this apartment, this car, things given to him by people he didn't know, paltry things that were supposed to make him whole, return him to society. His doctor at the institution said he should start over, too, consider these things his things, start building from there.

There's a chance you'll never know who you are, he petitioned. *You should start looking at your current life as your life, not as a holding pattern.*

⁂

The amnesiac realizes one day that the farmer must have cut the maze when the corn was low, while he could still see across the whole field.

So much for the farmer being a genius, the amnesiac thinks.

⁂

The amnesiac one day pictures a red tricycle, a particularly old, rusty red tricycle with a tear in the seat and the left handlebar grip missing. The pedals squeak and some of the spokes on the large front wheel are bent, others missing. But the amnesiac can see this tricycle and is sure it is his, or was his, that it was something he owned, probably as a child, in his past life. The image reoccurs several times a day, and soon, the amnesiac pictures himself as a boy, riding it up and down the sidewalk in front of his house, or at least a generic house, with rose bushes lining a white picket fence, a pie cooling on a side window. The amnesiac remembers losing the handlebar grip, taking it off one day, throwing it at a rabbit, and never retrieving it. He remembers how the torn leather of the seat poked into his leg, how for a while, someone had fixed it with black electrical tape, but that the tape, at some point, peeled off and no one ever fixed it again. He remembers his legs getting too long, his knees knocking the handlebars, and then someone, a dark, mysterious figure, picking up the red tricycle and placing it in a shed, replacing it with a two-wheel bike, a present with a bow, a random two-wheel bike the amnesiac cannot remember. The amnesiac recalls crying about his red tricycle being taken from him, being placed in this old shed. The amnesiac, in the corn, cries now for his red tricycle, feeling the painful irony: the one thing he can remember is something that he missed.

⟡

One day, when the amnesiac comes upon a couple in the maze, a beautiful girl in a cashmere sweater, accompanied by her obviously bored boyfriend, he introduces himself.

I'm the scarecrow, the amnesiac says.

Hello, the beautiful girl says.

Her boyfriend, staring at the amnesiac, at his corn clothes, corn shoes, and corn hat, doesn't say anything.

Nice to meet you, the girl says, and soon, they are gone.

The amnesiac considers this girl his friend. He thinks about Theo, how the girl should dump her current beau and date Theo instead, that she could come around more often that way, visit almost every day. Theo is a nice guy, likes corn mazes, and will inherit a huge farm one day. The amnesiac imagines the girl as Theo's wife, the future farmer's wife, selling cider and apples and pumpkins and gourds in the market in the barn. The amnesiac imagines an envelope, stuck to an ear of corn down a random passageway, inviting him to Theo and the girl's wedding. Hopefully, the wedding would be after harvest, after the maze is cut down, so the amnesiac could attend. The wedding between Theo and the pretty girl in the cashmere sweater is a reason for the amnesiac to get out of the maze. He thinks about it a lot, and the next time he sees Theo, he asks, *How long till the big day?* which makes Theo make a funny face. But the amnesiac remembers he has a lot on his mind, that the amnesiac is the least of Theo's problems. *If only I could be so lucky,* the amnesiac thinks.

⟡

The amnesiac can't remember much about what he calls his Between Life—that life after the past he can't recall and before his existence in the maize. He will never go back to that apartment, he decides, his food rotten, his power shut off, his rent long past due, government checks waiting in his mailbox. He doesn't want to stay in the maze, but he also won't go back to that. That was never his life, or anyone's.

What he has to do is figure out a third option.

He has plenty of time to consider this, what he'd like to do if given the chance to start over. Until then, he will learn to embrace the corn, the dirt, and the sky.

This is not a holding pattern, he tells himself, then walks straight ahead, coming to a wall of corn. There are two ways he can go. One is the way to the way out, the other leads nowhere but here.

For the amnesiac, the two look exactly the same.

The Deep

Anthony Doerr

TOM IS BORN IN 1914 IN DETROIT, a quarter mile from International Salt. His father is offstage, unaccounted for. His mother operates a six-room, under-insulated boarding house populated with locked doors, behind which drowse the grim possessions of itinerant salt workers: coats the colors of mice, tattered mucking boots, aquatints of undressed women, their breasts faded orange. Every six months a miner is laid off, gets drafted, or dies, and is replaced by another, so that very early in his life Tom comes to see how the world continually drains itself of young men, leaving behind only objects—empty tobacco pouches, bladeless jackknives, salt-caked trousers—mute, incapable of memory.

Tom is four when he starts fainting. He'll be rounding a corner, breathing hard, and the lights will go out. Mother will carry him indoors, set him on the armchair, and send someone for the doctor.

Atrial septal defect. Hole in the heart. The doctor says blood sloshes from the left side to the right side. His heart will have to do three times the work. Lifespan of sixteen. Eighteen if he's lucky. Best if he doesn't get excited.

Mother trains her voice into a whisper. *Here you go, there you are, sweet little Tomcat.* She moves Tom's cot into an upstairs closet—no bright lights, no loud noises. Mornings she serves him a glass of buttermilk, then points him to the brooms or steel wool. *Go slow,* she'll murmur. He scrubs the coal stove, sweeps the marble stoop. Every so often he peers up from his work and watches the face of the oldest boarder, Mr. Weems, as he troops downstairs, a fifty-year-old man hooded against the cold, off to descend in an elevator a thousand feet underground. Tom imagines his descent, sporadic and dim lights passing and receding, cables rattling, a half-dozen other miners squeezed into the cage beside him, each thinking his own thoughts, men's thoughts, sinking down into that city beneath the city where mules stand waiting and oil lamps burn in the walls and glittering rooms of salt recede into vast arcades beyond the farthest reaches of the light.

Sixteen, thinks Tom. *Eighteen if I'm lucky.*

⁂

School is a three-room shed aswarm with the offspring of salt workers, coal workers, ironworkers. Irish kids, Polish kids, Armenian kids. To Mother the schoolyard seems a thousand acres of sizzling pandemonium. *Don't run, don't fight,* she whispers. *No games.* His first day, she pulls him out of class after an hour. *Shhh,* she says, and wraps her arms around his like ropes.

Tom seesaws in and out of the early grades. Sometimes she keeps him out of school for whole weeks at a time. By the time he's ten, he's in remedial everything. *I'm trying,* he stammers, but letters spin off pages and dash against the windows like snow. *Dunce,* the other boys declare, and to Tom that seems about right.

Tom sweeps, scrubs, scours the stoop with pumice one square-inch at a time. *Slow as molasses in January,* says Mr. Weems, but he winks at Tom when he says it.

Every day, all day, the salt finds its way in. It encrusts washbasins, settles on the rims of baseboards. It spills out of the boarders, too: from ears, boots, handkerchiefs. Furrows of glitter gather in the bedsheets: a daily lesson in insidiousness.

Start at the edges, then scrub out the center. Linens on Thursdays. Toilets on Fridays.

He's twelve when Ms. Fredericks asks the children to give reports. Ruby Hornaday goes sixth. Ruby has flames for hair, Christmas for a birthday, and a drunk for a daddy. She's one of two girls to make it to fourth grade.

She reads from notes in controlled terror. *If you think the lake is big you should see the sea. It's three quarters of Earth. And that's just the surface.* Someone throws a pencil. The creases on Ruby's forehead sharpen. *Land animals live on ground or in trees rats and worms and gulls and such. But sea animals they live everywhere they live in the waves and they live in mid water and they live in canyons six and a half miles down.*

She passes around a red book. Inside are blocks of text and full-color photographic plates that make Tom's heart boom in his ears. A blizzard of toothy minnows. A kingdom of purple corals. Five orange starfish cemented to a rock.

Ruby says, *Detroit used to have palm trees and corals and seashells. Detroit used to be a sea three miles deep.*

Ms. Fredericks asks, *Ruby, where did you get that book?* but by then Tom is hardly breathing. See-through flowers with poison tentacles and fields of clams and pink spheres with a thousand needles on their backs. He tries to ask, *Are these real?* but quicksilver bubbles rise from his mouth and float up to the ceiling. When he goes over, the desk goes over with him.

⁂

The doctor says it's best if Tom stays out of school and Mother agrees. *Keep indoors,* the doctor says. *If you get excited, think of something blue.* Mother lets him come downstairs for meals and chores only. Otherwise he's to stay in his closet. *We have to be more careful, Tomcat,* she whispers, and sets her palm on his forehead.

Tom spends long hours on the floor beside his cot, assembling and reassembling the same jigsaw puzzle: a Swiss village. Five hundred pieces, nine of them missing. Sometimes Mr. Weems reads to Tom from adventure novels. They're blasting a new vein down in the mines and in the lulls between Mr. Weems's words, Tom can feel explosions reverberate up through a thousand feet of rock and shake the fragile pump in his chest.

He misses school. He misses the sky. He misses everything. When Mr. Weems is in the mine and Mother is downstairs, Tom often slips to the end of the hall and lifts aside the curtains and presses his forehead to the glass. Children run the snowy lanes and lights glow in the foundry windows and train cars trundle beneath elevated conduits. First-shift miners emerge from the mouth of the hauling elevator in groups of six and bring out cigarette cases from their overalls and strike matches and spill like little, salt-dusted insects out into the night, while the darker figures of the second-shift miners stamp their feet in the cold, waiting outside the cages for their turn in the pit.

In dreams he sees waving sea fans and milling schools of grouper and underwater shafts of light. He sees Ruby Hornaday push open the door of his closet. She's wearing a copper diving helmet; she leans over his cot and puts the window of her helmet an inch from his face.

He wakes with a shock. Heat pools in his groin. He thinks, *Blue, blue, blue.*

One drizzly Saturday, the bell rings. When Tom opens the door, Ruby Hornaday is standing on the stoop in the rain.

Hello. Tom blinks a dozen times. Raindrops set a thousand intersecting circles upon the puddles in the road. Ruby holds up a jar: six black tadpoles squirm in an inch of water.

Seemed like you might be interested in water creatures.

Tom tries to answer, but the whole sky is rushing through the open door into his mouth.

You're not going to faint again, are you?

Mr. Weems stumps into the foyer. *Jesus, boy, she's damp as a church, you got to invite a lady in.*

Ruby stands on the tiles and drips. Mr. Weems grins. Tom mumbles, *My heart.*

Ruby holds out the jar. *Keep 'em if you want. They'll be frogs before long.* Drops shine in her eyelashes. Rain glues her shirt to her clavicles. *Well, that's something,* says Mr. Weems. He nudges Tom in the back. *Isn't it, Tom?*

Tom is opening his mouth. He's saying, *Maybe I could—* when Mother comes down the stairs in her big, black shoes. *Trouble,* hisses Mr. Weems.

Mother dumps the tadpoles in a ditch. Her face says she's composing herself but her eyes say she's going to wipe all this away. Mr. Weems leans over the dominoes and whispers, *Mother's as hard as a cobblestone but we'll crack her, Tom, you wait.*

Tom whispers, *Ruby Hornaday,* into the space above his cot. *Ruby Hornaday. Ruby Hornaday.* A strange and uncontainable joy inflates dangerously in his chest.

Mr. Weems initiates long conversations with Mother in the kitchen. Tom overhears scraps: *Boy needs to move his legs. Boy should get some air.*

Mother's voice is a whip. *He's sick.*

He's alive! What're you saving him for?

Mother consents to let Tom retrieve coal from the depot and tinned goods from the commissary. Tuesdays he'll be allowed to walk to the butcher's in Dearborn. *Careful, Tomcat, don't hurry.*

Tom moves through the colony that first Tuesday with something close to rapture in his veins. Down the long gravel lanes, past pit cottages and surface mountains of blue and white salt, the warehouses like dark cathedrals, the hauling machines like demonic armatures. All around him the monumental industry of Detroit pounds and clangs. The boy tells himself he is a treasure hunter, a hero from one of Mr. Weems's adventure stories, a knight on important errands, a spy behind enemy lines. He keeps his hands in his pockets and his head down and his gait slow, but his soul charges ahead, weightless, jubilant, sparking through the gloom.

In May of that year, 1929, fourteen-year-old Tom is walking along the lane thinking spring happens whether you're paying attention or not; it happens beneath the snow, beyond the walls—spring happens in the dark while you dream—when Ruby Hornaday steps out of the weeds. She has a shriveled rubber hose coiled over her shoulder and a swim mask in one hand and a tire pump in the other. *Need your help.* Tom's pulse soars.

I got to go to the butcher's.

Your choice. Ruby turns to go. But really there is no choice at all.

She leads him west, away from the mine, through mounds of rusting machines. They hop a fence, cross a field gone to seed, and walk a quarter mile through pitch pines to a marsh where cattle egrets stand in the cattails like white flowers.

In my mouth, she says, and starts picking up rocks. *Out my nose. You pump, Tom. Understand?* In the green water two feet down Tom can make out the dim shapes of a few fish gliding through weedy enclaves.

Ruby pitches the far end of the hose into the water. With waxed cord she binds the other end to the pump. Then she fills her pockets with rocks. She wades out, looks back, says, *You pump,* and puts the hose into her mouth. The swim mask goes over her eyes; her face goes into the water.

The marsh closes over Ruby's back, and the hose trends away from the bank. Tom begins to pump. The sky slides along overhead. Loops of garden hose float under the light out there, shifting now and then. Occasional bubbles rise, moving gradually farther out.

One minute, two minutes. Tom pumps. His heart does its fragile work. He should not be here. He should not be here while this skinny, spellbinding girl drowns herself in a marsh. If that's what she's doing. One of Mr. Weems's similes comes to him: *You're trembling like a needle to the pole.*

After four or five minutes underwater, Ruby comes up. A neon mat of algae clings to her hair, and her bare feet are great boots of mud. She pushes through the cattails. Strings of saliva hang off her chin. Her lips are blue. Tom feels dizzy. The sky turns to liquid.

Incredible, pants Ruby. *Fucking incredible.* She holds up her wet, rock-filled trousers with both hands, and looks at Tom through the wavy lens of her swim mask. His blood storms through its lightless tunnels.

He has to trot to make the butcher's and get back home by noon. It is the first time Tom can remember permitting himself to run, and his legs feel like glass. At the end of the lane, a hundred yards from home, he stops and pants with the basket of meat in his arms and spits a pat of blood into the dandelions. Sweat soaks his shirt. Dragonflies dart and hover. Swallows inscribe letters across the sky. The street seems to ripple and fold and straighten itself out again.

Just a hundred yards more. He forces his heart to settle. *Everything,* Tom thinks, *follows a path worn by those who have gone before: egrets, clouds, tadpoles. Everything everything everything.*

⚜

The following Tuesday Ruby meets him at the end of the lane. And the Tuesday after that. They hop the fence, cross the field; she leads him places he's never dreamed existed. Places where the structures of the saltworks become white mirages on the horizon, places where sunlight washes through groves of maples and makes the ground quiver with leaf-shadow. They peer into a foundry where shirtless men in masks pour molten iron from one vat into another; they climb a tailings pile where a lone sapling grows like a single hand thrust up from the underworld. Tom knows he's risking everything—his freedom, Mother's trust, even his life—but how can he stop? How can he say no? To say no to Ruby Hornaday would be to say no to the world.

Some Tuesdays Ruby brings along her red book with its images of corals and jellies and underwater volcanoes. She tells him that when she grows up she'll go to parties where hostesses row guests offshore and everyone puts on special helmets to go for strolls along the sea bottom. She tells him she'll be a diver who sinks herself a half mile into the sea in a steel ball with one window. In the basement of the ocean, she says, she'll find a separate universe, a place made of lights: schools of fish glowing green, living galaxies wheeling through the black.

In the ocean, says Ruby, *half the rocks are alive. Half the plants are animals.*

They hold hands; they chew Indian gum. She stuffs his mind full of kelp forests and seascapes and dolphins. *When I grow up,* says Ruby. *When I grow up . . .*

Four more times Ruby walks around beneath the surface of a Rouge River marsh while Tom stands on the bank working the pump. Four more times he watches her rise back out like a fever. *Amphibian,* she laughs. *It means two lives.*

Then Tom runs to the butcher's and runs home, and his heart races, and spots spread like inkblots in front of his eyes. Sometimes in the afternoons, when he stands up from his chores, his vision slides away in violet streaks. He sees the glowing white of the salt tunnels, the red of Ruby's book, the orange of her hair—he imagines her all grown up, standing on the bow of a ship, and feels a core of lemon yellow light flaring brighter and brighter within him. It spills from the slats between his ribs, from between his teeth, from the pupils of his eyes. He thinks: *It is so much! So much!*

⁂

So now you're fifteen. And the doctor says sixteen?

Eighteen if I'm lucky.

Ruby turns her book over in her hands. *What's it like? To know you won't get all the years you should?*

I don't feel so shortchanged when I'm with you, he wants to say, but his voice breaks at *short-* and the sentence fractures.

They kiss only that one time. It is clumsy. He shuts his eyes and leans in, but something shifts and Ruby is not where he expects her to be. Their teeth clash. When he opens his eyes, she is looking off to her left, smiling slightly, smelling of mud, and the thousand tiny blonde hairs on her upper lip catch the light.

⁂

The second-to-last time Tom and Ruby are together, on the last Tuesday of October, 1929, everything is strange. The hose leaks, Ruby is upset, a curtain has fallen somehow between them.

Go back, Ruby says. *It's probably noon already. You'll be late.* But she sounds as if she's speaking to him through a tunnel. Freckles flow and bloom across her face. The light goes out of the marsh.

On the long path through the pitch pines it begins to rain. Tom makes it to the butcher's and back home with the basket and the ground veal, but when he opens the door to Mother's parlor the curtains blow inward. The chairs leave their places and come scraping toward him. The daylight thins to a pair of beams, waving back and forth and Mr. Weems passes in front of his eyes, but Tom hears no footsteps, no voices: only an internal rushing and the wet metronome of his exhalations. Suddenly he's a diver staring through a thick, foggy window into a world of immense pressure. He's walking around on the bottom of the sea. Mother's lips say, *Haven't I given enough? Lord God, haven't I tried?* Then she's gone.

In something deeper than a dream Tom walks the salt roads a thousand feet beneath the house. At first it's all darkness, but after what might be a minute or a day or a year, he sees little flashes of green light out there in distant galleries, hundreds of feet away. Each flash initiates a chain reaction of further flashes beyond it, so that when he turns in a slow circle he can perceive great flowing signals of light in all directions, tunnels of green arcing out into the blackness—each flash glowing for only a moment before fading, but in that moment repeating everything that came before, everything that will come next.

⁂

He wakes to a deflated world. The newspapers are full of suicides; the price of gas has tripled. The miners whisper that the saltworks are in trouble.

Quart milk bottles sell for a dollar apiece. There's no butter, hardly any meat. Fruit becomes a memory. Most nights Mother serves only cabbage and soda bread. And salt.

No more trips to the butcher; the butcher closes anyway. By November, Mother's boarders are vanishing. Mr. Beeson goes first, then Mr. Fackler. Tom waits for Ruby to come to the door but she doesn't show. Images of her climb the undersides of his eyelids, and he rubs them away. Each morning he clambers out of his closet and carries his traitorous heart down to the kitchen like an egg.

The world is swallowing people like candy, boy, says Mr. Weems. *No one is leaving addresses.*

Mr. Hanson goes next, then Mr. Heathcock. By April the saltworks is operating only two days a week, and Mr. Weems, Mother, and Tom are alone at supper.

Sixteen. Eighteen if he's lucky. Tom moves his few things into one of the empty boarders' rooms on the first floor, and Mother doesn't say a word. He thinks of Ruby Hornaday: her pale blue eyes, her loose flames of hair. *Is she out there in the city, somewhere, right now? Or is she three thousand miles away?* Then he sets his questions aside.

⁂

Mother catches a fever in 1932. It eats her from the inside. She still puts on her high-waisted dresses, ties on her apron. She still cooks every meal and presses Mr. Weems's suit every Sunday. But within a month she has become somebody else, an empty demon in Mother's clothes—perfectly upright at the table, eyes smoldering, nothing on her plate.

She has a way of putting her hand on Tom's forehead while he works. Tom will be hauling coal or mending a pipe or sweeping the parlor, the sun cold and white behind the curtains, and Mother will appear from nowhere and put her icy palm over his eyebrows, and he'll close his eyes and feel his heart tear just a little more.

Amphibian. It means two lives.

Mr. Weems is let go. He puts on his suit, packs up his dominoes, and leaves an address downtown.

I thought no one was leaving addresses.

You're true as a map, Tom. True as the magnet to the iron. And tears spill from the old miner's eyes.

One blue morning not long after that, for the first time in Tom's memory, Mother is not at the stove when he enters the kitchen. He finds her upstairs sitting on her bed, fully dressed in her coat and shoes and with her rosary clutched to her chest. The room is spotless, the house wadded with silence.

Payments are due on the fifteenth. Her voice is ash. *The flashing on the roof needs replacing. There's ninety-one dollars in the dresser.*

Mother.

Shhh, Tomcat, she hisses. *Don't get yourself worked up.*

Tom manages two more payments. Then the bank comes for the house. He walks in a daze through blowing sleet to the end of the lane and turns right and staggers through the dry weeds till he finds the old path and walks beneath the creaking pitch pines to Ruby's marsh. Ice has interlocked in the shallows, but the water in the center is as dark as molten pewter.

He stands there a long time. Into the gathering darkness he says, *I'm still here, but where are you?* His blood sloshes to and fro, and snow gathers in his eyelashes, and three ducks come spiraling out of the night and land silently on the water.

The next morning he walks past the padlocked gate of International Salt with fourteen dollars in his pocket. He rides the trackless trolley downtown for a nickel and gets off on Washington Boulevard. Between the buildings the sun comes up the color of steel, and Tom raises his face to it but feels no warmth at all. He passes catatonic drunks squatting on upturned crates, motionless as statues, and storefront after storefront of empty windows. In a diner a goitrous waitress brings him a cup of coffee with little shining disks of fat floating on top.

The streets are filled with faces, dull and wan, lean and hungry; none belong to Ruby. He drinks a second cup of coffee and eats a plate of eggs and toast. A woman emerges from a doorway and flings a pan of wash water out onto the sidewalk, and the water flashes in the light a moment before falling. In an alley a mule lies on its side, asleep or dead. Eventually the waitress says, *You moving in?* and Tom goes out. He walks slowly toward the address he's copied and recopied onto a sheet of Mother's writing paper. Frozen furrows of plowed snow are shored up against the buildings, and the little golden windows high above seem miles away.

It's a boarding house. Mr. Weems is at a lopsided table playing dominoes by himself. He looks up, says, *Holy shit sure as gravity,* and spills his tea.

⋅⋅⋅

By a miracle Mr. Weems has a grandniece who manages the owl shift in the maternity ward at City General. Maternity is on the fourth floor. In the elevator Tom cannot tell if he is ascending or descending. The niece looks him up and down and checks his eyes and tongue for fever and hires him on the spot. *World goes to hades but babies still get born,* she says, and issues him white coveralls.

Ten hours a night, six nights a week, Tom roves the halls with carts of laundry, taking soiled blankets and diapers down to the cellar, bringing clean blankets and diapers up. He brings up meals, brings down trays. Rainy nights are the busiest. Full moons and holidays are tied for second. God forbid a rainy holiday with a full moon.

Doctors walk the rows of beds injecting expecting mothers with morphine and something called scopolamine that makes them forget. Sometimes there are screams. Sometimes Tom's heart pounds for no reason he can identify. In the delivery rooms there's always new blood on the tiles to replace the old blood Tom has just mopped away.

The halls are bright at every hour, but out the windows the darkness presses very close, and in the leanest hours of those nights Tom gets a sensation like the hospital is deep underwater, the floor rocking gently, the lights of neighboring buildings like glimmering schools of fish, the pressure of the sea all around.

⁂

He turns eighteen. Then nineteen. All the listless figures he sees: children humped around the hospital entrance, their eyes vacant with hunger; farmers pouring into the parks; families sleeping without cover—people for whom nothing left on earth could be surprising. There are so many of them, as if somewhere out in the countryside great farms pump out thousands of ruined men every minute, as if the ones shuffling down the sidewalks are but fractions of the multitudes behind them.

And yet is there not goodness, too? Are people not helping one another in these derelict places? Tom splits his wages with Mr. Weems. He brings home discarded newspapers and wrestles his way through the words on the funny pages. He turns twenty, and Mr. Weems bakes a mushy pound cake full of egg-shells and sets twenty matchsticks in it, and Tom blows them all out.

He faints at work: once in the elevator, twice in the big, pulsing laundry room in the basement. Mostly he's able to hide it. But one night he faints in the hall outside the waiting room. A nurse named Fran hauls him into a closet. *Can't let them see you like that,* she says, and wipes his face and he washes back into himself.

The closet is more than a closet. The air is warm, steamy; it smells like soap. On one wall is a two-basin sink; heat lamps are bolted to the undersides of the cabinets. Set in the opposite wall are two little doors.

Tom returns to the same chair in the corner of Fran's room whenever he starts to feel dizzy. Three, four, occasionally ten times a night, he watches a nurse carry an utterly newborn baby through the little door on the left and deposit it on the counter in front of Fran.

She plucks off little knit caps and unwraps blankets. Their bodies are scarlet or imperial purple; they have tiny, bright red fingers, no eyebrows, no kneecaps, no expression except a constant, bewildered wince. Her voice is a whisper: *Why here she is, there he goes, OK now, baby, just lift you here.* Their wrists are the circumference of Tom's pinkie.

Fran takes a new washcloth from a stack, dips it in warm water, and wipes every inch of the creature—ears, armpits, eyelids—washing away bits of placenta, dried blood, all the milky fluids that accompanied it into this world. Meanwhile the child stares up at her with blank, memorizing eyes, peering into the newness of all things. Knowing what? Only light and dark, only mother, only fluid.

Fran dries the baby and splays her fingers beneath its head and diapers it and tugs its hat back on. She whispers, *Here you are, see what a good girl you are, down you go,* and with one free hand lays out two new, crisp blankets, and binds the baby—wrap, wrap, turn—and sets her in a rolling bassinet for Tom to wheel into the nursery, where she'll wait with the others beneath the lights like loaves of bread.

⁂

In a magazine Tom finds a color photograph of a three-hundred-year-old skeleton of a bowhead whale, stranded on a coastal plain in a place called Finland. He tears it out, studies it in the lamplight. *See,* he murmurs to Mr. Weems, *how the flowers closest to it are brightest? See how the closest leaves are the darkest green?*

⁂

Tom is twenty-one and fainting three times a week when, one Wednesday in January, he sees, among the drugged, dazed mothers in their rows of beds, the unmistakable face of Ruby Hornaday. Flaming orange hair, freckles sprayed across her cheeks, hands folded in her lap, and a thin gold wedding ring on her finger. The material of the ward ripples. Tom leans on the handle of his cart to keep from falling.

Blue, he whispers. *Blue, blue, blue.*

He retreats to his chair in the corner of Fran's washing room and tries to suppress his heart. *Any minute,* he thinks, *her baby will come through the door.*

Two hours later, he pushes his cart into the post-delivery room, and Ruby is gone. Tom's shift ends; he rides the elevator down. Outside, rain settles lightly on the city. The streetlights glow yellow. The early morning avenues are empty except for the occasional automobile, passing with a damp sigh. Tom steadies himself with a hand against the bricks and closes his eyes.

A police officer helps him home. All that day Tom lies on his stomach in his rented bed and recopies the letter until little suns burst behind his eyes. *Deer Ruby, I saw you in the hospital and I saw your baby to. His eyes are viry prety. Fran sez later they will probly get blue. Mother is gone and I am lonely as the arctic see.*

That night at the hospital Fran finds the address. Tom includes the photo of the whale skeleton from the magazine and sticks on an extra stamp for luck. He thinks: *See how the flowers closest to it are brightest. See how the closest leaves are the darkest green.*

⁕

He sleeps, pays his rent, walks the thirty-one blocks to work. He checks the mail every day. And winter pales and spring strengthens and Tom loses a little bit of hope.

One morning over breakfast, Mr. Weems looks at him and says, *You ain't even here, Tom. You got one foot across the river. You got to pull back to our side.*

But that very day, it comes. *Dear Tom, I liked hearing from you. It hasn't been ten years but it feels like a thousand. I'm married, you probably guessed that. The baby is Arthur. Maybe his eyes will turn blue. They just might.*

A bald president is on the stamp. The paper smells like paper, nothing more. Tom runs a finger beneath every word, sounding them out. Making sure he hasn't missed anything.

⁕

I know your married and I dont want anything but happyness for you but maybe I can see you one time? We could meet at the acquareyem. If you dont rite back thats okay I no why.

Two more weeks. *Dear Tom, I don't want anything but happiness for you, too. How about next Tuesday? I'll bring the baby, okay?*

The next Tuesday, the first one in May, Tom leaves the hospital after his shift. His vision flickers at the edges, and he hears Mother's voice: *Be careful, Tomcat. It's not worth the risk.* He walks slowly to the end of the block and catches the first trolley to Belle Isle, where he steps off into a golden dawn.

There are few cars about, all parked, one a Ford with a huge present wrapped in yellow ribbon on the backseat. An old man with a crumpled face rakes the gravel paths. The sunlight hits the dew and sets the lawns aflame.

The face of the aquarium is Gothic and wrapped in vines. Tom finds a bench outside and waits for his pulse to steady. The reticulated glass roofs of the flower conservatory reflect a passing cloud. Eventually a man in overalls opens the gate, and Tom buys two tickets, then thinks about the baby and buys a third. He returns to the bench with the three tickets in his trembling fingers.

By eleven the sky is filled with a platinum haze and the island is busy. Men on bicycles crackle along the paths. A girl flies a yellow kite.

Tom?

Ruby Hornaday materializes before him—shoulders erect, hair newly short, pushing a chrome-and-canvas baby buggy. He stands quickly, and the park bleeds away and then restores itself.

Sorry I'm late, she says.

She's dignified, slim. Two quick strokes for eyebrows, the same narrow nose. No makeup. No jewelry. Those pale blue eyes and that hair.

She cocks her head slightly. *Look at you. All grown up.*

I got tickets, he says.

How's Mr. Weems?

Oh, he's made of salt, he'll live forever.

They start down the path between the rows of benches and the shining trees. Occasionally she takes his arm to steady him, though her touch only disorients him more.

I thought maybe you were far away, he says. *I thought maybe you went to sea.*

Ruby parks the buggy and lifts the baby to her chest—he's wrapped in a blue afghan—and then they're through the turnstile.

The aquarium is dim and damp and lined on both sides with glass-fronted tanks. Ferns hang from the ceiling, and little boys lean across the brass railings and press their noses to the glass. *I think he likes it,* Ruby says. *Don't you, baby?* The boy's eyes are wide open. Fish swim slow ellipses behind the glass.

They see translucent squid with corkscrew tails, sparkling pink octopi like floating lanterns, cowfish in blue and violet and gold. Iridescent green tiles gleam on the domed ceiling and throw wavering patterns of light across the floor.

In a circular pool at the very center of the building, dark shapes race back and forth in coordination. *Jacks,* Ruby murmurs. *Aren't they?*

Tom blinks.

You're pale, she says.

Tom shakes his head.

She helps him back out into the daylight, beneath the sky and the trees. The baby lies in the buggy sucking his fist, examining the clouds with great intensity, and Ruby guides Tom to a bench.

Cars and trucks and a white limousine pass slowly along the white bridge, high over the river. The city glitters in the distance.

Thank you, says Tom.

For what?

For this.

How old are you now, Tom?

Twenty-one. Same as you. A breeze stirs the trees, and the leaves vibrate with light. Everything is radiant.

World goes to hades but babies still get born, whispers Tom.

Ruby peers into the buggy and adjusts something, and for a moment the back of her neck shows between her hair and collar. The sight of those two knobs of vertebrae, sheathed in her pale skin, fills Tom with a longing that cracks the lawns open. For a moment it seems Ruby is being slowly dragged away from him, as if he is a swimmer caught in a rip, and with every stroke the back of her neck recedes farther into the distance. Then she sits back, and the park heals over, and he can feel the bench become solid beneath him once more.

I used to think, Tom says, *that I had to be careful with how much I lived. As if life was a pocketful of coins. You only got so much and you didn't want to spend it all in one place.*

Ruby looks at him. Her eyelashes whisk up and down.

But now I know life is the one thing in the world that never runs out. I might run out of mine, and you might run out of yours but the world will never run out of life. And we're all very lucky to be part of something like that.

She holds his gaze. *Some deserve more luck than they've gotten.*

Tom shakes his head. He closes his eyes. *I've been lucky, too. I've been absolutely lucky.*

The baby begins to fuss, a whine building to a cry. Ruby says, *Hungry.*

A trapdoor opens in the gravel between Tom's feet, black as a keyhole, and he glances down.

You'll be OK?

I'll be OK.

Good-bye, Tom. She touches his forearm once, and then goes, pushing the buggy through the crowds. He watches her disappear in pieces: first her legs, then her hips, then her shoulders, and finally the back of her bright head.

And then Tom sits, hands in his lap, alive for one more day.

Six

Circling in the Air

David Driscoll

TODAY I WATCH WHITEY-TIGHTEY LINE. Whitey-Tightey Line is not real name, just name we use at factory. Real name is White Cotton Briefs. I am Inspector Number Seven. I work here long time. Too long, maybe, but this job is not so bad. I sit on stool over conveyor and watch for anomaly. I use Special Technique. Special Technique is pick spot on floor or paint chip on side of conveyor and spread out vision so it is big, big—like looking down from mountain top. In this way I see underwear three at a time, like looking at photo. Special Technique is very good for concentration, and sometimes I go very deep. Sometimes it looks like underwear is glowing, and sometimes I think threads are made of light. Sometimes vision drop away completely so there is no seeing and no hearing. This is very mystical state. I can always spot anomaly, though. Like now.

I press red button and conveyor stops, use Trigger Fingers to pick up whitey tightey from conveyor and transfer to Anomaly Bin. Trigger Fingers is metal pole with pinchers on end. Very handy for moving anomaly. Very easy on back. This anomaly is label sewed to front panel. This is functional anomaly. Functional anomaly means underwear still work fine but still is anomaly. If someone opens three pack of White Cotton Briefs in Boca Raton or Minneapolis and sees label sewed to front panel they will not like this. They will go back to store and ask for refund. They will see sticker says Inspected by Number Seven and shake their heads. I do not think they will call factory to complain but this is not the point.

There is soft electronic BONG sound, and blue lights come on, fade away. Five o'clock. When I first start work here there is whistle. When I first start work here we have sixty inspectors and five foremen. This is long time ago. Now we have four inspectors and one foreman. Now there is machine for everything. They have machine test waistband elasticity and machine check reinforced seam. They even have machine poke metal finger through jockey slot. Someday they invent machine detect anomaly and then poof—no more inspector. This is not so bad for me, maybe. I have retirement. 401K in toilet, but still this is not a problem. I have son who is cardiothoracic surgeon in Miami. He does not come home so much, but still he is good boy.

I hang Trigger Fingers and hard hat on hook number-seven. Way down at other end is Inspector Number Fifty-Two. Inspector Number Fifty-Two is enormous man. He has hands big like tennis racket and square head like Frankenstein. Also he is deaf. Inspector Number Fifty-Two works here sixteen years and never says one word. He is nice man, though. Inspector Number Fifty-Two gives me pat on shoulder on way to locker room.

Inside locker room I throw jumpsuit in laundry bin. On Monday it will be clean and folded in front of locker. I put on flannel shirt, and this feels soft on arms and shoulders, but buttons are very small today, and it takes big effort to push through buttonhole. I tuck shirt into jeans and zip up then attach belt buckle from Big Sky State. I have never been to Montana, but it is my dream to go. Open spaces. Wild West. I would like very much to see rodeo and grizzly bear. Someday maybe I will go.

Inspector Number Fifty-Two zips duffle bag and throws over shoulder, gives me second shoulder pat on way out of locker room because this is Friday ritual. On most days it is one pat but Fridays it is two. I sit down on bench in front of locker and bones feel very heavy. My job is not so hard, maybe, but I am not spring chicken. I look inside locker and still there is fishing hat. It looks very far away. I have not been fishing in a long time.

Outside of locker room keys jangle, and I look up. Foreman Doug is on landing in front of office, and his boots go PONG, PONG, PONG on metal steps. Foreman Doug is trying to fix collar of coat, and this is not going so well.

"Have a good weekend, Wang," he says. Wang is not real name. Wang is nickname. Real name is Xiang. This means circling in the air. Long time ago I think

I will take American name like Sam or Eliot, but old foreman calls me Wang, and this is end of story.

"You, too, Foreman Doug," I say and give comical salute.

Foreman Doug is still fussing with collar on way to exit. "Oh, Wang." He stops and turns around. "I've been meaning to ask you, how is the wife doing?"

I feel face go hot and look down at cement floor, but this is not dignified so I look up. "Much better. Thank you for asking," I say and smile champion smile.

Foreman Doug grins, and upper lip sticks to upper teeth. He looks like maybe he has strain, but this is how Foreman Doug smiles sometimes. "Glad to hear it," he says. "Whelp, see you Monday."

I nod and wave, but Foreman Doug is already halfway out door. It slams shut behind him. It is five-o-eight, and I am alone in worker area. Many years ago, inspectors used to stick around and shoot bull, maybe go for beer. Many years ago there was other man from Hunan Province work at factory. He was not from same hometown, but we knew many same people and many same places. It is nice to sit in break room after work and talk before going home. Maybe this does not happen now because there are only five employees, but I think it is more than this. I think people do not like each other so much these days.

Outside is twilight already and sky is very beautiful so I look up. Clouds are purple going down to pink and red and orange near roofs of row houses across street. There are many power lines in my way, and this is not so beautiful, maybe, but I pretend these are musical score for sunset symphony, and this is nice idea. I set lunchbox on roof of subcompact and unlock. I drive same subcompact for fifteen years. Paint is faded maybe, and there are cracks in dash, but still is in very good condition. I set lunchbox in center of backseat, and this reminds me of son when he is very small. I do not know why this is so, but it gives me good feeling every time.

I make left out of lot, very slow so undercarriage does not scrape on asphalt. The clouds to south are gray only, and there is smear of rain connecting them to earth like maybe painter have hiccup. I drive two minutes and first drops hit windshield. Five minutes later it is raining, and I am stuck in traffic with rest of the world. This is not so bad, maybe, but this is not nicest part of town. On one side of street there is empty lot with falling down fence and weeds tall as trees. Also there are three big piles of dirt, and one of them has rusted coil of wire on top like maybe it is halo for giant dirt angel buried up to forehead. Next to dirt pile there is section of concrete pipe big enough to drive subcompact through.

Also there is abandoned backhoe. It has rusted spots like old banana. Other side of street is not much better. Other side of street is strip mall with big parking lot and three empty stores, one 99 Cent Emporium, and one supermarket. Sign says Tiger Co-op, but nobody cooperating in there. On corner there is bus stop and blonde woman standing in rain. She has pink cashmere sweater on and gray skirt and newspaper overhead like tent to keep her dry, but this is not working so well. I turn on blinker and pull over to curb. I lean into passenger seat, and I see legs through window. I roll this down and shout, "Hey lady, you need lift?"

She bends at knees and waist and looks down at me. She is very pretty lady.

"I'm waiting for the bus," she says.

I shake my head. "Bus not coming. I pass two miles back. Bus have flat tire."

Lady looks at me with worried look and then stands up on tip toe and looks down street like maybe she will see bus this way and know I am big liar. Lady bends back down and looks in window but does not say anything.

"I drive ahead five miles, just like bus," I say. "You need lift?"

Lady glances over shoulder in other direction now and looks back at me. Her lips are pressed in wavy line like she wants opinion on what to do, but I am only one around so she is out of luck.

"You are getting wet," I say, and this does trick. Lady takes careful step so heels don't sink in mud and turns sideways so she can get down from curb in skirt.

"Oof," she says and swings legs into car. She pulls door shut and rolls up window with vigorous motion. "Thanks so much for stopping," she says. "I don't know what I would have done."

"This is not a problem," I say. "I drive straight ahead five miles, just like bus." I turn on blinker and look in mirror. Big woman in big brown van waves me in. I give her thumbs up through rear window, and I am thinking now people are not so bad. I am helping this lady, and the woman in van is helping me. Strangers helping strangers sometimes, even though they say this is a cruel world.

"What a day," passenger lady says. I look down and see wet newspaper folded on floor mat. I prefer she throws in trashcan back by curb, but this is not end of world. "I'm Linda," she says and holds out hand.

"Hello, Linda. You call me Wang." Linda has dry hand, like belly of lizard.

"Nice to meet you, Wang." Linda blows air out of mouth and lips to make sound like horse. "What a day," she says again. "What a week."

This is only small talk so I do not say anything. "How far you go, Linda?" I ask.

"About ten blocks," she says. Linda pulls down visor and checks makeup in mirror. She squeezes damp curls in fist and then folds up visor. "Who cares anyway?" she says and looks at me with bright smile. She has big white teeth. "I don't think I could have stood out there another second," she says. "It's getting cold already."

I nod because this is true. Next week I will need coat.

"I can't believe how fast summer went. And now fall is going, too." She has wide eyes like this is very scary thing. "I'm not ready for snow. Snow," she says again. "It's incredible to think there will be snow again soon."

I do not know if this is so incredible, but still I nod.

"So, is this your job, Wang?"

"Is what job?"

"Driving around saving damsels in distress?"

I laugh because this is nice joke.

"No. I am inspector," I say.

Linda's eyes go big again and she adjusts in seat to face me. "Like a police inspector?"

For a second I think maybe it is funny to say this is true and talk like I am on TV show where they use words like double homicide and drink coffee out of foam cups all day long, but instead I say, "No. I am inspector like quality control. In factory."

"Oh," she says, but her face is still bright. Linda seems like maybe she is very chipper lady.

"And what do you do, Linda?" I do not really care to know this, but this is polite thing to ask.

"I work for a lawyer," she says and rolls her eyes. "It's totally boring. Answer phones and make coffee, basically."

I nod and look forward and watch wipers squeak like metronome on glass. We are stopped at red light, and Linda looks down side street through passenger window. It is very gray outside. Gray on gray in gray world except for little red dot of traffic signal that has ring around it like planet because of water on window. I can only see small corner of Linda's cheek and back of head, but this is very forlorn image. Very beautiful. I watch water run down glass like streams branching. My light turns green and I step on gas, drive right into back of big, black SUV.

I look at Linda who has hands like little claws in front of open mouth, and I think of woman in horror film rated B. A man climbs down from SUV, and he is big as Montana. He walks to back of SUV and looks down, pulls moustache. He has cowboy hat and cowboy boots and plaid shirt unbuttoned to hairy solar plexus and sleeves rolled up to elbows. Man gives a little nod to self and walks up to window. I have rolled it down but do not remember doing this.

"You folks all right?" the man asks.

I nod, and his eyes flick to Linda.

"Looks like my trailer hitch punched a hole in your bumper," he says.

"I am very sorry," I say.

The man shakes his head. "No skin off my back. I just wanted to make sure you folks were all right."

I look at Linda and back at man. "I have insurance information," I say. "I will pull over and call police."

I see man's eyebrows bunch together like fuzzy caterpillars inching along. "I don't see why we'd need to do that," he says. "Unless you want a ticket to go with that hole in your bumper."

I feel Linda's dry hand on forearm, and she leans toward driver's side window. "No. We definitely don't want that. Thanks for being cool," she says. She smiles very flirtatious, and the man smiles back, also flirtatious.

"Don't mention it," he says. "You folks have a good day." The man taps door and there is CLICK, CLICK from huge ring on finger like maybe he wins Super Bowl, but probably it is only college graduation ring. I watch man walk back to SUV. There are wet drops on shoulders of plaid shirt, and he does not look back when he climbs into cab. I watch until hazard lights go off. SUV drives away, and there is honking behind me. I look in mirror to see man leaning over steering wheel of hatchback. He has both palms raised in air, and mouth is open with very annoyed look. He looks like young college professor maybe. He has tan sport coat and black tie, long brown hair, and wire-rimmed spectacles like John Lennon.

"Wang," Linda says, "are you all right?"

I nod because of course this is not a problem.

"Do you want to pull over for a minute?" she asks. She is talking to me like I am a child, and I do not understand this. There are cars passing me on right and left. The man behind honks again. I have hands at ten and two. I listen to wipers, steady like metronome.

"I'm sorry," I say to Linda.

"Don't worry about it," Linda says. "It was just a mistake. Happens to everyone."

"I am very safe driver," I say.

"I'm sure you are," Linda says.

"I never have accident," I say.

Linda nods.

"You could ask wife, but—" I tighten hands on wheel. Wipers go up and down, up and down. Man behind us honks again. "We should go now, maybe," I say.

"I think so, too," Linda says. She watches me, but still I do not put car in D until Linda reaches forward and presses button to turn off hazard lights. She smiles very encouraging, and I put car in D. We drive ahead and everything feels very strange, like this is same car I drive for fifteen years but also not. I do not know how accident happened. I saw brake lights on SUV, but still I drive forward like maybe I want to see what happens.

"Maybe I am very tired," I say to Linda.

"Me too," she says. "I didn't sleep well last night. I had terrible dreams." She is still nervous. She is talking fast. "Do you ever have dreams where there is someone in your house?"

I nod because I want to agree but cannot remember a dream like this.

"Then you know how terrible they are," she says. "Last night I dreamed there was a man in my house. A huge man. He chased me upstairs, and I fell down beside the bed. He had a nylon stocking over his head so I couldn't see his face, but I could see the hate there. It was the deepest kind of hate. It just kept on going. Bottomless hate. He had this rope in his hand like he was going to strangle me, and I tried to plead with him to leave me alone, but all that came out was this gobbledy gook that even I didn't understand. The more I tried to talk the crazier it sounded, and then it was like I was choking on my words. I couldn't breathe, but not because the man was strangling me. He hadn't even moved. He was standing stock still in front of me with the rope in his hand, but it felt like it was around my neck. It was such a terrible feeling. I was so frightened when I woke up. It felt so real."

Linda looks down at floor mat like she is staring into dream, and she has hand near collar bone like she is still afraid of choking. She looks at me with worried expression again, and I wish she would not have told me this. What am I supposed to do with this information? I am not therapist. I am not even friend.

Linda looks through windshield and says, "Oh, oh. I should have gotten out two blocks ago."

I turn on blinker and pull up to curb.

"I can't thank you enough for this, Wang." Linda has palms pressed together in front of heart. "You saved me. You really did. I mean, I would have been fine out there in the rain, but I needed someone to do something like this. You can't understand what this means to me."

I nod and smile, but it is very hard to look at her because she has look on face that is very full. I do not know how else to describe this, but it is too full for me, and I think maybe she wants to give me a hug and then she does. It is awkward hug because I have one hand on steering wheel and other hand on gearshift, and I am feeling hot and too close to Linda and so I give her pat and gentle push back into seat. She is reaching for door handle but still looking at me like I am someone very special.

"Wait," I say and reach onto floor mat behind passenger seat. I hold up small umbrella. "Take this," I say.

Linda wrinkles up face. "I'm not taking your umbrella," she says. "No way."

"This is not a problem," I say. "I have two." I reach back and pick up other umbrella to show.

"Nuh uh," she says. "You've done too much already."

"You take," I say and drop umbrella in lap. "It is extra. Also it is not nice umbrella. It is promotional gift. Free, you know? You take. What I need two umbrellas for?"

Linda looks down at umbrella in lap, and there are tears in her eyes like little moons, but also this is uncomfortable for her now, too, and she wants out of car just like I want her to leave.

"You're a saint, Wang," she says. "Take care." Linda leans forward quick and gives me peck on cheek like schoolgirl kiss. She pulls open latch and steps into rain. I watch umbrella bloom above her head, and she is off walking down sidewalk. She has left wet newspaper on floor mat, but this is not big deal. I set other umbrella on floor mat behind passenger seat where it is all alone now. I look at lunchbox sitting in backseat, and again it reminds me of son when he is small boy, only now he is angry, but I do not know why. He is sitting with arms crossed on chest and face turned to window. I shake my head at this. It is only lunchbox.

It is dark by the time I reach hospital, and parking structure is full of gloom and humidity. There are many empty parking spots on either side of ramp because most employees and visitors are gone for weekend. I take spot on third floor close to pedestrian sky bridge. I turn off ignition and put fingers on headlight switch, but I do not turn off. Instead I stare at lights, bright like spotlights on concrete wall. Engine goes TICK, TICK, TICK, and this is only sound I hear. I turn off headlights and pull out key, and for some reason this feels strange, feels like serrated knife on bone.

Pedestrian sky bridge is very bright, too bright. It has tubes of fluorescent light running along curved glass ceiling, and whole place glows like maybe you are going to heaven instead of just going to hospital from parking structure. Through glass I can see street below. There is woman in white coat with blue umbrella walking along sidewalk. Asphalt in street looks oily and slick. In the middle of street there is empty wheelchair. I do not see this at first because maybe I do not expect to see, and it looks very strange. I do not want to think about how it got there. Something about this bothers me very much.

Hospital is nice hospital for hospital but still is hospital. There are many windows and skylights in atrium, and also there are many plants. They do renovation so maybe you think this is new hospital, but it is not new hospital. You can see this if you look where walls join floor or if you look at paint on doors which is cover-up coat. I press elevator button and ride up to oncology floor. On oncology floor I keep eyes on tile. On oncology floor everyone has cancer. Maybe doctors, nurses, and visitors do not have cancer when they go home, but on oncology floor they do. This is something I discover in faces. This is why I watch tile.

Wife's room is dark inside, but door is open so I step in and close without sound. I cannot see, but I know this is not wife in bed. I know this even before eyes adjust because this is not wife snoring. It is old man. It is bald man with ring of white hair around back of head and spots on forehead and arms. I am very embarrassed for walking into wrong room, but when I turn to go I see sign near door that says this is not wrong room, and now I am very angry with nurses for not calling to tell me they move wife, and now I am very worried because I know it is more than this, and in my mind I am running down hallway, screaming wife's name, but my body is still in room with old man, and my hand is still on doorknob because it will not turn. It is wrist and not doorknob that will not turn. This is very strange experience, like maybe I am having stroke. Then I hear wife.

"Xiang," she calls. "I'm here." It sounds like wife is very far away. Like maybe she is calling from below floor or through walls from other room. But this is only because I am not listening. Wife is inside old man. This is very clear.

I stand beside bed and look into old man's open mouth. His teeth are very smooth and worn down and yellow and there is much metal from dentist. His tongue is inside mouth like slug, and this is very disgusting thing. I hear wife again. "Xiang? Can you hear me?" I picture wife very small inside dark cave. She is calling out with hands around mouth for amplification, and this is not so easy to take.

I take pillow from chair next to bed and hold one inch above old man's face with both hands. My palms are sweaty and arms and shoulders hurt from so much tension. Even breathing is not so easy, and I jump when there is bright flash outside of window. I look up and there is jagged lightning bolt reaching down to earth. It is purple but also it is white, and I count one, two, three, and there is thunder to rattle glass, and I can feel this in my chest. It is storm in earnest now, and I see other flashes inside clouds. I hear wind howl as it squeezes through tight spaces on exterior of hospital. This sounds like desperate animal looking for place to hide, but there is no place to hide, so wind must fight. It fights through trees across street and tries to rip traffic signal from concrete. I watch pizza box turn like saw blade beneath streetlamp, and grocery bag chases through air like ghost. I set pillow back on chair next to bed, and I do not hear wife next time old man snores. I know wife is not inside old man. This is good thing, I know, but still it is one more loss.

I am quiet on way out of room, and I am thinking of many things. I am thinking of days long ago with wife and days before, when I was small boy in Hunan Province, how I grow into man there, and then one day I meet wife and we are married and this seems like normal thing to do, but in truth it is strange thing to do. You live with wife for long time, maybe fifty years, and maybe you pretend that you will die on same day but this is not what happens. Maybe for some people it happens this way, and sometimes I think they are luckiest people. I live with wife for fifty years, and I do many things for her, and she does many things for me, some of them thinking things even. Why do we do this? Why do we not do these things for ourselves so we do not have to try when we are so old? This is something I do not know.

I am standing by elevator, and there is Korean girl beside me. I give her small nod and she has polite smile. She is very pretty girl. Make good wife for son in

Miami. Elevator dings, and I hold out arm for her to go first. I hold out arm because this is polite thing to do and girl goes into elevator. We are going to same
floor, and maybe she is also walking to parking structure, and for me this is nice
idea. I do not know if we will have conversation, but it is nice to have someone
to walk with. It is not so far, maybe, but still it is nice.

Down to Bone

Roxane Gay

WHEN I AM FIFTEEN, MY FATHER rapes my best friend Shelby while she is sleeping over. She tells me the next morning when I find her in my bathtub. I find him downstairs, sitting in a chair, leaning back on two legs while he drinks his morning coffee. He looks up, raises his mug, and says, "Be glad it wasn't you this time."

⁂

Every morning, I write a list of everything I know to be true. Some days this list is short. Other days it is longer. Jesus turned water into wine and for that he was a hell of a guy. My father loves to sing this fact loudly while cradling a paper-wrapped bottle of wine, dancing like a fool on the living room couch. Bruce Springsteen and Johnny Cash are the only men who make any music worth a damn. There is no such place as Iowa. My father told me the name was made up for the aptitude test they give to kids in grade school—to weed out the dummies and send them where they belong, he said. When we drove across the country to see the Grand Canyon, he gave me sleeping pills at the Illinois border and told me they were vitamins. I didn't wake up until we had nearly crossed into Wyoming. When I asked if we had found Iowa, he got angry. "How many times do I have to fucking tell you?" he said. He pulled onto the shoulder and slammed on the brakes, his tires leaving a long snake of rubber on the pavement. It was dark save for the occasional beam of light speeding toward us. He turned on the dome light, and spread open his wrinkled, stained atlas across the steering wheel. He grabbed my hand and used my fingers to point to a black smudge in the middle of the country and then he hit me with the atlas until it got damp and started to tear apart. There is no such place as Iowa. I know that now.

❧

I grew up in Hancock, Michigan, in the northernmost reaches of Michigan's Upper Peninsula. For most of the year, Hancock is dark and cold and strangled beneath a thick blanket of ice and snow and profound sorrow. There's a small university the next town over and not much else. It is a forgotten place on the shores of Lake Superior, far from anywhere. It is a hard place filled with hard people left behind when the last of the copper mines closed. What's left lingers, persists, refuses mercy.

❧

My father doesn't fuck me in our house anymore, out of respect for my dead mother's memory. My father fucks me because she haunts him, because he misses her and still sees her and smells her. I'm only doing what a good daughter does, he says, what a good daughter should. He takes me to the nicest hotel in town, once or twice a week. He pretends he's a better man than he is. He wears his best suit, carries his briefcase, and checks in alone like he's in town on business even though we only live a few miles away. Then he calls me on my cell phone, tells me the room number. He tells me to hurry because he needs me now. I open my car door. Some days, I throw up in the parking lot, and then I stare at myself in the side mirror and apply a thick coat of my dead mother's lipstick. The door to his hotel room is always propped open, and he is sitting on the edge of the bed, his tie hanging around his neck. He looks up and smiles. My breath sours in my mouth. He says, "You look just like your mother," like he's paying me a compliment.

❧

My mother never laughed but she smiled a lot, pressing her thin lips together, the edges curling up slightly. She had long black hair that she loved more than anything. When I sat next to her, I would braid myself into the thick strands until she shooed me away. On Saturday mornings, she spent almost an hour in the shower, carefully washing the week away. Afterward, she sat on the bathroom counter, parted her hair into four perfect sections and dried each one before twisting it into a knot and pinning it to her head. On Saturday nights, she and my father went to The Junction, a bar with loud music and cheap drinks at the intersection of two country highways. When she left the house, her hair was always piled in crisp, dark curls, and the air around her was thick with perfume. She would pat me on the shoulder and then walk slow and sexy out the front door. My father would smack her ass with a heavy hand and say, "Look at my lady," like he was somehow responsible for the impression she made. She loved me as best she could in a family where no one knew how to play their parts properly.

⚜

I hope Shelby will never speak to me again, but that would be too kind. She never comes to my house again, but demands that I spend hours after school with her each day in the stifling air of her bedroom. She recounts each detail of what my father did to her in the hallway just outside my bedroom with her pressed against the wall, her left arm stretched out, frantically scratching at my door. She tells me how he smelled, and how his skin crawled against hers, how even though time has passed, everything still hurts. As if I don't already know. For months afterward my father will ask after her. He'll say, "Whatever happened to that one girl?" He'll hitch up his pants, pour himself a glass of wine. "Why doesn't she come around anymore? You do something to her?" He'll laugh and grab me by shoulders, squeezing until he leaves finger-sized bruises along my collarbones. He'll tell me, "You'll have to do."

⚜

I met my grandfather only once before he died. He was short and fat and indelicate. We came home and found him on our couch, watching an episode of *Matlock,* his coarse laughter filling the family room. When my father cleared his throat, his father looked up at us, then at me standing between my parents, and said, "You're a pretty little thing." He patted the empty space next to him on the couch. My father put his arm around my shoulders, held me close, his chest rising and falling against my arm, faster than I thought possible. He kissed me on my forehead, told me to go up to my room. I ran to the top of the stairs and crouched quietly, listening as my mother offered my grandfather a drink and my father told her not to offer his father a goddamned thing and then the three of them argued for hours about everything that had ever gone wrong between them. At dinner that night, I sat next to my grandfather who told me nice stories about my father as a little boy. My grandfather slept on the couch that night, snoring loudly. The next morning, my father walked me to school, holding my arm too tightly. As we said our goodbyes, he told me, "Nothing my father ever says is true."

⊹

I am not an only child. Once upon a time, I had an older sister, Lena, who was sixteen years older. She could have left when she turned eighteen, but she didn't. She went to college the next town over and even when she graduated, she still stayed. Lena had dirty blonde hair and always chewed gum. She liked cars and Yooper boys and eating snow and when she sang, she sounded just like Pat Benatar. Lena slept with me in my bed, her back against the wall, my back against her chest, our legs threaded together. I never was good at sleeping at night. I would stare at the tree just outside our bedroom window, listening to the warmth of her light snoring against my neck, how her breathing stopped and her body tensed as our house settled into its age. When his shadow loomed over us, she would kiss my shoulder, and slip out of our room. In the morning, she would be wrapped around me again, her fingers curled into tiny fists. When I was nine, I found her floating in a tub of scarlet water, her arms crossed over her chest.

⊹

For most of his life, my father has worked in construction, renovating old mining houses so they can stand up to the harsh Upper Peninsula winters. On weekends, he would take my sister and I to whatever job site he was working on. We'd bring a thermos filled with soup and another filled with coffee and a boom box with a tape player and he'd blast Bruce Springsteen songs. He would strut around in his flannel shirt and dirty jeans and boots and say, "I'm the fucking boss." He'd laugh like he said something funny. He taught us how to use a hammer without hurting our thumbs and how to tear down drywall without making a mess. He taught us how to scavenge for cabinet fixtures and doorknobs and copper that he could sell for extra money. My father was very well suited to tearing things apart, to breaking a home bare. At the end of the day, he would load his truck with everything worth anything and we would pile into the front seat, warming our hands over the heater.

⚜

My family went on vacation once. I was eleven. My father took us to Mackinac Island to stay at the Grand Hotel because my mother's favorite movie was *Somewhere in Time* and she loved Christopher Reeve before he fell off a horse and later died. For a year, my father set aside $50 a week. It was the only time in his life that he saved anything. That summer, after school let out, we drove five hours on two-lane highways singing Johnny Cash songs, our feet hanging out the car windows. When we finally arrived in St. Ignace, wrinkled and hoarse, my father parked our car at the dock, and we took the ferry across Lake Huron to the island, where cars weren't allowed. My mother spent weeks carefully packing our suitcases with our nicest clothes and once we checked in she unpacked everything to avoid wrinkles. When she finished, she clasped her hands together, smoothed her hair, and stood by the window staring out at the lake and everything clear and blue and bright in the world. When my father stood behind her, she looked up at him, cupped his chin with one hand, her fingernails gently scratching his beard. I think she loved him.

⚜

The best part about running is the feeling that the wall of muscles stretched over the frame of bone protecting you is going to tear apart. I join the track team in the ninth grade because the coach sees me sitting in the stands every afternoon, watching the team practice. He lopes over to where I sit, says he wants to see me run, asks if I have any gym clothes. I'm wearing jeans, a T-shirt, a pair of Converse. I tell him I'm fine in what I'm wearing. He shrugs, fingers the stopwatch hanging around his neck. I don't wait for his prompt. I start running around the track, slowly at first, feeling my legs stretch into a steady pace. After a few laps, I run faster, and then faster still until everyone around the track stops to watch me. All I feel is the wind wrapping around me, drying my tears before they fall to the ground. I don't stop for anything, not until I hear a loud piercing whistle. I fall to my knees, gasping for air. "You're on the team," the coach tells me.

⚜

My first boyfriend is a redhead named Cooper Koskiniemi. We both have long last names that start with "K," so we meet because it's a small school and our lockers are adjacent. It will take him four weeks from the first day of sophomore year to ask me out. We go to dinner at Pizza Hut, flicking toppings off our slices, chewing on the rims of the thick red tumblers and then we go to the movies and spend most of it groping each other and sharing Junior Mints. We're with Cooper's older brother Pete and Pete's girlfriend because Cooper doesn't have his driver's license. They keep giving each other high fives. I catch Pete staring at me more than once. After the movie, the four of us are standing on the sidewalk, our fingers greasy with butter. Cooper reaches for my hand, warm, slick, a little sweaty and he holds it like he really cares. He asks me what time I have to be home and I tell him it doesn't matter. The four of us pile into Pete's Blazer and we drive out to the overlook where everyone from school hangs out. Lots of people are up there doing things that need doing in the dark. We can hear Pearl Jam and Notorious B.I.G. and R.E.M. coming from the parked cars around us. Cooper and I head into the woods, looking for a quiet spot. It is October and cold. We are shivering. He pulls me into a bony embrace, says he'll keep me warm. When he asks, I tell him he's my first because that's what he wants to hear. We do everything but kiss because that I don't do. After I break up with him, he spends the rest of the year leaving angry notes in my locker. Eventually, I carry all my books with me from class to class, my spine curving more and more beneath the weight of it all.

At sixteen, what I love most is working at Burger King in Calumet because behind the counter, in my polyester uniform, I can be a completely different person, someone who helps people and knows things. Colin, the evening manager, is twenty-one, impossibly tall with shaggy hair and dark eyes. He is in college and he too knows things. He likes showing me how to assemble Whoppers and drop frozen French fries into the bubbling vat of oil without getting burned. He teaches me how to make new dishes after closing, using chicken tenders and pickles and mustard and tomatoes. During our breaks, we sit behind the store between the dumpsters, giving ourselves brain freeze from racing to see who can drink their milkshake the fastest. Colin asks me out on my third day, the first time I get to use the cash register with the little pictures that will help me help the customers get their food their way. When I tell him no, he's still nice to me. After that, he drives me home at the end of my shift every night. He tells me about his classes and what it's like being in college, living away from his parents. He invites me to the house he shares with four other boys, and we play video games with his roommates. We sit on his porch swing, rocking back and forth, smoking cigarettes and drinking Dr. Pepper. Day after day, week after week, I wait for him to ask me out again but he never does. Colin lets me fall asleep against him while we're watching movies in his bedroom, and he never tries anything. Before the year is out, he's all I ever think about.

⁂

My grandmothers died before I was born. My mother died when I was fourteen. My sister died when I was nine. Sometimes, I sit in the attic in the center of a semicircle of their pictures, with my father's mother, stern, her hair swept into a tight bun staring into the camera with an icy expression. With my mother's mother, holding her only child on her hip, trying to cover her face with her free hand. With my mother on the beach at Mackinac Island, her impossibly long black hair covering half of her face as she dances in a circle. With my sister, wearing cutoffs and a tank top, hanging upside down from a tree branch sticking her tongue out at me, a month before she died. I look at these pictures, and try to memorize their features. When I die, there will be no one left who knows any of us were here.

⁂

When I turn seventeen, my father decides to learn how to cook. My mother has been dead for three years. He wants me home at six sharp, sitting at the dinner table, wearing something nice, preferably a skirt. He works from my mother's worn copy of *The Joy of Cooking* and, over dinner, he recites some of the bits of wisdom from the book like, "Tea: the cup that cheers without intoxicating." He pours us each a glass of wine and talks about how the wine complements the dish. I sit across from him and smile and force his food down my throat. I drink the first glass of wine quickly, the second more slowly, and by the third glass of wine, it is easier to play along. When we are done eating, he never lets me do the dishes. He tells me to make myself comfortable in the living room so I sit on the couch, watching *Jeopardy*, drinking more wine, until everything is so blurry that I don't hardly mind when he sits next to me, pulls my hand, then my head into his lap.

I threaten to tell someone about all the things that are wrong between my father and me when we are in our usual hotel room, lying on a Sleep Number bed. I'm watching The Discovery Channel, a documentary about English kids with horrible diseases that guarantee they will die young. My father is messing with the bed controls, adjusting the bed's firmness, laughing and making vulgar jokes as the bed groans from the exertion. I hope that this is how my mom must have seen him sometimes—silly and rakish and charming. When he grows bored with this new toy, he reaches for me, the old toy, starts running his hand down my thigh. I've stopped shaving my legs. It's been three weeks and now, he's noticing. "What the fuck is this?" he asks. "Are you some kind of dyke now?" I slap him away, my hands leaving bright red streaks against his pale chest. I gather the sheets around me. The English kids are about to fly to the States to meet a specialist. Their parents are hopeful. It's heartbreaking.

I tell him to fuck off, that I can do what I want with my body. He laughs again, but this time, it sounds mean. "You're my kid and I can do whatever I want with you." He grunts, stretches himself out of bed, shows me a document from his briefcase certifying he owns me. He owns everything I will ever do. I believe him because he's been right about other things. Then he throws me over his shoulder, carries me to the bathroom and dumps me in the tub. It's better this way, I think, not knowing what happened to those English kids. This way, they're still alive and they can still hope that it will all turn out okay. My father throws a razor at me. He tells me to make myself presentable.

When my mother's mother died, she left me a trust fund that would pay for four years at State with something left over. In August, at the end of a cold summer when all it did was rain and all my father did was drink his wine and take me to our hotel room where he would tell me that he couldn't let me go, he drives me the eight hours downstate to Lansing, gets me settled in my dorm room, meets my roommate, her parents. He gives me a crisp hundred-dollar bill, kisses me on my cheek, the stubble of his beard tickling my cheek. He tells me he'll see me at Thanksgiving. I watch him get into his car and pull away, but I don't wave. That night, after my roommate falls asleep and the room is silent but for the gentle whistle of her breathing, I double check that the door is locked and crawl into the narrow bed covered in the sheets Colin helped me buy. At Thanksgiving, I have to go home because I won't turn eighteen until April of my freshman year. Colin picks me up in his beat-up green Volvo. I hold his arm for the entire drive back. I am silent. When we arrive, Colin wants to come in, help me with my bag. I tell him no. If he meets my father, he will know the truth about us.

My father has a new girlfriend, the first one since my mother died, the first once since me. Tammy. She is a waitress with red hair who wears too much make-up and always has a Coors Light in her hand. She's in her thirties and has four kids of her own. She's sitting on the couch watching *Wheel of Fortune,* shouting the wrong words at the TV screen. She looks up and says, "You must be Ken's daughter," and I say, "The one that's still alive." My father emerges from the kitchen, wiping his hands with a dish towel. He nods in my direction, smiles, says maybe we'll go for a drink at the Ramada later. I go up to my room, close the door. I try to remember how to breathe. I try to forget how to sleep.

⁂

Every morning while we were lying in bed, my sister Lena said, "I love you like you're my own. Do you understand what I'm telling you?" I would nod eagerly. I would say yes. She kissed my cheeks and hugged me until I couldn't breathe, and then we would get ready for the day. She was a pretty girl, popular, but she always spent her free time with me. When Lena turned twenty-one, she bought an old Toyota Land Cruiser that drove in only three gears for $500. On the weekends, mostly during the summer, she would make us lunches of ham and cheese sandwiches and Cheerios and grapes and take me to the ruins of old, long-abandoned mines. We would climb through the rusty skeletons, finding old lunch pails and carts and all the things that get left behind when something dies. She would chase after me and carry me on her shoulders and laugh with me like I was her very best friend. Sometimes, we'd go to campgrounds. We'd sleep on soft quilts in the back of her truck. In the morning, we'd hunt for thimbleberries and hike to waterfalls where we would swim. Lena took pictures of the ruins. She said that they weren't as dead as people thought. She would get the pictures developed at the photography shop downtown by flirting with the skinny boy who worked behind the counter, leaning toward him in her tank top, one leg crossed over the other, popping her gum in his face, and then she hung her pictures up on our bedroom walls. Sometimes, I would find her sitting cross-legged on the bed, staring. I would ask her what she was looking at. She would just smile and hold me, close her eyes and smell my hair. She would let her breath fall against my face and tell me that she was giving me her *sisu,* the Finnish word for a fierce strength that endures. The last time I step foot into my father's home, Lena's pictures are the only things I take with me.

⁕

I write my lists in red notebooks, labeled by week, by month, by year. I hide these notebooks in the attic beneath the floorboards in a secret place my mother showed me the summer before she died. She had lost her hair by then. Her skin was waxy and thin, her breathing ragged and shallow, but she pulled down the staircase into the attic and took me up into the dusty space flooded with light and showed me photo albums from her childhood. She showed me her favorite hiding place. She said, "You're going to want to hide things from your father." In high school I wrote one thing I knew to be true over and over, until my hand ached: *When I turn eighteen, I will leave. I will leave and I will not look back.* When I was younger, my father would read me stories before bed. He would always leave out the happy endings.

⁕

When I graduate from college, I often hope for a phone call from a concerned nurse telling me that the old man is on his deathbed. I hope he will beg for me. I will rush to him and sit at his side and hold his hand and we will cry as he whispers acts of contrition. I won't forgive his trespasses. No. I will watch as his body betrays him. I will watch as he breaks down and makes a mess of himself. I'll watch as he dies in his own filth. In my notebook of things I know to be true, I often write that I know he will die alone and beggared. Most days, though, I cannot write this truth.

⁕

Colin and I need my birth certificate before we can fill out the application for our marriage license. That's how I find out. I see the truth, typed in neat black letters, and the whole world opens up, spilling into my arms.

⁕

My father lives with his wife Tammy and her four sons. There is a before and an after. There is his family and that family. If it weren't for one or two phone calls a year, phone calls my husband takes, I don't know that my father would remember that in the before, he had a wife and two daughters he broke bare. My husband and I live in Minneapolis now but three or four times a year, I'll drive the seven hours. I'll park across the street from that house. I'll watch the window of the room where he used to come for Lena until he had stripped her to her bones. I will close my eyes. I will see her, my real mother, clearly, staying when she should have left, holding me and kissing me with her bubble gum breath, telling me she loved me like I was her own, begging me to understand what she is saying. For the rest of my life I will want only one thing—to tell her yes.

Eight

Starry Night

Lania Knight

JAMES IS WAITING ON THE GRAVEL BAR throwing stones, and I'm face down, floating on the top of the water looking for crawdads. I can feel every rock slap the surface. I'm watching them fall to the creek bottom. But I pull my face out when I see James' two white feet beneath me. He manages to shove me under anyway. He's the only cousin I ever get to spend time with. And he sucks.

I'm sorry, he says. Okay?

No! I scream it at him. Asshole! *Ein Sheisskopf!*

Where'd you learn that word, he wants to know.

As if I'd be stupid enough to admit that I know some German. That I've been studying online while he's been busy living in Göettingen on his dad's chemistry fellowship.

Everyone knows that, I say.

He squints at me. Can I borrow those?

I tell him no but then I hand him the goggles anyway. He puts them on and goes underwater but doesn't stay long. After accusing me of having a watermelon head, he has the nerve to ask if I'll adjust them. I take them and pull the stretchy rubber strap, trying to think of some way to extract payment from him.

So, how do those German girls kiss?

Don't be stupid.

You don't even know, do you?

Why do you have to be so weird? I leave for a year and my cousin's turned into a freak.

Yeah, well you'd be a freak too.

But you used to be kind of normal.

When?

Before you started acting like a girl.

I am a girl, stupid. That's when I dive away from him in the shiny spandex swimsuit Aunt Jane bought me. When I surface, he's ready with his hands cupped together to slam a wall of water into my face.

I liked it better when you were a boy, he says.

I grab him around the neck and dunk him, reminding him that I'm still as strong as he is.

Dad wants to know that night when we're setting off fireworks what did I do to piss James off and I tell him maybe we've outgrown each other and then I think about aiming my Roman candle at James' face. But I don't because I have a whole bag full of army tanks and screamers and a rocket thing that has a head attached on top that looks Middle Eastern and I don't want to lose my one chance a year to blow shit up. Dad says you can't outgrow family and I pretend like I can't hear him over the noise and finally he leaves me alone.

Aunt Jane and Uncle Bill come to get James the next day on their way back to St. Louis and stay all morning. I try to hang out in bed pretending I have a headache, but Aunt Jane peeks in my door and sees my new swimsuit hanging over the chair and asks if it fits.

I hate the built-in bra, but I say sure and I wrap myself in my blanket.

She sits on my bed and tries to talk to me about how everything's going to be okay.

I want to tell her that no, I don't really think everything's going to be okay, and that nobody seems to understand me, especially not Dad. But I just rock inside my blanket and lean into her when she hugs me.

Give it some time, Aunt Jane says, and she talks me into telling Uncle Bill and James goodbye. I follow her out to the living room, scuffing my feet on the bare plywood floors. Uncle Bill shakes my hand, like he always does, and James drags me out onto the porch to try to wrestle me to the ground one last time before they leave. I pin him under my knee, but I let him up before the adults can see. Dad comes out on the porch looking like he's ready for me to stop doing things like wrestling with my cousin. So I pack a lunch and some water as soon as Uncle Bill's SUV disappears between the oaks on either side of our gravel drive. I'll be back later, I shout over my shoulder as I leave. Too bad if he wants more explanation than that.

My family lives on a farm. We have lots of woods surrounding the fields where my dad grows alfalfa and pumpkins and tons of vegetables. When we were younger, James and I liked to pretend we were soldiers. My dad's farm is close to the Missouri River, and even when I was young I knew a lot about the river and the geology of our land, which lies at a sort of intersection of bottomland and bluffs that are characteristic of the northern edge of the Ozark Plateau, and that we have all these cool places to explore . . . because I homeschooled . . . which was probably why I was a little weird and maybe too lonely and didn't understand that James didn't really care about karst topography or how male bats like to hang out on old shagbark hickory trees when they leave the maternal colony. But his favorite place was this one ridge I found where you can see all the way across Hartsburg to the river. It's not really on our land, but I like to go there anyway.

James used to love it when I showed him places like that. We'd hide out, pretending we were in foxholes making our way across imaginary battlefields. One day when we got to the top of that bluff, we made a pact. I would be a boy, and James would initiate me. He gave me a new name, Jamie, instead of the way boring Jenny I was born with, and taught me things like how to pee standing up and how to turn my eyelids inside out. It gave us equal footing. Sometimes I'd mess up, though, and tell him I wanted to kiss him. Mom never knew about the kissing thing, but she seemed to like it that James and I were close. She had a cousin who died when she was young.

When James and I would come back from hunting the pumpkin fields, Mom would feed us carob-sorghum bars and soy milk and ask for details about our enemy sightings. How do you decide whether to shoot them or take them hostage?

We usually just shoot them, James would say. And I'd try to put in my two cents, but then Mom's questions would start getting too weird, like did we know spent uranium was a neurotoxin and a teratogen, and could we identify the symptoms of Gulf War Syndrome? She took the fun out of war. I never asked if that's what her cousin died from, and by the time she got sick with cancer, it seemed like a stupid question anyway.

⁂

When summer is almost over and I've been trying for weeks not to think about James, my dad, my little brother, and I plan a trip. We decide to camp at Pulltite and then canoe on the Current River, something we haven't done in a long time. But then Aunt Jane calls. Can James stay with us for the weekend? She and Uncle Bill are going to another chemistry conference. They don't want to leave James home alone. Charlie, my little brother, is the only one who is happy because he gets to ask his best friend to come camping.

Which makes things complicated. All day Dad has been either lost in some other world (I'm pretty sure he's getting high, but I don't let on that I know) or he's been grouching about the under-ripe tomatoes I picked. Generally, Dad's a sweet guy, but I've been getting anxious lately when he gets like this and I keep quiet because I don't want to give him one more thing to worry about. I was the one who begged to go on this canoe trip.

Finally Dad leaves the field muttering about reorganizing the camping gear—how many canoes? how many tents? how much food? I know that everything is gonna be fine, even if I can't convince Dad, but by the time James shows up, you'd think it was all in ruins. I'm out in the field picking tomatoes (making sure they're ripe), trying not to notice James sitting on the front porch of our house drinking lemonade and watching the circus unfold near the van. I don't have to be out here sweating. But I am.

James is looking my direction, or at least, I think he is, but he's too far away for me to tell if he's actually looking at me. I stand, shading my eyes and daring him to come out to the field. Butt hole. *Dummkopf.* I've got to learn the German equivalent for asshole.

By evening, Dad is yelling at anyone who comes near the van, so there is a pile of shit by the back tire where we've all left whatever he's asked us to get and then dumped it because he couldn't figure out what to put where and ended up saying Just put it on the ground, Damn It.

I make tofu and noodles for dinner—loaded with tons of vegetables—and for once James hasn't complained that there isn't any meat. Mom was a vegetarian, and even though I eat hamburgers any chance I get, I've tried to be respectful that Dad wants to keep doing some things the way Mom did them. I almost can't remember what her dinners tasted like, but I'd never tell Dad. He still sets a place for her at the table sometimes.

Tonight, though, James is sitting in Mom's old place. He's different again this visit, not as big a change as when he first got back from Germany, but there's something about him I can't quite figure out. He's quieter and he doesn't say all of that German shit anymore, but he still reminds me too much of the asshole he was earlier in the summer. So I don't even look at him the entire meal.

It's dark and Dad's got a gas lantern going on a table by the van. I sit next to him and hand him a glass of iced herbal tea. It's got that raw sugar stuff in it I tell him and he drinks it all in one gulp and his body just kind of melts into the picnic table. I think he might have found his stash—as if he ever lost it—because I smell that sweet/sour scent of marijuana that I've been able to recognize since I was young. I just hope James doesn't come out here and smell it on Dad. I know better than to offer advice or condolences, so I squeeze Dad's shoulder and bring the empty glass back to the kitchen.

I announce that I'm going to bed. James will be sleeping on the extra bed in my room and I hope he gets the message to be quiet. We used to have a guest room sort of place where he would sleep when he stayed during the summer, but Dad took apart the floor back in February and has never finished laying down the new wood slats since tilling and planting started in March. Our house is really old and only two rooms are totally redone—the kitchen and Mom and Dad's bedroom, which was pretty smart of Dad because it was the one thing that made Mom smile when she came home to die last year.

I actually don't mind that the drywall in my room has never been taped or mudded. I'm sort of hoping Dad won't ever get around to it because I turned my art project last fall into a panoramic view of St. Louis and it covers three of my walls. The part where I started by the closet opening (no door yet) isn't so good, but by the second corner some buildings and trees are actually recognizable. I decided to model it on St. Louis since it's got two huge rivers colliding just north of the city and it's got so many cool old brick buildings. I went a little wild on the architecture after Dad took me and Charlie to this kids' museum that had a display of all these architectural remnants from buildings that had been torn down in St. Louis—door knobs, crown molding, fascia, gargoyles (my favorite), and stained glass windows. I stuck a few glow-in-the-dark stars along the top edge of each wall, sort of a lame attempt at what *Starry Night* might look like if Van Gogh had gotten the chance to paint St. Louis on unfinished sheetrock.

I'm staring at the glowing stars, making up stories about what's happening in St. Louis-on-the-Wall tonight. I keep thinking I'll hear James come in and then I'll never get to sleep, but I do sleep. He has to shake me awake in the dark and I can't figure out who he is.

Breathe, he says and I squeeze his shoulders, choking on the dream that's vanishing with his voice. But when I wake later, I can't remember which part was real, and then I see him in the other bed, and the sun has drowned out my sheetrock stars with morning.

⁕

Mom always used to drive the first leg down Highway 63, but now Dad drives the whole way and we make a few extra stops. Central Dairy has enormous scoops of ice cream on sugar cones for really cheap so we always find a shady place to park where we can watch the van and our camping gear from inside the dairy bar.

On the road, Charlie and his friend play a hand-held video game, and James and I are in the back listening to music on our separate sets of earphones. He's likely got some Seattle grunge band sound-alike going and I'm relaxing to a techno re-mix of an Irish singer. James' taste in music is pretty bad.

We've got a car-top carrier, and there are three bikes mounted to the back bumper, so once we hit the hilly roads further south, the van whines on every upward climb. As a rule, we're opposed to SUVs (which I secretly think would better meet our family's camping needs), so I sit in the back, uncomplaining about the noisy ride and thankful for my own private world provided by technology and the music industry. Neither of us has said anything about last night. I'm kind of in a bad mood because of all the packing and because I found one of my sticker stars on my bedroom floor this morning. Either it's a bad omen or it's just my cousin being an asshole. Or both.

I wake up from my nap to James punching my leg and so I elbow him and push him over to the far edge of the seat with my feet. You're taking up too much room and you snore he says and I just rearrange my pillow and shove on him again. And anyway we're going to stop to eat in Salem. So wake up.

Whatever.

I'm starving and I've got to pee but of course I don't tell him. Dad pulls into a gas station and we all tumble out of the car. Dad has some bad hat-head and I'm trying to catch my reflection in the window to make sure I don't look as bad as he does. I do and he isn't happy about re-opening the van so I can get my cap from the backseat. I hate baseball caps and this knit thing that Charlie gave me last year makes my head hot, but I pull it on and notice James looking at the local array of newspapers and flyers by the front door, and he's got on a knit cap too. He doesn't say anything when he sees me and I lose my nerve about calling him a copycat.

The bathroom is locked so I wait in the hallway trying not to piss myself. It's a one-seater and the floor is a mess and I stare at the graffiti and make sure not to touch anything after I dry my hands. James is waiting outside the door and moves aside to let me pass. I'm kind of tired of giving him the silent treatment but I don't know how to say let's be friends without sounding completely stupid.

We eat hummus veggie sandwiches at a white picnic table set on a small patch of grass between the gas station and a real estate office. Dad looks tired and I offer to drive but he laughs and says he'll get us the rest of the way there since I'm still underage, and I start dreading this last part of the trip—it's when I usually get car sick and I don't want to puke. We work our way down Highway 19 and when we turn onto EE, I switch out my techno for some old reggae my dad recorded when he spent time in Jamaica in the '70s and I try not to notice our 25 mph curvy descent into the Ozark National Scenic Riverway. Charlie's friend ends up hurling onto his lap but there's nowhere to pull over until we get to the campground, so I stick my face into the crack of an open window on my side and concentrate on the black dude's voice in my ear singing about Babylon (but it sounds like bobbylawn) and hope my puke doesn't make a trail down the side of the van.

We set up the tents first. Always. I didn't really puke, but it takes me an hour to feel normal and I'm less than thrilled about setting up camp. Dad's got the medium tent because the small one has a rip (Dad's apologized like three times about not seeing it when he loaded the gear) and that means all the kids sleep in the big tent. I consider offering to sleep by myself, but I'm not ready to spend an entire night alone. I throw my sleeping bag way over into a corner of the big tent and set up Charlie and his friend in the middle. I figure James can set up his own damn air mattress.

The last time James and I were here, he was bigger than me and when we were swimming, he had to bring me back from the big rock once because I couldn't make it all the way across by myself.

But this time, I'm making sure he sees that I can handle the water just fine. I get in about three good dives before he swims my way and pulls himself up. We take turns, mostly ignoring each other, but then he sits and watches me awhile.

Your dad didn't seem too happy about me coming on the trip.

I'm treading water and I have to look up at him and the sun's right behind him so I have to squint but I still can't quite see his face. It's not you, I say.

He seems lonely.

He hardly ever leaves our property, I say.

It's been a year, James says. Mom thinks he should let go.

I let the current carry me several feet downstream and it takes me awhile to get back to the rock.

Jamie.

What, I say. No one has called me that in a long time. To everyone else, I've been Jenny.

I'm sorry about all that boy stuff I used to make you do.

Tears sting my eyes before I can dunk my head underwater. When I come up, he dives right over my head and I watch the length of his body as it glides beneath the blue blue sky.

Race you back he says and he swims toward the boys. I'm several feet behind him but I watch his shoulders rotate in the current and wish that he'd just drown. My face feels hot, so I wait in the water. I tell Charlie to bring me my goggles and I spend the next hour helping them fill buckets with crawdads while James looks for rocks along the gravel bar. Maybe he remembers that time I told him about how Missouri used to be an ocean and our state fossil is the crinoid and you can find these rocks that are embedded with ancient sea lilies and sometimes the segmented stem crumbles away and leaves an empty space. I watch him and hope he's looking for a rock with a hole in it. But then I realize he's probably not.

That night around the campfire my dad brings out his guitar (he'd almost forgotten to pack it) and he actually convinces me to sing this old John Prine song about Muhlenberg County that he taught me when I was a kid. I haven't sung it in years and Dad has to play it in a new key because my voice sounds different. Charlie's been learning the penny whistle and so Dad sings some old war songs and the evening gets really mellow. Until I leave for the bathroom and James decides to come with me. Maybe he thinks since we had a kind of sort of conversation at the river, everything is okay between us.

I remember when you used to sing that he says. You should be in choir.

You have to go to church or school or something to be in a choir I want to say, but I don't because I'd never tell my dad he doesn't do as good a job teaching me and Charlie as Mom did, and I don't want James thinking I wish I went to public school like he does. So I just say I'm not really that good of a singer and leave it at that. He turns off his flashlight and makes some comment about the stars and how they never look like this in St. Louis. I want to point out Ursa Major and Lyra and Sagittarius, but I don't. Until he asks if I know any of the constellations. Even then, I only show him the Big Dipper because it's so obvious, and then he asks me if I want to smoke some pot and I want to know why does he think I smoke pot.

Your dad gets stoned, doesn't he?

Yeah, my dad gets stoned I finally say to James. And I ask him when did he start smoking.

When I was in Germany, he says, we hung out a lot with this other family and the teenage daughter hooked me up.

I'll bet. I say it before I can stop myself.

You want to try it he asks again and I say sure. We go to this small outdoor amphitheater where they give educational talks on bugs and spiders and shit and sit straddling a bench, facing each other. He's got a tight little joint and after just one hit I know it's going to be a good night.

This is really good I say when I finally release my breath over our heads. I watch the stars emerge through the smoke.

I take it you've done this before.

Once or twice I say and I laugh as if I'm already high. We pass it back and forth a few more times and then I lie back and watch the shimmering sky. He lies back too and his knees are touching mine and I'm so turned on I could scream.

Are you still a virgin he asks and I'm not even sure he's talking to me because this pot is so much better than anything I've ever smoked.

Yeah I say. It's hard to come by good sex when you homeschool in Hartsburg fucking Missouri. I'm laughing and I roll off the bench and then I keep laughing until I've pulled my knees up and I'm rocking myself and then I'm not laughing anymore.

Hey James says. Like his voice is from one of those stars and his hand reaches across the whole sky to touch my shoulder. He wraps his arms around me and I'm curled up into him, and even though I'm as tall as he is somehow he is bigger than me. I hold onto him and it comes to me that the dream last night was real. It's Mom and I'm going from room to room carrying her, telling everyone she's gonna die if we don't do something, and she keeps getting smaller and then when I'm standing in the unfinished guest room I look down at her and she's a teddy bear in my hand and then she's gone.

When I can breathe again, James and I are lying on the ground staring into the trees at the edge of the amphitheater, into them and beyond to the starry night.

Arschloch, I say and he starts laughing. I've always wanted to call you that, I say, and I pull away from him. And I've always wanted to kiss you. But I don't say that part.

I think you got all the weirdness genes he says.

Yeah, you got the normal mom and the normal dad. The normal childhood.

Everybody's fucked up in their own way he says and I want to know how he's fucked up but then he moves toward me and I can feel the gravel beneath the wooden benches pressing into my face. His lips touch my skin near my mouth, like he can't quite find me, and I'm hoping my mom won't mind this or Aunt Jane or Dad or Uncle Bill, but I start crying again and James pulls me closer and awkwardly strokes my hair until my breathing matches his.

You wanted me to do that, didn't you?

Yeah, I say. Weird, huh?

It must have been all that vegetarian crap he says and I can't stop the sound that comes out of me, part gasp, part sob, but I'd thought I was laughing.

When we walk back to camp, James reaches over and presses something into my palm. It's curved and hard and warm from his body heat and I hold it to the sky and see a single star pulse through its jagged opening. Where maybe a segmented stem fell out a million years ago.

Nine

Peter Torrelli, Falling Apart

Rebecca Makkai

WHEN CARLOS ASKED WHY I WOULD risk my whole career for Peter Torrelli, I told him he had to understand that in those last three years of high school, Peter and I were the only two gay boys in Chicago. Because I really believed it, back then, and twenty-five years of experience proving otherwise was nothing in the face of that original muscle memory: me and Peter side by side on the hard pew during chapel, not listening, washed blind by the sun from the high windows, breathing in sync. It didn't matter that we weren't close anymore, I told Carlos. The point was, he'd been my first love. I'd never actually loved him, but still, listen, believe me, there's another kind of first love.

It was during one of those long lectures or concerts or assemblies that Peter and I had discovered our common neurosis: the fear of magically switching bodies with the speaker or singer or priest, and then having to improvise an exit. I would slide toward Peter on the pew, open a hymnal, and above "A Mighty Fortress Is Our God" scribble in pencil: "Tuba player?" Peter would look up to the stage to watch the fat Winnetka sophomore puff his cheeks like a blowfish and write back: "Stop playing—no one misses a tuba." "1st Violin?" I wrote. "Feign a swoon," he'd write back. And then he'd mouth it to me, relishing the "oooo" of "swoon." We joked about this fear, but really I think it bothered us both—this idea that we might suddenly be thrust in front of our peers and examined. It doesn't take a psychotherapist to figure out why. Peter later claimed the whole reason he became an actor was that the only way he could enjoy a play was from the inside.

Everyone else knew it was his looks. I hadn't understood until we were sixteen what it meant to turn heads. I'd considered it a figurative expression. But when we stood in line at Manny's, or walked down Dearborn toward the bus, he was a human magnet. He was the North Pole. The girls at school would feel his sweater and tug his necktie. He said he had a girlfriend back east, that she was Miss Teenage Delaware, and everyone believed it. How could he *not* be onstage with that dark, sad face, that ocean of black hair, those sarcastic eyes? By the time we graduated, he'd done two seasons of professional summer stock. I was the varsity soccer goalie, and he was a movie star walking among us. When we sat together in chapel we looked like the kings of the school, and nobody knew any different.

And then the next day we were thirty-eight years old, and Peter fell to pieces. During a matinee of *Richard III*, in the middle of the second act, my friend abruptly and forever lost the ability to act. He said later it was something about the phrase "jolly thriving wooer," the strangeness of those words as they left his mouth, the pause a second too long before Ratcliffe entered. Since Peter told me all this, I've read the page twenty times in my Signet Classic—which is how I know that Peter's next line, as Richard, was "Good or bad news, that thou com'st in so bluntly?" It was a line he'd have made foul jokes about backstage. "And I said it," he told me. "But it came out in this *voice*, like all the costumes had fallen away, like I was some kid in eighth-grade English and I had to read my poem out loud. It was just *me*, and there was no character, no play, just these words I had to say. You know our whole thing about leapfrogging into someone else's body? It was like that, but like I suddenly leapfrogged into myself." He said he could see each face in the audience, every one of them at once, smell what they ate for lunch. He could feel every pore of his own skin, and the ridiculous hump strapped to his back. Backstage, they knew something was wrong even before he started to shake. By the end of the next scene, the understudy was dressing.

Peter told me this the next week over lunch. Actually, he told me many times, over many lunches in the following year, as if through the retelling he could undo something. We met every other Thursday at The Berghoff, where he'd have root beer and I'd have two pale ales and we'd both eat enormous plates of bratwurst and chicken schnitzel and noodles with butter sauce. We had set these lunches up two years earlier, very formally. We'd been in and out of touch for ages when we found ourselves alone on the living room futon of a boring party in Hyde Park, drunk, wondering aloud if knowing each other when we had acne was the reason we'd never dated as adults. We had kissed just once, sophomore year, after a SADD meeting when we stayed behind to pick up the leftover flyers. I didn't know he was gay. I hardly knew *I* was. He came over with the green flyers in a stack as if to hand them to me, but when I took hold of the papers he pulled them back and me with them. The only person I'd ever kissed before was a girl named Julie Gleason. Afterward he said, "You're pretty dense, aren't you?" That was it. We didn't talk for two weeks, and then we were best friends again, before the paper cuts on my palm had even fully healed.

I had looked at him that night at the party—beautiful and grown up, with a beer bottle sweating against the leg of his jeans—and said, "I never see you anymore."

He said, "Yes, I'm slowly becoming invisible." Peter was the kind of guy who would try for any joke, any chance to flash his perfect orthodontia. Even when it wasn't funny, you had to appreciate the showmanship. And then he looked at me seriously, which was rare at the time. "We *should* get together and talk. I mean regularly, because I miss you. It would be like therapy." I should have known I would always be the therapist. I told him once that he was the Gatsby to my Nick Carraway. He flashed his teeth and said, "Yes, but I throw *much* wilder parties."

And like stupid little Nick, I ended up trying to fix things. If I hadn't spent American Lit distracted by Zach Moretti and his amazing forearms, I might have registered that these stories never end well.

Let me say, Peter had been brilliant. Chicago breeds its own stage stars who stay local even if they're good enough to go to New York, and he was one of them. When I saw his Hamlet at Chicago Shakespeare, all memories of Mel and Lord Larry vanished in a celluloid fog. He was the right age, the right build, and those eyes could turn like lighting from irony to terror. I wonder how that colored our friendship, that I saw him simultaneously as Peter and Hamlet. If nothing else, it made me more tolerant of his ramblings and neuroses.

After the night he froze up ("The Night of Which We Shall Not Speak," he called it whenever he spoke of it, which was constantly), he took sick leave for a week, then tried again. If anything, he was worse. He quit before they could fire him, and spent the next two months looking for work. He walked into each audition knowing everyone in the room had heard about his big dry-up. It couldn't have helped.

A few months later, Peter moved to southern Wisconsin and took a job doing dinner theater, and our lunches became less frequent. In late November 2005, almost a year after The Night of Which We Tended to Speak Obsessively, we sat near a window in The Berghoff and watched the year's first snow collect in the street. He told me about his new role as Bob Cratchit in something called *Let's Sing a Christmas Carol!* The director wanted British accents from everyone. Peter could do a perfect one, of course, but not without sinking further into the hollow cadences, the glazed eyes, the strangling sense of the ridiculous.

"Most of them sound southern, it's terrible," he said. He was on caffeine today or something worse. He was literally bouncing on the springy seat of the booth. "The eleven o'clock number is, I shit you not, called 'God Bless Us Every One.' Jesus Christ, you should hear it, it sounds like Scrooge drops by Tara for pecan pie." Every time I saw him he talked faster, as if he were running out of time. He still flashed the smile, but perfunctorily, as if displaying his incisors for the dentist.

When our food came, he finally asked me a question so he could stop talking and eat his schnitzel. "How's life in phone-a-thon land? Are you giving away thousands of tote bags?"

I worked in special events for NPR, and for several years before we officially reconnected, Peter and I would run into each other in the restaurants of the monstrous tourist trap on Navy Pier where Chicago Shakespeare and Chicago Public Radio both live. Once, after we'd drifted apart for a few months, our lunch parties at Riva joined together, and when someone introduced us and said we might hit it off, we started laughing so hard Peter dropped his wine glass.

"We're doing better than last year," I answered.

"I've been telling everyone in the Land of Moo about the Republicans trying to shut you down. I'm going to assemble an army of cheese heads for your defense."

"Thank you, Peter. That's thoughtful."

Peter started mixing all the food on his plate: schnitzel, potato, creamed spinach, kraut.

"So, what about trying my shrink?" I said. "She's good. I wouldn't lie to you."

The old Peter would have cued up his German psychiatrist impersonation, drawing the attention of everyone around us, but the new Peter just stared at his mixed-up food. "She might be good, but how far is she from Kenosha, the epicenter of the theatrical world?"

"She's here in the city, and that would be good for you."

He agreed to call her and then told me about his great-uncle, who, after undergoing electroshock, became obsessed with licking copper objects. I wanted him to ask about me, to ask about Carlos, who was moving out of my apartment in gradual increments and breaking my heart in painful slow motion. I'd have to find someone else to complain to.

"Listen, though," said Peter, "I'm on the mend. If I had more serious roles again, that might do it. I mean, I was never a comedian, and that's what they're asking me to do."

As much as I didn't believe his optimism, I was glad he wasn't giving up. I constantly pictured him hanging himself from the closet rod of his cold little apartment, or drinking something medieval and poisonous. Maybe I'd just watched his Romeo too many times.

"I've got an offer for you," I said. I'd thought about it in the car on the way there and decided I couldn't ask him. I decided it several times, in fact, but now here it was, coming out of my mouth. "I want you to do some on-air work for me." He nodded, eyes wide, as he mashed his food and listened to me explain the project: in cooperation with the Art Institute, we'd commissioned twenty local poets and authors to write short works relating to the museum's crown jewels—a mystery writer casting one of the little Thorne rooms as a crime scene, a Pulitzer-winning poet extolling Picasso's man with the blue guitar in sonnet. The poems and stories would hang beside the art, and my job was to find actors to read them aloud at the gala opening and then record them for NPR and for the museum audio tour that people could rent with headphones. My brilliant idea had launched a two-year nightmare of collaboration with a hateful little man I'd come to call Institute Steve, and somehow I'd ended up in charge of the reading part. "It's December thirtieth, if your show is done. The thing is," I said, grabbing for the only available out, "the other actors might be people you knew."

"People I *know*, Drew." His face stilled itself long enough to shoot me one of his complicated, devastating looks: part annoyance, part sarcasm, part glee

that he'd caught me saying what I really thought. "I'll do it, if you don't think I'd embarrass you."

And so the Rubicon was crossed.

He left with Dr. Zeller's business card in his pocket and both of our leftovers in Styrofoam boxes. He was eating plenty despite his meager paycheck because he got free food at the dinner theatre, but every night he had to choose between chicken a la king and Lake Superior whitefish.

I stayed behind to pay the bill, and as I waited for the busboy to come back, I pressed my cheek to the dirty, cold glass of the window beside me. I felt like I needed to wake myself up. I had just risked my career on his ability to be Peter again, to jump back into himself, and I strongly doubted he could do it.

The next time we met for dinner was before the Art Institute event. I had more important things to do, but I'd been in earlier to see that my interns were on task, and I wanted to make sure Peter was ready and calm. The Berghoff was right around the corner, and I knew neither of us would get a chance to eat the shrimp and strawberries at the reception. He'd been down a couple of weeks before to record at the studio, and I'd been relieved at how good he was, at least without an audience. I'd invited him over then for dinner with Carlos, who was still hanging around to see what further damage he could inflict on my psyche, but Peter had an audition in Milwaukee with the Kinnickinnick Players for *The Night of January Sixteenth.* He hadn't gotten the part.

Tonight Peter looked skinnier and pale and had a soft stubble he might have been growing for insulation, the way he sat there in his coat and hat, his jaw shaking against the cold. To put it delicately, he looked like a few friends I had in the 1980s who are not with us anymore. I got the waitress to bring us some tea as soon as we sat down. He held the cup, letting it warm his hands, but didn't drink any. It was all over the news that The Berghoff would be closing in a couple of months. We'd stood outside in the cold for forty minutes just to get a table. People around us were taking pictures, touching the menus as if they were the faces of dying lovers.

"I went to your shrink," he said. "Twice. You didn't tell me she was beautiful. Like Juliette Binoche. And we're *very* optimistic." He was warming up enough to lay his woolly hat on the table.

"Great," I said. I couldn't keep from staring at how his brow and cheekbones stuck out sharply from his face, how his skin stretched over them, shiny and translucent. He went on and on about the therapy, about opening himself up to pain, about finding his core. I barely listened.

"So, how's Carlos?" he said once we'd ordered dessert.

It was too late in the meal, and he was too far behind on the story. "Not great, but you know," I said, confident he didn't care enough to press further. To be safe, though, I changed the subject. I said, "So, I had a dream about The Berghoff last night. I was running around downtown, trying to give everyone vitamin shots because of this disease I'd exposed them to. It was wartime, with tanks in the streets, and if people didn't get these shots they were going to die. I had to find everyone I ever slept with and get them to come to The Berghoff to get this shot. So I'm knocking on doors, but people have moved, and by the time I find Carlos he tells me he won't take the shot, he'd rather die. He's lying there in the snow, dying, and he goes, 'You can't save them all, Drew.' And I woke up screaming. I mean, what the hell *is* that?"

"Dreams don't mean anything," he said. "I used to believe they did, but they really don't. Random synapses." As I signed the bill, he dug into his apple tart like someone just rescued from the wilderness, his eyes wide with the wonder of sugar and crust. He chewed so fast it looked like his teeth were chattering. He gestured behind me with a jerk of his eyes, and I turned to look at the next table, pretending to get something out of my jacket pocket. I assumed he meant the teenage girl with a roll of fat hanging over the back of her low jeans. She was with her parents. "What would you do?" he said. His mouth was full of tart.

Sometime after high school, the game had evolved away from musicians and actors, and we (or at least Peter) had begun obsessing about leaping into regular people's lives, about how to fool their families. I was tired of it after twenty-five years, but this wasn't the day to put him in a bad mood. "Okay. Pretend to get sick so I don't have to go to school, and spend the whole time doing aerobics. I could get fifteen pounds off, at least. Do I get to be myself again after?"

"Presumably."

"Then I finish reading Proust."

Peter took a sip from his root beer bottle, and I noticed his hand shaking. I wondered briefly if it was Parkinson's, if the whole personality shift was that easy to explain—but Peter was such a hypochondriac, he'd have thought of that already. "You're so fucking boring," he said. "I'd run that fat little ass right into the street right now and see if I could stop traffic. I'd see how many laws I could break."

"You could do it right now," I said. "You could run out there and just ruin your life. Nothing stopping you."

He put his napkin on his plate and stood up. "I thought that's what the museum was for."

As we headed in the front doors of the Art Institute, the last regular museum visitors of the night were bundling past the stone lions and out into the cold. "Did you ever read that book when you were a kid?" Peter said as we walked through the emptying halls. "The one where the kids run away and live in the Met?"

"And they bathe in the fountain," I said.

"That's my new plan. I want to camp out under some dinosaur bones and just—" He let his sentence trail off, as if the suits of armor we were passing would explain the rest. I imagined them as a hundred failed geniuses, hiding behind the glass, starved down to thin, steel exoskeletons. They knew what he meant.

We stopped at the Chagall windows, stood for a minute in the warmth of their thick blue light, then headed into the special exhibit hall. I left Peter staring at a messy Klee while I talked to Lauren, my boss, who had hated the idea of this event from the time I brought it up two years before and was waiting for everything to fall apart. Her over-plucked little eyebrows arched up her forehead as she asked me why half the writers weren't there yet. I went to check on the champagne, and once the evening started moving I lost track of Peter among the tablecloths and microphones and whining interns, and finally among the rush of people and coats. Half were Art Institute supporters with vintage bracelets or Frank Lloyd Wright neckties, and half were NPR junkies with professor haircuts. Some might have been both, God bless them.

I knew I should have introduced Peter to the other actors, told him where to be, but leaving him alone was my small way of shaking him by the shoulders, of telling him to grow up. When I saw him again, he was talking to one of the actresses he knew from Chicago Shakespeare, a woman who'd just returned from off-Broadway and chopped her hair short. She was laughing at something he said, and he was teetering back and forth on his feet, as if he might at any second lose a lifelong battle with gravity. He was laughing too, but the way his skin stretched on his jaws, he looked deathly.

I took the microphone and welcomed everyone, but my voice could never command a room; people still milled and talked and jostled for position. I introduced the five actors, and it wasn't until they came and stood beside me that I noticed Peter still had his puffy green coat on, his hands shoved down in its pockets. I wondered if he was punishing me for leaving him alone, or if he was so thin under there that he didn't want to frighten people. In high school, he would take his shirt off at every opportunity, claiming it was hot out at sixty degrees. I'd assumed back then that his dark skin was from Italian genes, but now I saw it must have just been the sun.

The two other men were dressed in sleek sweaters, and the two women wore silk blouses and pants. Audition outfits, like Peter used to have dozens of. He looked now as if we'd found him on the street at the last minute.

We started with the first painting, Caillebotte's *Paris Street; Rainy Day,* and the short-haired actress read a brief story by Stuart Dybek called "Rainy Day Chicago." When she finished, the crowd moved across the gallery to a tiny Picasso, where one of the men read a poem called "Triangle Woman." We'd pulled a miracle, getting the Art Institute to move so many of its own crowd-pleasers into one exhibit; they'd wanted to highlight lesser-known works, things they would pull from some vault, but most of the writers agreed to the commission only if they could choose the painting. We'd asked the writers to e-mail us their wish lists, and *Nighthawks* topped almost every one. It was something about the loneliness, the coffee, the silence—everyone wanted to lay private claim to that one desolate corner of the universe. In the end, no one got it because it was on loan in New York. How could this one object embody loneliness, I wondered, when people crowded shoulder to shoulder around it, shared it, traded it, paraded it around? If Hopper's little coffee counter was lonely, it was in the way a prostitute was lonely. Or an actor.

I had a hard time paying attention, and I stood there thinking how flat the readers all were, how little grace they showed compared to Peter in his prime. He played Edgar in *Lear* one summer up in Evanston, in the park by the beach. He was beautiful in a red shirt, and his voice made every line sound like something you'd been on the verge of remembering, if you'd only had time.

Peter's first reading was for my least favorite story, as well as my least favorite painting in the entire museum. A very young, way-too-hip fiction writer from Bucktown named Sam Demarr had e-mailed us that the only painting he felt like writing on was "the one with the giant gum." I'd actually loved it as a child—that enormous pack of gum floating over the city skyline. Now I hated how the gum hovered there, out of proportion. It had nothing to do with the city below it, no shared color palette, the garish green wrapper rendering the brown skyline drab and uniform. On one of our first dates, Carlos and I had stood there joking that it was based on a true story, the Giant Gum Crash of '72. Since then, I'd always thought of the gum as about to land, to flatten the unsuspecting workers below, so I'd found it particularly funny that the story Sam Demarr had submitted was called "The Gum Flew Away." Demarr himself was standing there at the side of the room in dirty khakis, smirking at his wine glass.

Peter pulled a tube of papers from his coat pocket and unrolled it so he could read the top one. The other actors held theirs in the black folders we'd sent them in. "First, all the gum flew off," he read, "leaving Chicago in its spearmint dust. Then the department stores floated away." Aside from the fact that his papers were visibly shaking, Peter sounded like himself, strong-voiced and in full control of the English language. This story suited his flat, ironic delivery. I'd chosen it for him specifically because it was monochromatic and free from dialogue. "The hot dog stands were next," I heard him say. For all my daydreaming about finding myself stranded on stage, this was the closest I'd come to feeling as if it were my own energy propelling an actor, as if when I stopped focusing, the whole thing would fall apart. Peter was gesturing around now, with the still-shaking papers, backing toward the wall and away from the old ladies in the front row. Even his legs were bouncing, and it finally occurred to me that maybe it was drugs making his limbs and voice and eyes jump around like that. It didn't seem like something he'd do, but who was I, anymore, to say what Peter would do?

And then as he read the line about the mayor launching himself off the Hancock tower, Peter actually put the back of his hand against the painting and swept it up the canvas. The gasp from the crowd was so loud and so high that I couldn't tell where it stopped and the alarm started. A security guard I'd barely noticed trotted from the room, and another stepped forward, speaking into a radio. Peter froze, and I could feel his stomach flip. I could feel the sweat sticking the papers to his hand. The alarm was turned off, and people started talking quietly.

"And this is why we didn't broadcast live," Lauren whispered beside me. She was glaring at me like I'd done it myself. The Institute coordinators were talking in a cluster while two guards and a woman in a suit came hurrying in, asking Peter to step aside so they could inspect the painting for damage.

The crowd just looked embarrassed, all touching their faces but waiting politely for the reading to resume. Sam Demarr seemed to find the whole thing hilarious. Peter had stepped aside, but he was still up there in front of everyone, the only movement coming from his eyes, which jumped around liquidly, looking for their chance to leap free from his face once and for all. One of the guards talked with him in what should have been a whisper, but everyone could hear. He asked for his name, his driver's license, copied everything down on a big clipboard. If the guard took any notice of the waiting audience at all, it was as an audience for his own fine performance. And I thought, maybe that's what I would have done, if I'd leapfrogged up there into Peter's body, if I needed to get away before anyone realized I was a fraud: I'd hit the painting and make the show stop. But Peter had his lines right there, and he knew what to do.

It was a good five minutes before the woman in the suit stepped away from the painting and signaled that we could continue. She stayed there, though, in the corner of the room, frowning. I assumed she'd have a long night of paperwork ahead of her now, a lot of calls to make. I felt bad for her.

I took the mike again and said, with a big fundraising grin, "Now you've heard what fine security your contributions support!" Lauren was at the front of the crowd, shaking her head at me over and over to show how disappointed she was, as if I hadn't gotten the message yet. "We're going to try that one again." I waited for a meek laugh from the audience and then turned toward the actors. Peter looked at me with those blank, jumpy eyes. He hadn't done it on purpose, or at least he didn't think he had. He looked like he didn't even recognize me, like I was just another blurred member of his audience, watching and breathing and waiting for him to fail. I'm still not sure what I felt, standing there. Maybe I felt my heart break, or maybe I felt Peter's heart break. When you've known someone that long, when you formed yourself around his personality, back when you were just a fourteen-year-old lump of clay, isn't it really the same thing? Aren't his heart and your own somehow conjoined? Perhaps that's what I could never explain to Carlos: ours was a kind of first love that wasn't aimed at each other, but somehow out at the world. We were forever side by side on the chapel bench, watching the show. Peter whispered something to the short-haired actress and handed her his papers. He held up his open hands to the audience in apology, ten pale, bony fingers, then walked around the people and out of the exhibit.

"The Gum Flew Away," the woman read, the clarity of her voice a reassurance, a wiping away. "By Sam Demarr. First, all the gum flew off, leaving Chicago in its spearmint dust. Then the department stores floated away."

I thought of following Peter out. I'd done it so many times before, chasing him down as he stormed from a party, calling his name five times until he finally turned to look at me, tear-streaked or red-faced on the wet sidewalk. "He didn't mean it," I'd usually say, or "You're just drunk," or "We all love you." I never said that I did. Just all of us, meaning everyone at the party, everyone he'd ever met, everyone who'd ever seen him from across the street. It wasn't true anymore; the world didn't love him, just I did, and I had the feeling that even if I could say that, it wouldn't be enough. And even if it were, then what? What would I do with that responsibility? And now Lauren, who was still my boss if I was lucky, was finally shooting me a look of conspiratorial relief. "*Actors,*" said her face. "I know," said mine.

It hit me like a wall of cold water that I wouldn't see Peter again, that he'd avoid my calls until he drifted to another city to try again and fail. Someone would hire him at a third-tier regional theatre on the basis of his résumé, and he'd last one show, if that. He probably wouldn't know how to give up.

After the readings, I propped myself up at the microphone and said my bit about membership and shortening the pledge drive with early donations, and Institute Steve said something I couldn't follow in his nasally little whine, and I got a drink in my hand. It was cold enough outside that I wanted to drink just so I wouldn't feel the bone chill on the way home. I chatted up as many people as I could stomach over the wine and shrimp. People didn't want to talk to me, though. What they wanted was to meet the actors, these instant, small celebrities who had become important merely by commanding attention for twenty minutes and possessing nice faces. "I saw you in *Phaedra* at the Court," a woman said to one of the actresses, who smiled graciously. "It was just gorgeous. You wore that red dress. Tell me your name again."

Another woman asked the actor who'd read the Stuart Dybek piece to sign her program. She didn't seem to notice Dybek himself standing a few feet away, laughing with a friend and wiping his glasses on his tie. If the actor found the request strange he didn't show it, signing his name on the margin of the paper. Peter would have written something like "Peter Torrelli is *fabulous*. Love and kisses, Pablo P." Or the old Peter would have, the one who knew magic.

I felt the wine go to my head, and I felt relief that the whole thing was over. I drank more wine to shut out the suspicion that I was glad Peter had left. I got through the next hour and walked out into the cold, relieved to be drunk and half expecting to find Peter there on the sidewalk, eighteen years old and scribbling in ballpoint pen on the knee of his khakis. He was gone, and there were just people waiting for buses and people waiting for taxis, everybody waiting to leave.

It was like that after our kiss sophomore year, the way I stood frozen thirty seconds and then ran after him into the cold night, one of my duck boots untied, my left palm bleeding in parallel paper-cut stripes. He was gone, and I'd stood under the school's archway entrance looking to see his breath in the air, thinking it would tell me which way he went. I thought, if he ran back inside I'll follow him, and I'll kiss him again. If he got a cab, there's nothing I can do.

He *had* found a cab that night, as he probably had now. Or maybe he'd slouched all the way down Adams, his parka blurring him into the frozen crowd, the crowd sweeping him onto the train, the train shooting him up north and off the face of my earth.

This is the way it happens: First, my friend floats away, leaving Chicago in his dust. Then he leaves me—no breath above the concrete, no voice in the air to catch and hold so I can jump into him, so I can steer him back. Then The Berghoff closes, and the radio stations all shut down. The school chapel folds its benches and windows and flies away. The frozen sidewalks peel up like strips of gum. The skyscrapers drift like icebergs into the lake, up the St. Lawrence, and out to sea. The citizens grab for something to save, but it's all too cold to touch. The mayor holds a press conference. "We can't save it all," he says. In a month, they've all forgotten. Standing in the empty streets of their empty city, the people look up and say to no one in particular, "Something used to be here, something beautiful and towering that overshadowed us all, and it seemed very important at the time. And now look: I can't even remember its name."

Ten

In Which a Coffin Is a Bed
But an Ox Is Not a Coffin

Brenda K. Marshall

THE WINTER OF 1881 FOUND Frances Bingham reluctantly arranging for her move from the spacious comfort of her father-in-law's bonanza farm on the Dakota prairie to her almost-completed new home six miles away in Fargo. The arrangement that had suited both Percy and Frances since she had joined him in Dakota three years earlier—in which Percy insisted that he would soon leave his job as a newspaperman for the Fargo *Argus* to make a new start back east, and Frances, in turn, reasoned that it made no sense for her and their son, Houghton, to move to Percy's two rooms above the *Argus* in the meantime—had come to an end with Percy's newfound respectability as Fargo's delegate to the upcoming Fifteenth General Assembly of Dakota Territory. A man with a promising political career, Percy now insisted, must have his own home in Fargo, and his wife must live in that home with him, and not with his sister and father-in-law nearby.

Frances could not disagree, of course. That she had married Percy not for the opportunity to live with him but to be near his sister, Anna, was logic she was unlikely to share, no matter that her plans, her patience, her desire had come to naught. An incautious advance, the slightest pressure of Frances's lips and a tightening embrace during a good-night kiss of over a year ago had changed in a moment the easy friendship between the women. Where once Frances had dreamed of heat and passion, of sinking into the very being of Anna, of moving past clothes and skin until she had claimed spirit and soul, these days she would have been satisfied with a little warmth. What she encountered as she reached out, however, was less a reserve than the ghostly chill of absence.

And then there was the young Norwegian housekeeper, Kirsten, whose warmth and spirit seemed to grow in direct proportion to the waning of Anna's, and who, upon entering a room, was certain to search for Frances, only to become suddenly unable to meet the older woman's eyes. So Kirsten went about her business, blushing all the while, entering, retreating, and discovering soon thereafter another reason to be near Frances, which drew from Anna yet another sigh. Sometimes the complicated algebra of emotions, the looks and the looking away and the sighs and the silence drove Frances from the passive dramatics of the house to the bustling farmyard, to Little Carl's cookhouse, to Jack Shaw in the machine shed, to the barn to stand among beasts whose only longing was for hay. And so, despite her indifference to her appointment in Fargo with Ferdinand Luger regarding a final furniture order, Frances was grateful for a reason to be outside, breathing air unencumbered by sentiment or passion or memory or expectation or hope.

She was pulling out of the second barn in the carriage, her favorite bay, Raleigh, in the harness, when Little Carl stepped out of the door of the crew cook house with his hand raised to stop her.

"Where do you think you're going?" he asked.

The presumption of the question, Frances knew, was her own fault. She had been admonished several times by Percy for her readiness to mix with the farm help, but Percy was rarely around, and Frances had grown fond of the odd little cook.

"I fail to see how that is your concern, Carl, but since you have asked so politely, I am on my way to Fargo to conduct some business at the Luger Furniture Company."

"You don't want to do that."

Frances looked down at Little Carl from her upholstered seat. As a matter of fact, she was very little interested in furnishing the house in Fargo (and every bit of it on credit, at that), but even Little Carl, whose powers of perception Frances had found at times to be disconcerting, would not have presumed to speak to her quite so personally.

"And why is that, pray tell?"

"Weather."

"Carl," Frances said, completing her unspoken thought with a sweep of her arm that took in a dozen outbuildings and the field beyond where several head of cattle had been turned out to graze upon the remnants of the cornstalks there. An overnight dusting of snow lay lightly upon the frozen ground. It was a gray February day, but in no way threatening.

"Miss Frances, every bit of me hurts today. I can't barely move my neck, and that is as sure a sign as any that a storm's coming."

"I am sorry for your discomfort, but my neck feels fine, and the sooner I get going the sooner I can return. Now, I am certain that you have something better to do than . . ."

A call across the yard from Jack Shaw to "wait only," interrupted Frances. Silently, Frances and Little Carl watched him hurry toward them. Here was "that Jew, Jack Shaw," a figure far more offensive to Percy than the cook, no matter that he was one of the most valuable workers on the place, a genius with machinery. More importantly to Frances, he was a man with a ready store of tales of a life and a land far away. Silently pleased with the trust that had grown between them, she spent hours in the machine shed watching Shaw move from plow to harrow to binder with his tools as he talked about the young man who had left Russia as Yitzchok Chavinitz, arrived in New York City as Isaac Chavinitz, but stepped off the train in Fargo as Jack Shaw.

"Are you going to town?" Shaw asked.

"No."

"Yes."

Shaw looked from Little Carl to Frances before he said, "If the answer is yes, Mrs. Bingham, maybe you will make it for me a little easier and take instead the wagon. A shaft is out on the well pump. If you could only pick up the part from Henderson's?"

"Of course," Frances said, turning an arch smile on Little Carl.

"Only wait a minute and I will get the wagon hitched up," Shaw said, turning to go.

"Give us Dan," Little Carl called after Shaw, who stopped and looked up at the sky for a moment before nodding and striding on.

"Us?" Frances asked.

When they reached the furniture store on the corner of Broadway and NP Avenue, Little Carl helped Frances out of the wagon and then got back in for the short trip across the street to Henderson's Hardware. He would pick up the pump shaft there and then move on to Goodman and Yerxa's for the other supplies that he had suddenly remembered needing back in the Bingham headquarters farmyard. He was to pick Frances up at the home of Dr. and Lydia Harkness in three hours. In the meantime Frances and Ferdinand Luger would visit the new house to take some final measurements, after which Luger would drop Frances off for her visit with Lydia Harkness.

But Frances had been in the company of the doctor's wife for less than thirty minutes when her friend rose to answer a knock on the door, returning almost immediately to inform Frances that there was a diminutive man bearing a singular resemblance to a rabbit who was insisting that Mrs. Bingham "get her things and get to going right now." And indeed, when Frances went to the door, Little Carl was standing there with his nose twitching in the air, looking as if he were about to thump a boot against the porch floorboards to warn of impending danger. For a moment Frances considered instructing him to wait for her in the wagon while she returned to the parlor to finish her tea, but she knew that the thought of the little man huddled out there in the cold would be too disconcerting. So she accepted her astrakhan coat and hat from Lydia Harkness, and after an apology for such a short visit, followed Little Carl to the wagon. The day had darkened and the wind had a new bite to it, but not one snowflake fell from the sky.

"I am sorry if your aches have increased, Carl," Frances said as he set Dan on his way. "But I really must insist that in the future you hold to the schedule we have agreed upon. Your caution is misplaced and your insistence impertinent."

"Mrs. Bingham," Little Carl said, the formality of address telling Frances that his mood had not improved while in town, "I hope that's exactly what you're still thinking when we get home. If it is, I'll say my sorrys then. Here." He reached under the seat for the buffalo robe there.

Frances did not speak for the first half hour of the drive home, at first because she did not want Little Carl to think that she took lightly his presumption, and then because she realized that the day was too quickly falling into dark, the air had grown heavy, and Dan had begun to toss his head and snort in concern.

"Get up, Dan," Little Carl said. "Here it comes."

It came dramatically, with huge flakes dumped upon their shoulders, as if a chute had opened from the sodden air above, releasing the moisture it was no longer able to hold. Within minutes Little Carl's rabbit fur cap had collected enough snow to make it appear doubled in size. Frances pulled her hat further down over her ears and the buffalo robe up to her neck. Her eyelashes were thick with snow. The world had become white, the sky and the land distinguished by texture only. Coming into the trees along the Sheyenne, Frances realized by the temporary protection they offered the extent to which the wind had picked up. Even here the road was getting harder to distinguish from the space around it, and they were almost upon the bridge before they saw it before them. Still, Frances felt a surge of relief to know that the bulk of the trip was behind them and there remained no more than two miles yet to travel.

A blizzard may be described objectively by references to wind, to snow, and to dropping temperatures. A man or woman caught outdoors gauges its progress and severity in the gut. The snow that had been driving directly into the face of Dan and the wagon seemed to begin to swirl, and what once was north Frances thought could be just as easily west, or maybe south. Frances swallowed back the panic of vertigo and looked hard toward the ground to her side of the wagon. She thought she could see where the taller tufts of dried grass by the side of the tracks formed a darker shadow. Holding fast to this image Frances felt her dizziness recede.

Twice Frances heard Little Carl call out a hoarse "gee" to Dan and felt the wagon shift to the right, although neither time had Frances lost the shadow that she had believed were the snow-mounded grasses beside her. She did not know that the wagon had stopped completely until Little Carl yelled something at her, but even though she was sitting close enough to him to feel his body next to hers, she could not catch his words before the wind carried them away.

"What?" she turned and yelled back.

"He's losing the road." Frances felt Little Carl's breath against her chin as he shouted. "I got to get down and lead."

Little Carl did not wait for Frances's reply and in a minute was lost beside the moving dark before her that was Dan. Frances closed her eyes. Her toes and fingers burned, and she tried to wiggle them within her boots and mittens. Bending over her lap to point the top of her hat into the wind, Frances reached up to give her nose a squeeze under her muffler, and was grateful to feel it sting. For several minutes Frances rode like that, eyes shut, almost completely covered by the buffalo robe, aware that there was not one thing that she could do that would change her situation.

And then something felt different. Sickened now with panic, Frances lifted her head from the buffalo robe and squinted into the dark that was alive with swirling razors of ice and snow. It took her a moment to catch her breath against the wind. She could see nothing. No light remained in the day, no shadow below her promised that she still was upon the road, no body beside her said that she was not alone. There was only the assault of the blizzard and the sound of her own voice, tiny against the storm, yelling, "Carl! Carl! Carl!" It wasn't until she felt the wagon seat tilt beneath her that she realized that the wagon had come to a stop and Little Carl was yelling into her ear. They had lost the road. He had no idea where they were. He was giving Dan his head and hoping that the horse could sense his way back to the barn. "Just hang on," he yelled. Frances felt Little Carl lift his arms and bring the reins hard down upon Dan's rump. The wagon jerked forward once again. The robe lifted away from her side, and Frances felt Little Carl climb under its protection. Together they rode on, directionless, inside a freezing tent of darkness.

The disorientation in space lent itself to a similar confusion in time, and Frances could not have said whether it was an hour or several hours later when Little Carl stirred next to her. For a moment she was alone again under the robe, and then Little Carl was back, shouting that she needed to get down. Exhilaration and gratitude surged through Frances. It did not matter that she was in pain, her fingers and toes numb, her back aching from leaning close to her knees to stay warmer. Soon she would be in her bed, with Kirsten placing warmed bricks at her feet and Anna gently chafing her hands.

Trying to help Frances down from the wagon, Little Carl stumbled and they both fell to the ground. Despite the deep cushion of snow the fall was jolting and hard, their bodies too cold to absorb the shock. Frances was the first to regain her feet. Turning in a full circle she looked for the lights that surely must be burning in the Bingham house, or in the supervisor's house, or in the bunkhouses. But all was dark. She felt Little Carl grab her around the waist, and move her toward an insubstantial shape before her, and then she was inside a pitch-black space no warmer than the wagon, but sheltered from the force of the wind, if not its howl, exaggerated now by whistling and creaking. She could sense Little Carl moving nearby.

"Carl?" she asked, surprised to find that her mouth refused to properly shape the word.

"Just a second," Carl slurred. "Got matches. Just can't . . ."

"What?" Frances said when Little Carl did not finish his sentence and then did not speak at all.

"Can't get my fingers to work. Hold on," and then there was a tiny light and Frances could see a pair of small, disembodied hands moving away from her before the room returned to darkness. A small thud told her that something had fallen to the ground. The clink of metal upon metal indicated that Little Carl had found a cabinet. Then again there was a tiny light, and then more, and then there was Little Carl's face behind the candle that he held in his hands.

"Where are we?" Frances asked, an involuntary shudder punctuating her question.

"Hold this," Little Carl said, handing Frances the shaking candle while lighting another from its flame. "Over here. Hold it up."

Turning in a circle in unison with Little Carl, Frances could see that they were in a claim shanty not quite half the size of her sitting room. Newspaper-lined walls heaved and fluttered. The floor was packed dirt. There were two handmade chairs of twisted saplings and board odds and ends. A three-legged stool. A table of three separate rough planks resting on two sawhorses. Two wooden crates nailed to shiplap served as a cupboard. On another crate sitting upended beside the stool there was a kerosene lamp with no kerosene. A small cook stove stood at the opposite end of the shanty. The wood box nearby was empty. And in the corner, where Frances expected to find a bed, there was a long, deep, pine box.

"Old Andy Cooligan. I'll be damned."

"Who? What? Carl, where are we?"

Instead of answering her question, Little Carl asked one of his own, speaking slowly to keep his words recognizable. "Don't reckon Dan would fit through the door, do you? Probably be OK up against the shanty out of the wind, but we could use his heat. Here, hold this. Careful, don't drop it. Got to get him unhitched at least. See if you can get a fire started."

Everything that happened in the next hour should have taken ten minutes. Unhitched, Dan would not be led away from the small space out of the direct force of the wind that he had found against the shack, and Little Carl had little faith that the clumsy knot he tied would hold the horse to the wagon should he decide to wander off later in the night. Hugging his way against the shanty so that he would not lose his way back to the door, Little Carl returned to find that Frances had not started a fire.

"There's newspaper to get it started," Frances moved her arms toward the walls, "but not a stick of kindling. I tried and tried to break apart those chairs, but . . ."

"But you didn't have a proper tool," Little Carl said, lifting the pump shaft that he had dragged in behind him.

With the cupboard crates, the wood box, and the three-legged stool broken up and the stove lit, Frances began to feel safer, if not warmer. Little Carl, she noticed, could not stop the shivering that had begun the moment he first entered the cabin. His face was wet, as was the top of his undershirt, whether from melting snow or perspiration Frances did not know.

"You look like you are soaked to the skin, Carl," Frances said. "I think it might be wise to take off your inside clothes and let them dry next to the stove. You can roll yourself up in the buffalo robe in the meantime."

The look of horror that met this suggestion almost kept Frances from repeating it, but the man was visibly shaking and could not stop his teeth from chattering.

"I am serious. I think that given the situation we may relax proprieties for the night."

"Wh-wh-what makes you think we'll be going anywhere t-t-tomorrow?"

The thought that this blizzard would extend beyond the morning had not occurred to Frances, although she had grown accustomed to storms lasting much longer. Once again she took careful stock of their situation. The shanty clearly had not been inhabited for a while, and there was no food or water there, although there was snow aplenty to melt, and there were several bags of flour and cornmeal under a tarp in the wagon, as well as a tub of syrup, another of molasses, and a crate of tinned fruit. Much more frightening was the limited supply of burnable wood. Then Frances realized that Little Carl had turned her from the topic.

"It won't help anything to have you come down with a fever from sitting in wet clothes."

At this Little Carl stood and shrugged out of his winter coat and laid it by Frances's boots and mittens next to the stove. Then he reached for the tattered blanket that they had found at the bottom of the long homemade box in the corner.

"I don't know what good that does, Carl. You're still shivering. At least take the robe. It's so much warmer. Give me the blanket."

"Blanket's liable to be pretty l-l-lively," Carl answered.

Had Little Carl's refusal had to do with warmth, Frances would have continued to argue. Instead she said, "How do you know that this is Cooligan's claim shanty? Where is he? Where are we?"

Little Carl nodded toward the corner where the large box sat. "Cooligan m-m-mucks out stalls at Hadley's Livery in Fargo during the winter in exchange for a place to sleep. He proved up the claim a couple of y-y-years ago so he don't have to live here between harvesting and planting. I guess he just ain't got 'round to putting up something more permanent. He's the only settler I know said to sleep in a c-c-coffin. Didn't believe the stories myself, but there it is. That puts us . . ." Little Carl's sentence was interrupted by a violent shivering fit, after which he seemed to forget that he had been speaking.

"Are you all right?"

"Chilled through is all."

"That puts us where?" Frances prompted Carl.

"We must a' got turned around pretty soon after crossing the bridge. We're over a mile north and still east of the farm. No wonder Dan kept trying to get left on me."

"It isn't much," Frances said, looking around at the walls that continued to shudder in the storm, "but we were lucky to find it. Thank you, Carl." It was meant as an apology.

"Thank Dan," Little Carl said. "There's going to be more than one frozen soul thawed out in hell after this storm. It c-c-come on about as fast as any I've seen. Stand up for a minute, Miss Frances, so I can bust up that chair. Then you can help me drag that box over here. Inside that box, next to the stove, and under the buffalo robe, and you'll be fine for the night."

"What will you do?"

"I'm going to bust up those planks and saw horses and then s-s-sit on this here chair and hope they keep the fire going for a good long time."

With the coffin arranged next to the stove, Frances was about to step in, but hesitated.

"You'll f-f-forget where you are once you're asleep." Little Carl paused before adding, "I promise not to put the l-l-lid on."

It was the first smile that Little Carl had bothered with all day, and it allowed Frances to admit why she was hesitating. "I was actually wondering how . . . Well, it doesn't seem quite possible to . . . Oh, dear," Frances looked away from

Little Carl, "we are indeed thrown into a rather intimate situation here, and, well, perhaps it would be safe for me to just step outside for a moment."

"It would not, so don't even think about it."

"But . . ."

"Here." Little Carl stood and walked the two feet with his candle to where the crates had hung, returning with a tin coffeepot. "I better go check one more time on Dan. I won't let loose of the wall." Shrugging back into his wet coat, Little Carl stepped to the door and opened it just wide enough to let himself through, but even that was enough to raise the tenor of the wind's howl from a roar to a shriek. When he returned Frances had arranged herself in the coffin with the buffalo robe tucked around her. She was still cold but no longer frightened. She had been silent for quite some time before suddenly asking, "Why does he sleep in a pine box?"

"Never heard. Maybe 'cause you never know when you're going to d-d-d . . ." Another convulsive shudder interrupted Little Carl. "Die," he finished.

Frances did not believe that she would fall asleep in a coffin on an earthen floor in front of a cook stove in a homestead shanty with the wind wailing and the walls threatening to come down around her at any moment. When she woke she didn't know if she had slept for hours or simply dozed off for a moment. Sitting up she could just make out Little Carl in silhouette, rocking in the blanket on the keg chair next to the stove. An involuntary shudder that shook his entire frame released a small groan, almost feminine in its pathos. One candle remained lit next to him.

"I am almost too warm here, Carl, with my coat and the buffalo robe as well."

Little Carl started at Frances's voice, and sat up on his chair.

"Which do you want?" Frances spoke again.

"I'm fine."

"No you're not, and you will do me no favors if you get sick on me here. I am counting on you to get us home. Please." Frances stood within the coffin and moved as if to hand the buffalo robe to Little Carl.

"Just hand me the coat, then, and get back under that robe."

Frances slept fitfully after that, her dreams filled with wondering whether she were asleep or awake. Often she believed herself to be watching Little Carl as he softly stroked the lamb collar of her coat as he continued to rock. Only when she realized that she expected to open her eyes upon Kirsten and Anna sitting before her was Frances sure that she had been sleeping. It was the sound of Little Carl bringing the pump shaft down upon the coffin lid in the corner that had awakened her.

The morning brought very little light to the windowless shanty, while outside the storm continued, undiminished. Despite Little Carl's warning the night before, Frances realized by her disappointment that she had expected the worst to be over. Little Carl had already emptied the coffee pot, fed Dan from one of the cornmeal sacks, and now was fashioning hard cakes of cornbread, flour, and water. Throughout the day, Frances attempted to engage Little Carl in conversation to help the time pass, but the forced intimacy of space was slowly lessening the ease that had developed between them over the years in the cookhouse. When Little Carl did talk it was to tell stories of past blizzards he had lived through, complete with details of how those who had not been so fortunate had met their deaths. Several of his tales were about men and women who were found in snow banks within feet of their houses, having fallen down and given up without knowing that they were so near to safety. Then there was the story of the entire herd of cows that had frozen to death standing up, and had remained standing in the subfreezing winter weather for two more months until they thawed and dropped one by one in the spring. Most disconcerting to Frances was Little Carl's account of a settler near Fort Thompson who, stranded unprepared in his claim shanty during a five-day blizzard, had slowly begun tearing down the studs of his home to burn, and was discovered after the storm huddled frozen into the northwest corner that was all that remained of his shack. This is when Frances learned that Carl was about to begin breaking boards from the wagon, now that there remained nothing inside Cooligan's shack to burn except the pine coffin. Despite Frances's insistence that she, too, could sleep wrapped in the buffalo robe next to the stove, Little Carl appeared to have taken it as a matter of personal pride that she not.

Not long after a second meal of cornmeal and flour cakes, while Little Carl dozed before the stove wrapped tightly in the blanket that had become pungent with the stove's heat, Frances lifted her head from her arms where she had been sitting in her box, aware that the sound of the storm had changed. She was about to speak, but then decided not to wake Little Carl, who had settled into a series of regular whimpers while asleep, but no longer shivered. A thump and scrape against the side of the shanty brought Frances to her feet and to the door. It opened inward, revealing a waist-high hard bank of snow. The snow had stopped and the wind had subsided dramatically and Frances looked out upon an expanse of frozen waves of white. Another loud thud from the other side of the shanty sent Frances scrambling over the bank in front of the door and around the corner, where Dan was doing his best to get free of the wagon. She had just taken Dan by the head when Little Carl appeared. Although he was smiling, the past twenty-four hours had taken a toll on his strength, and he did not argue when Frances offered to help lift the harness onto Dan.

The smiles quickly faded when it became clear that the horse simply could not gain sufficient purchase in the banks that had swirled around the leeward side of the shanty to pull the wagon free.

"If it were Raleigh, we could ride double," Frances said.

"If it was Raleigh we'd be dead about now," Little Carl answered, and then added, "and Dan don't strike me as being so particular. We can get on from the wagon. Do you want front or back? I ain't particular myself."

It was slow going for the big workhorse through the deep drifts, and it didn't take long before he was covered in sweat despite the freezing temperature. Within minutes of the ride Frances's fingers and toes were once again numb. Behind her she could feel Little Carl shiver. And then they were within sight of the big Bingham house, a towering square set into an island of outbuildings, surrounded by an undulating yet motionless ocean of snow. Slowly they moved closer, Dan now straining harder against the drifts, and only then did Frances allow herself to think about how miserable and cold and terrified she was. She thought she could make out tiny sparkles in each of the house windows, and wondered what they could be, shining into the whiteness of the day that was all light with nothing illuminated. A sudden half-start by Dan almost unsettled his riders, and Frances looked down upon a frozen ox lying on its side, half-buried in the snow, a lead rope around its neck.

"What was it doing out here?" Frances asked, and felt Little Carl shrug behind her in answer. Both knew that the real question had to do with what had become of the man or woman at the other end of the lead rope. They were almost past the frozen beast when it spoke.

Frances and Little Carl put their heels against the sides of Dan in surprise, starting the horse again. Then the frozen ox spoke again, in what Frances had come to understand was a Yiddish accent. "Mein Gott," came the voice, "Is it a person?"

"Who's there?" Frances shouted, and then added, "Where?"

The words that came back were muffled. "In here! Give only a look!"

"In where? Oh, my God, Carl. It's Jack. He's inside the ox. Jack, are you all right?"

"Can't move."

Little Carl spoke quietly into Frances's ear. "I'm half froze. If I get down, I'll never get back up. We need to leave him here and send someone back. Nothing we can do."

Shaw could not have heard Little Carl, and yet he spoke as if to answer. "No time."

Frances slid off Dan, doing her best not to knock Little Carl off in the process, but needing to reach up to steady him upon the horse's wide back nonetheless. Breaking through snow past her knees, she made her way to the side of the ox. She could see now that its throat had been cut and its belly slit. A frozen mound of snow-capped entrails lay nearby in the space sheltered from the wind by the ox's belly. Bending to the incision that gaped open three to four inches, Frances searched for a face within, but could see nothing but snow and a crusted black ice. She explained that she and Little Carl were on Dan, but that they did not have the wagon to tie the ox to. She would send someone out to rescue him as soon as they reached the farmyard. When Shaw did not answer, Frances called out his name. This time Shaw replied, but his words were difficult to make out and she had to ask him to speak again. He had to explain to her twice how to cross the thick wagon reins over Dan's chest, cross them again over his back, and then attach them to the rope around the ox's neck. "Only chance," he said. Again, what should have taken a few minutes seemed interminable. Frances had no feeling in her fingers and was using her two hands together like a single pincer. She had no confidence that the fat knot she had managed to tie in the reins would hold against the weight of the ox, even if the lead rope did not break.

And then there was nothing to do but to tell Little Carl to hold on, to give Dan another slap on his haunches, and to trudge behind the path flattened by the ox's carcass, for there was no way to get back onto the horse.

They were within fifty yards of the farmyard when Frances saw a handful of men plunging as fast as they could through the drifts toward them, and she dropped to her knees. She did not know which of the hired men picked her up and carried her to the house. Seeing the candles burning in every window, faint gleams in the early dusk, she wondered for a moment if it were Christmas. Over her bearer's shoulder Frances saw another man carrying Little Carl in precisely the same fashion, although he was struggling to be set back down. He seemed so small in the stock hand's arms that she wanted to call out to the man to be careful. Perhaps she did. A third man was leading Dan and his burden toward the barn while calling out to a fourth to bring a saw from the blacksmith shop. At the door of the Bingham house, Kirsten waited, gesturing and calling to Frances's carrier to hurry, and then saying something to him in Norwegian. The warmth of the house hit Frances at once, releasing her from consciousness.

The last thing she saw before she fainted was Anna asleep in the parlor, her head resting against the back of the sofa where she sat.

Eleven

Drunk Girl in Stilettos

Lee Martin

WE CAME UP ON HER SOUTH OF TOWN on the blacktop, Wink and me, this girl looking all whoop-de-doo in high heels, her hip jutted out, her thumb stuck in the air, begging a ride.

"Pull over," I said. We were running eighty in his Mustang GT, and it was going to take a while to shut it down. "Damn it, Wink. Now."

"Jesus, Benny." He pressed his lips together and squinted at me with his right eye. His left one—or the empty socket, I should say—had a black, satin patch over it. He owned an artificial eye made from acrylic, but he wasn't wearing it that day. The patch gave him a tough look that I suspected he secretly liked. The thin strap slanted down across his forehead. "All of a sudden you're a Boy Scout?" He was busting my balls, but he'd already put his foot to the brake. "Thought you were in a hurry to get home."

"Just do it," I said, and he did.

He was in one of his pissy moods and more of a mind to keep heading up the blacktop, but I saw a girl who needed a ride, and I knew what that was like. Let me say it plain: I've not always been an upright man, and, as a result, I've had to rely on the kindness of folks; some, like my mama, loved me, and some were strangers who didn't owe me the time of day.

We were maybe a hundred yards beyond the girl, and Wink was stubborn and wouldn't back up, so we waited while she came to us, teetering along on those spiked heels. I got out of the car and watched her come. In the sunlight, her bare legs looked whiter than they probably really were, but she was a fair-skinned girl. I could see that. She was wearing a short denim skirt and a black T-shirt with writing in pink letters across her chest. I could finally read the words when she came up alongside the car: "I'm shy."

A little straw purse dangling from her wrist had a picture of that cartoon character, Betty Boop. Her red dress—Betty's, I mean—was lifting up over her hip, and I could see her white stocking and the garter with a red heart on it.

"Hey, know what Lady Godiva said toward the end of her ride?" I asked the girl. I waited just long enough for effect. With comedy, like with women, the trick is in the timing. "I'm nearing my clothes," I said, but I could tell she didn't get it. I opened the Mustang's door, folded back the passenger seat, and motioned for her to get in back. "Her *clothes*," I said again, taking one more shot at the punch line, but again I got no reaction.

"He thinks he's a funny man," Wink said.

I bowed to the girl. "I'm Benny. I'm a funny man."

She had on big round sunglasses with white frames. She pushed them up on her head and stuck her face up close to mine. "I know who you are." I could smell the liquor on her breath, and for an instant I wanted to kiss her just for the taste of booze, even though I was too old to do that. She was just a girl, and I was on the downhill side of fifty. "You're Benny Moon."

"You've been drinking," I said.

"Yeppie." She pressed a fingernail into my chest. "But I know who you are."

"Everyone knows Benny," Wink said. "He's about as famous as they come round here. Aren't you, Speed Racer?"

Odds are you've heard of me. Back in the summer I got arrested for DUI. No big news there, just that I happened to be driving a bar stool at the time.

That's right. Welded to a frame and powered by a five horsepower Craftsman lawn mower engine. Topped out at 38 mph. Slick as can be. For a couple of weeks there, I drove it around. Didn't have much choice. I'd lost my license, and the only way to get from here to there was to hoof it or to ride that bar stool. We live in a dry town, and it's five miles to the nearest tavern. A man gets thirsty? Doesn't have a legal right to drive a car? You do the math.

Anyway, I'd been to Bridgeport to the Hilltop Tavern one day, a Saturday, and I made sure to start back to Sumner while there was plenty of daylight left.

Then I remembered that I'd left my billfold on the bar after I settled my tab. I tried to do a U-turn right there on Route 250. Guess I didn't cut my speed enough. Next thing I knew, I was down, scraped all to hell from the pavement, a knot on my head.

Then I made my mistake. Called 911 on my cell. Said I'd had a wreck. Said I was out on 250 just before King's Hill. The dispatcher wanted to know how bad I was hurt. "Bad enough to call you," I told him.

Then the ambulance showed up, and a county sheriff's deputy, and, well, one thing led to another, and before I could say snap, I was all over the Internet and on CNN and in newspapers coast to coast. Even Letterman and Leno and Conan and the other late-night funny boys were telling jokes about me. I was *that* guy, the drunk who wrecked his bar stool.

You'd think it would've made me feel foolish about myself, but I couldn't quite manage that. Truth is, it's taken me off the booze for good, near as I can tell—and what's a little ribbing compared to the grace of that? I'll be Speed Racer. I'll be *that* guy. I'll be an idiot forever as long as I can say I'm a sober man.

We drove on up the blacktop—Wink and me and the girl. It was a nice fall day—Indian summer—warm enough to have the windows down, sun filling the Mustang and shining bright on the hood, the fields flashing by—bare now except for corn and soybean stubble—and a few red and orange and yellow leaves still holding on to the maples and oaks and sweet gums in the woodlands. We were at that time of the year when things were letting go, giving up, hunkering down—soon there'd be snow and ice and the long freeze until spring—but for a while yet, there was sun and enough warm air to make me believe it all could last forever.

Wink had a CD in, the Drive-By Truckers' *Gangstabilly,* and we were just heading up the blacktop, almost to Sumner, the water tower and the silos of the grain elevator already in sight, and we were listening to "Late for Church": *All this hollerin' makes me wonder. Does a whispered prayer get heard?*

Sweet autumn day, sweet music, and now this girl and those stilettos. She seemed like a gift, the sort handed to you when you're not expecting a thing.

I'd been out at Wink's shooting up bottles and cans with my rifle, a Ruger 10/22, just target shooting to pass the time, and now he was running me home. We'd had a little tiff. He'd got off on a jag—just a lot of bullshit, really—about what it would take to get me drinking again. I told him not a thing. Ever. End of story. That was enough to make him set his jaw.

"Must be something," he said. "How about if you won the Mega Millions? Hell, even the Little Lotto." No, I told him, hitting the state lottery, not even the Mega Millions, wouldn't make me backslide. "What if you knew you only had a month to live?" Ixnay. "Finding yourself on a desert island with Madonna and a fifth of Maker's Mark?" He was starting to tick me off, picking at me the way he was, determined to prove there'd be something to touch a weakness in me and send me back to the bottle. No, I told him.

Then he said, "Okay. What about if some psychopath had a gun to my head, and the only way to stop him from pulling the trigger was if you took a drink. Surely you'd do it then?" Well, of course there'd be a limit to how long I'd hold out. I wouldn't let a man die, but Wink was too sure of too many things. He thought he knew me. His little game was his way of saying he'd bet good money that before long I'd be *that* guy again. That drunk guy. So I said to him, "Nah, not even then."

"All right, just be an asshole," he said. I tossed the Ruger into the back seat of his Mustang—didn't even bother to take out the mag—and we started up the blacktop.

Drive-By Truckers were now singing "Panties in Your Purse." That song about a woman called a whore and a tramp, her man catching her with her stockings in her hand and her panties in her pocketbook—a song I ordinarily never gave a second thought—now broke my heart to hear because of that girl in the stilettos. I guessed she was up against something hard and didn't need to be hearing a song like that. I reached over and changed the track to "Steve McQueen," *the coolest doggone motherscratcher on the silver screen.* Wink always sang along with that one. We saw that movie, *Bullitt,* and the chase scene through the streets of San Francisco, when we were thirteen, and that was enough to sell us on Mustangs and speed. We didn't know, then, that I'd turn into a drunk. We didn't know that Wink would get beat in a bar fight and lose an eye. He knocked my hand away from the CD player. "Who made you dee-jay? I was listening to that song."

Wink's a big man with a shaved head and rolls of fat on the back of his neck. When he wears that eye patch, he looks dangerous. I used to tell him jokes. *What did the brave pirate tell the fraidy-cat pirate right before the big battle, "Nothing to be scared of, matey. I'll keep an eye out for you."*

"Ha, ha," Wink said when I told him that one. "Ha-ha-frickin'-ha." He told me to can the crap. Said he'd had enough of my jokes. Said his eye was gone-baby-gone, and every morning when he looked at his face in the mirror, there wasn't a damn thing, far as he could tell, to laugh about. I thought I was just lightening things up for him, just playing the fool to give him a chuckle. It wasn't that way, though. He made that plain. He said in a hurt voice I'd never heard from him, "Damn it, Benny. No matter what slips and shakes you've had, you're still a whole man. I'll never be that. Never again."

So I backed off. Stopped telling those jokes. Even resisted the one about the man having dinner in a restaurant and noticing the beautiful woman eating alone at the table across from his when, all of a sudden, she sneezes and her glass eye comes flying out. Wink was my friend and had been for years. If he wanted me to stop, I'd stop, and if he wanted to switch that Drive-By Truckers CD back to "Panties in Your Purse," I'd let him do that, too, despite what I thought about that girl and what she didn't need to hear.

I was disappointed in myself—I'll admit that—on account there was that girl and I should have done right about her. A *drunk* girl. Trust me, I know what it's like to be loose from right thinking, to be hard on the end of a bad shake, to reach for that bottle and not give a fiddler's fart about anything else. But like I said, Wink was my friend, no matter the little spat we'd had, no matter how bad he wanted to make me feel by acting like it was only a matter of time before I went back to being a drunk. He'd stuck by me through all my drinking days, stuck by me when I'd been an embarrassment and everyone else had given up on me—everyone except my mama who got down on her knees by her bed each night and sent a prayer to heaven for my redemption. I'm not sure what it was that kept Wink at my side. Maybe he needed me in order to feel better about himself. As long as I was drinking, and as long as he stayed true to me, he could be the long-suffering friend who, though he might be maimed, wasn't—praise Jesus—a drunk. The girl tapped Wink's neck with the barrel of that 10/22. "Hey," she said. "What happened to your eye?"

Jeezy-Pete. She had that Ruger, her finger on the trigger. Luckily, the safety was still on.

Wink tucked his head toward his right shoulder to see what was poking him in the neck. "Shit fire." He jerked away from that 10/22, and the Mustang swerved over into the other lane for just a few ticks before he could bring it back. "Drunk girl with a loaded rifle."

He narrowed his eyes at me and gave me that what-the-fuck-you-thinking look I knew so well from my drinking days. "Now that's just exactly what I need."

"I'm just a little bit drunk." The girl put the barrel right up to Wink's temple. "But that doesn't mean you've got a right to treat me mean."

"Darlin'," I said, using my gentle voice, the one I'd heard so many women use on me when I was falling-down drunk and they were trying to coax me into bed so I'd sleep it off. "Sugar . . ." I reached around and took hold of that 10/22 by the stock. "Sweetie, you don't need to be playing with that."

I gave a gentle tug, and she let the Ruger slide out of her hands. I laid it across my lap, but that put the barrel in Wink's crotch. He gave me that look again, and I swung the rifle up and over and propped it between me and my door.

A loaded rifle uncased in a moving automobile in Illinois? Well, sure it was illegal, but I'd been in a hurry when Wink and I were done shooting. He'd given me that interrogation about what it would take for me to start drinking again, and I just wanted to hit the road and get back to my place as quick as I could. I've gotten good at being alone: I put on my white noise machine, close my eyes, and listen to rain, or ocean surf, or a babbling brook. I hear grace in the water; I hear forgiveness.

The girl was crying a little now. She opened up that Betty Boop purse and took out a wad of Kleenex, the kind that'd been in that purse forever and was now one big crumbling tissue biscuit. Little white flakes were falling off onto her shirt. I reached into my hip pocket and pulled out my handkerchief—white, freshly pressed that morning, and folded into a neat square.

"Don't cry, darlin'." I gave her the handkerchief. "Where is it you're on your way to?"

Wink jerked the Mustang across the road onto the opposite shoulder and slammed on the brakes. We were just out of the last curve before the straight shot into town. I could see the population sign—1,200—just up ahead and the city cemetery with its tall cedar trees and its monuments and mausoleum and the lake with the statue of Jesus rising out of it, his arms outstretched to gather you in if you were of a mind to let him—as I've been more than once when I've walked through that place in the twilight just for the peace of it.

"Get out." Wink was shouting. He had his door open, and he folded down his seat so he could reach the girl. He took her by her skinny arm and pulled so hard her sunglasses got all cockeyed on her face. "Hold a gun on me, goddamn it?" I heard her knees hit the floorboard. Then Wink jerked her out and she fell into the weeds and her sunglasses went flying. He got down there with her, lifted his patch, and said, "There. You want to know about my eye so bad? Just take a good look."

His socket was all scar tissue.

The girl was crying. "I didn't mean anything."

Wink let her go. "I don't care what you meant. You can just walk."

"Not in these heels." She stood up, took off one of the stilettos, and showed him the back of her heel. "I've already rubbed a blister."

It hurt my heart to see her broke down like that there in the turkey-foot grass and the milkweed and foxtail. I got out of the Mustang and walked around the front until I could lay one hand on Wink's shoulder. I had the 10/22 in the other. "How come you want to go and make a scene? We're almost to town." I clicked off the safety. "Don't you hurt her."

I asked the girl again, "Darlin', where is it you're going?"

"To the funeral home," she said, "for Jackie Frutag's laying out."

"Jackie Frutag?" Wink got to his feet. "You know Jackie Frutag?"

The girl nodded. "He's my daddy."

I put the Ruger's safety back on. Then I found her sunglasses in the grass. I studied her face, and everything came clear to me. "You're Lily, aren't you?"

That sobered her up. She gave me a shy grin. "How'd you know my name?"

I handed her the glasses and she put them on top of her head, the stems stuck through her thick brown hair. "Your daddy used to be a friend to us. I haven't seen you in a good long while."

There was a time when Jackie ran with me and Wink. This was back in the day when we were too young to know a damn thing, even though we thought we did. Jackie Frutag—scrawny mutt with long stringy hair and a little knobby chin. We called him Pygmo because he couldn't have been more than five foot two, and that was in his Dingo boots. We all worked pipe for Marathon Oil for a few years and spent most of our nights helling around. Then Jackie married a Bridgeport girl, Cathy Catt, and got religion. He started lay preaching for the Church of Christ, where my mama went, and she made sure she let me know what a miracle it was that he'd turned his life around and had a little girl now, Lily, and wasn't she just the most darling thing.

I got tired of it in a hurry—Jackie Frutag stuck in my face as an example of what a man could do with himself if he took a notion. I'd see him uptown on a Sunday, coming out of Piper's Sundries with his *Evansville Courier.* He had his hair cut, of course, and most generally he'd have on a pair of dress pants, a short-sleeve white shirt, and a necktie. Cathy and Lily would be waiting for him in the car, and they'd head off to church. Sometimes he gave me a nod. Once he tried to talk me into coming along with them, but I told him I didn't want his religion. I told him I was just fine with living the way I was.

If I could, I'd let him know now that he was right—there was a peace to be found—but I couldn't on account he was laying corpse up there at Sivert's Funeral Home, and his girl, liquor on her breath, was on her way there.

"Jesus," Wink said. "Jackie Frutag. I bet he'd turn over if he could see you drunk and dressed like that."

Lily smoothed her denim skirt over her legs. She tugged at the hem of her T-shirt. She slipped her blistered foot back into that stiletto. "I don't have to stand here and listen to you talk to me like that."

She was a tender-hearted girl. I could tell that. In spite of the liquor and the Betty Boop purse and those stilettos and all her tough talk, she was a girl who'd lost her daddy.

"Where in the hell you been to be drinking the day of your daddy's wake?" Wink shook his head at her. "And you a preacher's kid."

She'd been to a party in the country. "Just a party," she said, like she knew there was no way to explain the logic of a girl going out on a drunk with her daddy just dead and here she was still a little lit the day of his laying out.

Wink was disgusted. No matter what he thought of Jackie Frutag and his Bible shaking, he couldn't get cozy with the fact of Lily's disregard. "You ought to think more of your daddy than that." He snapped his eye patch back into place. "You ought to have more respect."

But it wasn't like that, I wanted to tell him, and would have only I didn't want to say it in front of her. She was just at a loss—or at least that's the story I told myself. She didn't know how to face the fact that her daddy was dead, so she tried to go on like the world was running its regular course, like there was nothing she had to accept. Trust me, I wanted to say. I know the extremes we'll go to so we don't have to face the truth, particularly when that truth is the ugliness of our own living. Eventually, though, we come to the facts. Jackie Frutag was dead. She was his daughter. Drunk or not. Stilettos or not. Short skirt and T-shirt or not. Betty Boop or not. She had a place she needed to be.

Then she said, "Mama told me if I came to the funeral home, she'd have me arrested."

"Now, darlin'," I said. "Why in the world would she do that?"

As soon as the words were out of my mouth, I knew it was a stupid question. How many times had my own mama threatened to call the cops when I was drunk and out of hand? "Benny, I don't want to do it," she said one night, when I was in a craze. I'd already ripped the curtains down from their rods because I couldn't stand to be in my own skin and didn't know any way to say that but by tearing something all to hell. "But I will," she told me, "if I have to. Believe me, Benny. I surely will."

A family is a family up to a point, and I'm lucky that my mama, turning toward her last days now, believes in forgiveness. Since I'd got sober, I'd heard about Lily's troubles: the meth, the scrapes with the law for writing bad checks, the shack-up boyfriend in Lawrenceville, and the rumor of an abortion. "Such a shame," my mama said. "And Jackie and Cathy just the best people you could know."

It was plain that the Frutag family had their rough spots, and now here we were—Wink and me—in the midst of their drama.

"I've not been the best daughter." Lily flipped her sunglasses down. "I guess you know that. I'm sorry you're mixed up in it now."

Wink gave me one of those looks again, and I knew he was thinking that if I hadn't insisted on stopping to give the girl a ride, we'd be long up the road—smooth sailing—and nothing at all like this to deal with. What could we do now? Leave Lily there along the blacktop to walk the last half mile into town? Carry her on to the funeral home and wish her well? Put her back in the Mustang and drive her somewhere away from the mess of her life?

A car rounded the curve behind us, and we watched it come. A shiny new white Cadillac Escalade, one of those 70K-plus SUVs. It slowed down just enough so the people inside—a man and woman I didn't know—could give us the once-over as we stood there on the wrong side of the road. The woman, an older lady with her gray hair swept up on her head, actually pointed at us. The man—he was wearing a black beret—turned to follow her pointing finger, and there we were, two men in Carhartt bibs and thermal undershirts. Two rednecks, one of them wearing an eye patch and one of them holding a rifle. Two scruffy-assed, potentially psychopathic men, and a girl in a short skirt and heels.

The Escalade went on past, toward town. The brake lights came on once, as if the man was trying to decide whether to stop. Then he sped up and was gone.

"Come on," I said, ashamed now on account of those looks from that man and woman, but determined, too, not to let them tell us who we were. "Wink, this lady needs an escort."

There comes a time when you have to own up to your life. That's what I was thinking as we all got back in the Mustang, and Wink drove nice as could be into Sumner. We drove past the cemetery and that statue of Jesus with his open arms. We drove past the first houses. They had pumpkins on their front porches, corn stalks gathered up into shocks, bales of straw, scarecrows posed this way and that. The Borla x-pipes on the Mustang guttered along, making that rumble that would wake you from your bed with your heart fluttering if you heard it in the middle of the night. Wink didn't have any music playing now, and I listened to the somber rumble of those pipes, and I heard Lily draw a deep breath and then let it out as the funeral home came into view.

Cars were parked up and down the street, and people were on the sidewalk— women taking men's arms and walking with ginger steps over the uneven concrete and the leaves that had fallen there, children holding parents' hands and skipping along because they were too young to understand exactly where they were going.

I knew the feeling. My first day without a drink was a snap. I thought I had clear sailing ahead of me. I thought I could just walk through a door, easy as pie, into a brand new life. The next day taught me I was wrong, and the next one after that, on and on. Then finally I reached a place where the life of a sober man seemed right to me, and little by little I moved away from the drunk man I used to be.

Then this day came, and Lily flagged us down on the blacktop, and because of her, I called back what it felt like to be about to walk into a group of people and have everyone stare because you were who you were and they were who they were, and the difference was something they'd never let you forget.

"I can't go in," Lily said. She put her face in her hands and started to cry. "I just can't."

Wink pulled the Mustang in behind the Escalade, which was empty now. The man and woman who had looked us over were nowhere to be seen.

"This is your daddy's laying out," I told Lily. "This is a day that won't ever come again. You need to be present." I reached back and snapped my fingers next to her ear. "You need to pay attention."

She took her hands away from her face. She dug around in her purse and found the handkerchief I'd given her. She dabbed at her eyes. She leaned across the console, looking for her reflection in the rearview. Wink turned it so she could see. She patted at her hair. "All right," she said, "but I don't know that I can do this alone."

Wink said he wasn't going in there. He said he hadn't signed on for anything like that. He bristled for a tick, and then he turned a little shy. He ducked his head and touched a finger to his eye patch, tugging down on the corner, resettling it, and for an instant I felt the kind of life he had.

"I'm not dressed proper," he said.

"Me either." I slapped at the legs of my Carhartts. "But you know what, Wink? It doesn't matter a flip as long as our hearts are in the right place. Even Jackie would tell you that."

"Please," said Lily.

And that's how we ended up at Jackie Frutag's laying out, Wink and Lily and me. We walked in big as day. I didn't care how we looked. I didn't care what people would say.

They had Jackie in the main visitation room, the long center room with rows of folding chairs and the comfortable armchairs and sofas along the side. The double doors to the room were open, and we stood in the vestibule, looking in at the people who'd come. They stood in little groups or sat on the folding chairs. A few folks were gathered at the casket. I looked for my mama, who I figured would be stopping by, but she wasn't anywhere I could see. Cathy was sitting on a sofa near the casket, her hands in her lap, fiddling with a handkerchief. She had on a dark dress and black stockings. She'd always been a pretty woman, and she'd come to middle age in a fine way: just a sprinkle of salt in her brown hair, a few lines around her eyes. Jackie lay in the casket, his eyes closed, his hands folded and resting on his stomach.

I took in the smell of all those fresh flowers—all the gladioluses and mums and carnations and roses. I listened to the murmur of voices and felt the carpet under my feet.

"There's your mama," I said to Lily, and I nodded my head. "You ought to go up and let her know you're here."

"I'm afraid," Lily stuffed her sunglasses into her purse. "I won't know what to say."

"That's easy." I cupped her elbow and gave her a little nudge forward. "Just tell her you're sorry for the hurt you've brought her. Go on, darlin'. Just start there."

The woman from the white Escalade was signing the guest register. The man, his beret still on his head, stood a few feet away from her, waiting. He was wearing a black suit and one of those white shirts without a collar, the sort that buttons right at your Adam's apple. He had on a pair of black loafers with tassels, and he seemed fascinated by them on account he kept tapping first one foot and then the other, staring down at his feet to watch those tassels jounce.

The woman turned around and saw us. She had on dressy black pants and a black wool poncho that tapered down in a vee. Half-frame reading glasses perched on her nose, and she squinted at us over the tops of them.

"We saw you on the highway," she said.

Her husband looked up from his loafers. "Were you having trouble? I wasn't sure whether to stop." I knew he was thinking about that Ruger. I knew he was trying to determine whether he should be afraid of us. "No, wait a minute. I know you." He chuckled. "You're that man. The one who drove the bar stool." He shook his head over my idiocy. "Lord a mercy. What a fool thing. What in the world were you thinking?"

Wink took a step toward him. "That's ancient history, mister." He poked him in the chest with his finger. "Leave it alone."

The man—he was ballsy for his age; I'll give him that—knocked Wink's hand away. "Are you some kind of goon?" he said. "Is that why you wear that eye patch? Are you this fellow's henchman?" He laughed, tickled, I guess, on account he thought he was being a funny man. "I bet you don't even have a reason to wear that patch. I bet it's just for show."

Wink said, "That's right. I'm his henchman."

He said it in a low, even voice like that was a word he was used to saying every day of his life. He said it like he was stating a fact and there wasn't anything funny about it.

But the man laughed again. A little chuckle. "Henchman," he said with a smirk like it was a word that people like him owned and didn't belong on the tongues of people like Wink and me.

Something went through me, then, the feeling I used to get when I'd stagger out of a bar, maybe puke on my shoes, or piss myself, or fall over on the street and end up scraped and sore, and I'd hear people laughing, or worse yet, not saying a thing; they'd just stare, and when I caught them, they'd look away like

I wasn't right there in front of them. Standing there in that funeral home, I got that old sick feeling of hating myself and the life I had. I let that man with the beret get to me even though I thought I'd squared things with my drunk life and was moving on.

I took Wink by the arm and pulled him back, so I could get up between him and the man. I reached up and tore that beret from the man's head—he was all-over bald—and shoved it into his hands. "Take off your lid, brother. This is a funeral home."

That's what did it, set off a chain of events that went too fast for anyone to stop. If I had to do it over again, maybe I wouldn't have—maybe I'd have just told that man, no, there'd been no trouble out there on the blacktop, thanks for asking—but there's no use wondering about it now. What's done is done, and all I can do is tell it, plain as I can, the last part of this story, the part that'll haunt me forever.

The bald man slapped that beret back on his head, and I said, "Maybe you didn't hear me." I snatched the beret again, and this time I stuffed it into the bib of my Carhartts. "Do you need a lesson about respect? And another thing, I don't like the way you talked to my friend."

I looked around for Wink, but he was gone. I felt alone, then, hung out to dry, but I didn't have time to feel sorry for myself on account the man was giving me what for.

"Respect," he said, with a snort. He looked me up and down. "A man like you is lecturing me about respect?" He gave me one of those exaggerated laughs— *Ha, ha.* "Look at you," he said. "Ridiculous."

That's when I took him by the throat. I'm ashamed of it now. He was an old man who happened to be in the way of everything that ailed me. I grabbed right above the top button of that ridiculous shirt, and I told him to shut up. I told him he didn't know anything about the sort of man I was.

Maybe I didn't either. Maybe that's what I was about to find out.

The man's wife screamed. The people in the visitation room turned to see what was happening in the vestibule.

Cathy rose from the sofa and saw Lily. The white handkerchief fell from Cathy's hand and she froze, like she was afraid to move one way or the other for fear that what she was seeing might disappear.

That's the last thing I saw before the funeral director put his face in mine. He was a blond with one of those tanning parlor bake jobs. He tried to loosen my hands from the man's throat, but I hung on. Then he got me in a headlock. He wrestled me away from the man, and we sort of scrabbled across the vestibule until we knocked into the guest register stand and we both went down.

Everything was a flurry of feet to me and the rising of people's voices. The funeral director still had me in that headlock, twisting me around, and every once in a while, I caught a glimpse of someone's shoes. The carpet smelled of some sort of floral cleaner, and the funeral director had on too much pine-scented aftershave—something from Avon, I'd wager. Probably some of that Wild Country that my father always wore. I heard a man say, "What in the world?" and another man said, "He's a drunk, you know."

Then a woman screamed. Everything went quiet, like all the air had gone out of the place, and that's when I heard it, the sound I knew so well, the gentle click of the safety going off on my Ruger. I knew, without having to look, that Wink had been so pissed over what the man had said about his eye that he'd gotten the rifle from his Mustang and had it shouldered up now and ready to use.

"Let loose of him," he said to the funeral director, and then I was free. I rubbed at my neck. "All right, then," Wink said, and he swung that Ruger around, pointing it into the viewing room where people were scrambling to crouch down behind the sofas and chairs.

That's when I saw the most wonderful thing. Lily, still wobbly on those stilettos, was very patiently making her way up the center aisle. She stepped around folding chairs knocked cockeyed, waited patiently for those who were still trying to get somewhere safe. She made her way to her daddy's casket, and, once she was there, she reached her hand out and put it on top of his. She stood up straight, her back to all the ugliness we'd wrought behind her, and she had that moment, one she might not have had without me, without Wink.

"Put down the gun," I told him. I nodded toward the front of the visitation room.

He took the Ruger down from his shoulder. He rubbed at his good eye. He was seeing what I was seeing, the grace that'd come to someone we'd thought, only minutes before, was a drunk girl in out-of-place shoes looking for a ride up the blacktop. Now she was Lily. Now she had the chance her mama said she'd deny her.

"Mercy," Wink said, which was a no-good prayer on account of, at least in one sense, everyone was over for him and me. Of course you can't cause a disturbance and point a loaded rifle at folks in a public place and not pay the price for it, particularly after all the times I'd been arrested when I was drunk. Aggravated assault. *What would you expect,* folks would say, *from the likes of them?*

Lily, though, was at the start of something. I felt it in my heart. This was the day she'd start to turn everything around. Or maybe that was only my hope talking. I really don't know a thing now about what happened to her after the county sheriff carted Wink and me off to jail. I just remember seeing her mama easing up beside her at the casket. She put her arms out and gathered her in, her little girl—the one she'd swore she'd disown—and they held onto each other.

I'll carry the picture of that to my grave, and though I'm sorry for all the fright we brought folks that day, I can't say I regret it. I can only hope they finally saw the good that lay on the other side of what we did. I hope my own mama knows it, too.

She was outside the funeral home, just arriving, when the sheriff brought me out in cuffs.

"I'd do it now," I said to Wink.

He was in front of me in the company of a deputy. "Do what?" he wanted to know.

"Have a drink."

A million drinks. I'd have drunk myself to death to keep my mama from seeing me in trouble, the way she'd seen me so many times.

"Oh, Benny," she said. She lifted her arms a little like she might try to touch me, but, of course, she couldn't. The law had me, and, when that's the case, you don't have many choices.

"Benny," she said, "is that you?"

Like she'd been waiting. Maybe I'd been gone on a long trip somewhere—I closed my eyes an instant and made it true—and now here she was, glad in the heart.

I'd tell her to take me home, and we'd have a good laugh over how at first she hadn't seemed to know me. "Oh, I did, too," she'd tell me. She'd lean over and whisper in my ear. "You didn't have me fooled. I knew it was you all along."

Twelve

The State Bird of Minnesota

Charles McLeod

LUDD LIVED WAY OUT ON THE NORTH SIDE of the lake. No one really ever went over there. His cabin was built up right to his dock, and in the summer Ludd would often go swimming. He was bearded and awkward, an oaf of a man, but in the water he was something to look at. Ludd could hold his breath longer than anyone I've known. You could watch him dive in, go take your meds, and when you came back Ludd would still be down there.

His dock's pilings were dressed with what he'd found while submerged: fishing lures, the handlebars from a children's bicycle. There too was a raft Ludd had fashioned from logs and the tanned hides of animals—badger and deer and foxes. Late afternoons, as the light bowed and stretched, Ludd would untie and drift until sunset. He lay perfectly still, his arms at his sides, legs brought tightly together, and when the light hit the lake at just the right angle, and turned the water golden and orange, Ludd and his vessel looked set ablaze, his raft transformed to a pyre.

Winter our cabins were the only inhabited. The whiteouts were constant, the lake like a field. On warm days the temperature reached up to zero. Icicles as long as stalactites hung from the rain gutters. A service road was cleared each month by a bulldozer, though neither of us had any use for it. By Thanksgiving I'd taken out the battery from my pickup. Ludd didn't even have a driver's license.

I considered those months, and still do to this day, as a time of very deep privacy. The smallest of things—a goshawk overhead, the tracks of a wolverine left on a snow bank—would linger and echo in the halls of my mind well into the reaches of evening.

Halloween weekend, my only autumn there, a blizzard had started near lunchtime. I was excited for the quiet the snowfall would bring; I was trying to get to know myself better. Near dusk I heard noises past the living room's window. With two fingers I parted the slats of the blinds and saw Ludd kneeling by the side of my cabin. Some minutes later he thumped up the steps in moccasins he had handcrafted. I opened the door and gave him a nod. Ludd nodded back at me. In his hand was my garden hose. Ludd had coiled it.

"Cold gets up through the spout," Ludd said. "Burst all your pipes open."

I was embarrassed and took the hose from his hand.

"Don't hear this poorly but once the snows come, I like things to be kind of quiet. Flooding means maintenance and maintenance means people. And I'm not a people sort of person."

He was so much to look at I forgot to speak. Ludd was six-eight or six-nine, and must have weighed close to three hundred. His beard was jet black and ran the length of his neck. His long nose looked sharp at the tip of it. Ludd's eyes sat so wide apart from each other his lashes almost met with his sideburns. But what I mean to say is when Ludd's gaze met your own, it seemed also he was looking around you, that something urgent stood always in his vision's middle distance, constantly demanding his attention.

"I put rags in your faucets. Keep 'em covered 'til spring."

"Okay," I told him.

"Good enough?" Ludd concluded.

"Good enough," I said back.

Ludd nodded his head and walked down the steps. I saw him again seven months later.

In St. Paul I'd been married and held a nine-to-five job. I worked for a firm that managed wholesale securities. I was expected to take clients' money and invest it somewhere so that it could make more money, which would in turn be reinvested so the process could repeat. The first symptoms of breakdown occurred at the four-year mark. In my truck in the company parking garage, I wept often and for no real reason. At night at the dinner table, across from Michelle, I would forget that I was supposed to be eating.

"What's wrong?" she would ask.

"Nothing," I would say. But what I was thinking was, "Something's coming. I don't know what it is, but there's something on the way. And you and I are powerless to stop it."

I slept less by the week, and then not at all. In the blue light of predawn, waiting out the alarm, I began to grow paranoid. In a closet or crawlspace or down in our basement, someone was waiting. Most often these men had tools of some sort, carpenter's drills or thin-nosed pairs of pliers with which they meant to enter into my brain, and redirect its circuits and pathways. Still later I believed they already had, and that they were following me to check on my progress.

"Are you seeing anything? When you close your eyes?" All the nurses' scrubs were the color of lilacs.

"Sometimes I see birds, eagles or geese. They're flying north, but their wings are on backwards."

In the psych ward different doctors asked questions from a list. Is there unresolved grief? Are you addicted to drugs? Have you recently experienced the death of a loved one? But it was none of these things, and the inquiries dwindled, and after a month the chief resident halved my dosage. Six weeks later I signed off on my release.

I was sick, and then I got better.

The one modern amenity I knew Ludd possessed was a battery-powered amateur radio. All summer long, from Ludd's side of the lake, came a tinny extravagant music, accompanied by the extremely high voice of a female. At first I thought the language in which the woman sung to be Mandarin or Korean. Later, I decided it was Hindi. Ludd kept the volume up so he could listen while adrift, and when the wind blew from the north, the sound would carry all the way to my cabin.

The western edge of Minnesota holds grasses common to the prairie: bluestem and dropseed and miscanthus. Much of the rest—the Central Lakes, the Arrowhead—is coniferous forest. There is also, however, a thin band of deciduous flora: swamp ash and bronze birch and poplars. It was in the northern pocket of this biome on which the lake sat. We were closer to Manitoba than Minneapolis, right on the borderland's border.

Ten cabins in total circled the shore. The land was state land, and the dwellings still stood due to a grandfather clause—they had been there before anyone decided the area needed protecting. This clause also meant no renovations could be done; there was no flipping of property. The structures would remain in their original form until time or climate destroyed them.

The last week of May Ludd took to the lake. Patches of ice still clung to the shore; I stood watching from the porch of my cabin. Ludd was bare-chested and wearing camouflage shorts. The length of his beard and chest hair was uniform. He gave me a wave and then ran the dock's planks in a loping, staggered sort of gallop. It was like watching a sack filled with marbles roll down a hill. Ludd crashed into the water then emerged supine, swimming in a perfect backstroke.

Later that morning the music came on. I decided to go ask Ludd about it. The summer crowd would not show until later, in June, and none of them ever really stayed long. Nearly all came with children and aside from the lake, the area held no attractions. Most made the trip because their parents had done so, as had their parents before them. The properties were less places of escape than heirlooms they'd been forced to inherit.

Ludd's cabin was an A-frame of unpainted cedar. Humps of snow bunched at the base of the roof, inches from the tarpaper shingles. An overturned wheelbarrow, its belly rusted through, lay next to a wash basin wrapped in sheet plastic. Behind the structure stood a wide grove of bur oaks, the forest continuing north all the way into Canada. Around the oaks' trunks different items had been tied: old license plates, the belt chain from off of a hot saw. The front door of the A-frame opened onto Ludd's dock; there was no way to reach it from the lakeshore. I turned the cabin's back corner to find a window to knock on and ran chest first into the barrel of Ludd's rifle.

"Heard you coming," Ludd said. The gun's action was bolted.

My time in an office had trained me to always be wrong. "I'm sorry," I said. I put my hands in my pockets so Ludd wouldn't notice them shaking.

"I've got an errand to see to. Is there something you need?"

"I came over to ask about your music."

Ludd swung the gun's barrel onto his shoulder. "It's bothered you," he said.

"It hasn't," I said. "I just want to know what language it's sung in."

Ludd looked at me with his strange, distanced eyes. He was dressed in all black: tight-fitting pants and black logger's boots and a thick, ribbed ebony sweater. "It's Tagalog," Ludd told me. "Filipino. Comes in daily from outside of Quezon. I pick it up low-band on my Ten-Tec."

"Alright," I said, and started walking away. I felt stupid for being so eager.

"A person who turns on a gun is dumb, crazy, or brave," said Ludd. "And you're not the first or the last of them."

I stopped walking and spun on the back of my heel. Ludd was smiling at me. His teeth were a mess, not aware of each other; they sprung from his gums at all angles.

"Where's your wife?" Ludd asked. "You got on a ring." He pointed the gun's barrel at one of my pants' pockets.

"She's in the Twin Cities. But she's not my wife anymore. Or she is, I guess, for a little while longer."

Ludd looked toward my cabin, then north to the woods. Two hours southwest, in the town of Roseau, my divorce papers waited in a PO Box.

"You been out to the shrub-carr? I'm headed that way."

I shook my head no; aside from day hikes down a deer path I'd found, I'd spent much of the wintertime reading.

"You're welcome to come but we got a long walk."

"I don't want to intrude."

"You already did that," Ludd told me.

From the lake we wound east through high manna grass and a shrub layer of alder and dogwood. New buds dotted the trees' narrow boughs. Red mottled soil sucked at our boot soles. Wild mint grew next to grape fern and patches of bugleweed. We walked single file, everything still, only the two of us moving. The late morning light turned the air a bright gray. Our plumes of breath curled, then vanished.

A compass was built into the stock of Ludd's rifle, though he never once needed to use it. He'd lived wild long enough that the landscape meant more. The wetlands were his grocery, his drugstore, his strip mall. Over the course of my time—one year—at the lake, Ludd would on occasion impart pieces of knowledge. I learned seeing geese before May meant a drought year was coming. I learned the berries from a winterholly bush could cure fever. But to me Ludd's facts were only that—facts, data that was interesting but useless. The things that he knew how to put into use I could never have implemented.

After an hour of walking the wood opened on to a flat, wide meadow. Thin turns of water striped the low field. The clearing stretched out ahead of us for two or three acres. The fog had burned off and the warm sun felt good. Ludd let me catch up and then raised his arm, pointing with a finger.

"Across there," Ludd said. "See where the high willow starts? Animals want to be on the edges."

"Where did you learn how to use a ham radio?" My grandfather had once owned a Ten-Tec.

"Air Force," Ludd said. "I was stationed at Clark down on Luzon until '90."

"You used to fly planes?"

"No, I fixed air conditioners. Other stuff, too. Patched circuit boards and built fuse boxes. But mainly it was A/C units. It was hot down there."

"They taught you all that while you were enlisted," I said.

"Learned it before I went in," Ludd told me.

"Where?"

Ludd slung his rifle from off of his shoulder and knelt on one knee. "Princeton," he said, and then fired.

I wasn't prepared for the report of the gun. The sound stunned me, and for a moment I panicked. In an arc, like a wave, my old life rose up and washed over me. Here was the nurse, her long-tipped syringe. Here were the imagined footsteps of men, moving quickly up our staircase in the nighttime. My back tensed and I shuddered. I couldn't catch my breath. I'd shut my eyes without realizing I'd done so. When I opened them again, Ludd was headed for the high grass on the far side of the clearing.

What Ludd had shot was a moose, a fully grown bull. It lay dead on the ground, its head peeking out past the stalks of the willows. Its long body was gaunt. Mange patched its fur. Ludd had put a bullet through one of its eyeballs.

"They drop their antlers in autumn, after they mate. Conserves energy for winter."

Ludd kicked the beast and for a moment it twitched. I looked at the animal's lean, umber muzzle. There was a patch of bare skin just under its nose that was freckled with blood spatter. I hadn't seen the creature at all, and didn't know how Ludd had.

"What are you going to do with it?" I asked.

Ludd shook his head. "Can't get it back. Weighs half a ton. Stay here a second. I'm going to go check on something." Ludd handed me his gun and walked back through the willows. I was still breathing hard, my heart high in my chest. It seemed to me against Ludd's ways to kill something and leave it. I didn't understand, and wouldn't for years, why he had shot it in the first place.

From behind me, back on the fringe of the wood, came a shrill eerie clucking, followed by a rapid series of honks. I turned in time to see a pair of large black and white birds, loons, leaving their hiding spot in the shrub brush. They flew out over the meadow and then circled back in the lake's direction. They had yet to drop their coarse winter coats and their undersides were the purest of whites, and I tried to imagine what must be at work for nature to change the very color of something, to better ensure its survival.

When Ludd came out from the willows his pants were two-toned, wet all the way to mid-thigh.

"Did you see them?" he asked. He was grinning again.

"The loons," I said.

"The state bird of Minnesota," Ludd answered.

In remembering my marriage one sequence of images returns to me over and over. These depict man's early attempts at building machines meant for flight. One sees these contraptions on commercials, sometimes; they are used popularly as symbols of failure. The film reels, grainy and sepia-toned, show a pair of people in the cockpit of some laughably faulty apparatus. There is the plane with the too-long, tri-tiered wings; there is the plane with the giant umbrella, its pumping locomotion believed by its makers to be enough to lift their craft skyward.

Where I live now, on the Gulf Coast, I encounter sometimes the sort of couple I'd once been a part of. They are costly and loud and see the earth as little more than something to keep well below them. In the bayou's June heat they wear black linen suits and hatch plans to develop the floodplain. Their shoes are sharp-tipped and look sleek as jets. Cell phones sit on their hips like missiles.

Soon after my return from the ward, Michelle decided our days together were numbered. She herself was a lawyer and while there was love, there was also a blueprint that had not been followed correctly. Weakness of character equated to a flaw in design. Our machine would not leave its runway. The securities firm, unsure of how to proceed, let me go via a check in the low sixes. My third Monday home Michelle returned late from work with a brief that she had assembled. This document outlined, in tedious detail, the reasons for our impending separation. There were pie charts and bar graphs that showed, in full color, my drag on our upward mobility. Our living room a court, my wife made her case, pacing the carpet like she was waiting for takeoff.

"In the term *power couple* which word comes first?" she asked me.

I couldn't argue. But I also didn't care. On the coffee table in front of me, I'd opened the paper to the classifieds. In black block letters was the ad for the cabin. ESCAPE TO THE NORTH, read the posting.

Everyone's an inventor, whether they know it or not; survival, alone, is inventing, and our days and our weeks are like wire and bearings, and with each year we add to our chassis. We may not know why we're building but we build anyway. And on occasion, the things we are able to create force others to stop and take notice.

One of Ludd's bombs blew the arm off a child, a sixth-grader named Tiffany Stevenson. Tiffany lived in a suburb of Denver. Her father, R&D for Lockheed Martin, was the package's intended recipient. Wrapped in brown butcher paper, the address in black ink, the square parcel was delivered to the Stevenson's doorstep. Alone in the house and on Christmas vacation, Tiffany could think only of presents. Curiosity rampant she brought the package inside, taking scissors from their place in a cupboard. With the twine cut, the bomb shifted and set itself off. Neighbors called the police. Paramedics were able to save her.

A second device was sent east to New Gloucester, Maine, the town housing the last community of Shakers. In journals found later, in the cabin at the lake, it was explained by Ludd that his reason for targeting this group was to lead to the Shakers' resurgence; Mother Ann Lee, the sect's figurehead and matriarch, had predicted a revival in Shaker theology once only five members remained in the congregation. This prophecy has turned out so far to be false; there are now four living Shakers, with no new constituents pending.

Ludd's final bomb had failed to go off; for two weeks it sat on a university campus, in the mailroom of the Biology Department. More than a half dozen students, in reports to the media, said they remembered picking up the package and moving it. The addressee, a professor doing research in Ghana, was located and flown home by the federal government. Later this man would receive minor fame for being part of the first team of scientists to clone, successfully, a zebra.

All of Ludd's parcels were sent the same winter, mailed from Roseau, Minnesota. The postal clerk, a woman I'd known by name, recalled Ludd clearly and easily. Capped in each pipe shaft with match heads and gunpowder were the hooves of wild animals, broken to shards and then sharpened, so that upon detonation the things Ludd had killed would in turn go on to kill others.

My last month at the lake the weather was gorgeous: warm, and with little humidity. Each dawn birdsong spilled from the wood; it stayed light to near ten in the evening. Families arrived with bright rubber rafts tied to the roofs of their station wagons. Mornings I fished from the shore near my porch, careful to keep my shadow behind me.

With my lease up and truck packed I went over to Ludd's, to tell him goodbye and say thank you. He'd asked little from me and offered a lot, and it's rare to find those sorts of people. A wooden Dutch door was on the cabin's backside; I'd knocked on it more with each season. I wouldn't say we were friends but a rapport had developed; we'd accepted each other as neighbors.

When Ludd answered that day there were nicks on his cheeks—he'd shaved his beard off completely. His jaw line was short, his chin near to his lips. To say he looked different wouldn't be quite enough; some crucial part of him had seemed to go missing.

"Beard's gone," I said.

"Summer," Ludd answered. Bags wrapped his brown eyes. His girth spanned the frame of the doorway. Behind him, the cabin's interior was dark; the structure had been built without windows. From the room's depths issued the noise of Ludd's radio. In place of the singing I'd so often heard were only the sounds of raw frequency, a low wash of static out of which climbed a high-pitched metallic sort of chirping. I realized this to be the component's transmitter, searching for a signal and failing.

"I'm leaving tomorrow. I'm moving away," I told him. Ludd held out his hand and I took it in mine. His long fingers crept up past my wrist bone. "Okay," he said, then let go and shut the door. It was the last time that I ever saw him.

The next morning I found the note on my porch. Ludd's handwriting was precise and looked very feminine, and at first I was confused about where the piece of paper had come from. What Ludd had left me was a quote by Thoreau, out of *Walden:*

A lake is the landscape's most beautiful and expressive feature.
It is Earth's eye; looking into which the beholder measures
the depth of his own nature.

Today, the lake is no longer a lake; it was drained, and then used as landfill. Its image and name appear on no maps. There isn't any water to swim in. The country needed somewhere to bury its trash, and the area fit these requirements. Gone too are the cabins, Ludd's and my own, along with all of the others. The land's still protected, is still state land, there's just been a change in what's being guarded.

They never found Ludd; they searched and they searched. They dredged the lake then went north into Canada, a phalanx of men moving over the earth and the nettles in navy blue windbreakers. A hotline was started, bloodhounds employed. I watched it all from my TV in Beaumont. I've been down in the bayou for nearly two decades. I'm the owner of a rig diving outfit. For good money my shop gives scuba tours of the oil platforms just off the Gulf Coast. I've had a nurse shark swim nose-first into the small of my back. I've found raw pearls at the bottom of the ocean.

I'm sure that he's dead, that Ludd took his own life or that some act of nature—a rockslide, pneumonia—took it from him, but there is also a small part of me that believes that if I returned to the north I could find him, or rather that Ludd would somehow find me, that he would emerge from the woods with long hair and his beard, rifle slung over his shoulder. But if we did meet I don't know what might happen next.

It's winter now, and I see the loons often.

Thirteen

The Five Points of Performance
Christopher Mohar

ONE: PROPER EXIT

Hempel and I leave the funeral home in his new Trans Am. This is his dream car, a '74 Super Duty with a 455 HO V-8, Olympic white with the powder blue phoenix decal on the hood. Sitting in the parking lot, he asks if I want to drive. I do, just not right now, so I ride shotgun. The upholstery is black, but not dark enough to keep me from seeing a brackish stain across the seatbelt.

We take Pierce Street to Shady Lane and get on County PD. Hempel has it up to 105 when we hit the railroad crossing by the Sawyer Feed Mill. This is a new type of airborne, but the feeling is similar—like I've swallowed a live snake, tongue flicking my tonsils, tail rattling my guts. When Willy was alive he told me it hit him like a premonition the instant before his boots left the steel. For me, it's not real until I hear the sound of wind snapping into rip-stop nylon, *thuk, thuk, thuk, thuk.* In the car, the feeling doesn't last. Just enough hang-time to freeze the world for a second, for one glance up to the billboard on the feed mill's steeple: a collage of advertisements papered over and peeled off again a thousand times—tatters of Goodyear Tires, a shred of a McCormick-Deering.

The rear wheels touch down first and the chassis bottoms out with a sound like a .38 on a steel plate. The tires don't blow like I think they might, but the

Trans Am fishtails and spins off through the gravel shoulder. We skid to a stop two feet from a pasture fence, the timbers weathered black, the barbed wire strung taut as sinew between bones.

Hempel steps out of the Trans Am without closing the door. He walks a perimeter around the car, kicking each tire, bending to look at the undercarriage. Then he slumps down on the hood, spread so the phoenix wings feather out from his arms, laughing uncontrollably. Then I'm laughing, too.

Then I get out and puke into the switchgrass.

⁂

The night I met Hempel, I watched him KO my best friend Willy in four minutes flat.

Willy was my neighbor across the fence-line since forever; we'd worn a path through the soybeans down to the dirt. After school we'd hunt frogs or sneak our GI Joes into the barn to douse them in Will Senior's tractor ether and set them ablaze. The barnyard dirt was seeded with blackened faces and melted camouflage limbs. Later, after I got my Dodge, we'd go mudding in the creek bottom and then sit in Willy's driveway drinking High Life and swinging our feet from the tailgate, which is what we were doing when Hempel showed up.

They were stepbrothers overnight. Will Senior got involved with a cocktail waitress he met out drinking in LaMont, and the next thing anybody knew she was pulling up in his driveway in a '87 Subaru stuffed to the sunroof with tank tops and *Peoples* and frost-covered TV dinners thawing water onto the floor mats. And Hempel, seventeen, riding shotgun, all sunburned biceps and tobaccoed teeth. He moved into Julie's old room; she had already left on a full-ride to Platteville, anyway.

It was Friday so the first thing Willy did was invite Hempel to the gym. The sky was darkening and Willy's eyes were raccoon-shadowed by the barn light as he leaned to my ear to say, "I'll kill him."

Then he hopped down and shook Hempel's hand, and we all got into the truck.

Grey's Gym was just past the town limits, to get outside the ordinances. It was nothing but a metal pole shed in a gravel lot edged with gnarled oaks. A single streetlight shone over the aluminum door. Inside, the pads were caving and the canvas was stained brown with spattered sweat. The ropes went saggy so quick that Grey kept a pipe wrench in hand while he reffed—strictly to tighten the turnbuckle between rounds. So what? It was the summer before our senior year and we didn't know what to do with ourselves besides drink and drive and beat the shit out of each other, so we decided to make one of the three official. We went every Friday.

Hempel and I stood watching Fat Larry pound the piss out of some welterweight while Willy snaked through the crowd to get on the signup-sheet.

"Nice place, huh?" Hempel said. "I've never been in a ring before."

I spit onto the concrete. Didn't look down from the fight.

"You know this guy?" he asked. Fat Larry had the welterweight on the ropes and Grey rang the bell to break it up. The fighters took their corners. After a while the next round started.

"You box, too?" he said.

I took a pull from my High Life. I took another pull.

"Some," I said. "Not like Willy. But this is our thing, coming here together."

Another bell, and Fat Larry climbed out of the ring. The welterweight was bleeding from the face.

"You got more beers in the truck?" Hempel said. "I figure we'll all need some after the fight."

"Yeah," I said. "You sure will."

He shrugged, "I've hit some bags." Grey waved him up. Hempel stripped his shirt and climbed under the ropes. The halogen barn lights buzzed like a beetle in the summer heat, and Hempel's hair burned phosphorus white. He was rope-muscled and tall; he'd have a longer reach than Willy. In the opposite corner, Willy was grinning the shit-eating grin of a kid who just popped his cherry or caught his first largemouth. He paced from post to turnbuckle as a captive bear might measure its cage. His canines showed when he spoke, and the bridge of his nose was crooked from being already broken several times.

Grey hit the bell. Hempel didn't do any float-like-a-butterfly bullshit, he just fought behind his jab and when he hit, he hit goddamn hard. You already know how this story ends.

The moment Grey called the fight, I pushed my way outside and jogged to my truck. I dug the tire iron from under my seat. I'd parked under the streetlight, and the few intact flakes of chrome-plate on the rusty metal burst from shadow to light as I spun the iron in my palm.

Leaning on the fender, I waited.

When Hempel finally came out, he wore his gloves tied together by the laces and strung over his neck like a gold medal. He walked to the passenger door, tossed the gloves inside, and looked at me through the glass. He didn't say a word, just stood looking until we both knew I wasn't going to do anything.

Then he came over to my side of the car, glancing down, kicking a tire.

"What, did you get a flat?"

I shoved the tire iron back under the seat.

When Willy came out, a black spider of thread clung to his eyebrow. Grey had given him six stitches. I found out later that this was why it took so long for Hempel to leave, too. He'd stayed to make sure Willy was alright, personally supervising each suture as Grey's veteran hands threaded and pricked needle through skin and pulled the line tight.

TWO: GAIN CANOPY CONTROL

I run my tongue over my teeth and spit into the grass. The way Hempel looks at me should make me feel sicker, but I allow myself to feel washed of something. Hempel might vomit, too, but instead he gets back behind the wheel. For most people there'd be several ways to respond to what happened, but for us there is only one: denial.

You are not human. You must never break.

We drive Gall Road to XX, Hempel slowing into turns and down-shifting out of them, and at its gentlest, this still puts your Adam's apple to the back of your throat. The Trans Am breathes like a dead god awakened. The trees are a decaying filmstrip in the slurred language of speed.

"You missed the turn," I say.

"We're not going back to Will's," he says. "Wipe your mouth. I don't want you dripping puke on my seats."

The sun smothers on the horizon and the sky goes dark. We're a half mile from Trader's and you can already see the neon glow. The parking lot is packed with Broncos, Blazers with lift kits and 44s, rusty-ass 300,000-mile Toyota pickups, rows and rows of Harley fastbacks. The gravel under the tires sounds like grinding teeth. Hempel's car lurches into neutral as he takes his hand from the stick to pull the black tie from his neck. He flings it into the miniature back seat, puts the car in gear, and we prowl forward.

Inside, all four pool tables are surrounded by bikers wearing CC Riders leathers. Some underage girls are playing darts with a couple of bros who circle like turkey vultures, timing their ass-grabs to throw off the girls' aim. Three chain-smoking Native women sit hypnotized by the video poker consoles. I recognize them from some tribal function in a past life, but I don't wave.

Hempel and I edge our way to the bar and nod to Job the bartender and order two shots of Wild Turkey and two beers. Our hands turn the condensation on the glasses to the color of dishwater. We lean on the bar, facing the door.

"We ought to go back to your mom's later," I say, "to see how she and Will Senior are doing."

Hempel raises his shot glass in the direction of the pool tables.

"Look at all these faggot bikers." He downs his Wild Turkey.

"To Willy, then," I say, and I down my whiskey, too.

"Look at these fucking back-country-ass hicks."

I look down at my Carhartts, my steel-toed Wolverines. The black ones, for the funeral.

"What does that make us?" I ask. Hempel looks at me like I just spoke Chinese.

"We're the Eighty-Sixth Airborne," he says. "We're All-American."

⁂

After our fight, the ride home from Grey's was silent. At Willy's place, I pulled over in the unmown grass at the bottom of the drive. Hempel got out. His mom's Subaru was empty now, parked in the rutted-out gravel by the tractor shed.

"Come on," Willy said.

"I want to hear the rest of this song," I said, and I kept the motor running.

You got to know when to hold 'em, know when to fold 'em, know when to walk away, know when to run.

With the headlights off, I couldn't see all the way up the drive, but I watched Willy walk until he faded into darkness. I flipped off the dial and sat in silence. My ears tuned in to the frogs and cicadas. I sat. I heard them both laughing, their voices distant, as if under water.

When I got out, the mosquitoes were thick. I swatted at my neck and my hand came back slick with blood. I walked up to where they stood together in a wide swath of yellow light cast down from the window of the farmhouse. Hempel had his shirt pulled up to his chin and was showing off a massive welt. He prodded Willy's hands up into a high guard, and then mimed out punches in slow motion: a feint, a cross, a finger drawing through the air to indicate locations of posts and ropes, his eyes rolling back with each imagined blow. A pause in the reenactment to probe a swollen jaw.

The two brothers shook hands, and Willy reached out and clasped Hempel's shoulder. I see now that the fight was a rite of passage—from that moment on Hempel was one of us. But at the time, I was awestruck. *He came uninvited into your house*, I thought. *He just knocked you out.*

They saw me and stopped play-acting. I was still in the shadows, but I could tell I must've looked bad from the way Willy eyed me back. Hempel brushed his fingers over his bone-white hair.

"Hey, come on, Joseph," Willy said to me. Then smiling to Hempel, he said, "He's been staring you down all night, huh?"

I walked into the light.

"Yeah," Hempel said, "he's one goddamn surly redskin, ain't he?"

When Hempel looked to Willy for confirmation, his smile dropped. Willy clamped his hand around the soft of Hempel's jaw and squeezed so his hands shook. Hempel's lips bulged like a carp.

"You don't ever say that. I don't care who you KO. Say it again, I'll kill you."

"Relax, I'm joking," Hempel said. "Sorry."

When Willy let go, there were four white fingers fading from Hempel's cheek.

On the ground sat a Styrofoam cooler of the type you get from a bait shop to keep your leeches cool. Hempel opened it and tossed one can to Willy, took another for himself, and walked over to me with a third one in his hand.

"Where I'm from, it ain't proper to drink with someone who you ain't met," he said. "I'm Travis Hempel."

My fingers slid against his on the bottom of the can as I took the beer.

"Joseph White-Eyes," Willy said for me.

"Nice to meet you," Hempel said, like he'd never seen me before in his life, like Willy never hit him, like the parking lot never happened. I knew it was a gesture of charity, but I shook his hand anyway. This was before Basic, but even then I knew that discipline is how you get by in the world.

"You know what this extra's for?" Hempel asked, as he went to the cooler for a fourth beer.

"I guess that one's mine, too," Willy said. Hempel laughed and lobbed it to Willy, who held the cold can against his damaged forehead. I didn't open mine, just looked down at the black cusps of my fingernails and the silver of the can, and back up at Hempel.

"What's wrong?" Willy asked. "You need a second can to cool your head, too?"

THREE: KEEP A SHARP LOOKOUT

We finish our beers and get another round, and when those are gone we get another.

"Let's play pool," Hempel suggests.

"The tables are full."

"No they ain't." And for the thousandth time in my life, I knowingly follow Hempel into a bad idea. He leads me across the bar to the pool tables and the biker gang.

Anyone in here could tell you who these guys are. Even when you don't know their names, you know their eyes. You know they grew up doing tranny rebuilds in their tractor sheds. Charred venison, cigarette burns, ditch weed grown between rows in the cornfield.

A tall, muscled biker circles the table trying to line up his shot. He has a crucifix inked on his bicep and black hair like the aftermath of a wildfire. Hempel and I are in his way along the outside of the felt, but we don't move.

I can feel his eyes on us and I know that if I could see myself, I'd have the same set jaw, the same forced squint, the same *fuck-you* bent to my eyebrows. I know some people think humans are God's great gift to the universe, that we're special because we can think up morality and technology and civilization and all that bullshit. But we're not. We're just pissing coyotes—we can smell our own.

"We've got next," Hempel says.

"Afraid not," Crucifix says, and points to the coin tray on the edge of the table, where quarters are waiting in numbered slots. Hempel scatters the coins to the floor. He picks up the nearest one and snaps it neatly into the first slot.

"Next."

Crucifix tosses his cue onto the table.

"You ought to learn some manners, boy."

"Who you callin' *boy*, boy?"

But before the biker can reach Hempel, I step between them. I feel his gaze skim my chest like the pulse of air in the wake of a bullet, but he stops where he is.

"You want something, sand-nigger?"

I bite my cheek not to say anything. I won't mention that my Iroquois blood is more American than he'll ever be. I won't mention the bigotry itself, because once you've seen a Chinook take a shoulder rocket, well, fuck *politically correct*. I don't know anything about that. All I know is someone had to do the job and I went to get it done. I didn't go in wanting to kill a thousand Hajjis, like some of these guys say. But sure, I felt like that sometimes. Still, I'll bite myself instead of talking because no matter how goddamn wrong he is, there are still two of us and a dozen of them. I don't have a death wish.

"What did you say?" Hempel says.

"I'm not ready for you yet," Crucifix says, "I'm talking to Taliban over here."

"You don't ever say that."

He gives Crucifix a right cross that drops him to the floor. Before the rest of the bikers can kill us, I've got both hands on Hempel's chest and I'm working him backwards out the door, my mouth stuck on repeat in a way that takes me a minute to realize it's my own voice.

"Get out, get out, get out, get out!"

⚜

The three of us survived senior year together. In the fall, we hauled old barn lumber up the ridgeline on Willy's back forty to build deer stands, and when Hempel saw an eight-pointer he couldn't pass up even though he'd already spent his buck tag on a spike, the three of us dragged the body together in a dead heat all the way back to the house. Winter was full of ice-fishing and blackberry brandy, Friday-night fights, girls that came and went, cut classes, and finally the snow melted away to bright March afternoons when we'd walk over Willy's fields with our .22s, finishing a six-pack each and standing the brown bottles at the edge of the field, aiming with iron sights. Hempel was the best boxer but the worst shot, and when he kicked up fountains of dirt that left the bottles standing, he'd say, "My aim ain't what it used to be." He said it over and over, every shot, and every shot I pointed out that his aim had never been shit to begin with, until finally Willy told me to shut the hell up.

The night we graduated, Kelly Turner had a kegger in her hayloft and when the cops showed up, Willy and Hempel and I fled into the cornfield, the papery leaves nicking our skin as we ran, as we crashed to the ground and lay in the dust, panting. We slept side by side, separated by dark corridors of cornstalks. We woke with dirt in our mouths.

When we walked out at dawn, our classmates were still passed-out in the hay. One keg floated but another was still sputtering, and we filled some empty Gatorade bottles with warm beer for the ride.

"What next?" Willy asked.

"Let's go for a swim," I suggested, even though I had the feeling he was asking for direction in a vaster, less immediate sense.

"I know a place," Hempel said, and I gave him the keys to my truck. He drove us out past the fuel co-op, down County XX, and pulled off into the ditch along the Ox Creek Bridge. The day was already warm, and as we came up through the woods, the sun glowed hot through the burr oaks. The pond was called "Pewitt's Hole," but the creek didn't have a name—it wasn't more than a seasonal channel for snowmelt. Runoff trickled together in a rocky bed, edging its way to the sheer face of a basalt outcropping and flooding the basin below.

This was where we shared our first free fall—not on a zip-line at Fort Bragg and not under the rotors of a CH-47. We stood in the cold creek up to our ankles with the currents urging our feet toward the precipice. When we leapt, we fell side by side with the falling water like sticks carried over in the stream.

Our feet stung with the impact, velocity your body could never have imagined when you were still grounded. For an instant the water was warm but our lean bodies cut deep below the surface, deeper than sunlight could reach, to where the cold shocked you, to where the bedrock held hostage the springtime cool of melted snow even as the days lengthened and the grass baked brown in the rising heat.

We surfaced, screaming. What could we say? There were no words to describe that feeling, that rush of blood to the head that comes from knowing what you're doing is stupid and dangerous and amazing—you're young and invincible, you can fall forever, you will never die.

I swam to the bank and scrambled back up the boulders, eager to jump again.

"Let's go," I said, but when I looked over my shoulder, neither of them had followed me. Standing in the stream, I inched my feet through the rocks until I could curl my toes over the edge. Below me, Hempel and Willy were swimming in lazy circles together, diving, disappearing, re-emerging nearby. Willy looked up and met my eyes. He was smiling but I knew, then, that something was lost. Hempel called to him, and they both dove under again.

A week later Hempel would enlist, and two weeks later Willy and I would do the same. Of course, I didn't know it yet. In that moment, all I knew was that the sun was on my shoulders and the current was tugging my ankles. I stepped forward and threw myself over the edge.

FOUR: TURN INTO THE WIND

Crucifix comes in with his right so close I feel the wind of it. I'm keeping my distance, shuffling on the balls of my feet, coiling my springs. He thinks he'll get close and just grind me. Over his shoulder, crowds of people are fanning out the front door of the bar. My feet slip loose over parking lot gravel.

Hempel bobs in my peripheral, in close with a biker stocky like a bulldog and another with limbs drooped loose as a scarecrow's. The tall one has a pool cue. They swing out of view, and I can't see what happens next, but I hear the wooden snap of the cue hitting, hitting, breaking.

Crucifix swings from both sides, but my jab sends him back a couple paces. He comes in straight and I feint left, slipping it, and put a cross to his chest. I'm covering, elbows in, dancing back in a wide arc, circling, putting distance between us, keeping him just off my right side, keeping him spinning to keep up with me. He screams something. His mouth seethes with teeth and spit. I take a low guard, my right tucked close to my chest, my lead hand just off my belt buckle, below his line of vision.

I breathe. Tighten my fist. When my left connects from below, he never sees it coming. My right follows straight to his teeth. I feel my knuckles cut on bone.

Stay down, I'm thinking. *Please. Just stay down.*

But there are three others around me and I'm taking fist after fist to the arms, then hard to the guts. I double over and when I get hit again, it's with steel-toes kicking the wind out of me. I taste whiskey and bile.

I'm on the ground. Hands over my head, knees pulled tight. Hempel is in a crawl, spitting black, and the Bulldog biker is on the ground too, clutching his nose with blood welling out between his fingers. Scarecrow kicks Hempel in the ribs. I stretch for the splintered pool cue.

Then I hear the gunshot.

Job the bartender is standing in the bed of a nearby pickup with a sawed-off .410 pointed heavenward. He breaks the stock from the barrel and chambers another shell.

"Get out," he says. "Get the fuck out."

And I think, *exactly.*

⁂

There is no such thing as an ex-paratrooper. Once you're in, you're in. But it doesn't happen easy. Even if you finish BAC and get your silver wings, you're still just another airborne.

Here's how it does happen: you load up a hundred pounds of gear on your back, flak jacket, pocket flares, wire cutters, radio batteries, Halazone tablets. You sit on a metal bench in the dark belly of a Hercules for three hours that are both the slowest and the quickest of your life. A few of you talk shit on movies you've seen or girls you've had, but mostly no one talks at all. Twelve hundred feet is so low you can smell the burning asphalt and wood cinder when you pass over a village. The sun stings your eyes when they open the hatch, so you can't see the ground before you jump, just a white rectangle burning in front of you like a doorway to nothing—maybe purgatory.

No, purgatory would be a blessing where you're going.

You free-fall. You might die. The harness cuts into your chest and the risers snap tight, and maybe now you won't. You try not to vomit; maybe you don't. When your feet are on the ground and you're still alive, you look around the DZ and realize you're in a wasteland with nothing but sand and rubble for days in any direction. Now you're a paratrooper. Now you're in this shit for life. If you die, you die a paratrooper.

You already know how this story ends.

We were stationed in Kuwait, and they dropped us outside Fallujah. How can I even begin to explain what we experienced there? The heat of a structure fire so great you'd feel it from inside a building a block away, your cheek pressed flat to the warm brick. The background pop of rifle fire like a constant horrific birdsong. The bedrock rumble of truck bombs. IEDs. A black Mercedes-Benz limousine, gloss-perfect and engulfed in flames, smoke pooling through the ruptured windshield. A man steps out from the car and takes off running down an alleyway, and after he rounds the corner you realize the reason he looked funny was, well, he was on fire.

You find a pair of flower-print high-heels abandoned in the street. When you pick them up, you see the flower-print is wet blood on white leather.

What else to say?

Willy took shrapnel from an IED and got airlifted out. He spent three days in a hospital in Kuwait City before they shipped him home to Mother of Mercy. Six days later, he passed out face-first into his breakfast cereal, and by the time they got him to the ER, he was DOA. Maybe they fucked-up his antibiotics, maybe it was drug-resistant. Hempel thought it was some kind of intentional biological warfare, but I thought typical SNAFU. Who knows?

The funeral was back home in Wisconsin. Hempel and I were pallbearers, along with his father and some neighbors. All the airheads were there, anyone who could get leave. Briggs came all the way up from Kentucky, but he didn't help carry the coffin, with his arm like that.

After the burial, all the airheads stayed, eyes on the ground. Lit cigarettes. When we sang "Blood Upon the Risers," I know a lot of the NAPs didn't get it. Maybe we should have waited for more of them to leave. Maybe it was a cherry move to let anyone overhear what we had to say.

Willy's sister Julie was the only one who listened through the whole song, and when we got to the *Poured him from his boots* line, she was staring at me with eyes like a cornered animal. But I know for a fact that Willy would have wanted it this way.

That song was like our motto.

Gory, Gory, What a helluva way to die.

FIVE: LAND

The Trans Am's fat tires burn then catch. With the T-top still down, the night air rushes liquid around us. Bar lights disappear and it's nothing but trees and country dark, our headlights flaring forward into the depths of it.

Blood weeps from the corner of Hempel's mouth, and blood that's not his own is spattered across his forehead. I look at myself in the side view, the red smeared down my neck. I can't find anything to clean up with that isn't already wet, so I grab Hempel's tie from the back seat. I hold it out for him, but he shrugs and wipes the gore off of his face and onto his bare hands.

"Those bikers were pussies," he says. "You hurt? I didn't feel a thing."

When he rests his hand back on the steering wheel, the blood has seeped into the folds of his skin like stain into the grain of a timber, outlining the whorls and triangles in a deep crimson, almost black in the radio glow.

"They talked a lot of shit, but I didn't feel a thing," Hempel says. "We're All-American. We're All-Fucking-American. Even if you do look like a raghead."

His hands are jittering. The car trembles back and forth between the center-line and the shoulder.

"Where are we going?" I ask, though I already know.

Hempel doesn't answer, just clutches and shifts, lets the hum and throttle of the Trans Am speak for him. The darkness makes it hard to know just how fast we're going, but even so, I can feel it. The road is straight and then banks into a turn, and Hempel uses the whole of the pavement, taking the inside of the curve, ignoring the painted lines. He levels the wheel and buries the accelerator. Between us and the gravel drive up to Pewitt's Hole is a mile of nothing but curves and hills.

"Why do you have to look like a goddamn raghead, anyway?" Hempel says. "It wasn't my fault. There was nothing I could do. It's *your* fault, you fucking raghead."

He kills the headlights.

"Stop!" I scream. "Stop the car."

I feel the engine vibrations through the seat, harder now. I see darkness. The wind cascades over the windshield and I push my arms through the current.

"Tell me," Hempel says. "Tell me there was nothing I could do."

I rip the stick shift out of gear—forget the clutch. The engine roars when the tranny hits neutral and the car slows. I reach for the light switch. Hempel doesn't get out of my way and he doesn't stop me. His arms are just dead weight. I'm sprawled out horizontally, stretched just far enough to reach the switch, the plastic knob slippery under my fingers. Dark shapes blur by us on both sides of the road. My seatbelt cuts into my ribcage with a sensation almost like the tightness of the harness, and I half expect to feel the impact of the risers snapping tight when the chute opens. I flip the lights back on just in time for us to see the fawn.

Hempel brakes and swerves, and the car's struts thump as the animal is caught in the front tire and sucked under the wheel. The body snaps, wet and dull between the pavement and the undercarriage. The Trans Am shakes, the air bitter with tire smoke, gravel sounding against the chassis as we leave the asphalt. We're slowing. I feel the Gs in my stomach. Slowing, but we're still moving pretty good when the front fender hits a tree, crumples, and pivots the car backwards. My head painlessly kisses the dash. We skid into a second tree, and the rear bumper wraps itself around the trunk on both sides, our bodies snapping hard into the headrests.

It's over.

I don't vomit this time. My eyes follow Hempel out through the open T-top and away from the car. The silence hits me, and I realize the engine is dead. I know it won't start again.

By the time I catch up, Hempel is forty yards down the road, kicking up dust in the shoulder gravel. He doesn't once look back at the car—his dream car, his '74 Super Duty with its 455 HO V-8, Olympic white with the powder blue phoenix decal across the mangled hood, with the headlights still on like lighthouse beacons, moths flicking out from the trees, and Hempel a matte-black silhouette in the beams. He walks into the road and follows the centerline paint, *dash, dash, dash.* I open my mouth, but nothing comes.

On the pavement, fragments of clear plastic and broken glass mingle with fur and gore. Hempel drops to his knees and picks up the fawn, not even a yearling, just the size of a puppy with white spots across its caramel-colored back and eyes black as deep-water stones. Blood wets fur like dew pearled on grass blades.

He cradles the animal with its tiny head curled on his shoulder as if it were a human child sleeping safely in her parent's arms. The tip of the fawn's tongue hangs from its mouth and blood drips from its lips onto Hempel's body, bleeding into the fabric of his shirt. Another drip lands in the same spot, and the spot gets bigger. One more spot among the other smears and stains matching.

"There was nothing you could do," I say.

My hand finds his shoulder. Hempel drops his face to the fawn's body, hugging it tight against his chest, and when he begins to cry, both of their bodies shudder as one.

There was nothing any of us could do.

Fourteen

The Baby Glows

David James Poissant

THERE IS NOTHING ELSE about the baby that one might call unusual, nothing uncharacteristic of other babies. The baby does not skip rope. The baby does not levitate. The baby cannot line up dominos across the kitchen counter with his mind. The baby just glows.

The baby is not bright like a fire or a star. His light is soft as a glow stick's, the kind you buy at a carnival and snap to make shine.

LUMINESCENT BABY SHOCKS WORLD! one headline reads. Another: FIRE BABY HOT TO MOTHER'S TOUCH!

The baby's body temperature is 98.6°.

It startles the mother to open the nursery door to a radiant cloud over the crib. Then, she remembers, takes him in her arms, and holds him the way any mother would hold any baby.

The baby does not glow *sometimes*. The baby is *always* glowing.

It's only unusual because it hasn't happened before. Stranger things have happened. Babies born with tails. Babies with extra arms or eyes. Pairs of babies born sharing a stomach. This baby has no extra parts.

The baby is not magic.

A glowing baby comes in handy. Cradling the child, the father travels downstairs in the night, finishes laundry, searches the pantry for snacks without flipping a switch. The mother doesn't like when the father does this. "The baby," she says, "is not a light bulb."

Nothing else about the baby glows. The baby cries normal tears, drools normal drool, and—it must be said—poops normal poop.

And what becomes of a glowing baby? Will he grow into a glowing boy? Will he become a man who glows on his way to work, who confuses pedestrians at streetlights? Will he marry, and, if he does, will his husband or wife wear a blindfold to bed?

He will require exclusive showings at movie theatres. He will cause headaches at airport security. Common sense says he will never be eligible for the draft.

Some think that the older he gets, the brighter the baby will be. Some say his luminosity will fade with age, like childhood allergies. Others wager he'll beam at this relative wattage until, until.

One doesn't like to consider it, but the baby will die. One day, the baby, whether baby or man or boy, will be laid into a casket, the casket lowered into the ground. By then, one imagines, the light will have gone out. But one never knows. Perhaps he'll glow past his last breath, the way hair is said to grow for days from the dead. Perhaps.

Do you see him there, glowing belowground?

See the grass that grows from the baby's grave. See it sparkle. And a new species of incandescent worm to be discovered not far from the cemetery. And the moles that feed on these worms, their noses stars already.

There they go, tunneling, rocketing through earth, chasing those tender, smoldering fingers of snout, clawing their way up and up, and out, and into light.

Fifteen

Splendid, Silent Sun

Yelizaveta P. Renfro

11/6

Claudette—

You'll never believe where I am—or rather, you've already surmised from the picture on the reverse of this postcard. Yes, Nebraska. You know, that state in the middle somewhere, just another corn-filled patch in the quilt of indistinguishable states that make up the interior. You see that farmhouse and the gently rolling fields of corn in the picture? That's why I'm here. To find that. Not that particular house, per se, but what it stands for: that open and uncomplicated life that's vanished in L.A. Nebraska. Just the sound of the word conjures up images of corn and wholesome tow-headed children and the Fourth of July. It's more American than apple pie, right? Of course you've never thought about it. You've never been here. It's the coasts for you. Fine. But for me, this bland Midwestern Americana is the exotic. I'm here to see it all.

Brian

11/7

Claudette—

I went on a little stroll today around Dudley's neighborhood and had the scare of my life. I was maybe three blocks from Dudley's house, just walking along, looking up at all these grand old houses with big porches and porch swings, as Midwestern as you please. And then, out of nowhere, came this awful buzz like an air-raid siren—or at least what I imagine an air-raid siren to sound like. The noise was all around me, coming from every direction, and for a minute I thought: Holy Jesus, the Soviets have launched their nuclear weapons at last, and here I am stuck in Nebraska! Nonsense, of course—how long has the Cold War been over now? When did the Soviet Union fall? I guess it was some vestigial fear from childhood, when the commies were the bad guys. Who are the bad guys now? I couldn't remember, as I stood there paralyzed, listening to that awful wail, waiting for the big old planes swollen up with bombs in their bellies to come roaring overhead. Would they be painted with swastikas, Muslim moons?

B

11/8 (#1 of 2)

Claudette—

I went back to Dudley's and waited for the sky to fall, but nothing happened. When he came home for lunch, I told him about the siren, and he just said, Yeah, it's the first Wednesday of the month. And I said, What's that supposed to mean? And he said, 10:15, they test the tornado sirens, that's all. So I had to let this sink in, and then I said, What if there's a tornado at 10:15 on the first Wednesday of the month, and everyone ignores the siren because they think it's just a drill? And Dudley just looked at me for a long time, and then he said, Man, you really need to chill, you never used to be wound so tight. Do I need to chill, Claudette? You tell me.

It's cold and gray here compared to back home. Compared to where you are. Compared to our L.A.-blue sky. That should be a Crayola color. The most beautiful blue in the box.

Brian

11/8 (#2 of 2)

Claudette—

Dudley lives in a neighborhood called the Near South. Go figure. He's bought this monstrous, old, drafty box of a house that he's fixing up. A prairie four-square, he calls it. Built in 1922. The wood floors and the stairs are cold and creaky as hell. There's a giant porch on the front with the obligatory porch swing. He says in the summer months people sit out on their porches. He knows his neighbors and his neighbors' kids and his neighbors' dogs. It's all very Midwestern and homey. The porch is sagging and the steps are crooked. It's a very old house. You would hate it.

So I'm here for two weeks. Did I mention that? For better or for worse, I plan to spend precisely two weeks here so I'll have time for nothing else. You know why, babe.
Brian

11/9 (#1 of 3)
Claudette—

I rode the bus all over town today. It's funny because I'd never ride public transportation in L.A. There was this old guy on the bus, wearing farmer overalls with no shirt underneath, hauling a giant bag of ancient jumper cables—there had to be thirty of them in there, all wound up like a nest of snakes, their connections all corroded. And he kept talking about the weather, to no one in particular. We'll have snow before Thanksgiving, he kept muttering, looking out at the sky, which was blue today—not L.A. blue, but a pale, tranquil blue. I couldn't gather whether snow before Thanksgiving was unusual here or not. I will have to ask Dudley. It was warmer and sunny—not a hint of impending winter weather. This city is full of parks that are full of kids. I don't remember the last time I saw so many kids out playing on the playgrounds. Maybe because it was a nice day. In L.A. every day is nice. No reason to go out and play. I kept waiting for someone to ask me where I'm from, but no one seems to notice me.
B

11/9 (#2 of 3)
Claudette—

Another thing happened today. The bus was going past this magnificent building, so I leaned over to the guy across the aisle and asked him what it was. He looked at me like I was crazy for a minute, then snorted and said, What? The penis of the plains? And then he laughed. And he was right, it is pretty phallic. See the picture on the reverse? And suddenly I pictured it rising up off the center of this nation, this great bold protuberance on a vast body, and it was like I could almost see where I was on the continent. Almost, but not quite. And it was like I could understand why, if you're stuck here in the middle of the plains, you'd want to build such a thing. And I know it's hard to see in the picture, but at the very top of the building, there's a statue of this "sower" who is sowing his seed all over the plains out of a great big pouch at crotch level. I am not kidding. You would have laughed your head off, C.

B

11/9 (#3 of 3)

Claudette—

I got off the bus at the next stop and walked to the building, which of course turned out to be the capitol. Duh. I wandered in and somehow got myself attached to a school tour with all these rowdy fourth graders. It was actually fun. I learned about this big blizzard they had here back in 1888 when a bunch of schoolchildren got lost. I learned that Nebraska is the only state with a unicameral legislature. Bet you didn't know that, babe. And they have a law that no one can build anything taller than the capitol. So it will always be the biggest cock on the block. There was this little Asian girl on the tour who kept wandering off and looking at things on her own. You could just tell she had her own agenda, wasn't interested in the "party line" being dished out by the tour guide. You could see she was a bright kid. Sometimes we ended up looking at the same things, me and her, like these mammoth marble columns. Just touching them with our hands. All these people live here, and they don't think about L.A. or people like me. Like you.

B

11/10 (#1 of 2)

C—

What is near? Near to what? Near to whom? To some vague, unidentifiable, unknowable, inscrutable presence, some central beating heart or intelligence of this city? What does it mean to live in the Near South? Is there a Far South? Is there a Near North? The Near South is meaningless unless it's in relation to something else. I said these things to Dudley today.

And what about the Midwest? Can one ever be in the middle of the West? Isn't something west only in relation to something else? Why not the Middle East or even Middle North or Middle South? Why not just Middle, Mid for short? Aren't we practically smack dab in the middle? We could call this place anything. This is where the action should be, not on the coasts, the boundaries, the peripheries, the margins. I said these things to Dudley too.

Dudley said: Did you come out here just to make fun of people? And I said: Who am I making fun of? I have not made fun of a single person.

Have I mentioned that Dudley is a native?

B

11/10 (#2 of 2)

C—

All I ever knew about Nebraska I learned from reading Willa Cather's *My Ántonia* some dozen years or more ago in a class on "regional writers," Cather being representative of the entire amorphous middle "region," of course. And actually, I don't remember anything about the book. So, one can deduce, I know nothing about Nebraska. Except for one thing. There's that image in the book of a plow emblazoned across the red face of the setting sun, and I remember that my prof talked about it forever. Why it's significant I can't remember now—only that it symbolized absolutely everything in the book, and a few other things besides. It was so saturated with portent it positively dripped. A man could spend his life studying that plow-sun hieroglyph and still not get to the bottom of it. Oh, and I think Antonia was pretty hot, back before she had all those kids. You think she's around? Instead of sitting on an Italian beach with you, I am here. Maybe I should look for my Antonia. I doubt you've read the book, so this all means nothing to you.

B

11/11

C—

Yesterday Dudley and I went down to the Haymarket for what is known as "game day." You can see what the Haymarket looks like for yourself on the reverse—old downtown, shops, brick streets. Now imagine the streets swarming with bodies dressed in red. No, that does not do justice. I don't think anyone can really understand who didn't grow up in a football-crazy town. Everyone is together for the same reason, dressed in the same color. It's almost worth it to wear red just to be a part of that. Dudley and I sat on the dock at the main intersection, drinking lattes and just watching it all. Uncharacteristically, Dudley is not much of a football fan. He told me a story about someone who came through here on the train, stepped off onto the platform on a game day, saw all the lunatics in red shirts, and promptly got back on the train, believing he had stepped into the middle of some communist rally. He couldn't remember who it was. Happened years ago. I even saw a big group of fans from California with matching shirts. Traveled all the way here for the game. Amazing, all the stuff that goes on that you never knew about.

B

11/12 (#1 of 2)

C—

My problem is that I cannot see the place I am from, the place I've lived my entire life. I can't see myself in that place. I am too big and too small. I am everything. My head is filled with myself. So I am not part of anything. I thought I would be able to see this place clearly, distinctly, because it was not part of me, but most days it's just another city. I see bits and pieces, faces, trees, buildings, patches of sky, but I cannot see the whole. Same problem.

I have this whole stack of postcards I've written you here. I haven't mailed a single one yet. Do you think I will? Ha, ha. Maybe I should give this series a title. Maybe "A Tourist in Nebraska." My seventh day here. And to quote an old song from our youth, I still haven't found what I'm looking for. Whatever that is. (You.)

B

11/12 (#2 of 2)

C—

I want to tell you a secret: cornfields are terrifying. All dead and dry now, rustling, whispering. Dudley took me a ways out of town to a corn maze yesterday. A maize maze. Ha, ha. They were getting ready to shut down for the year and there wasn't anybody else there. Dudley and I went off in different directions, and as I started walking through that moving, shifting, dead corn, higher than my head, I can't tell you how scared shitless I became. I can't explain it. Just think of *Children of the Corn*. Think of those other movies with cornfields. Someone lost in the corn. Something coming out of the corn. Someone being chased by something through the corn. UFOs in the corn. Why? Why does this most wholesome thing terrify us? But no. High-fructose corn syrup. That is not wholesome. Ethanol in our gasoline. Corn in our whiskey. Corn in our cows. Government crop subsidies. Not wholesome. There is too much corn. That is why we fear it.

B

11/13

C—

I went with Dudley to a reception for his boss tonight. He had won some local leadership award. So the boss gets up and makes a little speech. Talks about how he moved to Nebraska ten years ago to work for this start-up computer company. Says when he was offered a job in Nebraska, he had to pause a moment to figure out where the hell that was. From Boston originally. Says now he'll never leave. Says Nebraska's the best-kept secret in America. Says he doesn't want the word getting out, or else everyone will move here, ruin the place. Says we're safe as long as we stay part of flyover country. Har, har. The crowd laughed at all his jokes, his put-downs. I didn't get it. How is it funny to put yourself down? I thought about it. And I think I understand. They only pretend to make fun of themselves, but actually they're showcasing, in their secret code, their superiority. Their Midwestern modesty is a type of smugness.

B

11/14 (#1 of 2)

C—

Here is what Dudley said to me last night, almost verbatim: There is no such thing as a Nebraskan, OK? Not the way you're thinking of it, not as some unified honky white force, not as an identity that we all share, not as some secret society you can figure out, you with your L.A. sophistication, your cleverness. These are people. They live here. That's it.

We stayed up late on Dudley's porch, drinking Fat Tires. You never met Dudley. We were buddies at UCLA. My bud Dud. Both studied computer science. He went away to school, and then he moved back home. That was always his plan. And he's content. That's the thing that sickens me somehow. He's got his old house that he's fixing up. Family in town. An older married sister with kids. There are an awful lot of kids here, C.

B

C—

I just can't get to sleep tonight. There's a big fat moon hanging just outside my window. It's a bit drafty in here. Dudley says the windows don't seal properly. It's on his to-do list. We're a lot alike, Dudley and I. It feels funny to say that. He's lived most of his life here, and I was born and bred in L.A. As you know. We have similar jobs as database administrators at similar companies. But the sameness runs deeper than that. I can't explain it. You'd see it for yourself, if you ever met Dudley. Dude-ly, we sometimes called him. Or just Dud. We thought it was funny that we knew a guy from Nebraska named Dudley. Grew up milking cows, we used to joke, right off the farm. Truth is, Dudley's never milked a cow in his life.

When I scheduled these two weeks off, six months ago, I never imagined I'd be here. In this place. Without you, babe.

B

11/15
C—

Gargantuan prehistoric elephants once roamed all over Nebraska. I've been going around, picturing it all day, ever since I saw the amazing skeletons at the natural-history museum. You can't imagine how huge these things were. Their legs like giant cathedral arches. You could pass right under them. Stroll clear under an elephant and out the other side. Their tusks like twisted, curved tree trunks. Their skulls like bathtubs. All this life that clambered about here long before any of us. It makes me feel almost fine. Nebraska was a happenin' place if you happened to be a mastodon. So just to cheer myself up, from time to time I imagine this big-ass elephant lumbering down the middle of D Street, or peeking its head over the new movie theater downtown. Ten thousand years ago. That's when they all died. That's a long time. Three years seems like nothing. One, two, three, we're done. How does something like that just stall, give out? Can you explain this extinction in my head?

B

11/16

C—

While Dudley's at work I often find myself just wandering around his neighborhood, making bigger and bigger circles around his house as I become familiar with the streets. Today I passed by a tiny bookstore nestled into a residential block. Small blocky building with a tiny storefront window. You'd hardly know it was there. There were just three words stenciled on the window: Rare Book Dealer. I had a feeling for a second that I had found what I had come here looking for, but the place was dark, the door locked. And then the feeling was gone, and I walked on. And for some reason the goneness of that brief feeling made me start having crazy thoughts. Like maybe I'll stay here with Dudley indefinitely. Maybe I just won't go back to work at the end of my two weeks. I could sit on this porch for a long time. Just writing postcards to you. I could just sit here. For richer or for poorer. For poorer, with no job.

B

11/17

C—

Went to Dudley's parents' house yesterday for Pre-Thanksgiving. It was the only day the whole family could be together. Dudley's brother Mitchell was in town from Kansas City. They had the traditional T-Day spread. Dudley's sister's kids were into everything. How do you like Nebraska? people kept asking me. Oh, it's great, I'd say, grinning like an idiot. Because what do you say? And then Mitchell leaned over and said, It's nice to live here, but you wouldn't want to visit. And he grinned at me like we were sharing some secret joke that only outsiders can understand. So I grinned back, and we sat there grinning, clutching beers in our fists.

Maybe "Postcards from the Middle" would be a better title for this memoir-in-postcards or whatever the hell it's becoming. This is a substantial little stack I've accumulated. I ought to tie them all together with a shoestring or gather them up in a hobo pouch on a stick. I'll sling it over my shoulder as I travel the country, the modern-day bum with literary pretensions and a short attention span.

Happy Pre-T-Day, babe.

C—

It's suddenly turned so cold. Dudley has lent me a coat. He says, Get your ass in off that porch. But I think best out here. He says, You don't see anyone else sitting out on the porch. So I say, How else are they going to know I'm not from around here? I've got to set myself apart. There is even snow in the forecast. I'm more excited than any Nebraska schoolboy. I've never had a snow day in my life. I holler in to Dudley: I'm waiting for it to snow! Not missing a beat, Dudley bellows back: I don't want any frozen corpses on my front porch! My fingers are too cold to write more. It's that cold.

Of course I never meant to mail these. I've left no room for an address or stamp. Just covered the entire backside of each one in my tiny print. Maybe I'll wrap them all up in silver paper with bells, my gift to you.
B

I can mark the day it was all over, even though I didn't know it at the time. Hindsight and all that jazz. April 18. Our apartment. Remember our "low key" celebration? A cheese platter, some wines, some fruit. We were both too busy at work to do more than that in the middle of the week. Three years. It was significant. But we still had time. Time to celebrate, time to do things right. You were wearing that mocha blouse with the ruffled front. Your eyes brown, your hair brown. Claudette brown. All browns are your browns—you own them all. A whole walk-in closet full. A sleek leather living-room furniture suite full. Wall-fulls of modern art, selected for color, complementarity. Your cell phone kept going off. Work stuff, clients. You seemed distracted. Bored? Who the hell knows? You can read anything into a situation after the fact. The tiniest glance can portend the fall of civilization. A butterfly's wing can set off a hurricane. Something like that. A plow silhouetted against the sun can mean everything. In retrospect.

Ah, yes, in retrospect. And so I have caught the moment, trapped it in a jar, so it can never get away, even if it beats the hell out of its wings. And it was only this: You picked up off the counter the discarded wrapper from the extra-sharp cheddar. And you said, This cheese has been aged four years. And then you said, This cheese is older than our relationship. And that was it. And you know what, babe? People just don't say things like that unless the relationship is, in their minds, already over. What you meant was: this cheese will always be older than our relationship. This cheese is more substantial than our relationship. This cheese is just so much more than us. Our relationship is not worth a hunk of cheese. This cheese is older than our relationship. Indeed. That one comment—my plow against the sun.

11/19

My God, it's actually snowed! The jumper-cable farmer's predictions were right on! You'll never believe this stuff, so white, so clean. Crunch, crunch under your feet. Everyone out shoveling, hot breaths billowing out of their mouths. Clearing sidewalks and driveways, talking. This is Nebraska! This is America! And the hush, the incredible white hush all over everything. The quality of sound itself completely transformed, muted. I walked right down the middle of D Street, taking pictures of everyone out shoveling. The first pictures I've taken here. Yeah, I'm a tourist! I wanted to shout. And this is the greatest thing I've ever seen! But no one seemed to pay any attention to me.

And as to that question you posed six weeks ago on heavy card stock in that big periwinkle envelope: No, I will not attend your mid-winter wedding with a guy you've known for, what, three months. Sorry, babe. Now that's some young cheese.

11/20

My last day in Nebraska. How has it come to this? A day of slushy melting, of mud. The aftermath. There is always an aftermath. Maybe I will just stay here, in sickness and in health. In sickness. I've developed a cold. Probably caught it from all those toddlers at the Pre-T-Day feast.

I just couldn't get enough of the snow yesterday. I walked all over town, ended up in the Haymarket just after dark. This freezing, bitter wind came blowing in off the prairie, and I really realized for the first time that I was on the massive, dark, open Great Plains. With all that wind blowing right through Dudley's coat, chilling me to the core, I suddenly saw it all in my mind's eye. I had this grand, sweeping vision of the Plains, and the city, and the Haymarket, and all the people, and myself. There I was, part of something big, and for a moment I could hold it all in my head. My head was big enough, just for an instant. A flash.

11/20

This cheese is older than our relationship.
So are the shoes on my feet. So are my hands that touched you. So what.
This house is older than both of us put together.
This elephant is older than our nation. This tusk is older than Thomas Jefferson's bones.
This grief is older than our world.
This sun is older than our souls.
Eat your cheese, C. Eat a big honkin' hunk of stinky old cheese. Cram your mouth with it. At your wedding. Something old—why not make it cheese? I will be the something blue.
Is this too poetic for you, C? Never knew this side of me, did you?
I'll never ever mail this one, not in a million years.

11/20

Something strange just happened. Something I don't understand. I'm sitting here on Dudley's porch. It's close to midnight, and bitingly cold. The neighborhood was all quiet, and then suddenly someone ran out of the house across the street and started to yell.

I'm not having this goddamned baby! she yelled. And I could see she was just a girl, hardly a woman at all. And then this dark figure appeared in the doorway behind her. I thought at first it was a man. I thought he was going to calm her or contradict her or somehow squelch out her high-pitched, late-night woman madness. I thought he was going to restrain her, rein her back in. So there was someone there to control the situation. That's what I thought. And then I got a better look at the other person and saw that it was a woman, and her pose was relaxed. She wasn't there to control anything.

11/20

I guess this just goes to show you that despite my best efforts, I'm a chauvinist. Because when I realized that there wasn't a man on the scene, for some reason I stood up and stepped down off the porch, as though I was going to fix everything.

I'm not having this goddamned baby! the girl/woman shouted again. Then the other woman came down off the porch.

That's right, the other woman said. Shout it to the wind, girl! she said.

Goddamn it! the girl/woman shouted, how did I ever get in this mess? And then she began to cry. And something started to pull at my legs so I was walking into the street.

Hey! I shouted, do you need some help?

And then the friend of the girl/woman turned on me like some animal. This is none of your goddamned business! she screamed.

11/20

And it isn't. I see that now. Sitting here on this porch, I see that now. They've gone back inside. Their lives, gaping open to me for a moment like the private, moist wink of a wound, have nothing to do with me. There was no reason for me to interfere. There was no reason for them to say one word to me. So I'll sit here and mind my own business in the cold. I'll just sit here and wait for the sun to rise. A fragment of something just came to me: The splendid-silent sun. I was only an English minor. I can't remember where half the stuff I read is from. But I think that must be Cather. It must be about Nebraska. Those words could only be written about Nebraska. The splendid, silent sun. I will wait for it. A Nebraska red sun. It will come up, a red disk gliding up over the sharply pitched rooftops of the Near South, over the city, over the plains. And for a moment, I will hold it all, cupping it inside of myself like something splendid and fragile.

4:39 AM

Why does this feel like the end of everything?

Sixteen

Miscarriages

Shannon Robinson

AGAIN

You look familiar.

That is what the anesthesiologist says to me. She's petite, much younger than I expected, and has pale, smooth skin. I'm here to have a D&C. I had an abortion three years ago, but that was in another city. In a few minutes, this woman will take the clear plastic cup that she's now holding and place it over my nose and mouth; she will put me to sleep. I will have no memory of her doing so.

D&C is short for Dilation and Curettage. The initials are for delicacy as much as for convenience. It is the operation performed after a miscarriage, wherein the fetus (or dead baby, however you wish to think of it) is sucked out of your womb. A bit of vacuuming in preparation for the next tenant. If there will be one.

I don't have a reply for the anesthesiologist's remark, although I feel that I should. She sounds so casually certain. Oh, I say.

Maybe I just have one of those faces. I'm lying down on a padded table, dressed in a large, two-ply green paper gown. A hose attached to a circular notch on the gown blows in warm air, inflating me like a pool toy, making me feel both comforted and a little silly. I'm wearing purple socks, with teddy bears on them in a raised, rubberized pattern. The hospital provided them. These I will keep. I will wear them around the apartment for the next few days until the soles get dirty and I begin to worry about the state of the unswept floors.

The nurses have directed my husband, Sean, to another room that is filled with other patients' relatives, waiting. As a day-surgery patient, you're only allowed to bring one relative, and no children under twelve. So in other words, no children. We'd read that on the slip of paper given to me by the nurse at my pre-op examination two days ago.

I guess they don't want a bunch of crazy brats running around upsetting people, grinding cookies into the rug, Sean said, probably thinking of the sign we read on our first visit to the obstetrician's office, stating NO FOOD OR DRINKS. *But you can bring in that coffee, honey. It's got a lid,* the receptionist had told him as we hesitated in the doorway. Sean has an open kind of charm about him, so she probably would have let him bring in a melting popsicle.

SENBAZURU

I had this notion, following my miscarriage, that I would undertake an origami project of folding a thousand paper cranes. In grade school, my class read a story about a brave Japanese kid who folded a thousand cranes while in hospital, hoping to get well. I remember feeling both impressed by and jealous of the kid's dignity. According to ancient lore, whoever folds a thousand paper cranes will be granted a wish. I imagined a cinematic time-passage montage, wherein people would see me, patiently creasing small pieces of paper, bending and unfolding with gentle, nimble precision. Tiny paper birds would accumulate in our apartment. White birds, birds with the faint blue lines of notebook paper; glossy magazine-scrap birds, birds folded from the silver paper discarded from cigarette packs. It would become a joke among my coworkers at the library and my friends, that this was my Zen fidget, my quiet party trick. And then, after I announced that I was pregnant, I could explain what was with the months of folding. I would have a mobile of paper cranes for the baby's crib, perhaps even a framed print of a crane—a white bird stretched in flight against a powder-blue background—that people would mistake for a stork. Later, I would tell my child the story of my ongoing dedication, how I humbly willed him or her into existence.

I sat at my desk, turned on my laptop and went online to learn how to fold a paper crane. I found a set of directions that consisted of diagrams showing a step-by-step transformation of a square of paper into a bird with pointy wings. It seemed simple enough, once I finally managed to cut a piece of paper into a perfect square (I've always found it difficult to cut straight lines). But as I started following the instructions, I could only get so far before I was stumped. I tried a different website, a different set of diagrams. Again, I had a problem. Again I tried a different website. But each set of directions I found seemed to leave out a crucial opening step, or depict one step in abstract terms (Where is that arrow pointing, exactly? What do they mean by *fold the outer corners to the center?* How?) The online videos I found featured people whose hands occasionally obscured their operations. I folded, re-folded, unfolded and rotated the paper, smoothing it out and pushing aside the books and notes cluttering my desk so I had more space to work, but I just couldn't replicate any of the instructions beyond a certain point. I left my creased not-crane by the laptop. A paper diamond. A crumpled kite.

The kid in that story—I think she died at the end, even though she folded all those cranes. Radiation poisoning.

WOMB-AH WOMB-AH WOMB-AH

Oh, my empty womb. I understand it's the size and shape of a pear. But when I think of it, it's hopelessly abstract—more in my head than in my torso. I can only picture a cross-section diagram, done in different shades of red, isolated against the contrasting white of a page. A scarlet light bulb shape, with the pink fallopian tubes attached like alien arms, stretched in crucifixion. My friend Emmy knitted a uterus from a pattern she'd found in a feminist craft book. She showed it to me when I was hanging out with her one evening at her apartment. This was a year before my first pregnancy.

The fallopian tubes were the trickiest part, Emmy said. If you don't stitch them right, she explained, they won't stick out like they're supposed to. See? She tossed it to me and I caught it. A fuzzy pink ball.

It's nice and squishy, I said, and tossed it back to her.

Isn't it? It's my wandering womb. She demonstrated by moving it from one place in her apartment to another—a bouncing path from bookshelf to television top. Television top to back of couch, nestled beside a sock monkey. She also had a pillow that was a stylized vagina made with beige velour and pink satin. I avoided sitting near it.

BLOT

After the D&C, the maxi pad they have put on me while unconscious lives up to its name. It's thick, long, and fluffy. It strikes me as a relic from another era, a less elegant prototype. There's only a small spot of blood on it. I notice this as I'm getting dressed, readying myself to go home, still dreamy and slow with receding anesthetic. When I look back to the cot where I'd been lying, I'm surprised to see a large blood stain on the sheet. It's like a Rorschach, and I need to read it. Is it two elephants, walking side by side, one slightly ahead of the other? But no: diagnostic inkblots are symmetrical. This is just a blob. I cover it with a towel.

ROT

No one tells you that after you turn thirty-five, you start aging in dog years. I can see it in my own face, looking into the mirror right now. The wrinkles multiply and deepen. It looks like the skin over my knees is melting. I see the roots of the grey wires that have wandered in among the younger silky strands of hair, little by little. Covering them with dye over and over is like spreading pesticide on a lawn for a few dandelions, but what the hell. I've found that if you pluck out the interlopers, they grow back in to resemble antennae. Their coarseness makes them stand straight up from your scalp. I try not to complain. Compared to what I'll look like at seventy-five, these are my fresh salad days. *When I was green in judgment, cold in blood.* It brings to mind those sad pre-cut salads in a plastic bag, wilting bits of arugula and radicchio that always look like they're two days away from being clotted slime. You must use them up quickly.

After the age of thirty-five, on average a woman becomes 50 percent less fertile. You are born with all the eggs you will ever produce. This seems incredible, inaccurate. Like something that was believed in the seventeenth century, some misogynist bit of hokum. But no, it is true. A man's supply of sperm, like blood, like skin, keeps endlessly renewing itself, refreshed like a web page.

Yes, but consider the content of the Internet, says Sean. Some of the sperm could be complete losers. Some guys' spunk could be the equivalent of a MySpace page.

Now there's a comfort, I say.

QUESTIONNAIRE

Was this your first pregnancy? The nurse asks.

No.

She's holding a clipboard, rolling through a series of questions concerning my medical history. High blood pressure? Strokes? Diabetes? Migraines? Allergies?

Any piercings? Capped teeth? She goes quickly, because it's a long list and the information is redundant. I've been over this before.

Do you have any living children?

No.

I'm so sorry, dear. That's very difficult. I hope it works out for you soon.

I don't tell her about the abortion. I want her to keep believing that I'm a good person.

KITTY

I had a dream that we already had a baby—a teeny tiny baby, more like a miniature person, like in *Thumbelina*. But in the dream, the cat had killed it. The dream wasn't about this event, more like the dream was about this event being true. I had an image of the cat, carrying a limp little corpse in its mouth, like a doll. Or a vole. That was not part of the dream. That is the part of the dream that I imagine when I'm awake, because it was missing from the actual dream.

After I come home from the hospital (the actual hospital, this is not a dream I'm telling you about), I look at the cat as she sits beside me on the bed and think, *You are not a baby.* The cat stares back at me, absolute blankness in her melon-green eyes. She yawns and her ears fold backward, like insect wings. Her mouth a leer of fangs, briefly. She walks over to me and begins to purr, bumping her head against my hand. Sean and I have joked with people about the cat being a child substitute. It's something I need to joke about, often, in order to keep it sounding like shtick. The cat's ears pivot slightly, and then she runs off to the kitchen. Her footpads make thunking sounds on the hardwood floor. I've been overfeeding her again.

When I was a little girl, my family owned a black cat named Minou. I used to dress him up and push him around in my toy pram. He would struggle as I forced his paws through the sleeves of the little clothes, but once he was fully dressed, he became passive and resigned. My favorite game was to stand at the top of our steep driveway with Minou in the pram and then let it roll down the incline as I chased after it at a short distance, always catching onto the handle just before it reached the road.

DEAR

Dear. All the nurses refer to me by this. Like I am a little girl. Like I am simple-minded and adorable. But really: like I am fragile. Such efficient tenderness.

Step on the scale, dear. You can put your coat over here, dear. Here's a gown for you, dear. That's right, dear. After it is all done, when I wake from the anesthetic, they will offer me juice and cookies.

The atmosphere is the same as when I had the abortion. The kindest of assembly lines. I remember sitting in a room full of women, all of us waiting to have the same operation. It's a small space, more of a nook than an actual room, and we sit in a circle on wooden chairs. I look at everybody as they look elsewhere. An older Indian lady. A young Asian girl. A woman with blonde hair who looks a lot like me. No one talks. We all wear a uniform. Plush white terry-cloth bathrobes over open-backed cotton gowns. Paper slippers. I keep the white gauzy shower-cap in my pocket. Only one of the women is wearing it already, stretched over her braids. A soap opera is playing at soft volume on a television set, fixed high on a wall. I find it odd that a parenting magazine has found its way into the thick stack of reading material. I suppose some of the women here are parents already and just don't want more. Buncha sluts, I think to myself, but not at all with sincerity. I'm just trying to cheer myself up. Every twenty minutes, a smiling nurse comes and calls someone by her first name. Although the closed unit we're in is referred to as "outpatient surgery," no other kind of surgery besides abortion is performed here. A receptionist had to buzz me in through locked doors.

The baby would have been Sean's. I am five weeks along, which is barely longer than Sean and I have been dating. He has won a prestigious internship with a lab in Europe, one that he's worked for years to obtain, one that can't be deferred. We cannot have a baby now. The decision is mine, and I know it's the correct one. Sean holds my hand and we sit side-by-side on my green velvet couch. A love seat, ridiculously tiny, like sitting in the backseat of a car. It's the first piece of furniture that I bought with my own money and I will drag it with me everywhere I live. We live: Sean and I will marry a year from now. Somehow, when I told him the news, I'd expected him to be physically disgusted. But his face is gentle, like a man looking at a night sky.

NAMING

When I get pregnant again, for the second time, Sean and I celebrate. We make my favorite dinner, pasta puttanesca. Afterward, we move to the living room with our dishes of ice cream, and Sean gets comfortable by the coffee table with a pen and paper. Although it's our intention to draw up a list of names we want, what we compile is its opposite. We nix the names of ex-boyfriends and ex-girlfriends (even if the associations are positive). Followed by anything that smacks of pretension. And anything overly trendy. Him: anything too hard for girls (Veronica), too soft for boys (Tristan). Me: anything too soft for girls (Charlotte), too hard for boys (Carl). Sean records our non-choices in block letters, writing with his left hand and spooning ice cream with his right. For both of us, certain names have unreasonable, yet unshakeable associations. Although our prejudices contradict each other's, we are in agreement that names, in themselves, have the power to bestow flaws and fates:

LIAM—Small penis

ABIGAIL—Cow

ALEXANDER—Jock

JULIE—Joyless bureaucrat

GABRIEL—Dope-smoking underachiever

HANNAH—Gives blow-jobs so people will like her.
   (Is that true? Doesn't sound like the Hannah I knew.)
   (Maybe she just didn't want you to like her.)

ZACHARY—Mealy-mouthed tagalong

BRENDAN—Sneaky coward

MADELINE—Hypochondriac; fake peanut allergy

ANTHONY—Chronic bed wetter

OLIVIA—The kind of girl who poses for pictures with her toes
   pointing together
   (What do you mean?)
   (Like she thinks she's so *whimsical* and *precious*.)

KEVIN—Fatso

NATALIE—Clumsy

CONNOR—Will grow a beard to disguise the fact that he has no chin

MACKENZIE—Self-important tramp; never wears proper bra size

TYLER—Hyperactive

ELIZABETH—Insufferable micromanager

IAN—Republican
(Wait—Ian's a really nice guy. I've known a lot of nice Ians, Sean.)
(Are you kidding? *Ian* is not only a Republican, he's a queer-bashing
   closet-case Republican. That's who *Ian* is.)

LUCAS—Stupid; hates reading

MICHAEL—Needs a punch in the face

CAITLYN—Bitter backstabber

ANN—Doormat

(I think Ann's kind of cute. You know: Annie. It's sweet.)

(It isn't sweet. She's got body odor. She's a martyr. She's the kind of kid
   you have to force other kids to play with. Trust me on this one.)

DANIEL—Wimp

JENNIFER—Horse-faced anorexic

We are worse than any schoolyard bullies with these names, with our shout-ing and laughing. Kids can be so cruel, people always say. Who are we fooling?

There are certain names that we dismiss without pejorative annotation. These are the names with vices that we each secretly find glamorous and strong. Scrap-per. Smart-mouthed. Arrogant. Workaholic. Maneater. Ladykiller. Ambitious. Ruthless. Cold. Selfish.

NAMELESS

I am now eleven weeks pregnant, and Sean and I are at the obstetrician's office for my first ultrasound. In the waiting room, Sean sips his coffee and I talk about preserving the ultrasound image so we can show it to people later. The paper it gets printed on, I understand, degrades quickly, so we should make a photocopy.

In the room with the ultrasound monitor, the technician asks me to shift a little further down on the padded recliner. My feet are in stirrups, and a paper sheet is tented over my knees.

All set? Now, I'll take this and you can reach through and help me guide it in, she says. The wand looks a bit like a microphone, and I think about (just think about) pretending to sing into it (*Feelings! whoa, whoa, whoa*); I realize that I've made this joke before with a vibrator, with the same song. The paper sheet doesn't really cover me, but no matter: I wonder who I'm preserving my mod-esty for. Sean sits on a high stool, by my side. Maybe all these paper sheets will seem silly in fifty years. Then again, maybe they're a recent feature. My mother, who once worked as an obstetrics nurse, tells me that they used to shave off women's pubic hair and strap their arms down during delivery. I'm not so sure about the strapping the arms down part. My mother's been known to fabricate.

Not maliciously and perhaps not even consciously. I suspect her brain splits the difference between the disbelief she anticipates and the truth.

The monitor on my right shows a grainy image, which moves a little as the technician gently pivots the wand. In the center of the screen is a large black kidney-bean shape, framed by flecks of grey and white, like static snow on a television. I wait for her to interpret the image. What is the head, what is the body.

Normally, at this point, we would see growth in the fetus. But I'm afraid a fetus hasn't developed. I'm so sorry. I know that's not the news you wanted to hear.

The technician hands me a stack of tissues and in three seconds I need them. After soaking them I stack them and line up the edges, like it's important. I cannot look at her, or my husband as he rubs my back, or the obstetrician who comes in to confirm the bad news. I have let everybody down. My body has lied to everyone. I am my mother's child.

BIRDIE

Nine weeks into my pregnancy, I talk to my mother over the phone about my fear of miscarriage. So many of my friends have lost babies; I'm aware that it's a possibility.

If you're still barfing and your boobs are sore, those are good signs, she says. I can hear her television on in the background. She likes to watch the silver screen classics movie channel at night while she sorts through grocery store fliers and clips interesting articles from the newspaper.

How far along were you when you miscarried, Mom? I know that she did, at least once. I have it in my mind that she had a stillborn, but I don't trust that archival entry.

My mother tells me that she miscarried in the hospital at five months. A boy baby. I press for details. Did you get to see it?

He looked like a little bird that had fallen from the nest.

This is the most poetic thing my mother has ever said. It is also, to my knowledge, the only poetic thing my mother has ever said. She's sentimental, but that's not the same thing.

If he had lived, I probably wouldn't be here. My brother would have had an older brother and my sister would have had a younger one. Maybe I would have been that little boy. Later on, I look up images of developing fetuses in the book Sean and I have dubbed *What to Expect When You're Expanding*. A baby at five months would be the size of a cantaloupe (the book is fond of fruit comparisons). It must have died sooner.

THE CASE OF THE BLIGHTED OVUM

Blighted ovum. It sounds like something you'd encounter on the blasted heath, something that would prowl the moor. But it also sounds right, in that it sounds awful.

Following the ultrasound, the obstetrician explains: with a blighted ovum, although an egg is fertilized and implants, the embryo stops growing. Or it never grows at all. The placenta, however, continues to develop, and continues to secrete hormones.

In other words, my fetus is a phantom. It is a poltergeist, setting objects in motion when there is no one in the room, making malicious mischief.

I think back on the weeks of feeling pregnant, but not being pregnant. Once, after drinking a glass of water I had to run from the room to vomit. I kept a plastic bag of crystallized ginger in my purse, to nibble on when I felt queasy. I loved the fiery sweet taste, the melting grit of the sugar against my teeth. Even the burble of the coffee maker in the morning made me feel sick; like a properly cautious mother-to-be, I'd given up caffeine anyway—although I missed it, I needed it, I was so damn tired all the time. I felt dazed, but rather pleased with myself. Sometimes I practiced putting my hand on my lower abdomen in a demure, protective gesture. My secret. I felt like the hostess of a surprise party, hiding behind a couch, poised to spring out and toss glittering confetti.

OLD MODEL

My boyfriend, Brian, is showing me the vintage reproduction anatomy model that he's ordered off the Internet. It's a ten-inch, yellow-white nude woman, reclining on a bed as if sleeping, as if dreaming or perhaps thinking: her expression suggests rhapsody. Her neck arches and her right leg is slightly bent. She is beautiful, with brown wavy hair spread loose over her shoulders, framing her upper body.

The eighteenth-century original was life size, can you imagine? Brian asks. And she's plastic instead of wax. He taps her miniature thigh, lightly. Brian is a pre-med student with a minor in art history, so he's interested in these things.

But this is the best part, he says. With his index finger and thumb, he lifts away the top layer of her torso, a panel of breasts and belly. Underneath are colored replicas of organs: grey lungs, a red heart, a brown uterus. He lifts each of these out, and places them beside the model on his desk. She looks like one of Jack the Ripper's victims, poor thing.

And look. Brian uncaps the uterus to reveal a tiny beige fetus. She's pregnant!

She's suspiciously pretty, I say, trying to extract the baby. It's fastened in place.

There were lots of models like these. Pretty cadavers. They're called *medical Venuses.*

Yes, a woman like a dug-out canoe, very sexy, I say. Although it is erotic, in a way. Brian and I share a daydream—I'm not sure who communicated it or thought of it first—about him cutting me open on an operating table. Not hurting me, but seeing what other people could never see. A literal intimacy. He will write a poem about it, except that he will be the one on the table, dissected by an unseen hand.

Despite his original plans to become a plastic surgeon, Brian is now in pediatrics. We keep in touch, from time to time. He's married and has twin girls. I saw the photos in a group e-mail.

SECRET

At least I know I can get pregnant. Now that I've miscarried, I no longer have to remind myself never to let those words slip to Mom.

How can I tell my Catholic mother that I had an abortion? It is a mortal sin, such willful destruction of God's property. It is too much to tell. Given my mother's tendency for exaggeration, maybe the amount of mercy she already begs from God on my behalf will be in appropriate proportion. That's not a cheap shot, by the way.

NOTHING

The time that has passed while I was under anesthetic is not like time spent sleeping. It is a pure absence of existence. The film has been cut and thrown away. I have no dreams to serve as souvenirs. I have been somewhere else, somewhere empty.

Of course, that is not the case. I've been put under by the petite anesthesiologist and have lain on a padded table while the obstetrician and nurses tended to my body, reached into me and cleaned me out.

Coming off the anesthetic, I feel euphoric, like I'm being rocked in the bottom of a boat on a lake, warm under a lattice of leaves and clouds. The nurses have likely smoothed the edges with morphine. I'm lying in a cot, now in a different place from the operating area, swaddled in cotton blankets, with curtains drawn around the cot to make a small room. Through a crack in the curtains I can see the nursing station. A stout woman in lavender scrubs is making entries on a computer screen. Sean is standing on one side of my cot, and the obstetrician is standing on the other. Sean has always said that he looks like Santa Claus: maybe, in a hippy-intellectual kind of way.

It's good that you opted to have the D&C because there was a lot to come out. We got it all, he says. The operation went well. You won't remember any of this conversation, the doctor adds, smiling. He's partly correct. I don't remember any of it until Sean tells me what he said hours later, when we're at home.

TRYING

I'm drunk on my own hormones. For a change, Sean adds. Oh, ha haa, I say, putting a touch of British into the last syllable. But he's right. There were some bad old days. Not that Sean was there for them: he just heard. That was back when we both would have considered each other un-dateable, living rather loose and large. Now we're married and trying for a baby. We're ready this time. I've been off and on the pill for almost twenty years, but now I'm off. My last pack of pills is housed in the medicine cabinet, each blister pocket empty.

I'm having a feng shui consultation with my friend Celine. She walks around our apartment, making comments and offering suggestions as I take notes on a pink spiral pad that I bought at the dollar store for this very occasion.

You should really think about moving the bed so that your feet don't face the door. That's a classic feng shui no-no. It means death. Bad for baby-making. Celine squats to look under the bed and laughs as she nearly loses her balance, teetering on her high-heeled boots. And also, she says, you need to clear out all the stuff you've got stashed under here so the *chi* can circulate. What are those—old magazines? Get rid of them. Clutter's bad. Blocks energy.

Celine suggests that we buy some plants for in the bedroom and also for the other rooms in the apartment.

Live things are good! But make sure you water them. Keep them healthy. Nothing like a bunch of shriveled plants to put the kybosh on fertility, Celine says. She then tells me about a recent consult she did for another woman trying to conceive.

So I was walking through her house, and one of the first things I see, right off, is that she has a rotting pomegranate, right smack dab in the middle of her Children and Creativity area. Really! How long has that been there, I'm thinking. Talk about a *symbol*.

Huh, I say. But I wonder: Who eats pomegranates? Not that I'm doubting Celine's story.

POMEGRANATE

I have eaten a whole pomegranate once in my life. My mother brought a few home from the supermarket, moved by some rare whim. She placed one on a plate in front of me at the kitchen table and I examined it, running my hands over its shiny red hide, tauter than an apple's, gathered at the top in points like a tiny crown. Give it here, my mother said, and slit the fruit with a paring knife. She let me bend open the cut seam, which produced a faintly hollow cracking noise, and I marveled at the exposed seeds. I thought they looked like ruby teeth, clustered together in some luxuriously eccentric profusion. My mother tucked a linen dishcloth around my neck. It's messy, she said.

This was years before I read about Persephone. Her marriage and bargain with death. Her bereft mother. In the mythology book I won years later, as a prize for proficiency in Classics, there are charcoal illustrations of Persephone emerging from the underworld, her arms extending upward from a hole in the ground, reaching toward a weeping Demeter, and of the pomegranate, with the fatal seeds extracted and piled to one side.

(I ate all the seeds of the pomegranate, sucking each one white, a drop's worth of juice at a time. It's not that they were sweet, but that they were so beautiful and so many.)

Seventeen

American Bulldog

Chad Simpson

THE NIGHT BEFORE, HER SOCKS LEACHED rainwater from the carpet in the basement. The dehumidifier was running. The sump pump still churned. Everything important—her sewing machine table, the desk with her art supplies—was up on blocks from the previous fall, and Anna figured it might as well all stay that way, at least for now: It had rained for four straight days, and who knew how much water was going to seep through the foundation walls before it stopped.

In bed, after she changed her socks and was snuggled and warm under the covers, Anna hoped she would dream of floods—the biblical kind, of arks and utter devastation. But she woke up a little before five to the sound of rain against her bedroom window and with no memory of the previous night's dreams at all. Leslie the dog was at attention outside her bedroom door when she opened it.

"Come on, then," Anna said, and Leslie followed her to the three-season room, where Anna let him out into the dark, wet backyard.

She put on a pot of coffee, and before she went to retrieve Leslie, she lit the basement stairs and began walking down them to see what kind of damage may have been done overnight.

Halfway down to the turn in the stairs, Anna heard water sloshing. She heard a muffled buzzing sound that may have been the dehumidifier but sounded like it was coming from a long way off. When she reached the turn, Anna saw that at least three but maybe four or five steps were submerged in water. Her basement, dimly lit, looked like the edge of a lake.

The water was still, but Anna could feel a coolness coming off it. She rubbed her hands over her forearms and squinted her eyes. A clear plastic tub filled with wrapping paper floated past the front of the stairs and knocked against the wood-paneled wall.

There were things in the basement she wanted to get out of there before they were ruined—a quilt she was sewing for one of her adult grandchildren, a needle-point project she'd been working on for months—but she'd heard about people being electrocuted in situations just like this. Those people took one step into the water and never breathed another breath. Who knew how long it took somebody to find them, drifting facedown among the debris of their basements, bloated with floodwater.

Anna ascended the stairs and realized she was hiking up her nightgown with one hand, as if it were in danger of becoming wet.

When she reached the three-season room, she saw Leslie standing at the screen door, staring at her, waiting to be let inside. Anna opened the door and grabbed the towel she kept on the nearby patio table.

"Come here, you," she said, and the dog stood at her feet. Anna draped the towel over his sides and patted him down. Leslie shook himself once, and again, pelting Anna with sprinkles. Anna patted him a little harder than she needed to. She hated this little ritual. She hated being in such close contact with the dog.

She told Leslie to sit, and then she picked up each of his front paws so she could dry them off. When she was done, the dog stood, and Anna dried each of his back paws, too. "Get going," Anna said, and made a motion with her hand. The dog trotted off, and while Anna wiped flecks of mud and leaves from her hands onto the towel, she heard Leslie's nails clacking on the kitchen linoleum. She thought about the body of water in her basement—about the books down there whose pages were becoming swollen, about the way water warps wood. The flooding wasn't as bad around here as it was in places like Gulfport, where the rainwater had pushed the Mississippi beyond its banks and right into town. The whole place had been evacuated. The farmers near there were looking out on land their families had owned for over a hundred years and seeing nothing but river. Still, Anna was unnerved.

The coffee had finished brewing, and she poured herself a cup, then stared at the open door that led down to the basement. She brought her mug to her nose, hoping to lose herself for a moment in its aroma and warmth, but she could hear water through the door. She imagined more tubs floating by the stairs in the dim light, tiny aimless ships on a vast sea.

And then she thought of her projects again—the things that needed saving.

Leslie came into the kitchen and took his usual seat in front of the refrigerator door. The linoleum was heated, and the dog settled onto his belly and let his chin rest on the floor, as if there weren't anything at all wrong in the world.

Anna set her coffee cup down on the counter and walked over to Leslie. His eyes were closed, and already he was drooling a small puddle of spittle onto the linoleum.

"Hey, you," she said, nudging the dog with her foot. "Meathead. Wake up."

The dog looked up and tipped his head to the side, his tongue hanging stupidly out of his mouth.

Anna and her husband Leslie had spent forty-one years of marriage utterly pet-less, and had raised two kids who begged them on a regular basis for an animal of some kind they could take care of.

The kids at first wanted a dog, of course. But after Leslie said no way, after he complained about how dogs just tear up the house and then ask you to take them for a walk, the kids moved on to asking for other animals over the years. Cats, birds, even fish, which were almost no fun at all. Leslie had said that it was a slippery slope, that he didn't want anything with a beating heart inside his house except for his wife and the children she had birthed.

Anna had felt a little sorry for the kids. She'd watched Vicky, now married and living in Chicago and with grown kids of her own, check out and read from cover to cover each book on dogs shelved at the Galesburg Public Library. Vicky knew every breed's origins, and how well it could see and smell and hear. She knew what its tongue looked like. The girl's devotion, the depth of her knowledge, broke Anna's heart.

But Leslie would not give in, even after Michael for a while refused to watch any television show that did not feature in some way an animal. Even after the boy wallpapered his bedroom with pencil drawings of schnauzers and terriers he'd traced from Vicky's library books.

The kids' efforts at securing a cat or a parakeet or a goldfish were actually a little weak, Anna thought. All they ever really wanted was a dog.

But Leslie wouldn't have it.

That is, until right after he retired, when he returned from one of his drives to God-knows-where with a fully-grown American Bulldog leashed to his arm.

"What should we name him?" he asked Anna in the three-season room.

The back of Anna's hand drifted to her forehead. "Oh, Leslie," she said, not wanting the dog to step foot inside her house. It had beady eyes and one black ear. Its tongue was a wide pink stripe.

"Yes," Leslie said. "Ha! We'll call him Leslie."

Anna turned back toward the house. "You can call him whatever you want," she said.

And Leslie did call him, often. He called him into Anna and Leslie's bed at night, where the dog slept right on top of Anna's comforter, draped over Leslie's legs. He called him out to the car, and the two of them disappeared together for hours. When Anna and Leslie drove to church on Sunday mornings, the car smelled as if the dog were hiding somewhere in the backseat.

Everything Anna touched seemed to smell like Bulldog. It was the smell, Anna thought, of her husband's retirement, and it infuriated her.

Anna had retired several years before Leslie, and while she had enjoyed her time at home alone—mildly redecorating the place and taking up sewing and needle-point—she had been excited about Leslie's retirement. About the things they might do together, like going for walks or playing tennis. And then no sooner than he had stopped working for Burlington Northern, her husband had brought another beating heart into their house. Another thing to put a little distance between his wife and him now that they could be alone together.

And then, just months after he had brought the dog home—months of agony for Anna, who couldn't sleep right with the dog on the bed the way he always was, and who couldn't buy enough air freshener to cover up the dog's stink—Leslie her husband died of a heart attack after dinner one night as he sat in his recliner with Leslie the dog on his lap, one hand on the back of the dog's head, right between his differently colored ears.

Anna walked toward the basement door now and patted herself on the hip. She smiled at the dog. "Come on, boy," she said, realizing as she patted herself on the hip again that she was performing a kind of imitation of her dead husband. How many times those past few months he was alive had she seen him walk past her and say nothing and then start talking to the dog and patting himself on the hip or leg or lap?

Leslie trotted over to her, panting, spritzing the floor with drool.

"We're going down to the basement, doggie," Anna said. She hiked up her nightgown with one hand and began descending the stairs with a ball of fabric in her fist. Leslie followed tentatively behind.

At the turn in the stairs, Anna waited on Leslie, who froze with his hind legs still on the previous step when he saw the water. Anna wondered if the dog could sense some electrical current. If he could smell danger.

In the weeks that followed her husband's death, Anna had felt like she couldn't even grieve properly. Leslie the dog always wanted to be put outside. He was always wandering around the house, whimpering, looking for his true owner. More than once Anna caught the dog in the backyard staring longingly at Leslie's car in the driveway.

When Anna couldn't even walk past the dog any more without catching his scent and then thinking unkind things, unholy things, about her dead husband, she considered trying to pawn the dog off on Vicky or Michael, or on one of her grown grandchildren. But not one of them even thought to bring it up. When they did mention the dog, they had the nerve to say something about how lucky she was to have him around to keep her company. The idiots.

For a few months, Anna drove by the Knox County Humane Society with her window rolled down, imagining Leslie as one of the barking dogs inside, caged and far away from her. She drove by a couple of the city's parks and imagined taking Leslie to them and removing his collar, letting him run until he dropped while she drove away.

But Anna never carried out any of these plans.

It had been six months now of just her and the dog, and she loved him no more than she had before. She wanted him around even less.

"Just a little farther," Anna said, taking another step down. The dog looked at her as if he was uncertain, but it was clear to Anna that he was going to follow her, however reluctantly, if only, perhaps, because this was the first time he had ever heard her use a kind voice with him.

Anna pitied the dog for a moment for his stupid dependence on her attention. For his blind obedience.

She wondered if maybe she would have felt differently about the dog if she'd known him as a puppy. If Leslie hadn't acquired the dog when it was already an adult. It was hard for Anna to imagine hating a puppy, under any circumstances. If I'd known the dog as a puppy, she thought, I probably wouldn't do what I'm about to do.

Anna took another step down, and then another, until the water was just a few inches below her feet. Lit by the bulb over the stairs, the water shone a dull shade of green. Anna was certain now that she heard the dehumidifier running. The thing had to be submerged, but it was still buzzing out there in the dark, doing its best to take away the moisture that was trying to drown it.

She turned, and the dog was still back on the landing, staring at her. Anna patted her hip again. "Come here," she said. "It's OK."

The dog walked down the steps until he was just behind Anna, then positioned himself so that he was sitting on his haunches with his front paws out to the side. Still, he seems to want to please me, Anna thought.

When she had first begun to descend the stairs, Anna had imagined that she was going to have to pick the dog up but she remembered now that dogs like to swim. Dogs were always doing whatever they could to jump into some body of water.

Anna scooted over on the stair to give the dog clearance.

"OK, buddy," she said, her voice high and light. "Jump."

She waved her arm over the water beneath her, but the dog only stared at her hand, as if it might finally be offering him some kind of treat.

Anna brought her hand back to her chest. She bent her knees and bounced, waving her arm again. "Jump," she said.

The dog remained upright on the stairs, balanced on his long front legs.

Anna felt stupid doing it, but she placed her hands over her head, as if she were a diver. "Like this," she said, flexing her knees and leaning out a little over the water.

The dog took one more step down the stairs. He came to her.

It was as if he were telling her that he would comply, but that he wasn't going to jump into the water of his own accord. She was going to have to pick him up.

"OK, Leslie," she said. She hiked up her nightgown, and maneuvered into a firm position on the stairs, her back to the wall.

When she bent down to pick up the dog, he stretched out his head toward her hand. He wanted her to pet him.

"All right," Anna said. "All right." She scratched between the dog's ears, and under the dog's chin, and he pressed his face into her hand—hard, lovingly.

Well, dog, she thought. This isn't so bad. Maybe it wouldn't be so terrible if this were the beginning and not the end of our life together.

A quick burst of cool air hit her, and Anna stopped petting Leslie and braced herself against the wall.

The sun was just coming up now, and the basement was lighter than it had been. The things drifting in the water were taking on shape, becoming more defined.

"It's now or never," Anna said.

The dog seemed to stretch his neck out toward her as if asking for one more touch from her hand, but Anna bent and scooped her arms under him. He yielded himself to her, was willing to let her pick him up, but still, he was heavy. Anna had to set him back down.

She got behind him and again lifted him. He was between her legs now, suspended in the air, and Anna began to rock him, to get some momentum.

She counted, *One,* and wasn't sure whether she would be able to maintain her hold on the dog until *Three.*

On *Two,* her arms ached. She thought for a moment about whether, if the dog were electrocuted, there would be a sound. Or a smell. She wondered whom she would have to call to wade out into the water and remove the dog from it. Her arms began to give slightly, but by *Three* she had gained enough momentum, and she let the dog go.

The splash he made broke what seemed to be an immaculate stillness. Water splashed onto Anna's socks and gown, and she shivered. She held her arms to her body and rubbed them.

A moment later, Anna realized that she wasn't looking at the dog in the water. After he landed, she had turned and was looking back up the stairs, afraid to see what might have happened.

She listened hard—and for what? The sound of Leslie paddling his front paws in the water, scrabbling for the stairs? A sound like bacon in a hot skillet? She hoped she wouldn't hear anything like that. The thought alone made her sick to her stomach. She gripped her middle with both arms and burped up hot, acidy air.

Anna realized she didn't hear anything at all except for the dehumidifier buzzing, and she gasped. "God damn it," she breathed.

She turned around on the stair, expecting to find Leslie's dead dog body floating there in the water, drifting toward the plastic tub filled with Christmas paper. She was shielding her eyes with one hand, imagining not the dog but the wrapping paper. The wreaths of green holly against a red background. The plain silver, shimmering.

She thought about the first Christmas she'd spent without her husband, just a few months ago, and she realized she wanted nothing more right then than for the dog to be alive.

Anna brought her hand away from her eyes, and there was Leslie. He paddled silently in the water and stared up at her with a look on his face that made Anna think he was waiting for her to tell him what to do next. His dark ear was folded over on top of his head.

"Good boy," Anna said. "Good boy." She clapped her hands and patted her thighs. She couldn't believe how happy she felt. Her giddiness made her feel silly, or simple. But she patted her thighs again and again called out to the dog.

He began to reach for the stairs with his paws, paddling like mad, and Anna decided she couldn't wait for him any longer. She descended the two steps between her and the water.

A chill began in her toes and shot up into her legs, and Anna continued her descent. She walked down into the water until it reached her waist and Leslie put his paws up on her shoulders. His face was right there before her own, and she realized she was still moving forward. Clumsy and cold and wanting to hold the dog to her until he submerged her completely. Until he pushed her down into the freezing water and she held her breath there for a while, keeping her eyes open. She wanted to hold her breath under the icy water until her lungs burned, until she was good and ready to come screaming back to the water's surface, gasping for breath.

Eighteen

Twelve + Twelve

Christine Sneed

SOMEONE IN THE ALLEY THREE STORIES below my window was calling out to someone else and what he was saying was not very nice. Maybe he did because we were all stuck in an ugly, listless March, ice visible everywhere and clinging to our lawns like a dense gray scum. We were exhausted and cynical under cloudy skies, our pants cuffs perpetually caked in grit and mud, our car tires spinning and spinning on snow-choked streets. No one I knew was outside digging up the flower beds, and certainly no one was in the mood to offer spare coins to strangers distractedly ransacking their pockets for change to feed the meters. Instead, people were talking heatedly into mobile phones or looking down at their feet as they trudged, these unloved husbands and crash-dieters and stubborn musicians and disbarred lawyers who all huddled in on themselves because among their other hardships, winter hadn't yet ended and at this near-unendurable point, they just couldn't look each other in the face.

Griggs was in my kitchen on a Saturday morning, sitting right by the window with his coffee and *Tribune*, listening to an outraged someone down in the alley yell insults at a hapless someone else. I was in the other room and didn't hear anything, but when I appeared before him with my newly clean hair and skin, generally pleased with myself, Griggs smiled a little, shook his head and told me what he'd heard. He wouldn't say the obscenities because he was my father's friend and therefore a supposed role model. I looked at him dead-on, repeating what he'd said, adding the missing words. He didn't flinch or give me a disapproving look; he only nodded, as if expecting this. His daughter, born five years after I was, had died a year earlier while living in Spain. Four months after her funeral, he had started calling me because I was a girl, as he said, who had always impressed him with her maturity and self-possession. I was also a nurse, which was something I imagined that he felt he needed. He was divorced, and over the past seven years, had had a series of unsatisfactory girlfriends, some of whom had badmouthed him to his friends, disliked and possibly mistreated his cats (Harriet and Softie), rolled their eyes over his incessant chatter about Shakespeare, whose plays and poems he had taught for several years in a night class at a local university, made fun of his old, rusting car, and teased him about his hairy, hairy chest.

I had no idea where he had found these women or why he had been attracted to them. I didn't ask too many questions about my predecessors because I felt poorly equipped to handle the answers. At the hospital I had to spend most of the day asking patients questions that they often provided saddening answers for. In my private life, I had gotten into the habit of avoiding similar exchanges. But I knew the answer to one question I wasn't going to ask. The answer was yes. Griggs loved me. I loved him too, but I wasn't saying so to him or anyone else yet. Up until a few months ago, I had only thought of him as my father's friend and then after his daughter's death, my father's stricken friend—a kind, steadily aging presence; a shy joke-teller; a Christmas giver-of-books, usually about or by Shakespeare; a distance runner until his knees gave up; a former husband of the tall and busty LouAnne; a grieving father who would probably always be grieving (I expected nothing else) in some corner of his beaten heart.

He had met my father in college, when he was a sophomore and my father a senior. They had been in the same fraternity and both had almost been recruited for the basketball team. Griggs had turned to running and my father had turned to the commodities market at which had he had proven extremely successful—he had retired at 42, whereas Griggs had kept doggedly working away at his consulting job until he had amassed enough money and contacts to start his own small consulting firm, which meant that he could manage more and travel less. He was wealthy but was not openly impressed by this fact. His car really was rusting and eleven years old; he lived in a two-bedroom condominium that had no remarkable features; at the time of his divorce, he had given his four-bedroom house with its two-car garage and half-acre lot on the North Shore to LouAnne.

"What do you think inspires people to say such horrible things to each other?" he asked, looking down at the alley which was empty now except for the usual jumble of overturned garbage cans. He was dressed in a white-and-blue-striped button-down and a pair of jeans, his hair damp from the shower he had taken before mine. Weeks ago he had stopped looking as paternal to me as he once had. He was 54 and I was 30. The age difference was not so bad when I thought of it as twelve plus twelve, rather than two dozen or the daunting, flat penalty of twenty-four.

"Habit, maybe?" I said.

He shook his head. "Whatever it is, I wish we could get rid of it."

"Yes, and right after that we'll do in AIDS and cancer."

"I'd like to think that's possible too," he said.

I could have been gentler with him, and for the first couple of months that we had been seeing each other, I had been, exceedingly so. More than once he had awoken in the middle of the night and sat stiffly upright, tears coursing down his face. I would coax him back down and he would lie stiffly next to me, abject and wordless, while I stroked his hair and kissed his face and mouth. *You're recovering from a war,* I had said one night. *You're not yourself and won't be yourself again for a little while longer.* The war was being fought internally, of course, and when I told him something I had started to believe not long before he had arrived in my private life—that people love a good tragedy, provided it doesn't happen to them—he had agreed. It's always easier to manage someone else's pain, he had said.

His daughter Trish, his only child, was living in Sevilla when she was killed. She had worked for an international organization that sought to reconcile Christians and Muslims. A man, a Spaniard, had died with her, and Griggs had paid the expenses of his funeral too, though the wreck had not been Trish's fault; they had been hit by a drunk driver at two in the morning on their way home from Malaga, where they had been meeting with an imam who was trying to preach religious tolerance in his mosque. Trish had been loved by many in Sevilla and her friends had held a memorial service for her there. In Chicago, her parents had arranged for another. I had gone to the one in Chicago and had let Griggs hold me for a long time at the door; my father had witnessed this but had said nothing about it until a few weeks later. "I trust you know how upset he was," my father had said. "Still is. He's not functioning the way he normally would. He called here yesterday and asked for your number. You do what you think you should."

That was all he said and it took Griggs three and a half months to dial my number. For weeks we only talked on the phone but then he asked me to dinner and I knew right away what he was up to. It didn't bother me. In fact, I was interested, but at the time, it had all seemed very abstract, as if whatever happened would only be theoretical. I would learn from this and be someone with him I hadn't been with past lovers. My father had some idea what was going on but he didn't ask. My mother knew exactly what was happening but hadn't filled my father in. She said I was old enough to do as I wished, and so was Griggs. But if I wanted to marry and have children, I might want to find someone closer to my age. I had told her that I was in no rush for marriage or for kids, that I liked Griggs quite a lot, and for now, things were fine as they were.

He could not take his eyes off of the alley. The *Tribune* lay unread on his lap. "I've heard people yelling at each other down there before," I said. "It happens pretty often."

"Don't you ever want to call out to them? Tell them to stop?"

"Once in a while, but they're not always swearing at each other."

"I suppose not." He looked at me, opened his mouth then closed it.

"What?"

He shook his head. "Nothing."

"What? You have to tell me now."

He hesitated, his brown eyes not meeting mine. "You could come live with me, if you ever got tired of this."

I was startled but tried not to show it. We had never talked about this. "Thanks, but I'm okay here, sweetie. It's very nice of you to offer though." *Sweetie. Dear. Honey.* These were the words I used with my patients and now with Griggs. I think he liked them too.

He still didn't meet my eyes. "All right, Brynne. I just want you to know that you'd be welcome."

I felt sad for him but knew that he wouldn't have liked this. For a year now, plenty of people had felt sad for him, and many would never stop. He wanted to forget what had happened. He didn't want to forget Trish, but I think he wanted to forget that he hadn't seen her in almost a year before she died, to forget that he would never see her again. Over the past few months, I might have become the most important person in his life, and it was an oddly humbling thing to know that you mattered, that you were a favorite, possibly irreplaceable. We had been seeing each other for a little less than four months. We now spent three or four nights together each week. I'm not sure why I wasn't more open with my own parents about this.

One of the main reasons, I suppose, was that my father would never have been able to look at either of us the same way again. Maybe he would have started to dislike Griggs. Having lost his own daughter, Griggs was now taking his friend's. I could imagine my father seeing it this way. He was someone who liked ownership, someone who liked knowing exactly where the boundary lines had been drawn; he was not the kind of man other people fooled with either because along with having an incendiary temper, he was physically imposing. Griggs was too, in a way, but he was thinner, less fierce-eyed, and rarely did he seem to overwhelm whatever room he walked into. It wasn't like he and my father would have gotten into a fistfight, but I knew that Griggs worried about my father's reaction. Yet, inviting me to live with him indicated a new willingness to make our affair much more public.

"I'd better get going," he said, setting the newspaper on the table next to his coffee cup. "I'm supposed to have lunch with LouAnne today."

This didn't bother me; they were friends and, after twenty years of marriage, it seemed a sensible thing to be. What bothered me was that it was only ten A M. "You could stay a little longer," I said. "I'm not due at the hospital until two."

"No, I'd better go. I have to do some grocery shopping that I've been putting off all week."

"I'll see you tomorrow night?"

He nodded. "I'll be by around seven if that's still good."

"I could come to you. Your cats wouldn't have to be alone again."

"They're fine. They have each other." He paused, looking a little anxious. "Every other night isn't too hard on them, is it?"

"I'm not sure, but I really wouldn't mind staying at your place more. You don't have an alley either." I smiled, standing on my toes to kiss him goodbye. He put his arms around me and hugged me hard. He hadn't shaved, and his whiskers pricked my forehead.

"I'll miss you tonight," he murmured.

"I'll miss you too."

When he left, I felt a disorienting mix of loneliness and relief. We were a funny pair, I knew, people often eyeballing us when we went out. *What's going on there?* I could almost hear them whispering. *Is she a gold digger or what?* His daughter and I had liked each other but had only been acquaintances. I had already graduated from college before she started her freshman year. As kids, we had lived several towns apart and had only seen each other on rare occasions. Even so, as an adult, I had been interested in keeping up with her; her politics had impressed me, as had her fluency in Spanish, and her willingness to live in a foreign country where she helped to keep dangerous strangers from murdering each other. My closest girlfriend, a nurse too, thought it was creepy that Griggs and I were lovers—"Don't you think it's all a little incestuous?" she had asked early on. "Don't you think he's a little weird? Why did he start calling you? What's he trying to do? Pretend that you're her when you're together?"

I didn't think any of this, at least not anymore. He was genuinely curious about my life, my opinions, my desires; we rarely talked about Trish and he had once said that he had started thinking about me a few years before her death, inappropriate as I probably found this to be. Still, I understood my friend's concerns. At first I had wondered the same things about him. I had worried that he would try to get me to dye my hair to match Trish's or learn more Spanish or that he would accidentally call me by her name. But nothing like that had happened. He and I were adults, as my mother had said. We were a couple, one whose future together was as unpredictable as most couples'.

That afternoon, I went to work and no one I had been taking care of the day before in the ICU had died or else been upgraded to critical care. I had two elderly male stroke victims and a young woman who had fallen down some stairs and badly injured her spine. There was also a new admit, a teenage boy who had been in a car accident, his jaw now wired shut, both eyes so swollen with contusions that he couldn't see. His mother was with him and planned to stay for as much time as she was allowed. His father was in California, on business, and wasn't able to get back until tomorrow. The boy's mother told me this with obvious bitterness, while her son, body and jaw immobilized, could do nothing but groggily listen. I touched her hand and said it was a shame. I touched his hand gently too, checking his IVs; we had him on glucose and morphine drips. I also had to make sure his catheter was still in place; this was delicate work, especially with a fuming, stricken mother waiting on the other side of the door.

Few mothers wanted to think about a youngish nurse poking around their sons' precious genitals, but the good news was this boy's semi-conscious state. His parents could not yet understand their luck, such as it was. Many patients were in a coma when first admitted to my unit, and the only exit for some was through the back door, which once shut could not be opened again.

The name on the boy's chart was Mark McGinnis, his DOB showing him to be only a few weeks away from 17, both eyes bloodied plums, his mouth and cheeks bruised and lacerated too. He had spanked the windshield hard with his face and suffered a concussion. Seven of his ribs had been cracked against the steering wheel. He had crushed a kneecap and broken a femur, both wrists and his collarbone too. He had not been wearing his seat belt in an old car, one without an airbag. But he had not died. It wouldn't have been good bedside manner, but I wanted to say this to his mother who right then was more interested in hating his father. Mark was going to survive all of his injuries and perhaps be a humbler person, a better driver, a nicer guy. He would not forget this, any of it, not for a very long time.

I had seen hundreds of car crash victims. Like diabetics, cancer sufferers, and pregnant women, they kept hospitals in gurneys and syringes. Despite all of the crash patients, I hadn't really thought about the particulars of Trish's wreck until Griggs and I started seeing each other. What he didn't know was that I could picture her; whether I wanted to or not, I could see the paramedics, the ambulance, her bloody and broken body as they rushed her to the hospital. I had heard from my father that her neck had been snapped on impact, her chest crushed, her vital organs arrested under terrible pressure. That Griggs did not have the ability to see her as I could was clearly a blessing, and perhaps this was why I had first wanted to be near him. I could imagine something he shouldn't ever be allowed to imagine, and I wanted to protect him from it.

At eleven PM when my shift ended, Mark was in the care of the night nurses, and his mother went home for a few hours. I returned to my petless, chilly apartment and missed my boyfriend, which seemed a ridiculous word to use for a man in his fifties. His *Tribune* still sat on the table next to his half-full coffee mug. By now, he was probably sleeping; Sunday night was hardly the most animated time of the week, except sometimes for the ER staff with their end-of-weekend crop of desperate cases.

I ate a bowl of cereal and took a shower, my second of the day which I knew wasn't a good idea because it dried out the skin and brought on wrinkles faster, but I could smell the hospital in my hair, and tonight I didn't want to carry it into my sleep. Afterward, in bare feet and a warm robe, I went into the kitchen and was pouring myself a glass of water when through the old windows overlooking the alley I heard two people shouting. —*Fuck you, asshole!*—*Fuck you too, you asshole's asshole!* I peered down at them, keeping the lights off. Two men, one older, possibly a father and son. The older one was gesticulating aggressively, lunging forward and giving the other guy the bird with both middle fingers. The younger guy waved him off and disappeared around the corner. For some reason, the older guy didn't go after him. He dropped his hands, turned slowly on his heel and walked the other way. I called Griggs, woke him up and told him what I had seen. "Do you need me to come over?" he asked sleepily.

"No, no. I just thought you'd get a kick out of it."

"You could have saved it until tomorrow. I would have gotten a kick out of it then too."

"I might have forgotten to tell you."

"I doubt that." He yawned.

I told him that I was sorry to have woken him. He said not to worry about it. Hanging up, I felt irritated. Disappointed too. I had wanted him to insist on coming over. Not long ago, I knew he would have.

Perhaps I had begun the process of losing him. Maybe by not saying I would live with him or even consider it, I had made him think hard, harder than any time before now, about the impracticalities, the bravado, of our relationship. He would surely die before me, possibly long before. Or he assumed I would leave him when he started to look like an old man. And not yet having told him I loved him, maybe he didn't think I did. As the one supposedly with more options and less vulnerability, he might have thought that I should be the one to take the risk and say it first.

Fuck you, asshole! These incredible words, arriving in my head unbidden, made me laugh out loud—how horrible, how absurd, ever to say them to him!

I had trouble falling asleep and, in the morning, the phone woke me unceremoniously at eight o'clock. My first witless thought—Griggs was calling to apologize for last night, and I answered without checking the caller ID. It wasn't him. Instead, a woman, and at first I couldn't place her voice, but then I realized with a guilty jolt that the voice belonged to LouAnne. She said good morning very cheerfully, not acknowledging the sleep in my froggy hello, asked about my parents, and then in one almost indecipherably fast sentence said she wanted to know if I would like some of Trish's things. She had slowly been cleaning out her room over the past few months, and Griggs had already taken what he wanted. She thought that I might like some of Trish's books and some of her sweaters and blouses too because we were about the same size. "Unless you've shrunk or grown lately?" she said with a laugh. Parceling out her daughter's things to friends seemed to her a much better idea than giving everything to the Goodwill. "I'd like the people who knew Trish to keep her more tangibly in their lives," she said. "I hope you don't think that's too morbid."

"No, not at all. It's very kind of you to offer." I had no idea what else to say. She had to have known that Trish and I hadn't been very close; surely her daughter had had other friends who would have wanted her things. But it seemed rude to turn LouAnne down because how to decline a grieving mother's offer without seeming rude and insensitive?

Yet I knew that more had to be going on here. I knew that she had some idea of how long Griggs and I had been seeing each other. At yesterday's lunch, in a snit over the move-in offer I had turned down, maybe Griggs had said more about me to her than he had needed to. Was she jealous? Seven years post-divorce?

It wasn't unlikely. In her view, I supposed, I was too much younger and still capable of entrapping men in their 20s and 30s, so what the hell was I doing with a man in her age group? Let alone the father of her only, now-lost child?

But to offer me Trish's things seemed an odd way for her to remind me of my place in the dating hierarchy.

"If you have a little time this week, why don't you come over and take a look at what's here?" she said.

I wanted to put her off indefinitely but didn't know how. "If it's all right with you," I said, "next weekend would probably be better for me."

"How about Saturday morning if you're not working?"

We settled on this day. She didn't say a word about Griggs and me, but the two of us must have been in her head, making some kind of trouble. Maybe I was a self-absorbed fool to think that she spent much time worrying about Griggs and disliking me, but I felt sure that next Saturday would not be a blue-sky-white-puffy-cloud kind of day. I could already feel something combative and defiant rearing up in me.

I had the day off, having worked until 11 last night, and I spent the morning cleaning and then trying to read a library book. At one o'clock when Griggs usually took his lunch break, I called and told him about LouAnne's offer. Of the two of us, I was the only one surprised.

"She asked me what I thought at lunch yesterday," he said. "I told her that she should do as she saw fit."

"You don't think it's a little strange?"

He hesitated. "Well, yes, maybe a little. Do you even want any of Trish's things?"

"I don't know. Maybe if I weren't dating her father. It seems like LouAnne is trying to remind us that you could be my father too."

For a few long seconds, he didn't reply. "We can't all be as closely matched as Romeo and Juliet."

"That's a good thing, considering how they ended up."

"*Desire my pilot is, beauty my prize.* That's from *Lucrece.*"

"Never heard of it."

"Not many have. It's one of Shakespeare's first poems."

"I don't want to go over there on Saturday."

"Then don't. Tell her you've had second thoughts. She'll understand."

"I bet she'll be offended. Wouldn't you be?"

"No, I don't think so, but I probably wouldn't have asked you either. Sorry about this, Brynne." He exhaled audibly. "I can talk to her if you'd like."

It seemed risky to let him, but better than confronting her myself. "If you wouldn't mind," I said. Whatever was going on here was between them anyway, but I hadn't realized this until now.

We said nothing more about it that night when he came over, nor on Wednesday, the next night we stayed together, me at his place this time where I insisted his cats sleep with us, poor Softie and Harriet purring half the night, unable to believe their good luck at having two warm human bodies to huddle close to. On Friday I finally asked him if he had talked to LouAnne and he said that he had. "She understood. I knew she would. It would have been an awkward thing for you, obviously. She did understand this."

"I sometimes wonder why you two got divorced."

He gave me a wry smile. "I've told you why. We were like a pair of old maids. Lots of arguments and no sex."

"Someday that could happen to us."

He shook his head. "I won't live that long."

"Please don't say that," I said, my eyes closing involuntarily. "I don't like to think of either of us dying."

"Neither do I, but I do it anyway. What happened to that boy you've been taking care of? The one with all those broken bones?"

I hadn't kept Mark McGinnis and his car wreck from Griggs because he asked about my patients all the time, wanting to know their circumstances, what I had to do for them, who visited and brought along magazines and stuffed bears. I couldn't lie about any of this. He seemed to know that Trish's death, the way it had arrived, was unremarkable—except in its impact on those who had loved her. This seemed true of most deaths, as the hospital and its beggar's trade made clear to me every day. But I loved the place anyway. I loved knowing that many people, if not everyone, recovered. Some were better, more alive and hopeful, when they left than they had been at any other time in their lives.

"They moved him out of ICU a few days ago," I said. "His orthopede said he's healing well. He's very young so he'll heal fast. They'll probably let him go home in another week, but he's in for months of physical therapy. He'll have to use a cane for a while after he starts walking again but eventually he won't need it."

"That's very good news."

"He'll be fine, I think. I've heard his friends are coming to see him now that we've got him in a regular bed. That always helps."

"His whole life," he murmured, "is wide open and waiting for him."

I looked at him, at his kind, serious face. We were sitting across from each other at the kitchen table and I reached over to touch his hand. "Well, yes, it is," I said.

He smiled. "You're very good at what you do."

I wasn't sure what he meant. "Thank you, I try."

"You're succeeding."

When we were in bed later, in the sleepy, expansive time that followed sex, I lifted my head from his shoulder and told him I loved him, not wanting to keep it from him any longer. He looked at me and smiled as if wonderfully sad, saying he loved me too. "Very much, Brynne," he said. "I'm so glad you feel that way about me. I didn't want to assume."

"You could have," I said, running my fingers through the lavish dark hair that covered his chest.

"I'm not much of a gambler anymore. Maybe that's not such a good thing in this case." He paused. "I'm sorry about the whole thing with LouAnne. You must have wanted to clobber me."

"It was strange, but it wasn't your fault."

"I didn't know what to say when she asked me."

"No would probably have been best," I teased. "But really, it's okay."

The next day, Saturday, Griggs went into the office to work on his quarterly budget before we met up again for the night. I was baking a chocolate cake after craving one all week when the front-door buzzer barged into my apartment. On the intercom was the same female voice that had woken me at eight the previous Monday morning. "It's me, LouAnne Griggs," she cried. After a dry-mouthed, sucked-in second of panic, I buzzed her up, too dimwitted to think of a way to fend her off.

She had a plastic bag in her hand, a lump-filled bag that contained some things I did not want to see, let alone keep. I couldn't really believe this bad news, as if someone had just handed me a thousand-dollar fine for stealing a pistachio from the bulk foods bin.

Nonetheless, I think she felt as nervous as I did, her face flushed, her eyes darting around the living room where I led her to an armchair and offered her something to drink. Either Griggs hadn't talked to her or she had been intent all along on seeing me. The latter seemed most likely; Griggs didn't lie, as far as I could tell. "You have a nice little place," she said. "How long have you lived here?"

"About a year."

"You own it?"

I nodded.

"A good starter home."

"Yes, I suppose so."

She nodded, pretending interest in the black-and-white photos hanging on the walls—enlarged prints from a trip I had taken to Australia several years earlier.

"Paul is very taken with you," she eventually said, her voice uncharacteristically quiet.

"I guess I feel the same about him."

"I thought you might. He's an extremely nice man." She pulled a furry blue cardigan from the bag and held it up. "Our daughter never wore this," she said. "I gave it to her for Christmas a few years ago. I'd keep it if it fit me."

"It's pretty," I said, not really meaning it.

"I think you should have it."

My stomach lurched. I could have cried out in frustration but instead sat docilely, guts churning. "I don't know if Paul told you, but I don't think I can accept any of Trish's things."

"She liked you, Brynne. I used to think you two should get together more, but I know the age difference made it a little difficult."

"Yes, I suppose it did." I tried to smile. "You're very kind to offer me her things, but I really don't think I can take them."

"Because of you and Paul," she said flatly.

"That's part of it, yes."

"I need to say something to you, sweetie."

I looked at her, waiting, not trusting the endearment. The whine of a motor started up outside. A leaf blower, I thought, not a mower, not yet.

"If he asks you to marry him, don't say yes unless you plan to stay with him. If he marries you and you divorce him a year or two later, I don't think he'll survive it."

I stared at her. "We've never discussed marriage. We've only been together for a few months."

"Doesn't matter," she said, shaking her head. "I can see it coming." She reached into the bag again, pulling out a fistful of sweaters. "I want you to take one of Trish's tops. Just one. You can pick it out. I brought eight or nine."

Out of shock more than guilt, I finally agreed. I worried that she would have sat in my living room all day waiting for me to change my mind. She nodded with stern approval when I chose a lavender pullover, cable-knit, very pretty, but I doubted I would ever wear it. Trish probably hadn't worn it either; I had never seen her in pastels, nor in lipstick or eye shadow. Of the two of us, I had always worn the make-up and the Easter egg colors.

LouAnne left a few minutes later, apologizing for arriving unannounced. "Paul won't like that I did this," she said at the door. "I imagine you'll tell him. I suppose I would too, but please don't be mad at me."

"I'm not mad," I said.

"Maybe not now, but later you will be." She hugged me stiffly, with one arm, and then she was gone. I stood behind the closed door and let out my breath, my chest and stomach finally relaxing. I had been sweating too, my underarms nearly dripping with it.

I jumped when the oven timer went off, at first thinking it was the door buzzer again. After I pulled out the cake, I sat at the kitchen table and stared out the window, smelling the chocolate but hardly registering it. Cars drove in and out of the alley every few minutes, garage doors creaking open and closed, but there were very few voices, only a crying child, then his harried mother demanding that he hurry up and get into the van. I thought about calling Griggs to tell him about LouAnne, but didn't. I didn't know when I would tell him. I wasn't mad at her. I was surprised and a little chastened, but also a little pleased. It was as if she had called my bluff, one I hadn't known about until now.

After dinner that night and a piece of cake with too much frosting, Griggs said, "I'd like to see Mark McGinnis."

I looked at him for a long time, wondering if this might be a very unwise thing for him to do. I really had no idea, not even a theory. "I suppose I could take you," I finally said. "But I'll have to check to see if it's okay with him."

Griggs considered this in silence.

"I think he'll say yes," I said. "When I tell him about you, he'll probably say yes."

"No, no. Don't tell him about me. Just go by his room tomorrow and I'll follow you and you can go in and say hello. I'll poke my head in and pretend that I'm looking for you. That's all I want. Just to see him."

I had started crying but his eyes were dry. He looked purposeful, not desperate or bereft. "Are you sure you really want to do that?" I asked, my voice breaking.

"Oh Brynne, don't—please don't cry. I'm fine. I just want to see him. Nothing else. I won't try to befriend him or anything. I promise it'll be okay. I just want to see him for myself."

He kept looking at me calmly, and eventually I heard myself say yes. "I suppose you could come by tomorrow afternoon."

"That'll work," he said. "I won't do anything but say hello. Then I'll leave."

"If you're sure you really want to do this?"

"Yes, I'm sure."

We planned for him to meet me during my lunch hour. I agreed to walk down the hall on the third floor in the east wing with him several steps behind me, watching silently as I turned into Mark's room. With heart pounding, I would do it. I would do this for him and afterward, I knew that I would hold onto him in the hallway, not caring if other nurses or doctors were questioning the propriety of such a display. One or both of us would start crying and eventually we would have to stop. Not long after, he would leave and I would go back to work and we would both be different. We would see each other differently from then on, as if we had been in a speeding car heading toward another speeding, unsteady car, but somehow it hadn't swerved from its lane and hit us. Somehow we had been allowed to drive on without incident, down the rest of the highway, right to our street and into the garage. We had locked the car and walked into the house, and everything was there, the hall light burning, the curtains closed—everything was just as we had left it.

Nineteen

A Dry Season
Ian Stansel

MY FATHER WAS A FARMER. He woke before light and spent his days trying to guide and control the life that came out of the earth. The farm belonged to his family gone back three generations. Corn from the get-go. My mother stayed at home and had us children because we lived in the world and that was the way of it. In my very early years my mother was a lively woman. She took us out in the old Ford truck, pushing and pulling the shifter with such vigor I was in awe of the machine, that it did not fall apart under her power. Then that changed. She stopped taking us into town, leaving the job to my father or Robert, Father's farmhand, or even from time to time Robert's wife, Estelle. My mother stopped leaving the property and then one day she stopped leaving the house altogether.

We lived just outside of a town called Sycamore. Seventy miles from Chicago, due west. Seventy miles made a difference then, far more than it does now. It had been less than a decade since the end of the second war, and the suburbs, though growing fast with GIs and their young families, were still just a narrow collar on the city. I was the second and last child for my parents. My sister was Harriet. I was the one, though, that our parents had been waiting for—a boy—and it showed in the way they treated me, taking my side in fights between Harriet and me, giving me a stern talking-to for something that would have surely gotten Harriet a spanking or worse. From an early age I understood myself to be different from my sister.

One summer day, Harriet and I found ourselves, as we often did on summer days, bored enough to act like friends. We scratched hopscotch into the ground by the barn but quickly tired of it. We tried to get our dog, a black Labrador named Petal, to chase a stick, but she wasn't budging from the shade of the house. It was too hot and she was too old. We sat down next to her just as our father came out of the barn leading Grace, his best mare. She had a hitch in one of her back legs. "Goddamn it," our father said. "What the shit." Then he called out loudly for Robert. "Go on and play somewhere else," he said to us, waving his hand in no particular direction. "Robert!" he called again.

Harriet and I went around the side of the barn but stopped and waited at the corner, peering around. Robert came out of the house, where he'd been having lunch. His wife was there that day. Estelle often came out and visited with my mother, sometimes bringing vegetables or flowers from her garden. It was easy to forget that Robert worked for our father; most of the time they seemed like partners or even brothers—Father being the elder, of course. Estelle followed Robert out of the house but stayed on the porch, leaning against the whitewashed post, watching her husband and our father. Robert shuffled over to where our father had Grace's leg up, examining her hoof.

"What the hell did you do to this shoeing?" our father said.

"I had a little trouble with that one," Robert said, matter-of-fact. He stuck his hands on his back pockets.

"I can see that. What I can't see is how you were gonna reimburse me the price of a healthy mare after she goes lame 'cause of your half-assed work."

It wasn't like our father to talk to him that way. Robert's body slumped a little, but then he stood up straighter than normal. "I don't think it's quite that bad, Karl, come on. She'll be back to normal in a couple days."

Our father looked at him. "Well, then we can laugh about it in a couple days, but for now all I got is a lame horse." He turned his eyes back to Grace's hoof. "Christ," he said. "How short d'you cut this?"

Harriet and I headed out and wandered across the field, moving carefully through the rows of tender cornstalks that we could have trampled with one misstep. The stalks should have been higher by that point in the July, but we'd been suffering a hot and dry spell and everything was getting dwarfed by it. The sun was high and I had to squint to get any detail from the wash of green and brown and white in front of me. "Shoo-wee," Harriet said, referring to either the heat or the interaction between our father and Robert.

"No kidding," I said. Either way.

Harriet was twelve. I would be ten in the fall. She was already showing signs of having our mother's tall and lean physique. She towered over my short, chubby self. Every once in a while I would have to double-time a few steps to catch up to her. I promised myself that someday I would pass her up, gaining such height that everybody else would have to break a sweat to keep up with my long gait.

"What do you think Dad's got a bug about?" I asked.

"Well, it isn't just Gracie," Harriet said. "Even I know that hoof'll grow out in a few days."

"You think he just woke up on the wrong side of the bed?"

"I'll let you know as soon as I figure out how to read minds," she said.

"Come on."

Harriet breathed loudly.

The field sloped ever so slightly downward to a line of anemic sycamores. For the longest time I thought the town had been named after this meager grouping, not knowing they dotted the whole region. Past the trees the ground fell away and we slid and hopped down to the creek bed that edged the south border of our land. The east and west sides ran into the McComb and Wilson farms, and to the north was the gravel county road that took us into town.

The creek bed was made of smooth, rounded stones, settled enough that they held in place as we stepped. There should have been water, at least a little, for another three weeks. A few days before, I had been walking the field and I found my father standing at the creek's edge. He looked down at it and then up at the cloudless sky. He took his brown cap off his head and used it to shield his eyes from the sun. I approached and asked him what he was doing and he looked back down at the creek and said, "Minding the store."

"You think Mom's ever gonna come out?" I asked Harriet. Our mother hadn't been past the front threshold in seven months at that point.

"Like I said, if I get to read minds, I'll let you know."

"If I was Dad I'd make her go out. She's his wife. She has to listen to him."

"I'm going back," she said abruptly, and made for the bank of the creek.

"Don't," I said.

She stopped. "Don't what?"

"Don't go yet."

"Don't go yet, what?"

I got it and rolled my eyes. "Don't go yet *please*."

She came back and we resumed our progress along the edge of our property.

"You can't make a person do anything," Harriet said.

"Kevin Johnson made Shane Wilson eat a worm," I said. This was true—it had happened just before school let out for the summer.

"That's not the same thing," she said. "Anyway, he didn't have to do it."

"Kevin was gonna beat him up if he didn't."

"Yeah," she said, "so he could have taken the beating."

"I bet I could make you do something," I said.

"This is not a game I want to play." She was making a serious effort to sound like an adult in those days. "Just stop," she said, "or I'm heading back to the house."

"I bet—"

"Stop!" she almost screamed.

We continued to walk the creek bed. I slowed and let Harriet take the lead and then bent down and picked up a small stone. I tossed it, not hard, and it tapped her on the head, right on the part in her hair, where it split into pigtails.

"Ow!" she said, reaching back to rub the spot. "God, what was that for?"

She waited for an answer, but I said nothing. Then Harriet puffed out a breath and clambered up the embankment. I followed. She strode quickly back toward the house, but I didn't try to catch up. I wished she would change her mind and come back, but knew she wouldn't. She just kept getting smaller in the distance.

When I got back to the house the radio in the living room was on. Tchaikovsky. The only station in our area played Tchaikovsky every afternoon at one o'clock. And every day my mother would turn it on and raise the volume until the speaker buzzed and then go upstairs into her room. We got to know the composer's work well. Even from outside we'd hear it. When the piece was over, she'd come back down looking puffy in the face. None of us would say what we knew: that for some reason our mother went upstairs each afternoon and cried to Tchaikovsky. There are words corresponding to what ailed my mother, words that are known in our current cultural lexicon: agoraphobia, depression, panic disorder. But back then and back there we were at a loss. All I knew was that there was something wrong with her.

My father came in just after me. Normally he would just go do the work that took him farthest from the house, not returning until the music softened. But this day he walked straight to the radio and turned the dial until it clicked. Barely a beat passed before my mother issued a piercing scream from upstairs. Even after traveling through the bedroom door, down the stairs, and across the room, it was still enough to jerk my hands up to my ears. Our dad took the stairs two at a time while I tried to block that voice from my head. It was almost unbearable for the second that the bedroom door was open. But it didn't end. She stopped to reload her lungs and then once again bombarded the house. Every few seconds she would silence herself and our dad would plead angrily, and then the noise would resume. Finally he came slowly down the stairs, looking empty. He went to the radio and turned it up even louder than before.

"Dad?" I said, over the crescendo of strings. I wasn't sure what I wanted to say, to ask. Something about my mother, about adults.

"Is it important?" he said. I said nothing. "Later, then." He went through the screen door and then stopped. "Robert's in town tending to some business," he said. "Make sure the horses got water in their buckets."

He drove the truck to the far side of the field. There he got out and looked west to the Wilson farm. Two white arcs hung low over their fields. In recent years, many farmers had installed irrigation sprinklers. The Wilsons had done this the year before and recorded a banner harvest. This year, with the nonirrigated farms like ours suffering from the drought, they were practically set to do us in.

I dragged the hose through the barn to fill up the horses' water buckets. My father or Robert would have taken the buckets out to where the spigot was, but I knew that if I was able to lift the bucket, it wasn't enough to get the horses through the afternoon. I reached the hose through the gate of Grace's stall and watched the bucket fill. Then I pulled the hose back, placed a thumb over the stream, and shot a quick burst at Grace's rump. Her head shot up and a shake passed down her neck and withers. She looked at me, the whites of her eyes showing. I gave her another shot and she whinnied.

When I was done I found Harriet and Estelle back behind the house. My sister was perched on a sawhorse, her ankles wrapped around the legs to balance. Estelle stood in front of her. The music was still wailing through the open windows. Harriet and Estelle were talking to each other, but I could not hear them.

Then Estelle turned to me and said, "Well, there you are." I read her lips as much as I heard her. "How are you doing, sweetie?" Harriet looked at me with some kind of sad contempt. "Come on over here," Estelle said. I went to her and she put her hand on my shoulder. "You know your mama's just having a hard time, right? She's gonna pop right out of this just as soon as she can." It was clear that Estelle wanted it to be true, that she liked Harriet and me and our mother a great deal, and that she did want good things for our family. She was a decent sort of woman and I knew I should have felt comforted, but having this smiling face tell me that my mother was going to be okay only made it seem more uncertain. I looked up at her and waited for something further, but all she did was purse her lips into a tighter smile and tilt her head slightly to the side.

"If you ever need anything," she said, "if you ever need *anything*, you tell Estelle and I will just come running." She looked at my sister. "That goes for both of you. You say the word and I will be here." She pushed a lock of hair away from Harriet's face and behind her ear. "In fact," she said, "maybe we can go get some ice cream later."

Harriet smiled and just then the music went mute. Our mother appeared in the living room window, her face slightly grayed behind the screen. "Staying for dinner, Estelle?" she said. Her eyes moved to Harriet and then to me before landing on Estelle.

"Oh, I don't know. I'm not sure how long Robert's gonna be. Anyway, I don't want to put you out."

"I'll make enough just in case—chicken tonight," our mother said, and looked at me, as this was my favorite. Then she disappeared back into the house.

Estelle said to us, "Doesn't that sound good."

⁂

Harriet had gone inside to help our mother with dinner, and with Robert gone and my father off in the fields, I was again on my own. I thought about heading over to see what Shane Wilson was up to, maybe cooling off going under his dad's field sprinklers, but I remembered how my father had been looking out there and thought better of it. I also remembered how I hadn't stuck up for Shane when Kevin Johnson made him eat that worm, and how Shane had looked at me afterward. So instead I walked the field and the bone-dry creek bed, thinking about my mother and about Estelle and about how different two women could be.

In addition to the house and barn and silo, we had two outbuildings on our land. One of those was full of machinery and other equipment, but the second was little more than a shed, empty save for a few random items: a cracked bucket, a wooden box missing its top, various rusted-out crank drills and hammers, and a cup of nails sitting on a counter-high work space. It stood only a hundred or so yards from our front porch but had been in a state of ignored disuse for so long that it was barely seen, as though it wasn't even there. Like some browned-out shrub nobody had yet taken the time to rip up. I went there on bored afternoons to pretend it was a castle I had to protect, or the hideout of a thief I had to apprehend. On this day it was to be a cabin far off on a winter mountaintop. But as I got close, I heard something from inside and peered through a break between the wall slats. The blinding sun was lowering on the other side of the shed, slicing through the small room in shards. My father stood in front of the work space with his back to me, his pants slung low enough for me to see the pale skin of his rear. Two bare legs wrapped around his waist. He made slight movements. Though his head and shoulders hid Estelle's face, I recognized the long red-blond hair flung over his shoulder. She emitted a repeated noise, a faint *ha ha ha*. My father puffed short breaths through his nose, the same as when he chopped wood and hit the log clean.

I stepped silently backward a few yards, a safe distance. I was about to break into a run and hide behind a low berm on the other side of our driveway to wait until they came out. To see whatever I would see. I couldn't imagine. But before I could move away any farther I saw my mother in the doorway of our house, the screen open. She was in a black and yellow dress, her hair down just the way it was each and every day. And, like always, she wore that look of exhaustion on her face, that expression I could never quite understand or forgive. She raised a hand and waved at me with her fingers. Without thinking, I checked on the shed to see if anything could be detected from where I stood. Then she looked over at it. If there was any surprise on her face, any burst of understanding, it disappeared before I could register it. The little building remained still. But she suddenly seemed a bit sadder. She drew her eyes back to me and slowly raised her hand again and went inside the house, letting the screen door bang shut.

My mind darted back to the shed. I understood what I had seen. I'd heard talk of it at school with friends, though the details of the act as reported (usually by boys with older brothers) were always fuzzy and, as often as not, doubtful. For all that mystery, it was amazing how clear it was at the moment of witness. And though I could not quite comprehend why anyone would want to engage in the act, I understood my father wanting to be close to Estelle. Estelle laughed and

Estelle smelled good. Estelle, as far as I could tell, didn't know the first thing about Tchaikovsky, or care. Sex was for married people, for mothers and fathers, but somehow my nine-year-old self also had the inkling of an understanding of adultery, an understanding beyond the definition. I understood why. I sympathized with my father and Estelle. I took their side. It was okay what they were doing, maybe even good.

⁂

When I came back to the house an hour later, my family was just sitting down at the table, along with Estelle and Robert. My mother was at the counter, cutting a chicken into pieces. "I was calling you," she said.

"There he is," Robert said. I hadn't seen or heard his truck coming down our drive. I felt like I hadn't seen him in days, though it had been only hours since my father chewed him out by the barn. His thin hair had been freshly combed back.

"Where have you been?" my father asked.

"I was at Shane Wilson's," I lied.

"Admiring his daddy's fields?"

"No," I said. "I don't know." His face was like it always was: round and reddish and stubbled.

"All right, well, sit down there." He tapped on the table in front of my seat. "Get some food in you."

"Smells delicious," Estelle said to my mother, who told her, "I'm glad."

Estelle smiled and there was a moment where her mouth hung open and it looked as if she was going to say something else. But she didn't. She went back to looking at her plate, straightening the napkin on her lap. Her hair was pulled neatly back in a ponytail. A small blotch of red showed on the skin over her collarbone. Small enough that no one would have questioned it. It was a hot day. Skin goes crazy.

I turned and found my father looking at me. His hands were folded beneath his chin and he eyes were squinted.

"How is that Wilson boy?" he said. "Scrawny little thing, isn't he?"

"I guess so," I said.

"What was it that other boy made him do, lick a frog or some such?"

"Eat a worm," I said. I glanced across the table at my sister, thinking about the conversation we'd had earlier, thinking about that little rock I threw and how it sent her away. But she was looking out the window, her mind somewhere else completely.

"That's terrible," my mother said, dishing food onto plates.

"That's boys," my father corrected her.

"That's good protein, too, I imagine," Robert joked.

"Maybe he should put more in his diet," my father said, "get some muscles on his bones."

"He's just a child," my mother said.

"Must have dug deep to get a worm in these conditions," Robert said.

My father took a tug off a piece of bread. "Got them sprinklers," he said.

"Oh," Robert said, "that's right." As if just remembering that not every farm had the difficulties we did. Not every man was out tending to hard, dry dirt.

My mother served each of us before sitting down with her own small portion. Chicken and potatoes and peas. Even the peas tasted good. Everything my mother cooked tasted good. When she set my plate in front of me she paused to put her hand on my head, smoothing down my hair and then curling her fingers in, as if to take a little piece with her, to slide it into her pocket.

Our old Lab, Petal, walked across the room in her slow, arthritic gait. She carefully leaned forward, stretching her front legs and raising her rear. Her tail went up, giving us a view of her backside.

"Don't you wink your bung at me," my father said. Harriet giggled and then said, "Eww." "Karl," my mother said. Petal looked back at us and then let go a squeak of a fart. And that sent us all into fits of laughter, even my mother, though she tried to hide it. I laughed harder and longer than anyone else, tearing up, giggling uncontrollably at that slow, gassy old dog.

"We're gonna have to be going right after dinner," Robert said after a minute. "O'Connor's staying open so I can pick up that brake drum, but I got to get there by six."

"But what about ice cream?" Harriet said.

"What's this?" my mother said.

"Oh," Estelle said, "I mentioned maybe we'd go into town for some dessert. I hope that's okay."

"That's fine," my father said. "You go on over to O'Connor," he said to Robert, "and we'll get the kids their sweets, then you can meet us and be on your way." Robert looked at his wife, but Estelle just went about cutting and chewing her food. My father gestured at her with his fork. "She doesn't want to go over there. You kidding? O'Connor gets talking. Old man'll bore the woman to death."

"Yeah," Robert said after a moment. "I guess you're right."

"Don't suppose you want to come?" my father said to my mother.

"Maybe next time," she said. "Anyway, not too much room in that old truck of yours."

"Nothing wrong with that truck," he snapped.

"I didn't say there was, Karl."

"Yeah," he said. There was a pause during which none of us spoke or even looked up from our plates of food. There was just Petal clacking across the floor in the living room. Finally my father said, "Chicken's good," and took another bite.

⁂

A while after dinner we piled in, my father behind the wheel, then me, then Estelle with Harriet halfway on her lap. It was tight, but once we started, the wind through the windows cooled us and I liked being forced against my father's side.

We got into town and it was still hot and the ice-cream parlor was doing brisk business, the line to the counter a dozen people deep. As we waited I thought of how good this was, standing there with my father and Estelle, even with my sister. After a few minutes my father sighed and handed a dollar to Estelle. "We'll be outside," he told her. "Chocolate and chocolate," he said, pointing first to himself and then me. On the sidewalk, folks were heading to the pictures. My father set his hand on my shoulder and took me slowly against the general stream of people.

"Did I hear you threw a rock at your sister?" he said.

"I don't know," I said.

"Well, you can trust me that that's what I heard. Are you saying you don't know if you threw a rock at your sister or not?"

I said nothing.

"Listen to me here," he said. "You don't throw rocks at your sister. You know better than that." He took us to a bench. We sat down and he gestured vaguely back toward the ice-cream shop. "They'll see us over here," he said, as if to reassure me, and then continued. "Don't throw rocks at girls. There's a way men treat women. You need to protect them, son. Other people try to throw rocks, your job is to stop them. I know they can be a handful, but still that's no reason."

Estelle and Harriet joined us with our ice creams. We fit ourselves onto the bench and ate in silence. Robert showed up after we were finished and our father said, "All right, then," and the three of us got into the truck.

We took the long way, swinging a few blocks to the south before heading back up toward the farm. There were houses just off downtown, tall Victorians that people called the Painted Ladies. They were decorated with bright colors on the eaves and shutters and doors and window frames. Delicate woodwork spiraled and laced along wraparound porches. Each one was unique. Each one a testament to the early days of the century, when Sycamore and a thousand other towns like it were flush with money and spirit, established by men whose family names were known. They were built with precision and lived in with what I imagined was a kind of clean elegance. We stared as if we were looking at both the past and the future simultaneously, the what-was and the what-if. I indulged in fantasies of leisure and power. Servants. Underlings in vague business ventures. Cars in the drive. Sometimes a wife, though at the moment I hardly understood the use of one.

⚜

"This year we start home economics," Harriet said to our mother, who was sewing up a hole in one of my father's shirts. The three of us were in the living room and I was curled into the wingback, picking at the stiff metal links of an old horse bit. "And they're having all the mothers come in. A different girl's mother each week to help out with the class."

Our mother did not look up from her stitching. "That right," she said. Then, "Where is your father?"

"Checking on Gracie," I said. He'd been gone for a while by then. He hadn't even come in after we got back from town.

"I told Mrs. Samuels about what a good cook you are," Harriet said, "and she told me there'd be plenty of weeks we'd be doing cooking and baking. She said all the mothers would be choosing whatever they wanted to do. If they want to make a pie or cook up a casserole or, well, anything." She drummed her hands on the book in her lap. "Anything else, either," she went on. "It doesn't even have to be cooking. If you want to show the girls about that stitching or just keeping house, I'm sure that would be fine."

"Well," our mother said, and then paused. "Well, let's talk about that closer to schooltime."

"You could probably show everyone a thing or two about doing up a chicken," Harriet said, smiling.

Our mother nodded. "I'll keep that in mind." She bit off the line off the thread she'd been working into the shirt and tugged at the fabric, testing the strength of the stitches. Then she picked up a pair of jeans and went about re-threading her needle.

My sister left it at that and said she was tired. She kissed our mother good night and went to her room.

In the silence between my mother and me there hung information. Information I had, and information she had. And there was some we shared, but neither of us was quite sure what exactly that was.

"I guess it's about your bedtime, too," she said.

"Maybe she should bring Estelle to school with her," I said.

She finally looked up from her stitching. "Say that again?"

I tried to make it sound casual. Something that just made simple sense. But my face was hot. "Maybe Harri should bring Estelle with her to her class."

"Why would you say that?"

I shrugged. The smell of chicken remained in the air, warm and salty. I felt sick in my stomach. The radio was dead quiet in the corner. My mother kept her green eyes on me, waiting for me to say what she hoped I couldn't. "I looked over in the shed today," I said.

Her cheeks dropped. "I think it's time you head on to bed."

"I was gonna go in there and play—"

"Head on up to bed now."

"It was strange—"

"That's *enough*," she said sternly.

I held her gaze for a moment and then got up and went to the front door, pushed open the screen, and stepped onto our porch, letting the door thwack closed behind me. There were a million things I could not have known right then. I did not know, for instance, that we would survive the dry season that year, barely, and that my father would continue to eke out something like a living for years to come. I did not know that in three years my mother would be gone, having finally escaped the house by way of a rope and a sturdy beam. I did not know that Harriet would leave us, too, as soon as she could, off to college just after her eighteenth birthday, and later to her own family and life. Or that Robert would one day buy his own parcel of land, that our interactions with him and Estelle would be reserved to moments in town when my father refused to talk to either of them. And I could not see to the time when my father would pass and the farm would be sold off to real estate developers who would raze each building, starting with that shed, and tear out the crop without harvesting so much as a kernel. These events would come in their own time, but each and all of them are now wrapped up, inextricable, in what had just transpired between my mother and me. Even at the moment, though, I understood that something had been lost, that an absence was created that night by my own stupid cruelty.

My father sat on the porch swing. After a moment, music from the radio came on inside. Softly. My breathing became heavy and my body tense. I had to keep from crying. I wanted to scream and to put my small fists into my father's chest, his red face, but I stood motionless just outside the door, paralyzed with knowledge. The air was still hot. There were no clouds in the sky. He tipped his hat back off his forehead and kept his eyes out on the hard fields.

"This goddamn season," he said.

Twenty

Schnecks

Mark Wisniewski

BLESS ME, FATHER, FOR I HAVE SINNED; my last confession was—good Christ, I have no clue, maybe a year ago—no, I might have been here just before last Easter, though I couldn't swear to that on a bible. But here's one true thing, Father: I feel nervous right now. And to be honest I always feel nervous after fair-time, not necessarily on account of my own sins, at least not mortal ones, but still I'm always nervous after fair-time, which gets me to thinking, so this year I figured I'd try confession with you.

Which fair? The *State's* Fair. The one we just had in West Allis. To which I'm sure you went.

You're not pronouncing it correctly, Father. You said State when instead it's *State's*. As in the fair that belongs to the state, as in Wisconsin, so why would you say only *State*? Anyways I'm sure you've been there at least once in your past—

Never? Well, you should go. Next year you should go certainly. It's a wonderful time, especially for the younger set, and see maybe one reason I'm nervous now is, well, somehow the teens we employ at the Fair don't like me so much after we take down our tent for the year, and I have to admit this bothers me.

Pardon?

We have a wiener tent there, Father. For selling foot-longs.

Foot-long *wieners*, Father. We—my husband and I—have a tent to sell them right there, on the State's Fair's premises. Yes and like I say we sell foot-longs, which are delicious, especially with your dark mustard. And Father we also sell beer, which we have a license for—not always perfectly up to date but we always have one—and we slow-cook barbecue sauce so we can offer for another twenty cents *barbecue* foot-longs, and of course with foot-longs you'll want chips so we can sell you enough of those to cover the rest of the paper plate we give free, or you can have navy beans for another fifteen to thirty cents if I have patience to make beans ahead of time. Now and then I'll also manage to boil kapusta, which we've sold for as little as a dime extra depending, and from us you can also get genuine vanilla ice cream in those cute plastic cups, though I personally never eat ice cream—or for that matter sour cream—three-four hours before to after kapusta since this disturbs my gastric. So you see altogether we're in the business of making people happy.

And most people we deal with are. But, like I say, not always the teens employed by us. You'd think these kids would grin to work in our tent; in fact, during the winter, for instance at Christmastime, they beg me to hire them, and if I say yes they—*initially*—thank and sometimes even hug me knowing our workers are known to make good money for sixteen-and-mature-fifteen-year-olds. Also our workers often laugh and put in overtime, so they walk off with plenty of cash, Father, which brings me to one of the things that might be making me nervous, which is the night a number of our schnecks went missing.

Schnecks, Father. You know, the rectangles with white frosting—long johns, some call them? Which most people naturally love? In fact I can sell your foot-long, and I can sell your beer, but your schneck will sell itself and then some. Eat one schneck and you'll right away want another and never think twice about paying again. So you enjoy a second *schneck*? Who doesn't deserve two at least?

The point is my brother Gary fries schnecks at his bakery, and maybe you don't think schneck when you first order a foot-long, but we've found that, out of our State's Fair tent, schnecks do extremely well, especially early in your cooler days and again just before closing. People like schnecks so much we can without blinking move four dozen in an hour, so we stock them in our back room, which here I'll admit is just a curtained-off section of our tent.

And see my brother Gary is normally fine with donating to us these schnecks, but see this might be what makes me nervous: Gary wants to write our schnecks off as business losses so he need not report to the IRS as much profit, so he can save taxes every April. To which my husband Yashu says, *Taxes*? Are you nuts, Gary? Who pays taxes? This is my husband I'm talking about so I should watch myself; on the other hand I am in confession, and this is my Yashu: he always says *Taxes,* meaning, Who really pays them?

I realize that, Father. But need we give so *much* unto Caesar? Anyway Gary has said to my husband Yashu that he, Gary, pays taxes, and my husband Yashu sort of yells at him, maybe a bit tipsy from beer Yashu yells: You just make the schnecks and we'll sell them like they never existed, and we take only cash so who could know the difference? But Gary *still* says he wants to write off. He's a stickler like that, Gary. So I say to Gary, on the side this is, away from Yashu— and Father remember now, this is me talking to my blood brother—and with all that considered, I say: Listen, Gary, we can work this out, maybe slide some of our State's Fair cash flow your way—you know, pay you a few cents per schneck even though you're my brother and you normally just plain give. But *again* Gary says no. He says if we paid him even just pennies per schneck, he'd have to *report* rather than deduct, which would mean more federal than ever—and state!—so I say to him: Gary, no one pays *all* their taxes, so why you? Plus I also remind him we give him bonuses by letting him take as many broken foot-longs as he wants at the end of any State's Fair day, so you'd think he'd drive schnecks to us at the fair whistling Dixie, but what I just said brings up another thing that bothers me—boy I'll tell you, Father, this whole wiener and schneck business really does keep me awake at night.

It *is* stressful, Father. And on top of what I've just told you is this whole business of childhood labor laws. My understanding recently from what my husband Yashu heard from a well-read neighbor of ours is that under sixteen is too young for *any* job, which to me sounds like more of this garbage you always hear. I agree that when it comes to a shy, extremely thin, starved young girl in a crowded clothes factory stitching her fingers to a rusty old Singer in Czechoslovakia, this is obviously something we need laws passed to stop, but we're not talking about Czechoslovakia, or even Russia here; we're talking a *State's Fair.* In fact, we're talking the *Wisconsin* State's Fair, a family event wholesome people have enjoyed for decades, probably since John Hancock and those others *drew up* the states. Not to mention I've told all my nieces who work in our tent, and I always *will* tell them: Young ladies, there's a way to deal with men. There's a way to give men what they need without you yourself getting in trouble. It might not be exactly what some men want, but still they'll walk away from you happy, possibly even in love with you, and they sure as heck won't later call you a floozy or a whore or any of these types of names. I mean, Jesus Christ, Father, you don't want the rabbit dead, though on the other hand I understand there are pressures on a maturing girl nowadays; there are societal pressures and the pressures of her own bodily and romantic needs; these are all understandable, which is why a young lady should, at some point in her life, under the correct circumstances, *give* a guy something. But for God's sake, I say to the girls working for me, don't get pregnant! So with men do only what you have to. And of course remember, after you're done, to wash your hands. This is the advice I give, Father, and if these fifteen-year-old girls weren't working at our tent to hear it, they might *never* hear it, and *then* where would they be? Certainly a maturing girl's parents rarely talk about such things, Father. You and I both know that. It takes an aunt, or an aunt-like person, and often it also takes a situation like a State's Fair concessions tent—you know, where *sure* there's long hours but also a certain amount of laughter in the air, on top of plenty of extended family working toward a common goal.

What, Father? What's the common goal? Profit, I suppose. And, Father, I hear myself say the word profit in this church of yours and already I feel evil. But, if you could tell me, what is so wrong about profit? It's the heart of the American system, or so I was taught in school time and again, and America, from what I still many times hear on even cable news, has always been an extremely God-orientated country. In fact at the fair I always try, time allowing, to read the words In God We Trust on every dollar we take in—I agree trust isn't as strong a word as love, but once you start printing money you don't go changing it or you'll find yourself dealing with counterfeits. Which is another thing that stresses me but not in the sense of it being a sin I might have committed—more like one maybe committed against me.

But, yes, to get back to the point, we try to stock as many schnecks as possible, Father, and we sell them without prejudice, and we also sell the, watchamacallit . . . *near*-beer, which might be at the heart of what most bothers me today. Discount near-beer, this is; my husband Yashu knows a German who brings kegs of it in cheap from almost to Iowa, and I mean very cheap—I have no idea how, after his gasoline and oil, he affords to sell it to us as low as he does, but we don't ask, and what this near-beer does is allow us to sell to minors. To be perfectly honest with you, Father, there is a tiny bit of alcohol in this near-beer, but our inspector, who tends to be very tough on us, tells us it's legal for minors as far as he's concerned, and I don't think my husband Yashu is bribing him to be less concerned than otherwise, though I can't say this for sure, since Yashu is always walking out from that curtained-off stockroom and snatching twenties from the register used by the kids who sell for us. That's yet *another* thing that stresses me: that Yashu keeps snatching any bill larger than a ten and walking it back into our stockroom; I guess he doesn't trust our workers, but what kind of message does this send to these kids?

I tell him the message it sends is that as soon as they get a chance, they should pocket and keep any twenties they take in, since he figures they'll do it anyway. I mean, Father, when you don't trust your own provider, won't that lead to trouble down the pike? Who will you finally trust? No one? And what is Yashu doing with all that cash? Burying it in the backyard, he tells me, but that too stresses me since what happens if he passes on, leaving me clueless about just where to dig? Not to mention how do I know our cash is really under that sod—and not lost from him investing in stocks in the market?

Anyways, yes, the inspector says the amount of alcohol in our near-beer is fine for minors to drink, though I'd say don't let a toddler have it instead of soda since who can say these alcohol percentages are always correct—you get the gallons from near the bottom of the vat, which these gallons driven to us by the German probably are, and who knows *how* much as far as these percentages go. But what bugs me most about our near-beer, Father, is what my husband tells my nieces and nephews and such who work our front lines, and that is to charge underage teens at least an extra twenty-five cents per cup for this beer, and to hand cups of it over the counter to these underage teens as if you're dealing on the sly, looking both ways just before you hand over, as if you're watching out for police. This of course gets these underage customers all excited about drinking what they think is true beer but isn't. And Father, I'm telling you these underage customers then tell their underage friends like wildfire, and soon we have dozens of pimpled faces "sneaking up" to our tent, paying us extra for beer that's dregs if it has any kick to it at all, then rushing off like they're getting away with murder. Not far from our tent you'll see some of these teens giggling and carrying on as if they're drunk when in fact they aren't, which is fine I suppose, but there's something about this whole business of deceiving them that bothers me when I finally lay my head on the pillow. Maybe it's the irony of how Yashu and I use these kids' desire to drink illegally to get money from them legally. Or maybe it's that I actually do, in my heart of hearts, fear that the near-beer we sell has more wham than we and our inspector and the German believe.

But back to the missing schnecks. Though they have slightly to do with the near-beer. Come to think of it, they too have to do with the childhood labor laws I'm still not sure exist—and of course if those laws do exist, there's the question of whether breaking a law is always a sin. Anyways when it comes to our near-beer, one of my young nieces was the best of any of our workers at selling it—a real smiler, she—and my husband and I were all for her sales tactics, until roughly six months after one year's fair, when she left Wisconsin for Canada unmarried. Maybe I shouldn't confess to you what might be one of her biggest sins, but maybe she already confessed it in this very booth—not to mention if my family members could confess big sins for me, I wouldn't mind in the least.

Anyways this smiling niece of mine, whose name I won't mention—though for this discussion only, let's call her Joan—she started out as one of our barkers, which we would use back then. You know, you hardly see barkers around in these days of neon signs, but back then we'd use them, this niece of mine Joan one. What worked best, Father, was when our barkers yelled, *"Foot-long hotdogs, barbie-cue, ice-cold lemonade; Mom, we got Pop on ice; wienie, wienie, wienie!"*

I think it's cute too! And our barkers would shout it smiling and, Father, I'm telling you, it worked: Yashu was on the backyard late every night burying handfuls of twenties.

But I'm getting away here from possible sins. This-here Joanie, as I might have said, was my niece, and she ran off to Canada after the one summer she worked at our fair tent, and that was the same summer the man with the monkey walked around the fair. Much was said about this man months later, but that August everyone was just excited about him: by gosh he had a *monkey*, which as you know you don't see many of in Wisconsin except for at the zoo, where, back then, you paid to see that Samson the Gorilla, who, as you may know, scared more than charmed like your smaller monkey can. And this fellow at the fair *had* a smaller monkey, not exactly your organ-grinding type but along those lines, and by that I mean he—the *man* now, is to whom I'm referring—had people thinking his monkey was cute and therefore that he, the man himself, was a harmless sort. It's amazing how quickly people judge people by just one pet they take public; for example, who even nods at those who walk bulldogs? The point I'm trying to make here is you can imagine, *Father*, how this Joanie, at her age back then, took a shine to this man with the small monkey. She probably met him on one of her work-breaks away from our tent, where the smell of her blouses often suggested she smoked—though come to think of it in this church here, it could have been only the man with the monkey who smoked.

And I don't like to gossip, Father, but let's just say that when you have a young lady and a charming man and cigarettes and smiling and talking intensely against the deadlines of work breaks, the next thing the young lady knows, she can find her face flushed with what she believes is love—and then, *if she doesn't handle the man wisely,* she can find herself in the kind of fix she's been raised to avoid.

No, I can't say for sure she was pregnant, Father. Who can ever say *any* of these things for sure? What I can swear on a bible about is that a man did have a small monkey that year at the fair. And that it did escape from him, and that, as far as my husband Yashu and I know, it stole quite a few of our schnecks.

I think it escaped off the leash because the man wasn't watching it, and my theory says he wasn't watching because he and Joanie hid in our stock room until after we left for the night, at which point these two lovebirds, in the privacy of the darkness then in our tent, went ahead and, you know, made time.

And what gets me is Joanie wouldn't have *met* this man if Yashu and I hadn't encouraged her flirtatious ways with customers while she was selling for us the near-beer. Do you see how it's all connected, Father? My husband and I wanted more profits—and as a result an unwed niece finds herself with child? Do you see how a young woman pretends to watch for police while smiling and flirting and along comes a man with a monkey and she and the man get to talking and laughing, then chatting and serious flirting and kissing and on and on? Until she's pregnant and runs off to live in shame? In *Canada*? Claiming she went there to be an artist when in fact all she ever made creatively, as far as I know these many years later, was a vest made from plastic six-pack holders?

Father, *nobody* leaves her family and good, cash-paying employment to be an *artist*. Especially an artist in Canada. I don't care how much you like that French-Canadian accent, or how much you believe snow piled high around you will force you to make something from nothing people would pay to hang on their walls more than they would a stuffed bass. It just makes no *sense* to be an artist in Canada. If you ask me, it makes no sense to be an artist *any*where, but if you do happen to be that kind of a dreamer, I'm fairly sure you'd go someplace extra *warm*, like say for instance Costa Rica, where at least you'd save on sweaters, heating bills, and things of that nature such as shovels and salt.

Plus you have the many *colors* down there. For example those red and blue parrots. You need *colors* for art was what I was taught in school, especially your brighter colors, which is the main reason I never swallowed whole this Joanie's story about being an artist in Canada. I mean, come on, Father. You must agree with me.

You're not *sure,* Father? Okay, then here's another fact: when the police found the monkey, it had frosting on its lip. Or so it appeared to their eyes. Which proves the monkey ate at least one schneck, which pretty much proves he took ours, and how does a monkey steal and eat a good number of schnecks—at *night,* when the State's Fair is closed—unless that monkey's owner was in our tent, preoccupied with something that caused him to lose his head?

I realize that, Father. And if you say it's not my fault, I'll try to believe that. With the appropriate thanks to you.

No, Father. That's it. I really do think that's it for now. Other than, since we're on the subject of the State's Fair, Yashu and I have sometimes, when business has gotten slow, snuck in a few of our workers by using saliva to transfer those ink-marks they stamp on the back of your hand to prove you've paid your way in. But already—I mean before confessing this slight indiscretion—I was feeling more relaxed. Though right now I'll still ask pardon from God, as well as penance from you, Father. Unless you yourself could swear on a bible that nothing said here was a sin.

THIRTY OTHER
DISTINGUISHED STORIES

"A Deer Big Enough to Show" by Mike Alber. First appeared in *Hobart.*

"The Winner" by Charles Baxter. First appeared in *Tin House.*

"The Sea That Leads to All Seas" by Katie Chase. First appeared in *Prairie Schooner.*

"People Who Are Not Like Us" by Brock Clarke. First appeared in *Sycamore Review.*

"The Arrangement" by Tenaya Darlington. First appeared in *The Sun.*

"Repo Man" by Janice Deal. First appeared in *CutBank Online.*

"Clarity" by David Driscoll. First appeared in *TriQuarterly Online.*

"That Story" by Jack Driscoll. First appeared in *The Georgia Review.*

"Sky Riders" by Jack Driscoll. First appeared in *The Georgia Review.*

"The Truth of Matin County, Illinois" by James Gill. First appeared in *Crab Orchard Review.*

"Flirting with Normal, Flirting with Crazy" by Jacqueline Guidry. First appeared in *Nimrod International Journal.*

"Triumph" by Chris Haven. First appeared in *Hunger Mountain.*

"Four Calling Birds" by Michael Martone. First appeared in *American Short Fiction.*

"Believers" by Joe Meno. First appeared in *Southern Indiana Review.*

"Hunting Season" by Matthew Modica. First appeared in the *Antioch Review.*

"My Nonsexual Affair" by Andy Mozina. First appeared in *Ecotone*.

"The Village" by Antonya Nelson. First appeared in *TriQuarterly Online*.

"Bullheads" by Michael Noll. First appeared in *American Short Fiction*.

"The Klein Farm" by Jessi Phillips. First appeared in *Glimmer Train*.

"Telling Him" by Craig Planting. First appeared in *The Sun*.

"The Rivermutts of Pig's Eye" by Mark Rapacz. First appeared in the *Southern Humanities Review*.

"Horse" by Luke Rolfes. First appeared in *The MacGuffin*.

"Passion" by Christine Sneed. First appeared in *New South*.

"Student, Teacher" by Christine Sneed. First appeared in *Pleiades*.

"Five Rooms" by Christine Sneed. First appeared in *New Ohio Review*.

"Where He Went Under" by Richard Spilman. First appeared in *Prairie Schooner.*

"Cowboys" by Susan Steinberg. First appeared in *American Short Fiction*.

"Hymie and Ruth" by Daniel Stolar. First appeared in *Chicago Reader*.

"The Approximate End of the World" by Theodore Wheeler. First appeared in *Boulevard.*

"Like a Phoenix" by Erika T. Wurth. First appeared in *The Florida Review*.

CONTRIBUTORS

CHARLES BAXTER is the author of ten books of fiction and several books of poetry and criticism. He teaches at the University of Minnesota and lives in Minneapolis.

DAN CHAON is, most recently, the author of the short story collection *Stay Awake*. Other works include two novels, *Await Your Reply* and *You Remind Me of Me*, both national bestsellers, and the collection *Among the Missing*, a finalist for the National Book Award. He teaches at Oberlin College in Ohio.

RODERIC CROOKS is a fiction writer and librarian. He studied at the Iowa Writers' Workshop and is currently pursuing a doctorate in Information Studies at the University of California Los Angeles.

MICHAEL CZYZNIEJEWSKI is the author of the story collection *Elephants in Our Bedroom* and the chapbook *Chicago Stories*. His stories have appeared or are forthcoming in *Southern Review, Ninth Letter, American Short Fiction, Pushcart Prize XXXI,* and others. He teaches at Bowling Green State University, where he serves as Editor-in-Chief of *Mid-American Review,* and he received a 2010 Fellowship in Literature from the National Endowment for the Arts.

ANTHONY DOERR is the author of four books: *Memory Wall, The Shell Collector, About Grace,* and *Four Seasons in Rome.* His writing has won three O. Henry

Prizes, two Pushcart Prizes, the Rome Prize, the Story Prize, the New York Public Library's Young Lions Award, the Barnes & Noble Discover Prize, and a Guggenheim Fellowship. In 2007, *Granta* put Doerr on its list of 21 Best Young American Novelists. He lives in Boise, Idaho.

DAVID DRISCOLL's stories have appeared in a number of publications including *Mississippi Review, TriQuarterly,* and *Inkwell.* He is currently at work on a collection of short stories and a novel. He lives in Chicago with his wife, dog, and three cats.

ROXANE GAY lives and writes in the Midwest.

LANIA KNIGHT teaches creative writing and literature at Eastern Illinois University. She was born in Slidell, Louisiana, and grew up in East Texas. After leaving home at sixteen and dropping out of school, she had many adventures, including working on an organic farm in southern Boone County, Missouri.

REBECCA MAKKAI's debut novel is *The Borrower,* and her fiction has appeared in *The Best American Short Stories* for four consecutive years. She lives north of Chicago.

BRENDA K. MARSHALL is the author of two novels, *Dakota, or What's a Heaven For* and *Mavis,* and the academic book *Teaching the Postmodern.* She teaches in the Department of English at the University of Michigan. Originally from North Dakota, she lives outside Ann Arbor, Michigan, with her unlawfully wedded spouse of 25 years.

LEE MARTIN is the author of four novels, including *The Bright Forever,* a finalist for the 2006 Pulitzer Prize in Fiction, and *Break the Skin.* He has also written the memoirs *From Our House, Turning Bones,* and *Such a Life.* His first book was the short story collection, *The Least You Need To Know.* He teaches in the MFA Program at The Ohio State University.

CHARLES McLEOD is the author of a novel, *American Weather,* and a collection of stories, *National Treasures.* His fiction has appeared in publications including *Alaska Quarterly Review, Conjunctions, Dossier, Eleven Eleven, FiveChapters, The Gettysburg Review, Hayden's Ferry Review, The Iowa Review, Michigan Quarterly Review,* the anthology *Fakes,* a Pushcart Prize anthology, and on Salon.

CHRISTOPHER MOHAR is the recipient of a Wisconsin Institute for Creative Writing Fellowship, and his story "The Five Points of Performance" received the

2010 McGinnis-Ritchie Award for Fiction from *The Southwest Review* as well as the 2010 Larry and Eleanor Sternig Short Fiction Award from the Council for Wisconsin Writers. He teaches creative writing for the University of Wisconsin's Continuing Studies program and has previously been a metallurgical engineer, adult literacy tutor, busboy, lifeguard, and writing workshop instructor in a men's correctional institution. He lives in Madison, Wisconsin, where he is currently at work on a novel about meat.

DAVID JAMES POISSANT is the author of *Lizard Man*, winner of the 2011 RopeWalk Fiction Chapbook Prize, and of a collection of stories and a novel forthcoming from Free Press. His stories have appeared in *The Atlantic, Playboy, One Story, The Southern Review, New Stories from the South*, and two volumes of *Best New American Voices*. He lives with his wife and daughters in Orlando, where he teaches in the MFA program at the University of Central Florida.

YELIZAVETA P. RENFRO is the author of a collection of short stories, *A Catalogue of Everything in the World*, winner of The St. Lawrence Book Award. Her fiction and nonfiction have appeared in *Glimmer Train, North American Review, Colorado Review, Alaska Quarterly Review, South Dakota Review, Witness, So to Speak*, and elsewhere. She holds an MFA from George Mason University and a PhD from the University of Nebraska. Born in the former Soviet Union, she has lived in California, Virginia, Nebraska, and Connecticut.

SHANNON ROBINSON's fiction has appeared in *Nimrod International Journal, Sycamore Review, Crab Creek Review, Sou'wester, Gargoyle*, and *Whiskey Island*. Her short story "Miscarriages" won *Nimrod International Journal*'s Katherine Anne Porter Prize for Fiction, and her story "Everyone Has a Tell" was awarded the *Crab Creek Review* Editors' Prize. She has an MFA in fiction from Washington University and recently completed a residency at Hedgebrook. She is married to poet James Arthur.

CHAD SIMPSON is the author of *Phantoms*, a chapbook of very short stories. His work has appeared in several magazines, including *Timothy McSweeney's Quarterly Concern, Sycamore Review, Barrelhouse, The Collagist*, and *The Sun*. He lives in Monmouth, Illinois, and teaches fiction writing and literature classes at Knox College.

CHRISTINE SNEED's story collection, *Portraits of a Few of the People I've Made Cry*, won AWP's Grace Paley Prize for Short Fiction and has been nominated for a Los Angeles Times Book Prize in the first fiction category. Her stories have appeared in *Best American Short Stories, Ploughshares, The Southern Review, New England Review,* and many other journals. She teaches at DePaul University in Chicago.

IAN STANSEL is a graduate of Northern Illinois University and the Iowa Writers' Workshop, and is currently pursuing a PhD in Literature and Creative Writing at the University of Houston, where he serves as editor of *Gulf Coast.* His work has been published in *Ploughshares, Antioch Review, Ecotone, Barrelhouse,* and elsewhere, and has been shortlisted for *Best American Short Stories.*

MARK WISNIEWSKI is the author of the novels *Confessions of a Polish Used Car Salesman* and *Show Up, Look Good.* His fiction has won a Pushcart Prize, an Isherwood Fellowship, and a Tobias Wolff Award and has appeared in venues such as *TriQuarterly, The Missouri Review,* and *Best American Short Stories.*

GUEST EDITOR

JOHN MCNALLY is the author of three novels (*After the Workshop, America's Report Card,* and *The Book of Ralph*), two story collections (*Ghosts of Chicago* and *Troublemakers*), and two nonfiction books about writing (*Vivid and Continuous* and *The Creative Writer's Survival Guide*). He has edited and co-edited several anthologies on subjects ranging from baseball to superheroes. A native of Burbank, Illinois, John holds degrees from Southern Illinois University, the University of Iowa, and the University of Nebraska. He is Associate Professor at Wake Forest University and lives in Winston-Salem. He currently is at work on a long historical novel set in Chicago.

SERIES EDITORS

JASON LEE BROWN teaches writing at Eastern Illinois University and has received awards from the Illinois Arts Council, Academy of American Poets, and Illinois Press Association.

SHANIE LATHAM teaches writing and literature at Jefferson College in Missouri. She is Managing Editor of *River Styx* magazine.

www.ingramcontent.com/pod-product-compliance
Lightning Source LLC
Chambersburg PA
CBHW020053030726
47498CB00006B/1772